M000234470

# RECKLESS

GEMMA ROGERS

Boldwood

First published in Great Britain in 2020 by Boldwood Books Ltd.

Cover Design: www.judgebymycovers.com

Cover Photography: Shutterstock

A CIP catalogue record for this book is available from the British Library.

Paperback ISBN 978-1-83889-016-2

Large Print ISBN 978-1-83889-736-9

Ebook ISBN 978-1-83889-018-6

Kindle ISBN 978-1-83889-017-9

Audio CD ISBN  978-1-83889-014-8

MP3 CD ISBN 978-1-83889-733-8

Digital audio download ISBN 978-1-83889-015-5

Boldwood Books Ltd
23 Bowerdean Street
London SW6 3TN
www.boldwoodbooks.com

*To my beautiful girls, Bethany and Lucy, who are far too young to read this.*
*I hope to make you proud.*

# 1

It wasn't a collision. There was no crunching of metal or shattering glass, but the sound of tyres screeching across the tarmac drowned out the voice of Roman Kemp on Capital radio. I winced in my seat, gripping the steering wheel in an attempt to control the car as we skidded across the road. The back end of my Audi A3 swung out, shaking my daughter and I inside like rag dolls, before bumping against the grassy bank of the roundabout. The seat belt locked and dug into my chest, as the side of my head thudded against the window. I flung my arm out across Charlotte's chest, terrified she was going to fly out of her seat, as we came to an abrupt halt. Disorientated by the ringing in my ears, time slowed. Sharp, shooting pains flew down my neck, each movement drawn out in contrast to my racing heart.

'Are you OK?' I looked at my fifteen-year-old daughter in the passenger seat, gaping at me. She managed a nod as I patted her thigh.

I put my hands back on the wheel, knuckles white as I struggled to catch my breath.

'Mum, you OK?' Charlotte's face was ashen, eyes wide and now brimming with tears.

Head throbbing, I raised my hand to feel the beginnings of a tender bump, hidden beneath my hair. I flinched.

'Jesus, he was driving like a dickhead!' she exclaimed.

A car horn sounded, pulling me back to the moment, and I saw him through the haze of raindrops that littered my windscreen. The weather was unusually wet for the beginning of September. It seemed like it had rained for days, the ground was saturated. The driver of the old black, boxy-shaped Ford Fiesta that had pulled out, into my path, causing me to slam on the breaks and lose control on the slippery road, stared at me. We locked eyes; his, like Charlotte's, wide and panicked. He was young, just a stupid kid.

Teeth gritted, I tried to articulate the word that was forming. Rolling it around my mouth before I could spit it out. The car had stalled, but Stormzy blared out of the speakers relentlessly. I started the engine and lowered my window, ignoring the beeping behind me.

Watching him trying to start his car, to leave the scene. I could hear his engine turning over but refusing to come to life and give him an escape. Our cars were blocking both lanes of the roundabout, at a standstill, mine facing his driver's door.

Leaning my head out of the window as far as I could, pinned by my seat belt, I shouted, 'You absolute twat!'

He stared at me, open-mouthed as though he wanted to reply. But then his car sprang to life and he tore off, wheels spinning, still driving too fast for the conditions. The rain had stepped up a gear since we'd stopped, now hammering on the roof.

Cars were queuing behind me and horns of commuters on their way to work screamed impatiently. Not caring that I'd seen mine and my daughter's lives flash before my eyes only seconds earlier. No one had got out of their car to check we were all right. No one wanted to get wet.

Sighing, I manoeuvred the car into first gear, and slowly eased away. Indicating to leave the roundabout, unable to stop my hand trembling on the gearstick.

'Mum?' Charlotte's voice was stronger now, the shock ebbing away.

'I'm fine. Are you OK?' I saw her nod in my peripheral vision. 'What an idiot.'

My face contorted and I could feel the perspiration at the base of my spine seeping into my cream blouse. The drumming in my chest slowly returning to its natural rhythm. I didn't need this today. The first day of the summer term at a new school for both of us. I was desperate to make a good impression. Charlotte's navy uniform had been pressed, her brogues glistening. Her hair in a neat plait; mine smoothed and tucked behind my ears. Everything had to be perfect, but now I was a flustered mess.

Fifteen minutes later, after a slow drive in which I was reluctant to move out of third gear, we arrived at the car park. I felt like I'd held my breath the entire journey and was grateful to find there were spaces left. Even with the near accident we weren't late, having left the house in plenty of time. I parked away from the entrance; Charlotte hopping out as soon as the engine was off, desperate to leave the confines of the car. I followed, smoothing my clothes before closing my door, then opening it again.

'Really, Mum? Today?' Charlotte sighed, as I counted to four.

I bit down on my molars. There was no point in explaining again, it was a compulsion. An anxiety tick of sorts. The therapist I saw when it started had said it was a coping mechanism for times of increased stress. A repetitive action that helped me regain control of the situation and of myself. It had become second nature and something I did automatically now to feel calmer.

Charlotte didn't understand. Not today, on the first day at a new school. It was all about her. Wasn't that what all teenagers were like? I knew she was nervous as she pulled on her earlobe and twisted her plain gold stud. She rolled her eyes at me, her mouth giving way to a smile as she took in my proud stare.

'Good luck. Have a wonderful day. Text me if you need to, but don't get into trouble for using your phone.'

'You too, Mum.'

She turned on her heels and headed for the main entrance, out of the drizzle, leaving me behind. I knew it was going to be that way. I hadn't expected anything less. I retrieved my satchel from the boot and counted the number of times I locked and unlocked the car as I left the car park. The key fob hot in my hand. Always four, everything was four.

The sun broke through the clouds and there was a brief pause in the rain as I stood to take in the looming old building of St. Wilfred's Comprehensive, its red-brick two-storey exterior with peeling white sash windows situated on the largest grounds I'd encountered. It looked almost gothic from the outside, like an old boarding school. It was certainly big enough and I knew it would be a while until I found my way around. It was a new start in Rusper, just outside Horsham in West Sussex, where I would be teaching English and Charlotte would be going into year eleven. She'd turn sixteen in January next year and was going into her final year of high school. My stomach clenched at the enormity of it. This had to work, it just had to.

Groups of children gathered by the doors, a sea of navy blazers and white shirts. I waited until there was a gap and moved inside. The long corridor was brightly lit, white walls displaying artwork; mosaics and watercolours, and a trophy cabinet positioned outside the headmaster Mr Scott's office. His door was shut and I could hear muffled voices inside, so I decided not to interrupt.

'Excuse me, could you tell me where the staffroom is please?' I asked a girl loitering nearby. She was around Charlotte's age and wore thick black eyeliner around her chestnut eyes.

'It's the last door on the left, Miss,' she replied, pointing down the corridor, before heading in the opposite direction. I'd been inside the school before for my interview and had a brief tour, but only remembered Mr Scott's office.

I found toilets before the staffroom and slipped inside, grateful they were empty.

I imagined most of the teachers were already in their classrooms, preparing for the day ahead. I wanted a moment to tidy my hair and put on a dash of lipstick. The cream blouse and navy pencil skirt I'd chosen was my smart but functional outfit, until I saw how the other teachers dressed. In some schools, teachers wore suits, but in others their attire was more relaxed. I hoped it was the latter.

My face was still pale, the colour yet to return to my cheeks. The queasy feeling that had started in the pit of my stomach was drowned out by the throbbing of my head from the collision with the window. Spraying some perfume across my blouse, I took a moment to regain my composure. Pushing aside the anger bubbling beneath the surface at the other driver who'd been so reckless.

First-day nerves took hold and I zipped my bag open and shut, again and again. *One, two, three, four. You can do this, it's a new start, a new life in a new town.*

Just then a text came through on my phone. Sliding my finger across the screen, I saw it was from my husband David.

Good luck, you'll be fantastic x

Steadying my breathing until I felt in control, I pulled open the door and stepped into the busy corridor, almost colliding with the frowning headmaster.

'Ah, there you are. Welcome, Isabel.' He smiled, opening his arms wide and, for a worrying second, I thought he was going to envelop me in a hug.

'Izzy, call me Izzy. Sorry, you had someone in your office,' I explained but he waved me away.

'No problem. Now, Izzy, let me take you through to your classroom. As I mentioned before, you have a lovely year eight class that you'll be form room teacher for. You'll be known as 8C; they are all aged between twelve and thirteen. They'll be with you for about twenty minutes twice a day, each morning and afternoon, where you'll take the register. I looked after them for part of last year and they are a smashing bunch.' Mr Scott strode quickly down the corridor and I hurried to keep up. My skirt too tight at the knee to walk fast. Why did he look after a form? In my previous school that would have been unorthodox for a headteacher.

'Will I teach my lessons from the same classroom?' I asked.

'Yes, absolutely, that will be your classroom.' He glanced over his shoulder. 'Still raining out there?' I nodded, remembering my umbrella in the boot of the car.

'Afraid so, but I think it's slowing down. The Great British Summertime, eh,' I said, palms dampening as a tirade of bewildered-looking students pushed through the doors and ploughed towards us.

Someone bumped my shoulder and mumbled an apology.

'Stevens,' Mr Scott said sternly.

The boy turned around and my stomach plummeted to the floor like a sack of potatoes.

'Yes, sir?' he replied in a bored tone, his mouth in a tight smile.

'You bumped into Mrs Cole. Can you apologise please?' He hadn't seen me properly; hadn't registered me yet. But I saw him, clearer now he wasn't behind a windscreen. Blond shaven head, blue eyes, vaguely resembling a young Jude Law. Athletic-looking, he stood almost as tall as the headteacher. Our eyes met, and I thought I heard him gasp.

His smile faded, and he stuttered, 'I, I did.'

'He did,' I agreed, unsure why I was defending him. I eyed him coldly. He could have killed us this morning.

'Off you go and tuck that shirt in,' Mr Scott instructed, nodding towards his untucked T-shirt, before we carried on down the corridor.

As he held open the classroom door to 8C, I glanced behind me in the direction we'd come from. The boy, last name Stevens, was still standing there, staring at me. A permanent fixture in the corridor as students scurried around him. I paused, my hand briefly touching the small mound on my head. My thumping skull stepped up a notch. Mr Scott's voice was muffled in the background. As I crossed the threshold into the classroom, I took one last look down the corridor, sure I saw the corners of the boy's mouth curl upward.

## 2

I tried to focus on Mr Scott's voice, but he sounded like he was underwater. My head throbbed. I should take some painkillers. I would, when I was on my own. I took a deep breath and forced my mouth into a smile, trying to pull myself back to the present.

'As you can see, the children are very enthusiastic about English lessons here.' The classroom was bright and colourful with work displayed on the walls as well as many large images of well-known book covers. The faces of Matilda and Harry Potter stared down at us.

'Looks fantastic,' I agreed, and he grinned appreciatively.

'Right, I'll let you get settled. The register is here.' Mr Scott pointed to the black folder on my desk. He patted my shoulder before leaving and, as soon as he'd gone, I sank into the chair, relieved to be alone for a short while.

Tearing through my handbag, I unearthed an old packet of paracetamol and took two dry, swallowing hard. The chalkiness made me baulk. Shockwaves reverberated around my body as the revelation sank in. He was a bloody student. There were too many kids driving around in fast cars. They should raise the driving age to twenty-one. He had to be a sixth former, but even so, still a student. One that I had sworn at in public this morning.

The bell rang out, making me jump. I felt like a bag of nerves, barely holding it together. When had I become so weak? So anxious? I knew exactly when, but it didn't help.

I held the base of the seat, my fingers drumming on the wood. It was my anchor. *One, two, three, four. One, two, three, four.* I waited for the feeling to pass. Within seconds, the noise outside the classroom escalated, there were loud shouts, laughter and the stomping of feet.

Pupils darted into the room and sat at empty desks. Most of them looked happy to be at school; for some children, the school holidays were long, and school was their escape. Occasionally, it presented the only social life they had. There were always a couple of children slouched in their chairs, looking like they'd been dragged out of their beds ten minutes before the bell rang and this morning was no exception.

'Good morning, everyone!' I said loudly, ignoring my churning stomach. The beginning of a new school year was always the hardest.

The raucous class fell silent.

'My name is Mrs Cole and today is my first day at St. Wilfred's. Now, as you all had your first day this time last year, I hope you'll be extra helpful to me this week as I learn all your names.' The crowd of faces beamed back at me and I felt my shoulders ease.

I called each name from the register and everyone answered. I handed out planners and individual timetables to each of the children, who pored over them at their desks.

'Great, a full house today. So, who would like to tell me about their summer holiday?' I asked the class, my eyebrows arched expectantly.

For a few moments, no one spoke, until a boy at the back raised his hand. He had brown hair styled into a quiff and exuded the boyish confidence of someone popular amongst his peers.

'I moved to a new house, Mrs Cole, that was pretty cool. We had to have takeaway every night for a week as we had no oven.' He gesticulated wildly as he spoke, and I warmed to him immediately.

'That does sound exciting and, guess what, I moved to a new house too, but I wasn't lucky enough to have a week of takeaways.'

The class laughed and a couple of other children took their turn to talk about their time away. One of them went to Disneyland, which everyone was extremely interested in hearing about.

Twenty minutes flew by and before I knew it, the bell rang again and the children filed out of the door, most of them clutching their timetables, trying to ascertain where they were going next. The corridor outside bustled and echoed with shouts, but within a couple of minutes, I heard heavy classroom doors slamming and it was quiet once more.

I had an hour where I didn't have a class and was going to use the time to familiarise myself with the school and prepare what I could for the rest of the week. I was teaching a year nine class at ten o'clock and looked over my lesson plan. My iPhone vibrated on the desk and I smiled down at a message sent from my best friend Stella.

Knock em bandy

Despite the traumatic start to the day, I felt calmer after meeting my form room children. The school had been a good choice. David and I made the right decision to move, I could feel it. We previously lived in Wallington, a London suburb, but Charlotte got into a bad crowd. She followed around a girl called Lisa, started skipping school, her grades plummeted and she was finally suspended when caught smoking on the grounds. I wanted to get her out of there. David worked in finance and had been approached around Easter by his former colleague, Patrick, who owned part of a public relations company in Hove. David was interested in moving, hating the daily commute to London but nervous to jump ship, so gratefully declined. When Charlotte got suspended in July, David got back in touch with Patrick, and tempted with promises of less hours and more money, he made the leap and we searched for schools.

When we found St. Wilfred's, I was immediately impressed. The Ofsted rating was Good, and it had a sixth form attached with a variety of media courses available that I could see Charlotte would be interested in. During a tour, I got a feel of the place. Charlotte seemed keen and when I saw they offered the same GCSE options and the syllabus at St. Wilfred's was nearly identical to what she had been previously learning, it was a no-brainer. I enrolled her to start in the coming September. It was only by chance when I mentioned to Mr Scott that I was looking in the surrounding areas for a teaching position that he said they had a vacancy for an English teacher.

At first, I wasn't sure how it would work; Charlotte attending the same school I'd be teaching at, but she said it didn't bother her as long as I kept my distance. When I discussed it with Mr Scott, he said he wasn't fazed as it was Charlotte's last year, as long as I didn't teach her directly. David thought, if anything, it would be a good opportunity to keep an eye on her. To ensure she was on the straight and narrow.

Once committed, we found the perfect house in Rusper, amidst a row of five detached cottages that were surprisingly spacious on the inside, with a large gravel driveway and separate garage. I fell in love with the rustic fireplace and family kitchen. Our offer to purchase was accepted, we engineered the move during the school summer holiday, and everything seemed to slot into place. After the awful year we'd had, we saw it as a sign that we'd been given another chance to be happy.

Glancing back at the plan, I saw the year tens were going to be starting *Romeo and Juliet*, which, at fourteen and fifteen, was always met with lots of sniggering and lewd comments. Footsteps in the corridor caused me to look up and I saw a figure stride past the door, our eyes connecting for a split second before he was gone. I forced my gaze back to the sheet of paper and gripped the arm of the chair. The footsteps paused and resumed, this time back towards the classroom, until a head popped around the door frame.

'Miss?'

I was pretending to read, my knee twitching under the desk, but I glanced up like I'd only just noticed him.

'Hello?' My voice caught in my throat.

A sheepish grin emerged on his face and he stepped into the classroom. Towering over me. He had a strong angular jaw, piercing sky blue eyes and pearly white teeth. Good-looking without a doubt, but he knew it.

'I'm really sorry about this morning. It was you on the roundabout, wasn't it, Miss? I mean, I recognise your face, although you don't look so angry now.'

Impertinent little sod. By the look of him, I was sure he'd be able to talk his way out of anything, but remembering what I'd called him, I had to tread wisely.

'Was that you? You need to be careful, you could have killed yourself pulling out without looking.' He had the good grace to look suitably ashamed. 'What's your name?'

'Nicky Stevens, Miss, and I'm late for PE, but I wanted to apologise.' Flashing me an awkward smile, he left to go to his lesson. It could have been uncomfortable if he'd taken offence to being called a twat this morning. Would he be in any of my lessons? I hoped not.

\* \* \*

The rest of the day went as planned, although my mind wandered to Charlotte and how her first day might be going. My morning lessons were pleasant, the children were well behaved and at lunchtime I braved the staffroom. It was a large, square room, with one green three-seater sofa and two mismatched armchairs around an oblong wooden coffee table displaying various degrees of tea-stained rings. There was a kitchenette at the end of the room, with a fridge, a few cupboards, a microwave and a kettle.

I placed the Tupperware pot of cold pasta salad on the worktop and awkwardly introduced myself to the other teachers. Shaking hands with sweaty palms was never good, but no one commented. I always struggled to hide my nerves. There were two women and two men, one of whom was Mr Scott, taking up the kitchenette as the kettle boiled. Deep in conversation, they discussed whether there would be a snap general election as Boris had promised if a bill against a no-deal Brexit was passed by MPs.

The women were vastly different. One was a plump, friendly-looking lady with grey hair and a warm smile. I guessed instantly she was the art teacher from the way she was dressed, lots of colours thrown together and purple Doc Martens under a long tie-dye skirt, and I was right. She interrupted the debate and introduced herself as Matilda Brown, shaking my hand firmly. The second lady was short and wiry with glasses and a pointed nose. She smiled tight-lipped at me and limply grasped my hand as though she hated physical contact as much as I did. She was Ms Quinn, no first-name introduction, and was the maths teacher.

Next there was the scruffy history teacher, Mr Collins, first name Henry, who grunted a welcome and, lastly, Steven Scott, who'd come into the staffroom for the purpose of introducing me to the other teachers.

I cast my eye around the room; it seemed from the various attire that I didn't have to worry about what I wore, there was a mixture of formal and informal. I relaxed knowing I didn't have to conform either way and my previous work wardrobe would be fine.

Mr Ross, a latecomer to the staffroom, breezed in. He was the PE teacher, a no-nonsense Scotsman, who, as soon as we were introduced, asked me if I'd seen Nicky Stevens that morning. The mention of his name made me slop a tiny amount of tea over the side of my cup as my hand trembled. Apparently, Nicky had blamed me for his late arrival, as I'd accosted him on the way to his lesson. It was easier to agree than to explain I had almost crashed into his car this morning and he'd stopped to apologise.

It played on my mind throughout my last lesson of the day and I was grateful when Charlotte slunk into my empty classroom at ten past three, still trying to avoid being identified as the daughter of a teacher by her peers. She told me on the way home that her day had been OK, she was still working out who was who in the social hierarchy. I knew the move wouldn't have been easy for her; she didn't think there was a problem where she'd been before. Our relationship had been fractious ever since.

'How's your head?' she asked.

I gingerly touched the lump, the pain easing.

'Good, thank you. Can you believe *he* goes here?' I said, shaking my head.

'What, to St. Wilfred's?'

I nodded, glimpsing Charlotte's open mouth. 'He came to see me in my classroom to apologise.'

'I hope you told him to piss off,' Charlotte replied, without batting an eyelid.

I gave her a sharp look. 'No, I did not, funnily enough.'

The radio was turned up for the rest of the journey and as soon as we got home, Charlotte vanished to her room to boot up her laptop. Facebooking or Instagramming or whatever it was teenagers did that incurred so many hours online.

Our neighbour Mary popped round almost as soon as we got back, she'd introduced herself the day we moved in, having lived in the cottage next door for thirty years. Her and her husband Bob were retired. Since our arrival, she'd popped in every couple of weeks, delivering scones and cakes, much to David's delight. Today, a batch of still-warm blueberry muffins were handed over as she reminded me the bin men were coming tomorrow. We chatted for five minutes on the doorstep, Mary declining my offer to come in. I made a mental note to pick up some flowers for her.

I sat on the sofa with a mug of tea and a muffin. I had no homework to mark and no lessons to plan for tomorrow as I'd managed to get that done in my free period. The house was deathly quiet, the only noise from the clock ticking above the fireplace. David would be home later; perhaps we could watch a movie together. Crack open a bottle of wine to celebrate my first day. I headed into the kitchen to make a Bolognese sauce, humming to myself.

At half past five, as I was setting the table and about to dish up, David called my mobile.

'I'm sorry I've got a conference call with the US at six, shouldn't be more than an hour.'

I tried to keep my voice upbeat as I told him it was fine, but I knew he wouldn't be home before eight. If this was what his new job was going to be like, we wouldn't be spending as much time together as I'd initially thought.

## 3

When the front door opened, I glanced at the clock – it was quarter to nine, much later than I'd realised.

Charlotte and I had eaten dinner together, discussing Mr Ross, whom she declared as 'evil' because he had made them wear disgusting tabards in PE that had never been washed. She seemed totally unfazed by the transition to St. Wilfred's and I was relieved her day had been a good one. Afterwards, Charlotte went upstairs to do science homework on the periodic table. I cleared up and sat in the lounge, watching a true crime documentary; I loved them and fancied myself as a bit of an amateur detective.

David swooped in and kissed me on the forehead before going into the kitchen to reheat his dinner. I'd left it in the microwave, as I always did.

'How was your day?' I called, finishing my glass of wine and knocking back some more painkillers. My bump was now a dull ache, but irritating nonetheless.

'Busy, yours? How was school?'

'Fine, apart from some idiot on the road this morning. Charlotte seems to like it.'

'Great,' he said. No further conversation followed. He didn't even enquire about my journey to work.

He ate his dinner at the table, casually perusing the newspaper he'd brought home. When he finished, he flopped beside me in front of the television, stifling a yawn. It was obvious he was tired, but when I announced I was going to bed at ten, he didn't follow. Feeling slightly rejected, I cleaned my teeth and got into bed.

I knew David was anxious about making a good impression at his new job. He'd started three weeks ago, determined to hit the ground running. Whenever David encountered any stress, he would shut down and I'd have to wait for him to snap out of it. I gritted my teeth and rolled over, plumping my pillow with my fist. It wasn't just the pressure of his new job, or the recent move. He'd been distant for a while, but there was nothing I could do to fix it. I couldn't change the past, however much I wanted to.

The next morning, David had gone by the time I woke. He usually left for work early, preferring the quieter roads to the congested school run and said it was a less stressful start to the day. I wished I had that option, but I'd always been the one to do the school runs.

I woke Charlotte and we both got ready for school. The sky was overcast and as we left it began to rain again. The warmth of summer had abruptly ended with the start of the term. As a result, the roads were busy, and I arrived a little later than planned, although with less drama than yesterday's commute.

As I shook out my umbrella and hooked it onto the coat stand in the corner of the classroom, I noticed a cup on my desk. A Starbucks takeaway coffee cup, steam protruding from the hole in the lid. Bemused, I slid into my seat and picked it up. Latte had been ticked on the selection but there was no name written on the side. Instead, a yellow Post-it note was peeling off the cardboard as it was so hot. It had one word written on it in thick black capital letters.

*SORRY*

Was it for me? I frowned, who'd felt the need to apologise? Had I missed something, or was it meant for someone else? I was in the right classroom, wasn't I? I looked around at the now familiar pictures on the walls. Then I remembered the journey to school yesterday morning and the near miss at the roundabout. Surely it couldn't be? The boy from yesterday had brought me a coffee to apologise for his terrible driving?

I leaned back in my chair, staring at the offering. If it was him, the gesture seemed mature beyond his years. I braved a sip, pleased to discover it was a latte, the hot liquid burning my throat.

'You got it then, Miss?' came a voice from the door, startling me. A little of the hot liquid leaked onto my hand, searing my skin.

'Shit.' I scowled, raising my hand to my mouth. Heat engulfed my cheeks.

He leaned on the door frame, looking considerably pleased with himself, smirking at my loss of control.

'Sorry about that. I don't normally curse in front of students.'

His eyebrows lifted and I felt the onset of a hot flush, the silence making me squirm.

'Thank you, it's kind of you, but you didn't have to do that.'

'I did.' The bell rang and he turned to leave, our conversation finished.

The classroom swiftly filled with children chattering amongst themselves and throwing bags under desks as they slipped into their seats. I took the register and chatted to some of the children about how they'd found their first day back at school, all the time cradling the coffee, the warmth making my fingertips tingle.

It wasn't long before the year eights were replaced by year sevens, who all looked so little. Every year, they seemed to look smaller. Their pristine uniforms drowning them with backpacks bigger than they were. I couldn't believe Charlotte was that size once.

The lesson today had them writing stories with a definitive beginning, middle and end, all on the subject of 'growth'. The explanation I had given them at the start of the class was that 'growth' could mean any number of things, from plants growing, to how you could grow as a person.

They banded some ideas around between them and, after a few minutes of brainstorming, the class were fully engrossed, and the room fell silent. All the children had their heads bowed, scribbling away in their exercise books and occasionally raising their hands to ask a question.

I could hear a PE class outside, it sounded like football from the posts rattling and scuffling of trainers on concrete. It was still drizzling, and I didn't envy them playing outside today.

A loud bang echoed around the classroom and everyone jumped, heads snapping to the window just in time to see a football bounce off the narrow wall and zoom into the flower bed. I tutted – at that force, it could have smashed the window I'd left ajar to allow some fresh air in.

'Carry on, children, I'm going to close the window as they're a noisy bunch out there.' I walked over to the paint-chipped sash and pulled it down, spotting Nicky Stevens navigating the path between the flower beds towards the building. He was part of a mixed group, playing football in the tennis courts. Perhaps doing a PE A-Level? He had to be in sixth form if he was old enough to drive.

He grinned when he saw me, his walk becoming a swagger, and mouthed the word 'sorry' as he came closer. What must it be like to have that much confidence?

I couldn't help but smile at his nerve, but I did shake my head in disapproval. He picked up the ball and kicked it high over the wire fence of the court, back to his teammates, with expert precision. They didn't wait, carrying on the game without him. He turned back to award me another smile and stretched his arms over his head in a victory pose as he walked backwards. His rain sodden T-shirt rode up, showing a glimpse of bare torso beneath. Sitting dangerously low, his shorts revealed the V-shape of his hips and the trail of hair descending beneath.

My face flushed as he caught me looking. It was exactly what he'd intended.

I turned away quickly, cheeks now a vivid scarlet, and hurried back to my desk. My eyes darted around the room to see if anyone had noticed the exchange, but the children had resumed their stories.

What had just happened? How had I let myself get drawn in to that charade? Clearly, I had to be more careful with him. There was no doubt that display was deliberate, and I'd fallen for it. Even a rumour these days was enough to ruin a teaching career.

Nostrils flaring, I launched the empty coffee cup with the note still attached into the bin and sat down to drum my fingers on the underside of my desk. *One, two, three, four. One, two, three, four.*

\* \* \*

The rest of the day was uneventful in comparison. In the staffroom, I chatted with Matilda and Susan – Ms Quinn – over sandwiches. Susan had volunteered her first name this time, seemingly thawed since our last interaction. They gave me suggestions on restaurants and what there was to do in the area, some of which I'd already explored. Horsham was a market town and had a shopping centre, swimming baths, cinema and theatre. I loved to go to the cinema almost as much as I loved curling up with a good book.

I asked for directions to the leisure centre, hoping to go for a swim after school if I could rope Charlotte in too. I always kept a backpack of swim gear in the boot of my car, in case I got the opportunity. Where we used to live, in Wallington, I swam at the local pool three or four times a week, using it as my time to destress. Charlotte hadn't been interested in swimming for a few years now, but I persuaded her to come along and sit in the spectator section, nonetheless. It seemed as long as she had her phone and could connect to free Wi-Fi, she was happy. Plus, I couldn't deny wanting to keep an eye on her. I had to make sure she stayed out of trouble at St. Wilfred's.

Any time we spent together these days was a bonus. Since the hormones kicked in, it seemed mothers became public enemy number one and I was no exception. It was a challenge to say anything to Charlotte without it being misconstrued as criticism. I was often treading on eggshells. Although uncharacteristically, on the drive to the leisure centre, Charlotte shared that she had made a few friends and they'd already asked her what she was doing at the weekend. I refrained from gushing too much, fearing it might make her clam up. I had to trust she'd chosen more wisely this time as her old friends, Lisa especially, had led her down a path I didn't want to revisit. I wanted her to have a clean record at St. Wilfred's.

'Whatever you want to do, honey. I can always drop you in town if you'd like. I've heard there's a good cinema and a bowling alley.' Charlotte had always enjoyed the cinema too. I had been taking her to the toddler mornings on a Saturday since she was three, whenever there was a good Disney or Pixar movie out. Packing the bag with lots of treats would help to keep her sitting still for two hours, which sometimes felt like a marathon. We hadn't been to see anything for ages, the days when all it took was a bag of sweets to coax Charlotte to the cinema were long gone.

When we arrived at the pool, it was relatively quiet, except for a few boys showing off for Charlotte's benefit and making the lifeguard blow his whistle at thirty-second intervals. My daughter, at fifteen years of age, was becoming more attractive every day and it wouldn't be long before boys were knocking on the door. She had so much spirit, more than I had at her age. Dark and brooding, like her father, but when she got angry, she was as unpredictable as a firework. The transition into the teenage years had been a challenge.

I eased into a couple of lengths of breaststroke in a lane I had all to myself. Swimming was my favourite form of exercise; all stress would dissolve, and I'd allow myself to daydream. Gliding through the water, being weightless, was blissful and I even found the smell of chlorine heavenly. I contemplated my day and the move to St. Wilfred's. So far it had been a success and I was hopeful that it would continue. I had bridges to rebuild with David and Charlotte, but for the first time in a while, it felt achievable.

# 4

---

When we got home, Charlotte disappeared to her room; she wanted to ring her friend Lisa from her old school. I wasn't overly happy about it, but I understood that it wasn't fair of me to expect her to cut ties altogether. Plus, it was a fight that I didn't think I'd win.

Even though it was early, I poured myself a glass of wine from the bottle I'd opened last night. A reward for a good day. We were having chicken fajitas for dinner, but by the time it was ready, the kitchen was a mess. As I laid the table, David came in, dumping his laptop bag in the hallway and striding into the kitchen. He kissed me on the cheek and pinched one of the sliced peppers from the chopping board, tossing it into his mouth before I could object.

'It's lovely to have you home early,' I said, giving him a quick squeeze around the middle, but even my good intentions of being affectionate with David felt alien now. With the house move last month and new jobs for us both, there had barely been any time for intimacy. It felt like we were ships passing in the night.

'How's the job going?' It was David's third week in his new position, and this was the earliest he had been home from work since he'd started. Charlotte and I were getting used to eating alone.

'OK actually. I had to present some projected savings to the vice president yesterday, which is why I was late back, but it went well, and I think they are going to implement my suggested changes.'

I beamed at my clever husband.

'You're not the hatchet man, are you?' I laughed, but David shook his head.

'No, I leave that to someone in Human Resources,' he joked.

'I see.'

'What about you, how are you finding the rabble at St. Wilfred's?'

'Fine, they seem nice.'

We sat down to eat when Charlotte eventually emerged from upstairs, informing us that Lisa had been suspended already, in her first week, for fighting. Mine and David's eyes met, silently confirming we'd made the right decision to move schools.

After dinner, David changed out of his suit and he and I sat in the lounge to watch the latest satellite movie premiere, or rather, he stared at his mobile all night. By ten, I was yawning and ready for bed. Swimming had taken it out of me; I'd lost my stamina.

In the bathroom, I slipped on a silk nightie and cleaned my teeth, leafing through a book in bed until David came upstairs.

When he climbed in beside me, the mattress dipping and his body cold, he rolled onto his side to switch off the lamp. I gently pressed myself against his back, caressing the base of his neck with my lips. David reached behind and placed his hand on my thigh, patting it lightly. A minute later, I heard him snore.

I turned away, letting a sigh escape, and stared at the ceiling. I'd been dismissed. We had to get over this hump and there was only one way to do it, but I couldn't do it alone. We hadn't been together physically for over three months and the longer it went on, the harder it was to get back into. I hadn't spoken to David about it yet, hoping it was a blip and there would be no need for any awkward conversation, but it was fast becoming the elephant in the room.

Our sex life had been sporadic at best since last year. I'd accidentally fallen pregnant. A tummy bug had purged my contraceptive pill a few days before a rare night away. My best friend Stella had stayed over to keep an eye on Charlotte and we'd booked a night in a hotel in Brighton. It had been such a shock when we found out, as conceiving Charlotte had taken a year of trying and when we'd tried for another child it had never happened.

Although the pregnancy wasn't planned and the age difference between the children would have been massive, we decided it was a gift. But just before I reached the sixteen-week mark, I miscarried. We were devastated and it somehow fractured the relationship between David and I. I was grief-stricken, consumed by guilt and emotionally shut down. David tried to help me through it, but I became cold and detached. Eventually he gave up trying to console me and we'd been papering over the cracks ever since. It became something we never spoke about, although looking back now, we could have done with some counselling.

Charlotte wasn't told about the pregnancy; we were going to surprise her with the scan to show the sex of the baby. There seemed little point in upsetting her to tell her about a brother or sister she would now never have. I'd tell her when she was older. As a result of the miscarriage and complications during the operation to remove the remaining foetus left behind, doctors confirmed I would likely be no longer able to have children. Scar tissue in my uterus and cervix would mean getting pregnant could be problematic. At thirty-nine, I felt I was getting a little old, preferring to concentrate on the family I had already. But David changed, he'd said it was like having a winning lottery ticket snatched out of his hand. I'd pushed him away, sure he blamed me for the miscarriage. I'd tried to take good care of myself. I'd taken folic acid and extra vitamins; exercised, drank plenty of water, but I couldn't hold on to our baby. Now it felt like I hadn't just lost my baby, but my husband too.

I desperately missed how close we used to be. David was always affectionate, and I loved that about him. He never missed an opportunity to grope me in the kitchen, sneaking up behind me when I was doing the washing up and 'unarmed'. I'd been desired and I wanted us to get back to that place but wasn't sure how. Exasperated, I put my headphones in and listened to the latest Jane Fallon novel I'd downloaded, to drown out David's snoring.

\* \* \*

On Wednesday, Mr Scott requested a staff meeting after school, which worked out well as Charlotte asked to go home with one of her new school friends. She gave me the address and asked if I could pick her up on the way back. I was looking forward to meeting them. I was hopeful that Charlotte had learned from her mistakes and would make better choices in whom she spent her time with. The teachers gathered in the IT classroom, a looming room with high tables lining three of the four walls, a monitor and keyboard for each pupil stationed a few feet apart. We congregated at a bank of desks in the centre.

To start, Mr Scott introduced me to the remaining members of staff I hadn't already met in the staffroom and then moved on to discuss the addition of after-school clubs. He hoped we would have suggestions in our relevant areas of expertise.

Mr Ross, the PE teacher, proposed to coach a netball team after school on a Tuesday, in addition to the mixed football club he already held. I made a mental note to inform Charlotte, sure she would enjoy netball if she could be persuaded to sign up. Matilda asked if she could run a pottery class, to which Mr Scott agreed in principle, depending on the cost of the clay. Mr Collins, the history teacher, was a chess enthusiast and said he would find out if any of the students would be interested, before advertising a club.

I shifted in my seat, counting silently in my head as I felt my pace quicken. They'd been around the table, but I was yet to contribute.

'I could run a creative writing club, if you think any of the students would be interested?' My voice started strong but tailed off when everyone turned to look at me.

'Fantastic idea, Izzy, yes I think that has legs. Catch all those future authors and journalists.' Mr Scott clapped his hands together and I felt the prickle of perspiration on the back of my neck. I drummed my fingers on my thigh, counting, until the attention was diverted.

I agreed to advertise my club, to be held on a Friday after school for an hour, which only gave me two days to plan. My chest fluttered as though caged birds were inside at the prospect of running a class where all the pupils that attended wanted to be there.

The meeting concluded at half past four and, as we walked out together, Matilda invited me to join her and Susan for dinner. They were going to get a curry and I was disappointed I couldn't join, but it was too short notice and I had to get Charlotte. Next time I promised I'd come along if they gave me a date.

I wanted to make friends with my work colleagues as Stella had moved to Nottingham over the summer to look after her elderly parents. She was only at the end of the phone and I spoke to her often, but I missed having a girlfriend to go shopping or out for dinner with. These days, I seemed to spend much of my time alone.

Deciding it was a bit early to get Charlotte and not wanting to ruin their after-school fun, I ventured into town to find the library. If I could borrow some books on creative writing to have a read through in preparation for the class, it would be a good start. I hadn't run an after-school class before, so was nervous at the prospect although it was a subject I loved. If I was lucky there might even be some suggested exercises I could use.

I'd seen signposts to the library on my way to school, so I had a fair idea where it was and, after a couple of wrong turns, I eventually found it. Libraries were my favourite places; quiet and peaceful, where time stood still. The smell of books was intoxicating, and hours could be wasted leafing through the latest romance offerings.

Today, however, I went straight to the information section and avoided fiction altogether, knowing it was a place I'd lose time. In a peculiar slow sidestep walk with my head leaning to the right so I could read the titles, I found the section on creative writing. Many looked dated, and I took a few out of the bookcase, turning them over to read the back cover before returning them to their rightful places.

'Hello, Miss.' A voice from behind made me start and I almost dropped the book I was holding. I spun around to see Nicky, shirt now untucked, sporting a mischievous grin.

## 5

'Hi,' I could feel my chest reddening. It was where it began, before it crept up my neck, leaving a mottled pattern it its wake. *This is ridiculous, why am I blushing?*

'Nicky,' he said smiling, introducing himself.

'How are you?' I asked, trying to appear unflustered. What was he doing here? I expected him to be running around a football pitch or out with a girlfriend, not knee deep in books.

'Good thanks, what are you looking for?' His gaze travelled downwards to the book in my hand, nodding appreciatively as I raised it for him to see.

'You?' I asked, to be polite. I couldn't help feeling uncomfortable. Nicky's wasn't a year group I was used to dealing with. I'd never taught sixth formers before. They were practically adults.

'Sports Science, for my A-Level. I also need to learn about muscles and ligaments for Biology.' His eyes glossed over me and I pulled my jacket together. The action made his eyes glint. I felt like prey about to be consumed. Physically he was imposing, tall and broad, and I couldn't help feeling out of my depth, despite being twenty years his senior. 'They've got a coffee shop upstairs; do you want to get one?' Nicky asked.

My eyebrows shot up momentarily. He was so self-assured, as though he was talking to a girl his own age and not a teacher. Taken aback, it took a few seconds to formulate a polite but firm response.

'I'm not sure that's appropriate, Nicky, but thank you.' I turned to leave with the book still in my hand, my skin steaming beneath my clothes.

'It's not a crime, Miss,' he called after me as I hurried to the self-check-out machine, feeling foolish for leaving so abruptly.

I fumbled around in my bag for my purse, but before I could get my library card out, he was beside me.

'Chill out, Miss, it's only a coffee. I know you're new here and if you ever want anyone to show you around, let me know.' He shrugged and turned to leave.

I felt a pang of guilt as I watched him walk out of the door to his car. Perhaps I wasn't being fair, he was just trying to be kind. Likely an attempt to make amends for how we met. Almost running a teacher off the road wasn't the best first impression and I was sure he felt embarrassed.

Through the glass, I saw he'd parked his car next to mine. Had he followed me here? No, of course he hadn't, I was being stupid. The near miss the other morning had unsettled me around Nicky, despite this I could still feel the tell-tale thrumming of my pulse in my neck.

The self-service machine didn't work, and I had to register for a new card as the one I had was redundant in this borough. The man behind the desk was painstakingly slow and questioned every answer on my form as though I was signing up for an exclusive membership to some secret society. All the time, I tapped my foot, counting steadily to four as I breathed in through my nose and out through my mouth, waiting for the anxiety to disperse. I hadn't always been this way. I used to be confident, but it seemed the older I got, the more fearful I became. Counting, repetitive actions and swimming were the only things that calmed me.

As the librarian generated my card, and my tapping slowed, I consoled myself that Nicky wasn't on the list of A-Level English Literature students. I'd checked that morning, worried he might put me off. Blushing like a teenage girl whenever we spoke was embarrassing. The more awkward I felt, the redder I became. Something that had plagued me since childhood. Although as I got older, the episodes became less frequent. Until now it seemed. I didn't know why he made me nervous, something about his manner, his confidence perhaps?

Eventually I was handed my card and was able to check out the creative writing book. It was one I'd ended up with rather than chosen, distracted by Nicky's arrival, but it would have to do.

I typed the postcode into the Audi's satnav feeling silly about my notion of being followed, as Nicky had left the car park already. I took the directions to collect Charlotte, driving through a small newly built housing estate with picture-perfect semi-detached properties in a line. Amy's house had beautiful silver pots by the front door, filled with pink begonias. I was looking forward to meeting her mother, but Charlotte slipped out of the front door when I rang the bell, closing it firmly behind her.

She said she'd had a good time but didn't offer any more details. I had a feeling she wanted to keep her friends close to her chest. Worried that they'd be ripped apart if she formed any attachments I deemed unsuitable. I'd tried to explain, when we told her we were moving her out of Wallington, that I was only thinking of her future, but she'd refused to listen. She didn't utter a word to me for two weeks, her door was constantly being slammed, and I knew she was struggling with lack of control of her own life. It kept me up at night, worrying we'd made a mistake, but I knew I had to get her away from that crowd. I had visions of the police bringing her home, stoned out of her head, and social services intervening.

'Stir fry for dinner tonight?' I suggested, hoping Charlotte would agree. I wanted something quick and easy so I could have a soak in the bath. Charlotte seemed fine with that idea and reluctantly helped me get the ingredients out when we got home. We were making progress; my attempts at conversation hadn't been brushed off completely, although she rolled her eyes when I complimented her on how well I thought she was doing with the massive change. When I dished up, I still hadn't heard from David, so put a bowl in the microwave for him as usual.

Once we'd eaten, Charlotte carried on with homework at the dining table and I went upstairs to run a bath, adding a few drops of moisturising bath soak David had bought me last Christmas.

Slipping off my black ankle grazers and polka dot blouse, I stood in front of the mirror in my mismatched underwear. The once white bra had turned a light shade of grey. Perhaps it was time to go shopping. My figure wasn't too bad, a small paunch around the middle I hadn't managed to lose since having Charlotte, but my legs were long and slim. They were my best feature and I needed to get them out more often. Every year I promised myself I would wear more skirts and dresses, but trousers were like a comfort blanket. I wasn't as toned as I used to be, but if I got back into swimming, it would make a difference.

The reflection staring back at me wasn't bad for someone soon to be forty. I dyed my hair a mahogany red now as the greys were beginning to peak through, but I kept it short in an angled bob that was, according to Charlotte, on trend.

Sliding into the bath, I sighed and closed my eyes, the warmth soothing. Running my hand over my stomach and watching the water run off my skin, I enjoyed the sensation. I missed being touched. David hadn't touched me in months.

I remembered when our sex life had been fun and spontaneous. We were forever giggling, grabbing opportunities when Charlotte wasn't around. For a while, losing the baby had turned my body from a means of pleasure into something I despised. My chance of a baby had been snatched away and it took time to come to terms with the fact I'd never carry again. As soon as I felt ready, I began reaching out to David, trying to instigate some longed-for intimacy, but he seemed detached. When would he be ready? How long would I have to wait?

'Mum!' Charlotte shouted from the bottom of the stairs, jolting me from my thoughts, and I sat up so fast, water erupted over the side of the bath.

'What?' I shouted back, my voice so high-pitched it was unrecognisable.

'Where's my PE kit?'

I sighed and picked up the razor to shave my legs.

'It's in your PE bag in your wardrobe, already packed.' I had yet to get out of the habit of packing PE bags, making lunchboxes and putting away ironing. Charlotte had it way too easy and she knew it.

I didn't linger in the bath. I could feel my mood sinking, so got out and put my pyjamas on. I curled up on my bed, skimming through the creative writing book I'd checked out in a rush. It wasn't the best, quite dated, but I couldn't change it now. Luckily, the trip to the library hadn't been a total waste, there were some exercises on story planning in the book I could use. How many pupils would attend the after-school class? What if no one came at all? That would be embarrassing.

* * *

At school the next morning, I saw Nicky across the playground and my stomach lurched. When he saw me, he grinned and waved. I managed a weak smile back. I could see him watching as I walked into school. I hoped it wasn't because of the outfit I'd chosen.

As I had free rein over what to wear, I had decided to be brave and chose a classic grey shift dress with a red cardigan to complement it. When I bought the dress last year, it came in grey and red, but I didn't have the confidence to buy the red one. I knew it would be another of those outfits in my wardrobe I would put on, look in the mirror and then change into something else as the voice in my head whispered, '*It isn't you*'.

I'd ignored that voice, coming downstairs and earning a wolf-whistle from David, who was working from home. I'd smiled and rolled my eyes, refraining from challenging him on his empty promise. It has only been a light-hearted whistle, no desire burned in his eyes. I couldn't remember the last time there had been. Perhaps I could suggest couples' therapy? Would David be up for that? We needed to find our way back to each other.

Charlotte hadn't been quite as impressed when we'd got in the car. She didn't mention the dress but that wasn't a surprise. I could probably leave the house naked and she wouldn't notice. I chose not to dwell on it and instead slotted the netball class into conversation. Surprisingly, Charlotte appeared interested in signing up. It transpired that Amy was sporty, so she figured they could do it together. I was delighted Charlotte was having a good week and settling in well. With her happy, it took the pressure off and I could concentrate on making this move work for all of us. I'd make more of an effort with David to talk about the miscarriage and not gloss over it like we had been.

It was a day of Shakespeare. I was teaching *Romeo and Juliet* in the morning, then an hour on sonnets, followed by *Macbeth* in the afternoon, which was my favourite. A story so dark and twisted, I fell in love with the witches the first time I read it. I was more excited about my lessons than the weekend ahead, which was likely to be filled with finishing the unpacking. I hoped we could manage to squeeze in dinner and a movie, a suitable reward for completing the move.

It was my turn on playground duty, which Matilda kindly pointed out on the rota in the staffroom. I hadn't noticed there was one but wandering around outside at break time, making sure none of the children were up to anything they shouldn't be, wasn't much of a hardship. Plus, it was good to get a little fresh air and the circulation going. Left to my own devices, I'd sit at that desk all day.

The sun was shining, and I was a little warm in my cardigan but too self-conscious to take it off. It wasn't raining, which made a nice change. Playground duty on those days would not be fun.

Mr Scott came out to join me briefly, letting me know all the after-school clubs had been featured in the newsletter which had gone out to parents yesterday and posters had been put up too. He told me not to be discouraged if numbers were low this week due to the late advertising. Grateful for the support, I said I'd let him know the turnout next week.

When I was alone again, I carried on the circular route around the playground, taking the path towards the tennis courts where the boys played football. My skin prickled as I neared the crowd, apprehension creeping in, although I wasn't sure why.

Nicky jogged past me, saying something in passing that I didn't catch.

'Pardon?' I called and he turned around.

'He fancies you, Miss.'

I frowned, no idea what he was talking about.

'Him, Mr Scott.' Nicky shook his head at my lack of comprehension.

'Looking hot today Miss.' He gave me a wink and carried on jogging, rounding the corner and out of sight.

## 6

When I got home, David was still in the office upstairs. I could hear him on the phone laughing, but when he finished, he came down to make me a cup of tea and even asked about my day. What surprised me more was that he'd cooked a gammon in the slow cooker for dinner. Perhaps he was trying to close the gap between us?

Charlotte asked for help with a piece of maths homework she was struggling with, which was ultimately David's department. He was the numbers whizz, I had no head for figures. They sat at the table whilst I cleared away dinner, all the time Charlotte's phone buzzed continually from the worktop where it was charging. She got up to answer a Face-Time call and I was about to tell her to ignore it, when David interrupted.

'Its fine, honey, we're done, she just needed some help to explain her workings out.'

Charlotte disappeared upstairs as the shrill tone of landline rang out.

'Wow, Clapham Junction in here today!' David exclaimed as he picked up the phone.

It was Stella, finding out how our first week had been at school.

After exchanging pleasantries, David took his cue and left me alone in the kitchen.

'Yeah, it's been good actually. Charlotte is settling in well and seems to have made a friend so that's great. The head teacher is pretty laid-back and is happy to let me get on with it,' I said, sliding into a seat at the table.

'That's a relief then.'

'Yeah, although I almost had a car crash on the first day. A bloody kid pulled out on me at the roundabout.'

'God! Did you hit them?'

'No, thankfully it was a near miss, but my anxiety shot through the roof, and then, guess what?'

'What?'

'Turned out to be a sixth former at St. Wilfred's. Came to apologise the same day.'

'Awkward.' Stella giggled.

'Just a bit.' It was my turn to laugh. 'Anyway, how are you?' I continued.

'Before that, are there any fit teachers?' Stella asked, getting the formalities out of the way.

'No, afraid not.' I chuckled. My thoughts drifted to Nicky for a second, but I quickly pushed that notion away. There was no way I was going to mention him.

Stella told me how she was trying to readjust to living 'up North' again. The village she'd grown up in was beautiful and the people friendly, but it was hard work with her dad's dementia getting worse. She'd moved in to the family home to take care of her parents, leaving her job, and pretty much her life, in London behind her. I felt heart-broken for her.

My parents had retired to Dorking a few years ago to a picturesque bungalow in the heart of the Surrey hills. We visited often, although they were yet to come to the new house. Wanting to wait for us to settle in. With them getting older, it was another incentive for us to move closer, but Mum was a volunteer at a charity shop and Dad had taken up birdwatching, they were both busier now than before.

Stella said she hoped to visit in a few weeks, she was waiting for her brother Robert to come up from Battersea for a few days and take over until she could arrange some regular care. It sounded like she could do with a break. We had plenty of room and she and David got on well, so dates were pencilled in the diary before we said goodbye.

After the call, I found David in the lounge watching television and I flopped down beside him, regaling my conversation with Stella.

'You know she's always welcome to stay. I know her moving away has been difficult,' David said, resting his hand on mine. My skin warmed beneath; the touch welcomed like a comfy pair of slippers.

When we went to bed later, I tried to instigate some intimacy with David again. This time, he responded with a little more enthusiasm and we had sex for the first time in months. It was over quickly, which I had expected, but it felt more functional than passionate. Although David made the effort to hold me afterwards, I couldn't help but feel empty and unsatisfied.

* * *

Finally, Friday arrived and despite feeling apprehensive, I was looking forward to the creative writing class. A few of the students I'd mentioned it to had said they would come. The day flew by and every spare minute I had I reviewed exercises and tried to keep the palpitations at bay. Charlotte was going to go to Amy's again and I was relieved; she wouldn't have to hang around and wait for me. I made a mental note to check if any bus routes could take her home from school, so she had another way to get there in case I ever got caught up.

The last lesson wasn't great, and I had to have words at the end with one disruptive year-nine girl who insisted on talking over me at every opportunity. I wasn't stern by nature but had learned that, given the opportunity, children would walk all over a teacher if they could. I found if I nipped certain behaviours in the bud the first time they occurred, my pupils treated me with respect. After the girl left the classroom, a few eager students that had been loitering in the corridor as soon as the bell went came through the door securing themselves seats in the front row. I smiled at them warmly, pleased that not only had some students turned up, but I recognised several of them from my classes.

'Is this the creative writing class?' came a familiar voice.

I turned to look at the door, surprised to see Nicky standing there, filling the space, two students standing awkwardly behind him.

I felt the miniscule muscle behind my eye begin to twitch. I'd been relieved I didn't have to teach Nicky during the day, but I couldn't stop him from attending an extracurricular class. I nodded and waved him in, feeling my anxiety spike. He sat in the front row and plucked a notebook out of his bag and a pen from behind his ear.

I turned away, greeting five more students who wandered into the room, ascertained they were in the right place, and sat down. The turnout hadn't been too bad, eleven students in total and hopefully more next week.

Facing the group, I perched on the edge of my desk, fingers drumming the wood underneath, out of view, as I did a couple of rounds of counting. Realising I couldn't put off starting any longer without seeming odd, I took a deep breath.

'Welcome to the Creative Writing Class, thanks for coming today. In this class I'm going to aim to show you how to get the most out of your writing, using some exercises and tips that will help you focus on being more imaginative.'

I handed out a sheet of paper to each student. On it was a block of colour and the word RED written in large letters underneath. I gave Nicky his last, unable to mistake his eyes gazing up at mine as he took the paper. I turned away, moving back to my desk.

'I know some of you, but if we could go around the class, let me know your name and year group please.'

I glanced at Nicky, who was closest to the door, and he spoke without hesitation, his voice deep and ragged, like he'd smoked a packet of cigarettes before he came in.

'Nicky Stevens, sixth form.'

The rest of the group took their turn as I recorded the information, it was a mix of year sevens, nines and Nicky.

'Brilliant, thank you. OK, so today I want you to think about the colour red. How does it make you feel? What do you associate it with? I want you to write a six-line poem about the things you connect with it. Does it make you think of danger? Of love perhaps, or anger? It doesn't have to be an emotion at all. What about red apples, red leaves in autumn, red sunsets – whatever springs to mind. We'll spend most of the time working on this activity and we'll read them at the end.'

One of the girls at the front, Emma, raised her hand and I smiled at her.

'Does it have to rhyme, Miss?'

'No, Emma, not all poems rhyme and whether yours does is entirely your choice,' I replied.

They all started to scribble ideas in their notebooks and sat, occasionally chewing their pens, staring into space for inspiration.

What was Nicky going to write? I couldn't believe he was honestly interested in creative writing, assuming he was more of a sportsman. Why was he here? I let twenty minutes pass whilst I pondered the question, drawing a cluster of tiny squares on my doodle pad, before asking the students if they were ready. Most were, but some wanted an extra five minutes. It was already ten to four, the time had sped by, and I was keen to ensure everyone got to read their poem.

I asked Emma to go first and went around in a circle before coming back to Nicky. All of them had presented a well-thought-out poem in the time allotted to them.

'Nicky, what have you written?'

He glanced at me, his eyes displaying a vulnerability I hadn't seen before. Clearing his throat, he leant forward over the paper.

'Red is the colour of roses with thorns,

Of new beginnings and beautiful dawns,
Red is the colour of love at its best,
With romance and flowers, the courtship test,
Red is the colour of lust and of lies,
The two together a perfect disguise.'

You could hear a pin drop in the classroom. I was floored by what Nicky had written. The rest of the class eyed him suspiciously, as it was clear his poem was superior.

I shook myself out of my daze. 'Fantastic, Nicky, well done. Well done to everyone, they were all fantastic poems. Now it's almost time to go, but if you can, I would like you to write another poem for next week, but this time I want you to pick your favourite colour.'

The students gathered their books and started to make their way to the door, saying goodbye to me as they passed.

Nicky was the last one to leave, deliberately putting his things away slowly. Once the corridor fell silent, I was acutely aware we were alone together. I tried to push it to the back of my mind, but something about him unnerved me. His stare was penetrating, like he could see inside my head.

'That was amazing, Nicky, I had no idea you were so talented,' I said, watching his eyes light up at my compliment.

'Thanks, Miss, I like writing. I read a lot too. I'm not all about football, you know,' he replied, and I knew instantly I'd made the mistake of stereotyping him. From his tone, I assumed it was something others did too.

'I'm impressed, truly.' I zipped up my bag, resisting the urge to do it more than once, and put my coat on.

Nicky stood to one side and let me walk through the classroom door first. Chivalry I wasn't expecting from a teenage boy.

For a second, I thought I felt his hand on the small of my back, guiding me out of the room. So light, I wasn't sure if I'd imagined it.

## 7

He was so close, our shoulders almost touching, I could see stubble emerging through the pale skin of his jaw. I widened the gap between us, the awkward silence excruciating. The only sound were my heels echoing down the corridor.

We exited the school and he carried on with me to the car park.

'What are you up to at the weekend?' I asked, not being able to bear the silence any longer.

'Not much. I need to get some football boots and I'm probably going to work on my car, it needs an oil change.'

'I've got some shopping to do as well, I think,' I volunteered awkwardly, although I didn't.

'I'll see you later, Miss,' Nicky said, after we'd reached my car, heading off through the gates.

I got into the driver's seat and sat, mind whirling as I watched him walk away. I couldn't start the car, not until I wound down the windows four times. Talking to Nicky was like interacting with a man, not a boy. I was floored by how articulate his poem was, as though he was wise beyond his years. I was annoyed I'd typecast him so easily. I wasn't normally so quick to judge.

I drove to Amy's house to collect Charlotte. This time, I managed to have a brief chat with her mother on the doorstep. Louise was pleasant, a trendy young mum in skinny black jeans with platinum blonde hair. Standing next to her, I felt frumpy. She said Charlotte was welcome at her house any time. It was good company for Amy as she was an only child like Charlotte. The words stuck in my throat as I agreed. I suggested Amy came to ours for dinner one afternoon next week so we could return the favour.

When we got in the car, Charlotte told me the plans she'd made for the following day.

'Mum, if you can drop me into Crawley, a group of us are going shopping, then MacDonald's and perhaps the flicks, if we can all get into the fifteen-rated film. I'm not sure whether we all will, Katy is still fourteen, but I'll let you know,' Charlotte babbled, checking her phone for anything she might have missed in the last five minutes.

We'd given in when Charlotte started high school and let her have David's old iPhone when he'd upgraded. My husband liked to have the latest gadgets, the most recent phone, iPad and anything else that required software updates. He revelled in being a bit of a tech geek. Charlotte benefited from his cast-offs as I wasn't interested. In contrast, I just wanted a smartphone that worked, not caring about the year or model. Initially, I was worried about Charlotte having a phone, my main concern was hearing about children being bullied via social media outside of school hours. But we'd decided we had to trust Charlotte to tell us if that was ever the case. Plus, I wanted her to keep in touch with us whilst she was out, and so far, there hadn't been any problems.

She'd never missed a curfew or failed to let us know where she was, but she was always glued to the stupid thing. It was like an obsession and David and I regularly commented that we would have to get it surgically removed from her hand. We had a no-tech rule after eight at night, if anything to give her eyes a rest. The phone was placed outside her bedroom door and not to be touched until morning. David regularly checked her apps for anything untoward; he was much more clued up on it than I was.

'Sure, I'll drop you into Crawley and see what your dad has planned, otherwise I might do a bit of shopping too.'

Charlotte narrowed her eyes. 'This isn't one of those times where you stalk me around the shopping centre, is it? Mum, I'm trying really hard to make new friends and fit in and if they see you creeping about everyone will take the... mickey.'

I laughed, unable to get my head around the fact that I was now the embarrassing parent. I still felt like a teenager myself most of the time.

'No, of course not, you won't see me, I promise. Do you need any money for tomorrow?' Charlotte shrugged, her focus back on her phone.

I gave her twenty pounds when we pulled up onto the driveway and agreed to drop her to the large shopping centre at ten the next morning.

David was still at work, an unread text on my phone to say he would be late home. I asked Charlotte if she fancied a takeaway and was met with a loud shriek, so I ordered pizza. It took ages to arrive but was worth the wait. We couldn't manage an extra-large pizza between us, so there were leftovers for David.

I sent him a text to let him know and he replied to say thanks, then announced he was going to play golf tomorrow with his boss. Seconds later, another text came through asking if minded. I didn't have much choice by the sound of it. Sunday would fly by with chores, and the plans I'd made in my head of spending some of the weekend unpacking now looked unlikely. The house would remain unfinished for another week.

* * *

When Charlotte appeared the following morning, I couldn't help but raise an eyebrow. She looked grown-up in high-waisted jeans and a pretty, embroidered off-the-shoulder top which only just reached her belly button. Her face, however, was plastered with make-up and I couldn't stop myself intervening.

'Charlotte, why don't you let me do your make-up? You look like it's wearing you, not the other way around,' I said gently.

Charlotte blinked back tears and I cringed inwardly at my clumsy words. She hardly ever wore make-up, but it was obvious she had a new group of friends that did. I kicked myself that I'd never given her any tips.

'I can straighten your hair too if you like, we've got time,' I offered.

Charlotte had David's dark wavy hair, which she hated, so she softened at this and trudged upstairs to the bathroom.

I started with Charlotte's caked on make-up and once I had removed a lot of the excess with cotton pads, she looked much better. I added a bit of blusher and, after wiping away the thick black eyeliner, used some brown instead to frame her hazel eyes. It didn't look so harsh. I straightened Charlotte's long hair next, leaving it sleek with a few curls at the bottom.

She beamed at her reflection in the mirror and gave me a hug to say thank you. It was such a rare occurrence these days, I had to turn my face away, eyes pricking with tears. I squeezed my daughter tight. She was growing up too fast, fifteen already, but I longed to hold on to my little girl forever.

We were running out of time, so I threw on my favourite indigo jeans, and a crisp white shirt. Slipping my feet into ballet pumps, I grabbed the recycling to put in the garage on the way out. Charlotte jumped in my car on the driveway and I pressed the key fob to raise the garage door. When I lifted the lid of the bin to dump the collection of bottles and cans, I spied David's golf clubs tucked in the corner. If he hadn't taken his clubs today, then whose was he playing with?

I swallowed, my mouth filling up with saliva. A wave of nausea washed over me. Was he really playing golf?

I pulled my phone out of my pocket and composed a text to David.

Round the course yet?

'Mum, come on, we'll be late,' Charlotte called, interrupting my thoughts.

I pushed down my uneasy feeling and hurried to the car, not wanting Charlotte to see my trembling hands.

* * *

In the middle of Crawley town centre was a large shopping centre and I parked in the multi-storey. Charlotte was meeting her friends outside Boots which was on the ground floor. I left her there to wait for them and made her promise to text me once they'd arrived. I wandered into Debenhams, loving the selection of brands in one store: Principles, Coast, John Rocha, and spent the next hour trying on various items, including a purple wrap dress, a pale blue pleated skirt and a pair of shoes. All of which found their way into my basket.

I reasoned if I was going to be left to my own devices, I couldn't be held responsible for the spending. I felt a pang in my chest when I saw a mustard coat that Stella would love. We'd spend hours shopping, laughing our way around the department stores, trying on whatever we fancied. It wasn't the same alone. If she was here, I'd be able to tell her about the golf clubs. I couldn't stop thinking about them. I could ring her, of course, but I wanted to give David the benefit of the doubt before I threw him under the bus. Plus, Stella loved David and I was sure she'd come up with all sorts of reasons why he may have left his clubs at home.

I wandered into the underwear section; it was all so pretty, pastel green and peach, polka dots in pink and cream lace. I felt like a kid in a sweetshop, unable to remember the last time I bought something other than a functional T-shirt bra. Perhaps this was what I needed to inject some passion back into my marriage? I picked up a powder blue lace balcony bra and matching knickers and headed into the changing room.

When I finally left Debenhams, it was nearly lunchtime and I'd spent almost two hundred pounds. I hadn't bought myself anything in such a long time, I didn't feel guilty. Continuing on my splurge, I booked a hair appointment at a salon called Rush, just outside of the centre, one that Susan had recommended. My bob was growing out and the greys were peeking through.

Afterwards, my stomach twinged, so I headed back inside the centre and up the escalator to the top floor, where the food court was. When I got to the top, I perused the various options: Burger King, jacket potatoes, and noodles. I couldn't face any more fast food and by chance saw an outlet advertising baguettes and paninis towards the end of the food court. I ordered a sundried tomato and mozzarella panini and Diet Coke before heading to a corner. The food court was packed, there were hardly any free tables, but I lingered and managed to grab one that had just been vacated.

I unwrapped the panini, steam still rising from the filling and checked my phone. I wanted to see if David had text me back. No texts. Where was he?

I saw in my peripheral vision a pair of beige desert boots approaching my table.

'Hello, Miss. Mind if I join you?'

I looked up to see Nicky looming over me, a wrapped panini in one hand.

## 8

'I'm not sure about this, Nicky,' I said weakly. I felt my lungs tighten, the panic beginning to rise. My heart grew louder as though someone was turning a dial. It was one thing bumping into a student, but what if someone saw us having lunch together?

'You worry too much, Miss, what's the worst that can happen?' he said, as he slid into the chair opposite.

I shivered at the proximity. He smelt deliciously fresh; a scent that made me think of days spent on the beach at the Witterings. Family days with David and Charlotte. What if she saw us eating together? She was in the centre somewhere with her friends.

Nicky noticed me surveying the faces in the crowd, looking for another free table I could vacate to. The place was rammed. Was it so bad to sit together? What harm could it do?

'You don't need to keep watch, Miss.' I winced, my eyes glancing to the next table, wondering if they'd heard Nicky refer to me as Miss? It was awkward enough bumping into students outside of school without being addressed so formally.

'Stop calling me Miss, please, call me Izzy. Obviously at school you'll still have to call me Miss though.' I almost said Mrs Cole but for some reason I stopped myself.

'OK, Izzy, it's a nice name, short for Isabel I'm guessing?' he said, taking a small bite of his cheese and ham panini.

I nodded, mine was still too hot. I felt the urge to drum my fingers on the table but distracted myself by tapping my foot instead. I hated having to explain my compulsion to others, most of them looked at me like I was a freak.

'So, did you get the football boots?' I asked, remembering our conversation from yesterday and wanting to try and keep the situation as normal as possible.

Nicky shook his head. 'No not yet, I've been at football practice this morning, and I coach the under eights afterwards, so I've only just got here. I see you've had quite a trip so far though.' He leaned over and eyed the large Debenhams carrier bag by my feet. It was wide open, and the new blue lace underwear sat right at the top of the bag in full view.

I gasped and pushed the bag under the table out of sight, feeling my face glow crimson.

'I'm sorry, I didn't mean to embarrass you,' he said, biting his lip. I watched his complexion redden as he leaned forward and briefly touched my forearm before I pulled away.

I willed my face to resume its normal pallor, which was intensely difficult especially as a second ago he'd touched me like it was the most normal thing in the world.

'It's fine,' was all I could manage and, not knowing what else to do, I took a bite of my panini and sat chewing. The filling scorched the roof of my mouth as my tapping foot went into overdrive.

We sat in silence for a minute, concentrating on our lunch. I struggled to meet his eyes. I wanted the ground to swallow me up. Our meeting had been awkward to say the least without him having seen my new underwear to add to it. The panini was difficult to chew. Nicky's voice interrupted my thoughts.

'He's a lucky man,' Nicky whispered, eyes lowered to the table.

'Who?' I choked out, stifling a cough.

'The man you've bought underwear for.' Any hope I'd had of my face returning to normal went out the window as I felt the flames beneath my skin rise up again.

Nicky met my eye with a genuine smile before looking away. Our eating lunch together no longer felt harmless.

I shook my head, I'd made a mistake. Jumping up to leave, I knocked the table with my thigh. The half-eaten panini still in its wrapper on the table.

As I gathered my bags, Nicky grabbed my wrist to stop me, his fingers hot against my skin.

'Where are you going?'

'I'm not quite sure what's happening here, but you are a student and I am also happily married,' I said, wrenching my arm out of his grip, tiny blotches remaining where his fingers had been.

I strode away without looking back. Had I overreacted? I didn't know but I felt foolish, I was the adult after all, I should have known better. I should have gone with my gut and asked him to sit somewhere else.

\* \* \*

I drove straight home after my encounter with Nicky and had to go back out again to collect Charlotte from the cinema. The group of girls had been to see a comedy called *Good Boys*, all of them managing to get in the fifteen rating. By all accounts, Charlotte had had a fun afternoon with her new friends. I felt relieved she'd had a good time and seemed to be fitting in. They seemed like a nice crowd and I was glad it wasn't something I'd have to worry about with everything else going on.

David came home for dinner, although he declared he wasn't hungry. He and the boss had been out for lunch after their round of golf. I prickled at his hug and he asked me what was wrong.

'Did you not get my text?' I asked.

'It came through on the way home. I was driving.'

'I saw your clubs in the garage. How did you manage to play without them?'

'Yeah, I completely forgot to take them, but Patrick had a spare set.' He didn't hesitate to answer, and I didn't hear his voice waver at all. If he was lying, he was convincing. I narrowed my eyes, something didn't sit right.

When he went upstairs to have a shower, I picked up his phone, staring at the blank screen. Did I want to do this? Break the trust by going through his things? I knew it was crossing a line, but I had to know what he was up to or whether I was going mad. I unlocked the screen, grateful the passcode hadn't been changed and was still the last four digits of his parents' old home phone number. There was nothing to note in his messages or emails and I breathed a silent sigh of relief. I looked at a few other apps but just as I was about end my search, I had an idea. I clicked on the FindMyPhone app, a default app that is preloaded on all iPhones. I tapped Share My Location and selected my telephone number as the person to share it with. I closed down the app, hoping David wouldn't notice I could now trace him. We'd made sure we both had access to Charlotte's location as soon as she was given David's old phone. He'd shown me how to activate it, I wouldn't have had a clue otherwise. I was probably overreacting, blowing things out of proportion but now I'd know if David wasn't where he said he was.

On Sunday, I got up early and spent the day indoors, managing to finish the unpacking from the move. There were some decorative jobs David and I wanted done. Parts of the reclaimed oak flooring needed sanding and the butler sink in the kitchen was slightly stained, but the official move was complete. I'd overestimated what we had left to do as a lot had to go into the loft and the empty boxes were now neatly stacked in the utility room waiting to be collected.

Charlotte met up with Amy again, but this time they hung out in Starbucks. Apparently, this was something teenagers did now, which had bypassed me altogether. When I was the same age, it was a bottle of cider at the local park, snuck in after dark. So I was glad Charlotte was settling down; she seemed calmer since meeting Amy. Her new friends at St. Wilfred's were having a positive effect and I couldn't deny

I was relieved. I didn't want her to be as wayward as I was, and it was important to me that she felt we were a team at home.

As we'd barely spent any time together as a family over the weekend, we all decided to go for a Chinese on Sunday night. It was a cuisine we all enjoyed and our local one was only a ten-minute walk away. It turned out to be a pleasant evening, as we sat around the table feeling content. The mood was buoyant, even Charlotte laughed at David's awful dad jokes, but inside there was a knot in the pit of my stomach.

My run-in with Nicky was niggling at me, as it had done, in truth, since I'd left him on Saturday. With the start of the school week approaching, I felt on edge at the prospect of seeing him again. I could have handled things better, not run away like a coward. I found his intense stare overwhelming; attention wasn't something I was used to receiving. When I'd returned home from the shopping centre, the house had been empty, and I'd stuffed my underwear purchases under the bed. Even though they were a gift for myself and no one else, I'd been unable to look at them since. They were a reminder of an uncomfortable situation that I felt foolish for running away from.

That night I laid in bed, drumming my fingers on the side of the mattress in time with David's snoring, anticipating seeing Nicky the following day. I wasn't sure why I was anxious; he was only a boy, and nothing had happened. I probably wouldn't even see him until the creative writing class on Friday, if he wasn't too embarrassed to attend, but when Monday came, it seemed Nicky was everywhere I went.

After form room, I visited the school library looking for a copy of Shakespeare's sonnets and saw him, head bowed, searching the bookshelves at the far end of the room. I froze, watching him run his finger across the spines, brow furrowed, searching for something in particular. Should I leave? Scurry away unseen? Watching him deliberate between two books, the concentration apparent in his eyes, it hit me that he was just a student. I had nothing to feel apprehensive about. Wrapping my arms around myself I slipped into the adjacent aisle. It was a good opportunity to clear the air. We were two of four people in the library: Thomas the librarian, and another student at one of the tables, copying sections of text from a book the size of *War and Peace*.

I crept down the aisle until I was directly opposite and able to see him through the gaps in the shelves. Lines were apparent on his normally smooth forehead and he chewed his lip as he concentrated on reading the titles. I kept my voice low so I wouldn't be heard by the others.

'Hi,' I whispered, clearing my throat when he didn't look up straight away.

He frowned at me through the space above the books, his expression pinched. Without a word, he lowered his eyes, continuing the search.

I rubbed my clammy palms on my trousers.

'I'm sorry,' I continued, figuring it was the best place to start.

Nicky's shoulders slumped, his bravado slipping for a second.

'I should be sorry, but, it's just, you know... you can't blame me for trying,' he breathed.

I shook my head, unable to comprehend his audacity.

'I lost track of time, had to rush to pick up Charlotte.' The lie came easily, covering my embarrassment for running away and not dealing with the situation at the time.

'I see,' he said, lifting his chin. He seemed to see straight through me.

'How about we start again?' I offered, unsure whether to state the obvious, that I was married and unavailable, but I couldn't quite bring myself to say the words. I was assuming that he was interested in me, sure he was flirting, but maybe I'd made a mistake in thinking it was anything more?

'Sure.' He smiled, although it didn't reach his eyes.

'Do you not have a class?' I asked, changing the subject.

'No, it's a free period.'

'I better get back, I need to find a book about sonnets, mine has gone walkabout.' I turned to leave and felt his eyes burning on my back as I did. I was glad we'd cleared the air. It could have gotten extremely awkward, especially as he was in my creative writing class.

* * *

The day seemed to drag, and the post-lunch assembly didn't help. It was my first one – the teachers sat at the front of the hall, on the stage, and children sat on the floor in rows facing us. Year eleven and sixth form were the only students allowed to sit in chairs at the back of the hall. The whole thing felt invasive. Like we were under the microscope. Too many sweaty bodies crammed into the space, all eyes on us as though we were on display.

The hall was dark with lots of wooden panelling, air musty from lack of circulation and fresh air. After lunch, all I ever wanted to do was nap and trying to refrain from yawning whilst Mr Scott spoke was proving difficult. I clenched my jaw to stop my mouth from springing open.

Charlotte was sat on a chair at the back, her legs crossed. She looked bored too, twirling her hair around her finger. I couldn't blame her.

As I surveyed the faces staring at us, I saw Nicky in the last row, chewing gum, his eyes glistening. I looked away, and glanced back a few seconds later, catching Nicky wink at me. My muscles stiffened, body rigid as I turned my attention back to the words of Mr Scott. I avoided looking in Nicky's direction for the rest of the assembly.

# 9

Charlotte arrived into my classroom at the end of the day with a long face. She'd just come from maths and was frustrated she couldn't grasp a particular equation as quickly as her peers. My suggestion that we get ice cream at a nearby dessert restaurant was met with disgust.

'I'm fifteen, Mum, not eight,' she said, voice laced with sarcasm.

'Well, in that case, shall we go and do some shots instead?' This raised a smile and we settled on a visit to Starbucks in town. Charlotte showed me where it was, and we sat on a comfy green sofa right by the window.

I wrapped my hands around my caramel frappuccino, the cold making my fingers tingle. Charlotte was sucking hers loudly through a straw.

I could see why it was the cool place to hang out, there was a relaxed atmosphere. The buzz of people milling around, but it managed to be chilled out at the same time.

'So, any boys on the horizon that your dad and I need to worry about yet?' I asked.

'Mum, we are so not talking about this.' Charlotte shut down the conversation instantly. Why were teenagers so secretive? It was like as soon as she started wearing a bra and her period arrived she morphed into a different person. I remembered having crushes at Charlotte's age that my parents never knew about but they were one-sided, so there was never anything to act on.

'OK, but you're all right though? Nothing you want to talk to me about? I'm here if you do.'

'If you're going to tell me about the birds and bees again, please don't.'

I laughed and shook my head as I watched Charlotte squirm in her seat. It reminded me of when I was that age, although my mum never talked to me about anything, I had to find out from my friends. Charlotte did chat about school though and said she was going to try out the netball club tomorrow. I offered to pick her up after I'd nipped for a quick swim, but she wanted to get the bus.

Apparently, you could get the number 2 bus from outside the school and it stopped at the end of our road. My chest constricted and I knew I was being overprotective. Charlotte had to stand on her own two feet at some point. She'd hadn't had to get the bus at the last school. We lived five minutes away and she didn't even have to cross any roads, just walk along a footpath. It was no surprise she wanted a bit of independence. I'd seen it happen time and time again at school. Parents kept their children on too short a leash and were surprised when they rebelled. I always said when the time came, I would do the opposite, but now it was here, I understood how tough it was to let go.

I loved bonding moments with my daughter, they were few and far between these days, but I felt more like a team with Charlotte than half of a couple with David. Our wedding anniversary was approaching next week, and it would be sixteen years since we'd said, 'I do'. It seemed like a million years ago. I mentioned it at dinner later that day and David tried to cover the fact that he'd forgotten by leaning across the table to kiss my cheek.

'I'd have got less for murder,' he said as he took his plate to the sink and Charlotte snorted. I rolled my eyes.

'Why don't we go away for the weekend, all of us, to Center Parcs or somewhere?'

It was Charlotte's turn to roll her eyes. 'And be stuck with you love-birds? No thanks.'

David leant across and patted my hand, saying he'd look into it.

When we got into bed, David snuggled behind me and kissed the back of my neck. I arched my back appreciatively, groaning as he reached around to cup my breast. We were soon making love, although just as David finished, Nicky's face popped unwelcome into my thoughts. I sat up quickly and made my way to the bathroom, hiding out until I could hear David's light snores from behind the door. My fingers drummed my bare thighs as I sat on the toilet, trying to banish Nicky's face from my mind. Was it somehow related to my feeling that David's golf trip had been a cover for something else? I had to give him the benefit of the doubt. In all the years we'd been married he'd never so much as a looked at another woman.

After a while, I crept downstairs to the kitchen, not wanting to wake David or Charlotte, closing the door behind me. As I stood over the kettle waiting for it to boil, my chest tightened. Was I going mad? Imagining something was going on when it wasn't? No, I was sure he'd changed. At home it felt like we were acting. I was the Stepford wife and David, the solid provider. Had I fallen out of love with him? Had he stopped loving me? Maybe the miscarriage last year had broken us and been the final nail in the coffin. Could that be why David was never around? Perhaps he couldn't bear the pretence, the mundane daily routine and that was why he stayed away. Maybe it was why I felt so unsettled by Nicky?

I had to get him out of my head. I didn't want him intruding on my life, popping up wherever my subconscious decided. I began scrubbing my hands in the sink. Trying to rid the dirty feeling that had wrapped itself around me like a blanket.

David and I were strong, we'd get through it. We'd get away for a weekend and perhaps try and spice things up. Inject some passion back into our lives. Make us want each other again.

* * *

In the morning, I pulled the new underwear purchases out from where I'd stuffed them under the bed and put the peach set on. It lifted me in all the right places as I turned, admiring it in the mirror. A good bra worked wonders, it stretched me out and my stomach appeared flatter too. I chose the purple wrap dress, removing the tags. It felt good to wear a whole new outfit. The neckline was deep, but Charlotte said it looked fine with a necklace. I would have asked David, but he'd gone to work before I'd even woken up. I was hopeful he'd like the dress later, perhaps enough to see what was under it. The scent of his aftershave lingered in the bathroom. A new one, I hadn't smelt it before. The clear wrapping was still in the bathroom bin. Who was he wearing that for? David had stuck with the same aftershave since we'd met, Le Male by Jean-Paul Gaultier. I bought him a bottle every birthday, it had become a tradition.

I slumped onto the bed, gazing into the distance. If alarm bells weren't chiming before, they certainly were now. I snatched up my phone, typing 'how to tell if your husband is having an affair' into Google. According to the random magazine article I clicked on, I needed to watch for: working longer hours, new clothes or gym regime, taking more care with their appearance and decreasing sex drive.

I was still thinking about the list when I arrived into the staffroom and knew instantly I'd made a mistake with the dress. Mr Scott's gaze lingered a second too long before he blushed and looked away. After that, I felt self-conscious all day and couldn't stop rearranging the neckline, paranoid I'd look down and find it gaping. My anxiety in full force, I had to do almost everything in groups of four, sure some of the students had noticed I was off kilter.

When the day finally ended, I was desperate to destress with a swim. I bumped into Matilda in the corridor on the way out and we arranged to meet for a curry for next week. I felt a warm glow at being included, at least it was one night where I wouldn't be at home, waiting for David.

I saw a figure near my car as I approached. On closer inspection, I could see they were leaning on my driver's door. Who the hell was it?

My stomach churned audibly as I registered it was Nicky. He smiled as I drew nearer.

'I was wondering if I could get a lift, my battery is dead. Unless you've got some jump leads?' he raised his eyebrows expectantly. There hadn't been any boys as self-assured when I was his age. They were all awkward spotty teenagers back them, Nicky on the other hand looked more like a man than a boy.

'No, I don't have any. Don't you have any mates who can pick you up?' My words spilled out in a rush as I looked warily around the car park. It was nearly empty, but there were a few cars left and I was concerned how many teachers were still in the building and could be watching our exchange.

'OK.' He shrugged and turned to walk towards the gates.

I sighed, it was obvious he was disappointed, but I didn't want to be seen with him in my car. Plus, Charlotte was around somewhere, at netball practice.

When he'd left the school grounds and was out of sight, I climbed in the car and started the engine. As I pulled out of the gates and onto the main road, I saw Nicky walking along the pavement, his bag slung over his shoulder, bouncing with each step. Checking my rear-view mirror to ensure no one was behind me, I stopped beside him and lowered down my window. I was only giving him a lift, nothing more than that. As a teacher I should help out a student if they needed it.

'Cheers, Miss.' He hopped in and I pulled away.

'Where do you live, you'll have to direct me,' I said, gripping the steering wheel and turning up the air conditioning.

'Keep going down here,' he said, pointing when I needed to turn.

When we got to his house around ten minutes later, I parked a little way ahead of it. He lived in a terraced house, with a gravel front garden filled with pots of yellow marigolds.

'Who do you live with?' I asked, nodding back over my shoulder towards his house.

'Just my mum,' he replied, but didn't volunteer any further information and I didn't pry. I let out a silent sigh, feeling calmer now we
were a suitable distance from the school and less likely to be seen. I
had to clear this up now, make him see that there was a line he couldn't
cross.

'Nicky, I don't think you realise how much trouble you could get me
in. If someone was to get the wrong idea even, I could lose my job.'

He turned his body around in his seat, facing me, the distance
between us shrinking. Close enough to smell the minty chewing gum
on his breath and see that he needed a shave. My cheeks burned
despite the cold air pumping through the vents. His eyes wandered
down my body, taking in the purple fabric of my dress stretched over
my thighs before moving upwards. Observing the accelerating rise and
fall of my cleavage, his gaze eventually returned to my face, eyes
hungry. David hadn't looked at me like that in years.

'Just let it happen,' he whispered and moved in, brushing his lips
against mine.

I forgot myself for a millisecond, shocked that our lips had touched
before I shoved him back into his seat.

Nicky scowled, his eyes narrowed, fixed on mine.

'No, Nicky! I don't know how I can make it any clearer.' I gritted my
teeth.

He threw open the car door and grabbed his bag from the footwell,
flinging it over his shoulder.

'You're a fucking tease,' he spat, and I shrank back in my seat. In a
second he was out of the car, the door slammed shut.

I blinked back tears, filling my lungs with air, unaware I'd been
holding my breath. His demeanour shocked me. I rested my forehead
on the steering wheel, eyes closed and counting. Flicking the internal
lock; *one, two, three, four, one, two, three, four.* Carrying on until the
inside of the car was no longer blurry.

Going swimming didn't help me shake the feeling in the pit of my
stomach. I managed forty lengths, twenty more than usual in the hope

I could exhaust my body and my mind. I tried to erase what had happened. Was Nicky right? Had I led him on? I had to get my head together and focus on the job and my family. I had to stay away from Nicky.

## 10

The following few days passed in a haze, all I did was work and sleep. I couldn't help feeling lonely and isolated. I pushed thoughts of Nicky out of my mind and was grateful when I didn't see him at school. Perhaps he was avoiding me, as I was with him?

David worked late, always apologetic when he got home. On the FindMyPhone app, I saw he was at his office in Hove. Exactly where he was supposed to be. I was at a loss at what else to do. He hadn't mentioned going away and I knew he'd forgotten. We'd slipped back into that familiar routine; I'd leave his dinner in the microwave, spending my evenings marking or reading and was in bed most of the time when he got home. Charlotte spent an evening at Amy's, but otherwise she was in her room doing homework or on the iPad. I was bored and the house felt cold and lifeless.

I rang Mum often, checking to see how her and Dad were. Mum loved to tell me about the characters she met every day at the charity shop where she volunteered. An elderly gentleman came in twice a day, to see if anything new had been donated. Mum thought he was a bargain hunter, I told her he probably had a crush on a member of staff. We laughed.

The only other outlet for me was swimming and I managed to fit in a couple of trips to the pool. I was getting better at increasing my distance each time and enjoyed releasing my pent-up energy. I tried my best not to think about how David and I were drifting further apart. I felt powerless to stop it. Did I still love him? I thought so, but it wasn't the same as it used to be. Was anyone's marriage the same after so many years together?

I was thankful I had Stella to turn to. We had a couple of long chats over the phone, once Charlotte had gone to bed. Curled up on the sofa with a glass of wine, she knew me so well, she immediately sensed something was wrong. I tried to brush over the subject, complaining David was always working late and yet this new job was supposed to mean we could spend more time together. Stella had enough on her plate with her parents, so I tried to keep things as light as possible although she took the time to pacify me, reiterating that David was just trying to make inroads in the company. We were both looking forward to when she would come to visit. I was desperate for some girl time.

I felt a jolt to my core when Nicky came to the creative writing class on Friday. It was the first time I'd seen him since Tuesday, but he barely looked at me during the hour, not even when it came to reading out his homework, the poem on his favourite colour. I found it unnerving. He handed in the poem as he left. Placing the paper on my desk without so much as a glance at me.

David played golf again with Patrick on Saturday. He was going to be out all day. This time, he was being picked up, as his boss wanted to go for a drink after finishing the course. He left early, when I was in the shower, so I didn't see him leave. Over breakfast, we'd argued about him spending so little time at home. He was apologetic, claiming he had no choice, but I was infuriated. The tension between us was palpable and I considered throwing an accusation at him, that he was having an affair, but I was scared he'd say yes, admit he was and pack a bag, leaving Charlotte and I here alone, our family unit destroyed. I wasn't ready to contemplate that scenario.

When I'd dropped Charlotte off with Amy, I was at a loose end. I contemplated going back to the library or heading to Tilgate park, a renowned beauty spot, but my phone buzzed, reminding me of the cut and colour I'd booked at Rush for an hour's time. Shit. With everything going on, I'd forgotten my appointment. I drove into town and parked a street away from Rush at an NCP car park, dashing to get to the salon on time. Two hours later with the amazing Rebecca, I felt a million times better. She'd reshaped my bob and my hair was now a glossy red.

David strolled through the door after nine, halfway through a movie Charlotte and I were watching. He was tipsy, his walk had a slight lean, as it always did after a few pints. Unsurprisingly, he didn't notice my hair when he poked his head in to say hello. Shortly after, we heard the banging of pans from the kitchen. Was he cross I hadn't made any dinner for him? Now wasn't the right time to ask if he'd really been playing golf.

Charlotte shifted in her seat, the atmosphere suddenly tangible. When the film was over, David still hadn't materialised from the kitchen, so we disappeared upstairs together and left him to it.

I woke around eight on Sunday morning, sunlight filling the bedroom. The jarring sound of a magpie calling pushed me out of bed. I could hear David snoring downstairs; he must have slept on the sofa. No doubt he'd be hungover and grumpy all day. I'd woken already irritated with him and got on with my chores, managing to strip the beds, put some washing on, and hoover before he even came to.

David wandered into the kitchen as I was peeling the potatoes for a Sunday roast over the sink. The atmosphere unchanged from last night.

'I'm sorry.'

I had my back to him and rolled my eyes. 'What for?' I asked flatly, continuing to peel, not bothering to turning around.

'For being out all day yesterday, for coming home drunk and being useless today.' He wrapped his arms around my waist and buried his head into my neck, his breath hot on my shoulder. I had to refrain from flinching and spoke through gritted teeth.

'Where did you play?'

I felt David's arms stiffen for a second.

'Peacehaven.'

'Well, I'm glad you had fun,' I said, my voice dripping with sarcasm.

David sighed and gave up on his apology, returning to the front room.

\* \* \*

Monday came around again all too soon, but I leapt out of bed when the alarm went off. At least I could keep myself busy, my mind away from home. Our anniversary was on Thursday and I was waiting to see if David would remember. I'd already bought him a card and a sixteen-year-old bottle of single-malt whisky to match our sixteen-year anniversary and hidden them away in my wardrobe.

I immersed myself in my lessons and Mr Scott paused to watch, eyebrows raised, when he walked past and saw my year nines acting a scene from *Macbeth*. I'd used my free hour to borrow some costumes from the drama department and print out a scene for a small group to act out. It was a great way to get them to understand the text. Most of them loved it as it was unusual for them to be so active in an English lesson.

At lunchtime, I had some marking to do so stayed in my classroom whilst I ate a sandwich. Matilda popped her head around the door, an earnest smile spread across her face.

'Knock,' she said jovially.

I smiled and waved her in, still chewing.

'Hi, how are you?'

Matilda perched on the edge of a desk; folders clutched to her chest. Her style was so eccentric, I loved it. She wore her purple Doc Martens with black leggings, a tie-dye tunic and chunky beaded necklace. 'Good thanks, just checking you're OK as you weren't in the staffroom.'

I lifted the pile of marking, rolling my eyes.

'I've got so much marking today, I thought I'd try and get ahead. Still on for a curry this week?' I asked.

'Absolutely, I think Susan should be too. Wednesday work for you?'

I nodded enthusiastically. I was looking forward to it.

Matilda stood and headed for the door.

'Oh, by the way, you're popular today,' she said.

I frowned, no idea what she meant.

'Go and take a look at your car,' she said with a chuckle as she left.

I snatched my keys out of my handbag and hurried out of the building towards the car park. My car looked normal from a distance, but I could only see the rear as I'd parked forward facing. When I got around to the front, there was a small posy of flowers tucked underneath one of my window wipers. A pretty arrangement of carnations and gerberas in pink and orange. A card hidden in the middle of the display.

I looked around the car park before opening it, my ears growing hot. Who had given me flowers?

The card had one solitary word: *Sorry*

I assumed they were from David, although receiving flowers on my car was odd – surely, he would have sent them to our home or to the school office? Either way, it was a lovely gesture and I felt a warm glow spread through me as I carried them back to the classroom, lifting the bouquet to smell the flowers as I walked. Smiling to myself, I glanced over to the tennis court and spotted Nicky. Something about his stance made me stop in my tracks. Pressed against the wire fence, fingers curled through the gaps, he stared openly in my direction. The flowers weren't from David at all.

I looked around and could see no one watching, so raised the flowers slightly and nodded towards them in a questioning gesture I hoped he would be able to see. He gave a distinctive nod and my stomach plummeted. I dropped the flowers to my side, holding them by the stems so the blooms were upside down, petals fluttering to the ground as I walked. Intending to throw them into the nearest bin.

I glared at Nicky, although there was probably too much distance between us to see the irritation written on my face. He clearly wasn't getting the message.

## 11

On Tuesday, I didn't see Nicky out of the window at break time and he was nowhere to be seen when the sixth-formers had their PE lesson in the tennis court. The day was uneventful and after netball practice, Charlotte went back to Amy's house. Louise was going to drop her home later, so I took the opportunity and went for a swim. I hadn't had the chance to go after work the day before as I'd been cornered by Mr Scott who'd wanted to hear all about the creative writing club and by the time I'd shown him some of the planned assignments, it was gone four.

Halfway through my target of forty lengths, I paused to have a breather at the pool's edge. Squeezing the water out of my hair, I took off my goggles and wiped under my eyes in the hope my mascara hadn't run too much. A group of boys at the deep end were throwing each other around and hooting. I froze when I realised Nicky was one of them, the cold water disguising the goosebumps that had appeared on my arms. He caught my eye and smiled before I looked away. He didn't seem surprised I was there. Had he followed me here?

No, why would he do that?

I sank lower in the water until it covered my shoulders. He wouldn't come over, would he? In my swimsuit, I felt naked and exposed.

Trying to ignore the raucousness at the other end of the pool, I carried on with my lengths, failing to keep count, distracted every time he was in my field of vision. When he climbed out of the pool, his green shorts clinging to his thighs, I faltered, swallowing water and coughing as I reached the side. His shoulders were broad, and his smooth chest defined. Lean and toned, the sprouting body hair and middle-aged paunch still a couple of decades away. He towered above his friends by at least a foot.

When I finished spluttering, I stretched my arms and back, unable to tear my eyes away as Nicky rinsed himself in the poolside showers. He knew I could see him; I was sure of it, deliberately running his hands across his skin in a show meant for me. Then he was gone, headed for the changing rooms, without a single glance in my direction.

I felt my jaw tighten, my molars clenching as I threw myself into another ten lengths, trying to banish the inappropriate thoughts swarming around my head. Had David ever looked like that? Maybe when we first met, but, to be honest, I couldn't remember it. I had to concede Nicky was handsome. He knew it though. I could tell in the way he carried himself.

When I'd left it long enough to be sure he'd gone, I got out of the pool, turning my shower to as cold as I could stand.

* * *

David wasn't home when I walked through the door, but Charlotte's school shoes had been discarded in the hallway, so I knew she'd been dropped off already. It would have been nice to have the house to myself. I was worried my improper thoughts of Nicky, his green shorts clinging to him, would be written all over my face. My cheeks reddened as the image filled my mind and I shook my head to clear it.

In the kitchen, Charlotte hovered over a saucepan bubbling away on the hob. I lay my handbag on the worktop, looking around in awe.

Eyes wide, I surveyed the scene: the table was set, napkins and wine glasses had been put out as though it was a special occasion.

'I thought I'd make a start and surprise you,' Charlotte said, bouncing from foot to foot.

'I am surprised,' I replied, my voice high-pitched. I squeezed Charlotte to me and kissed the top of her head before she could wriggle away. 'What are we having?'

'Spaghetti and Caesar salad, is that OK?' Charlotte asked, chewing her lip.

A warm glow swept through me. She was growing up too fast. I nodded, wondering if I was being buttered up for something.

'Need any help?' I asked but was shot a withering look and waved out of the kitchen.

David strutted in, a triumphant smile on his face, announcing himself loudly. Perhaps he thought we should be grateful he'd made it home for dinner? I nodded at him as we passed and took my wet things upstairs.

From the bathroom, I could hear David and Charlotte talking. He sounded as surprised as I was that Charlotte was cooking dinner, although the menu might cause him to moan later when we were alone. David was like a caveman and any meal without meat was disagreeable.

I heard his footsteps on the stairs and busied myself emptying the washing basket. He leaned through the door to the bathroom. The smell of his new aftershave still fresh, like he'd not long applied it.

'How was your day?' he asked and kissed my cheek.

I felt myself stiffen at his touch. I couldn't help it. Everything about David annoyed me at the moment. It was irrational, but his voice, his face, his mannerisms, all got my back up. An image of Nicky's smooth chest invaded my mind and I pushed it away.

'Fine. Remember you need to be home by seven tomorrow, I'm going out for a curry with a couple of the teachers.'

He stared at me blankly and I sighed. I wasn't sure why I'd expected him to remember.

'I did tell you. Matilda and Susan... The art and maths teachers,' I said, waiting for the penny to drop.

David shrugged but nodded; I knew he didn't recall the conversation. He didn't remember anything outside of his own bubble.

'Sure, it's fine, I'll make sure I'm here.'

'Thanks,' I replied flatly. My knight in bloody shining armour.

His phone started to ring, and he turned away to answer it. I leaned in, to try and gauge who was on the other end. I was expecting a woman, but I heard a male voice asking David about derivatives. Had I got it wrong? I'd overanalysed before, thinking something was wrong when it wasn't. Was I putting two and two together and making five? My anxiety didn't help, my mind would go into overdrive and I'd conjure up all sorts of scenarios. None of which were likely in reality. But something had definitely changed. Perhaps I needed to bite the bullet and initiate some intimacy between us again. Normally a good tumble between the sheets would sort things, but I was about as enthusiastic about that as I was the weekly food shop.

That night, I climbed on top of him before he could give me an excuse and it wasn't long before he was hard and inside me. I closed my eyes and moved rhythmically. David was groaning beneath me, but I was going through the motions. I leant forward and kissed him, pushing my tongue into his mouth, but as hard as I tried, I couldn't get into it. After ten minutes, I began to move faster, knowing David wouldn't be able to hold off for long. When he was done, I locked myself in the en suite and sat on the toilet, shielding my eyes from the bright light. My mind whirred, thoughts of David with another women forced their way into my head and a crushing sensation enveloped my chest.

'You OK?' David whispered through the door.

'I'm fine,' I replied, as light-heartedly as I could manage. I emerged to muffled snores and resorted to earphones when I got into bed, hoping my audiobook would drown him out.

The next morning, standing in front of the mirror, I struggled to choose my clothes, eventually deciding on the blue pleated skirt. The sun was shining, and it looked like a nice day ahead. I matched it with a cream blouse and heels. A slick of cherry lipstick finished the look.

Charlotte commented on how nice I looked as we got into the car. She seemed happier since the move, likely due to her blossoming friendship with Amy. A different child to the one who was struggling to fit into the crowd in London. The one that was too easily led, too eager to please her friends and do anything to look cool. Receiving a genuine smile from her was so good to see and I didn't feel like I was the enemy any more.

Amy came to meet Charlotte in the car park. She was a pretty girl with long mousy-coloured hair and a large mouth which was almost always formed into a smile.

'Hello, Mrs Cole,' she said brightly, looping her arm through Charlotte's.

'Morning, Amy. You must come over for dinner this week if you're free, or next week. Let Charlotte know what day is best for you and we'll sort something out.'

'Thanks, Miss.'

The girls turned and walked towards the playground.

'Have a good day,' I called after them as I watched them whispering conspiratorially. Oh, to be that age again, young and carefree where your troubles were no more than studying for your GCSEs and which boy you fancied.

The first lesson of the day was A-Level Literature; they were studying *Tess of the d'Urbervilles* by Thomas Hardy. It was one of my favourites, so a pleasant class to teach. The sixth-formers were all keen and listened intently. It was a different feel in the classroom altogether to a younger age group. The students had chosen English Literature, so they wanted to be there.

I looked around the room, well over half of the class were girls, aged sixteen to seventeen. My thoughts turned to Nicky, as they had done much of last night. These were the girls he would be dating. There were some pretty ones too and I was sure he would be able to take his pick; or maybe he already had? He could have been out with every girl in the room for all I knew. I bit down on my molars, jaw clenched tight, wondering why the thought unsettled me.

* * *

When lunchtime arrived, I wolfed down half a sandwich and went outside for playground duty. The sun was warm, but there was a cool breeze which kept catching my skirt, pressing it against my legs as I walked. I moved in a loop of the grounds, leaving the tennis courts until last, walking straight past the boys playing football, smiling as I went.

Nicky stepped out from behind a striker, our eyes meeting before my attention was caught by a group of year eleven girls. One of them swearing, hands gesticulating at the other. I intervened and she apologised without argument.

In my peripheral vision, I could see Nicky waiting to catch my attention, but I pretended I hadn't seen him and carried on walking; stopping to talk to a group of girls sitting on the grass nearby. When I glanced over my shoulder, I saw he was still there, brow furrowed.

I didn't want to interact with him, it was best to ignore the attention. I tapped my fingers against my thigh, counting to four in my head, over and over again, as I carried on walking, leaving Nicky behind.

## 12

I had some marking to do when I got home before I got ready for my evening with Matilda and Susan. I'd prepared a lasagne, which was in the oven ready to go for Charlotte and David to share, and was watching the minutes tick by on the clock in the kitchen. Had he forgotten our conversation?

I opened and shut the dishwasher door. *One, two, three, four. One, two, three, four.* My stomach fizzed with anger. I hated being late. Charlotte was old enough to be left by herself, but if I could avoid it, I did.

David walked in at five to seven, muttering an apology that the traffic was awful, and I left as soon as he arrived, barely acknowledging him. Turning the radio up in my car, it felt good to be out, the sun was sinking slowly, but the wind from earlier had dropped. I arrived at the restaurant fifteen minutes later, the traffic *was* unusually heavy for the time of day.

Our table had been booked for seven thirty and I was the first to arrive. I was shown to our seats and offered a drink. The restaurant was called Cinnamon and had blacked-out windows, so you weren't unable to see inside from the street. The interior décor was a dusky pink with minimal lighting and soothing Bangalore music played in the background. Matilda had recommended the restaurant and when her and

Susan arrived ten minutes later, the gentleman who was front of house welcomed them like they were old friends.

'Hello, ladies, welcome back – usual?'

Matilda and Susan nodded, pointing in my direction and the waiter began to make their drinks. The restaurant was over half full, which was always a good sign midweek.

'Hi, Izzy,' Susan said and leaned awkwardly over the table to give me a hug as I stood. She looked glamourous in black trousers and a sequin embellished blouse. Matilda had toned down the colour combination for the evening, choosing red, in various shades, from top to bottom. The Doc Martens had been switched for red suede pumps.

'I feel like I'm being interviewed again.' I beamed at them across the table as they sat side by side.

'Well, we'd have you wouldn't we, Susan?' Matilda exclaimed.

The waiter arrived with their drinks, a tonic water for Susan and a pint of Cobra for Matilda.

'Cheers,' Matilda said, raising her glass, and we followed suit.

A basket of poppadoms arrived at our table and my stomach growled appreciatively. We gave our main course order to the waiter and dug in.

'So, how are you settling in to your new home?' Susan asked as she spooned some mango chutney onto her plate.

'Great, I love it. The house is bigger than we had before, so I have lots of furniture shopping to do, but it's beautiful. We lived in a more modern house before, but I fell in love with the cottage in Rusper on sight. It's so homely and the area seems nice.'

'It's lovely down that way, I used to ride horses there many moons ago,' Susan chipped in.

'How are you finding St. Wilfred's?' Matilda asked as I snapped a piece of poppadom and put it in my mouth.

'Kids are nice, and obviously the staff too. I think it was a good move,' I replied once I'd finished my mouthful.

Matilda told me she'd been at St. Wilfred's for five years and Susan even longer. It had changed so much apparently in the last two years, since Mr Scott had been appointed head teacher. Previously he had taught English, so it was his favourite subject.

'I didn't know that, so is that how the position came up? Did he move into the head teacher role?'

Matilda shook her head mid-mouthful and Susan leaned forward to whisper.

'The last teacher left in a hurry.' Her eyebrows lifted so high, I thought they might disappear beneath her hairline.

I mirrored Susan and leant closer, keen to hear what was not to be overhead by the other diners.

'Apparently she had an affair with one of the pupils,' Matilda hissed.

I froze, the blood draining from my face. I took a long sip of my lemonade before asking, 'Who with?'

'We don't know exactly, Mr Scott was very discreet and got her out in a hurry to save her reputation. I'm not sure how far it went, he didn't disclose the details to the staff.'

I didn't have to feign the horror Matilda and Susan expected to see. Had the student been Nicky? The question ate away at me, but the conversation swiftly moved on to a different topic, namely Mr Collins' lack of personal hygiene.

'I mean, he doesn't even wash that scruffy old jumper and he doesn't iron his shirts either,' Matilda boomed, getting louder the more lager she consumed. Our waiter kept bringing top-ups every time our glasses became empty. We didn't have to ask for another drink once.

The main courses arrived, and we got stuck in. Our food was delicious, and I was glad I'd worn my denim jeggings, grateful for the elasticated waist.

Matilda and Susan were an absolute scream. They knew everything about the school, from the caretaker having it off with one of the married dinner ladies, to the gossip that came out of the girls' toilets at break time. All too soon it was almost ten o'clock and, with full stomachs and Matilda a bit tipsy, we decided to call it a night, agreeing to make it a regular monthly feature. I was flattered they'd let me join their little get-togethers. I wanted to fit in as much as Charlotte.

We emerged from the restaurant in the middle of a heavy downpour, saying our goodbyes briefly before escaping from the rain. I'd managed to get a space outside by pure luck, having caught someone leaving as the satnav announced I'd arrived at my destination. Susan, who was driving tonight, had parked around the corner, so they hurried away as I jumped in my car, locking the doors as I always did before starting the engine. As I turned the blowers on to clear my steamy windows, I caught a glimpse of a shadow at the passenger door. A loud bang on the glass made me cry out, echoing around the car.

I squinted, trying to make out who it was, and then the window began to clear. I could see a dripping Nicky, bent over and grinning at me. My heart pounded at the scare, breath catching in my throat. Checking my rear-view mirror to make sure Matilda and Susan were out of sight, I lowered the window.

'All right, Miss.' His smile was wide, teeth beaming in the darkness, unaware he'd scared me half to death. Rain beaded on his forehead, collecting and running down his nose.

'Are you following me?' I asked, knowing we weren't near where he lived.

He didn't answer straight away, eyes narrowed as his hands rested on the door.

'No.'

I saw headlights in the rear-view mirror approach from around the corner.

'You'd better get in,' I sighed, unlocking the door, concerned Susan would see.

Nicky jumped in; he was drenched. The smell of cigarettes and a sweet amber-scented aftershave emanated from him.

'Are you following me?' I repeated. Nicky appearing out of thin air had spooked me, a mix of nervous excitement trickled through my veins.

'Yes,' he admitted. A glint in his eye.

I shook my head and, without waiting, pulled out of the parking space and drove down the main street until I found a side road. Turning in, satisfied we were inconspicuous in the poorly lit street, I parked up and cut the engine.

I turned around in my seat to speak, but Nicky was there, his lips on mine as he held my face, the urgency apparent. It was forceful and passionate, as though he'd been building up to it for a while. For a second, my defences evaporated. I leaned into him, my body betraying me as I pawed at his hooded top, pushing my hands beneath to feel his hot bare skin on my fingertips.

Sense finally prevailing, I pulled away. What the fuck was I doing?

'Wait,' I said breathlessly, resting my head back on the window. It was a mistake. I needed to think. I wanted air and turned on the engine so I could lower the fogged-up window. Nicky remained silent, his cheeks pink and hoody ruffled.

I stared at him, trying to make sense of what had happened. Watching the rise and fall of his chest. His head barely a few inches from the roof of the car.

'Izzy, I...' he tailed off.

'I need to think, Nicky,' I snapped, frustration boiling over.

He recoiled at my sudden outburst.

'This can't happen,' I breathed, smoothing my hair and straightening my clothes.

'Why?' He looked genuinely perplexed.

I felt my nostrils flare.

'There are a million reasons why. I'm married for one, it's my fucking wedding anniversary tomorrow. What are you, seventeen? I'm old enough to be your mother,' I ranted.

'I'm eighteen,' he said, grimacing.

For a second, I thought he was going to argue further, but instead he got out of the car. I watched him walk away, raising the hood over his head as he disappeared into the darkness.

'Jesus,' I sighed, checking my face in the mirror. I looked exactly like I'd been having a fumble, the skin red around my mouth from kissing. I sat for a while, not wanting to go home. The thought of looking David in the eye after kissing another man was unbearable, the betrayal weighing heavily on me.

*It was only a kiss,* the voice in my head whispered. There was absolutely no way I was going to let that happen again. I wasn't about to lose my career or my marriage over a boy half my age. I was no Mrs Robinson. The thought of the stigma attached to a teacher-student relationship made me shudder. I hadn't engineered this move to watch everything I'd worked for – the house and change of schools, as well as my relationship with Charlotte and David – go down the drain.

Goosebumps peppered my skin and I closed my window before starting the journey home. When I got there, David was sat at the oak kitchen table, fingers tapping at his laptop, engrossed in a spreadsheet. He raised his head when I dropped my keys, clattering to the floor in the hallway.

'Good curry?' he asked, eyeing me as I scooped them up.

'Lovely,' I replied and slipped off my shoes before heading straight upstairs to get changed, my waistband straining. I couldn't focus, even removing my clothes was a struggle as my mind raced, thoughts all of a jumble.

I sat in bed attempting to read until I heard David's footsteps on the stairs, quickly sliding the book under my pillow and turning off the bedside lamp. I feigned sleep when he came in the room, but I knew it was going to be a long night. My stomach was bloated with rich and spicy food and churned audibly, but it was my head that was elsewhere. I couldn't concentrate on the book; I felt so guilty. It was impossible to switch off. How could I have let it get so out of hand? A line had been crossed, personally and professionally, and, as much as I wanted to, I couldn't take it back. I relived the kiss again and again, every time I closed my eyes, like a five-second movie on loop. It was so real I could almost taste him on my lips.

## 13

David was heading out of the door when my alarm went off the next morning. I heard the handle being pulled up to lock the door as I came to. It was our wedding anniversary and the sky in collusion was grey and overcast. This time sixteen years ago, under a haze of bright sunshine, I was preparing for the happiest day of my life. Until Charlotte came along, of course.

Back then, I was so sure David was the one. He made me laugh; he was kind and handsome and I knew he'd be a fantastic father. All of this was before ambition took over and his career became the thing that drove him, excited him. He was climbing the corporate ladder and my career was put on the back burner whilst I raised our child. No discussion. I felt guilty, but playing the little wife at home and looking after Charlotte wasn't enough for me. Those years had been a struggle, but we'd made it through. David didn't understand; he thought I took it for granted, that I was lucky to stay at home and look after our child with no financial worries. It was why I kept quiet, not wanting to appear ungrateful, but I was jealous of my husband's professional success.

On reflection, I'd been feeling isolated for a while. As soon as Charlotte was old enough to play out with her friends, spending time with me wasn't on the agenda. I couldn't blame her, it was a natural progression, and I didn't want to be the one to hold her back. The pregnancy last year allowed David and I to find our way back to each other and to what was important. I got excited at the thought of extending our family, grabbing it with both hands, until Mother Nature stepped in and a second child wasn't to be. Now we seemed further apart than ever.

Once dressed, I dug out the card I'd written some weeks ago and the malt whisky, taking them downstairs to place on the kitchen table. There'd been nothing left out for me. I doubted he'd even remembered; romance had never been one of David's strong points. He was much more practical; for our sixth anniversary he'd even bought me an iron.

Charlotte raised her eyebrows when she finally came downstairs, around ten minutes before we were due to leave.

'Channelling Dad today, are you?' she smirked.

I'd power-dressed in a pair of grey wide-legged trousers, a white shirt and waistcoat over the top. I loved an androgynous look.

'Oh shut up, smart-arse!' I said, spritzing myself with perfume.

'Well, no one is going to mess with you today, dressed like that.'

'That's the intention,' I replied, winking. It was true, I had to make the boundaries clear, if only in my own mind.

'Mum, when can Amy come to dinner?' Charlotte asked.

'Tomorrow?' I suggested.

'Great. I'll let her know.' Charlotte began tapping at her phone.

The traffic was bad due to the imminent predicted rainfall, which thankfully didn't arrive until we were safely inside the school building.

My morning whizzed by with a review of the scene in Romeo and Juliet where they meet at Lord Capulet's feast, by year ten, followed by more declarations of love with year seven and their sonnets. The rain hammered on the classroom windows intermittently, the sky so dark we had to have the lights on.

At lunchtime, I was printing out the exercises for the last class of the day when Nicky walked in, drenched by the downpour which had disrupted his football game. His shirt was practically transparent and stuck to his skin. Rainwater dripped into a puddle on the floor where he stood. I opened my mouth to speak, but nothing came out.

'You're as bad as me,' he said, licking his lips and twisting the bottom of his shirt to expel the water. The ache from last night surfaced and I tried my best to ignore it.

'No, I'm not,' I whispered, more to myself than to him.

Nicky opened his mouth to speak, but the corridor and classroom filled with students sheltering from the rain.

'I'd better go,' he said, his voice low.

I knew I shouldn't, but I wanted to know how it would feel to have his hands on me, just once. It was wrong, immoral even, but it wasn't as if he was a child. Cheeks burning, I tried to focus back on the exercise sheets spread across my desk.

Charlotte came to my classroom after school had ended, the last hour had been painful for us both. She looked sweaty and dishevelled. I couldn't help but smile, she was usually impeccably turned out, not a hair out of place. Girls her age were always so concerned with the way they looked.

'What happened to you?' I asked.

Charlotte dropped her bag at my feet and tied her hair back into a ponytail. 'PE. We had the bleep test.'

I remembered it only too well, it was a form of torture that PE teachers kept for rainy days or when they were in a bad mood. Pupils had to run between two cones, from one end of the hall to another, whilst listening to bleeps on a tape, although by now there was probably an app for it. The number of seconds between the bleeps decreased as the test got harder, meaning the runners had to move faster between the cones. It was something I was never any good at and unfortunately for Charlotte, she'd inherited my not very sporty genes.

'Come on, let's go home.' I packed my things and we dashed to car as the rain continued to pour.

When we got home, there were anniversary cards on the mat,

posted by mine and David's parents, but there was no note or card from David and no message on my phone.

I rung Mum and thanked her for the card, staying quiet when she presumed David had bought me flowers. It was easier to go along with her assumption of him being the perfect husband than admit he'd likely forgotten. I said we'd finished our unpacking and I'd arrange Sunday lunch when she was free. Mum had a couple of busy weekends coming up, with a trip to the theatre and then dog sitting for her neighbour who was having a hip replacement.

I put the cards on the mantelpiece. A reminder for David if nothing else.

Out of principle, I refused to cook on my anniversary, so I let Charlotte pick a takeaway. She chose Chinese and I opened a bottle of wine when it arrived, pouring myself a large glass. Charlotte noticed the card and whisky on the table.

'It's not Dad's birthday, is it?' she asked, her face scrunched, horrified she might have forgotten.

'No, it's our wedding anniversary. We got married sixteen years ago today.' Charlotte put down her fork, her eyebrows raised theatrically.

'And Dad's not here?'

'Nope,' I said, taking a bite of a prawn cracker.

Charlotte looked more affronted than I felt.

'Happy anniversary, Mum.'

'Thanks, love.'

I'd resigned myself to the fact David had forgotten. Although when it got to half nine and he rolled in, it was the last straw. Charlotte was in her bedroom watching Netflix on her iPad and I'd sunk half a bottle of wine. Fuelled by the alcohol, I was no longer willing to let it slide.

'Hello, beautiful,' David said, coming into the kitchen. He took one look at my narrowed eyes and knew he was in trouble. 'What's up?'

'You're a twat, that's what's up.' I stood to put my empty glass in the sink.

'What have I done now?' he sighed, and I felt my jaw clench, looking pointedly at the table where the card and whisky bottle, decorated with a red bow, had been left.

He followed my gaze and the penny dropped.

'Happy anniversary,' I said sarcastically as I pushed past him to go upstairs.

'Shit! I'm sorry.' He followed me up and I shot him a look as we reached the top.

'Shh,' I hissed, not wanting Charlotte to hear us argue.

'I'm sorry,' he repeated, whispering.

I busied myself washing my face and cleaning my teeth as David sat on the bed. He didn't even try to explain himself, his head bowed. I wasn't interested in anything he had to say anyway.

'I'll make it up to you,' he said, eyes downcast, staring at his shoes.

I couldn't bring myself to speak. In that moment I despised him. When had he become so selfish, so engrossed in his own world that the lives of me and Charlotte seemed to run parallel to his?

I couldn't bear to look at him for a second longer, rolling over to face the window, putting my earphones in, but the narrator's words swam around my head, and I couldn't take them in. My mind was so full, I thought my skull might shatter from the pressure. Eventually, after fifteen minutes of oppressive silence, he stood and meandered downstairs.

\* \* \*

I woke up still angry. The mood from last night had followed me into the daylight hours. I'd struggled to sleep, tossing and turning, my mind and stomach churning simultaneously. David was still on the sofa when I came downstairs for a cup of tea. The anniversary card had been opened along with the whisky, of which a quarter had already gone. David was snoring and dribbling on my beautiful jacquard cushions and I scowled silently at him on my way back to the shower. I put on a black polka dot wrap dress with a statement necklace and heels. I'd show him what he was missing.

When I went to find Charlotte at eight, I assumed she was in her room, already dressed, but I was wrong. I found her still in bed, wrapped in her duvet with an extra blanket on top for warmth. She was shivering, eyes red, surrounded by used tissues.

'Don't you feel well?' I asked, stroking her fringe away from her clammy forehead.

'Feel rough, Mum. I'm really cold.'

I tucked Charlotte back in and retrieved the thermometer from the bathroom. Her temperature was a dizzying 38.9 degrees, high enough to warrant a day in bed. I popped downstairs and made her a Lemsip, leaving it on her bedside table.

'Dad's asleep on the sofa. He had a bit too much to drink last night. I'll leave him a note to stay home with you today.'

Charlotte nodded and closed her eyes to go back to sleep. I leaned down and kissed her damp head.

'I'll ring you later on, OK, text me if you need me. I'll keep my phone on me. Guess we'll have to have Amy around for dinner next week?'

Charlotte shrugged, which meant she must have been feeling rough.

I wrote David a note in large block capitals on A4 paper and left it on the floor in front of the sofa. I'd already seen his laptop on the kitchen table, so if he was intending to work at all, he could do it from home.

My mood, softened by Charlotte's fragile face, darkened when someone cut me up at the roundabout on the way to work. Today was not going to be a good day.

## 14

My English Literature sixth-formers were taken aback by my verbal annihilation of Alec d'Urberville in our character discussion that morning. It was lucky I was not on playground duty either, as the rowdy girls showing off to the boys outside my classroom window would have got a talking-to as well.

I called home at lunchtime, after hurriedly eating my sandwich and having a quick catch-up with Matilda and Susan in the staffroom. I hadn't told them about David, we weren't that familiar yet, but I texted Stella – I needed to vent to someone. I received a message back, a single word.

Dickhead

I had no doubt she'd ring me later.

Charlotte informed me that she was still in her pyjamas but had moved out of bed and onto the sofa in front of the television. Glued to the news reporting on the thousands of people gathered in London protesting against climate change. The four-hourly doses of paracetamol seemed to be doing the trick, but she still sounded full of cold. David had been looking after her apparently.

'I've got my creative writing class after school today, so I won't be home until later, OK?' It crossed my mind to cancel but it wouldn't look good to be missing a class so early on.

There was a loud sniff and a request for tomato soup for dinner which was what Charlotte always had when she felt poorly.

'Sure, I'll pick some up on the way home. Shall I get ice cream? Fancy a movie and some ice cream on the sofa tonight?'

The suggestion seemed to raise Charlotte's spirits. Perhaps a good rom-com and Ben & Jerry's, along with some TLC, was what we both needed to end the week.

I couldn't wait to get home; the creative writing class was a thorn in my side, and I berated myself for suggesting it to Mr Scott. In reality, I did enjoy it, but I was nervous about seeing Nicky. The thought of him made every nerve switch onto high alert. I remembered the kiss, my hands on his torso in a sheer moment of madness. I felt a tingling beneath my skin. I knew I wouldn't be able to look at him without blushing.

When the bell rang, sounding the end of school day, all the children hotfooted it out of my classroom and I nipped to the toilet. The woman staring back at me from the mirror as I washed my hands looked like a stranger, tired and slightly drawn. I ruffled my hair to get some volume into it and gave my neck a tiny spritz of perfume before dashing back to my classroom. Nicky was already sat in the front row, slouched in his seat, legs wide apart, smiling up at me. We were alone and the atmosphere in the room was laden with tension.

'Hi,' I said, perching on the edge of my desk, directly opposite him.

'Hi.' He licked his lips, a teasing glint in his eyes.

I felt the burn creep up my neck and breathed deeply to steady my legs which had turned to liquid.

The rest of the children entered the classroom in dribs and drabs, sitting down and chatting amongst themselves. No one appeared to notice the silent exchange between Nicky and I. Snapping out of my fantasy, I put my teacher hat back on.

'Good afternoon. Today I want to find out from you what your favourite book or books are and why. What makes them your favourite? Why are they memorable to you?'

Everyone got out their notebooks to commit their ideas to paper.

'For example, one of my favourites is *The Woman in Black* by Susan Hill. It's a fantastically haunting ghost story which builds tension slowly. It's eerie and unsettling and a favourite for many horror readers. There's no gore, but it makes the hairs on the back of your neck stand on end.' I smiled at the class and stroked the back of my neck, remembering the first time I'd read the book when I was a teenager. Since then I'd read it numerous times, even dragging David to see the stage show, which was not his thing at all.

Nicky gazed at me through his eyelashes, a twinkle in his eye. He looked mischievous, like he was thinking things he shouldn't.

'Emma, what's your favourite book, or one of them and why?' I asked, turning my attention to one of the year nine girls.

'Umm, probably *The Host* by Stephanie Meyer.' I recognised that book, Charlotte had read it when she'd finished the *Twilight* series.

I smiled warmly at Emma, who looked like she was feeling a bit shy about speaking in front of everyone.

'OK, so what makes it your favourite?' I encouraged.

'I love that it's got some science-fiction elements and a love story as well. The characters are really likeable.'

I nodded.

'Robert, what about you?' I gestured towards Robert, a year seven sitting in the back row.

'My favourite is *The Maze Runner* by James Dashner. I like the futuristic world and the monsters.'

Another two pupil's favourites were *The Enemy* by Charlie Higson and *The Fault in our Stars* by John Green. I had watched the latter with Charlotte, it was one of the many films born out of a good book. I had to say I'd enjoyed it immensely; however, the amount of tissues Charlotte and I had gone through was ridiculous.

'Nicky?'

'I enjoy the *Game of Thrones* books.' This got the other boys in the class nodding enthusiastically. I knew they were massive, but I hadn't managed to watch any of the popular television series and felt too far behind to catch up.

'I've not read any of those,' I admitted.

'They are full of fighting, wars between rival families for the throne. The stories are intricate, and the characters are bold and colourful. It really draws you in.' Nicky reached into his bag underneath the table and took out one of the books, holding it out to show me. Our fingers grazed as I took it from him, his as cold as ice.

'Thanks Nicky, I'll take a look.'

The rest of the class listed their favourites one by one and I looked up at the clock.

'OK, we've got about forty minutes. I want you to write me a story, no more than 500 words, and I want you to think about what it is you love about your favourite book. What engages you and keeps you turning the page, try to incorporate that into your own story.'

Everyone went back to jotting ideas in their notebooks, except for Nicky, who was staring at me as I rounded my desk and sat down, leafing through the novel, reading the blurb on the back and author recommendations at the front. Nicky's name was written neatly in blue ink on the top left-hand corner. I fingered the pages, knowing his hands had touched them too. I tried to read the first paragraph, but I thought I could feel his eyes on me. Glancing up, I was surprised to see his head bent over his exercise book. Inwardly I chastised myself. What the hell had gotten into me? He was just showing me his book. I put it down, pushing it to the edge of the desk, out of my eye line. I had to shift my focus to something else.

I compiled a list of what I had to do at the weekend in the way of marking and lesson planning and moved around the class, assisting the children with shaping their prose. Before I knew it, the hour was up.

'If you can finish your stories at home and bring them next week, we'll read them then. Have a lovely weekend.'

Most of the students were quick at putting their things away and wished me well as they strode past me into the corridor, keen to begin their weekends. Nicky was the opposite, moving slowly until the room was empty.

I grabbed the book and handed it back to Nicky who was still seated. Wrapping my arms around myself, sure he would hear my stomach somersaulting as I stood by his desk. The silence of the classroom was deafening. He took it without a word, leaning over and slipping it back in his bag which was on the floor by my feet.

Looking up, Nicky met my eyes, a knowing smile creeping onto his face. A perfect mixture of mischief and fun, I couldn't help but find it infectious. I felt his hand wrap around the inside of my calf. His touch made me start, but I didn't move away. I bit my lip as I allowed him to rub his thumb back and forth, caressing my leg. He held my gaze intensely as he slowly ran his hand upwards, towards my knee. Anyone could have walked in the classroom and caught us, but I'd never felt so alive.

Eventually I pulled away, walking back to my desk to pack up, still feeling the imprint of his hand on my leg. I shrugged on my coat and picked up my handbag.

'Have a nice weekend, Nicky,' I said as I left the classroom.

Behind me, I heard the screech of the chair against the floor and footsteps following. He maintained his distance until I reached my car.

'I'm parked around the corner, follow me?' His eyes were imploring.

He jogged away before I could say no, I had to get back. Every fibre of my being screamed it was a bad idea. I was getting into something I shouldn't. If I had any sense, I'd drive away from here, go home, back to the family I'd left this morning, but curiosity got the better of me. I got into my car and drove out of the car park. Nicky's Fiesta was already indicating to pull out from his parking space, so I slowed to let him go, flashing my lights.

We drove towards my home, heart racing as I wondered where he was taking me. When he drove past the turning into my road, I continued to follow him. Not sure why I hadn't just indicated and driven home. But what if he'd turned around? I didn't want him to know where I lived.

I chewed my lip, fingers drumming on the steering wheel in quick succession. What harm could it do? A quick chat and then I'd be home.

Nicky indicated for a turning on the left, and then left again into another car park, this one for playing fields. A desolate expanse of muddy green, with no playground in sight. Before I'd even parked, he'd jumped out and was heading to the block of what I assumed were changing rooms, keys dangling from his hand.

I got out of the car, and followed, lingering by the open door and peering inside.

'Come in,' he said from inside, as I surveyed the space. Wooden slatted benches around the edges, hooks upon the walls and open showers at one end. I shivered as I stepped inside, my head snapping around as he locked the door behind us. The room was cold and musty, an unpleasant smell of damp, sweaty football socks ingrained in the concrete. Overhead, the fluorescent light flickered furiously, matching my pulse. This was a mistake. I turned to leave, but Nicky stepped in front of the door, blocking my path.

'Wait,' he breathed, against my cheek. Slipping his hand around my neck and pulling my mouth to his.

All sense evaporated and I gave in. His touch was urgent, necessary; a need we both had to fulfil. Hands roamed my body, like he couldn't decide where to go first. I fumbled with the fastenings of his trousers and he gasped as I wrapped my hand around him. Lifting my dress, he pulled my knickers aside, pushing himself into me without hesitation. The wall, cold against my back, bare brickwork snagging at the fabric with each thrust.

It was quick, I came within a minute, but we stayed locked together, catching our breath. Eventually untangling and rearranging our clothing, eyes on the floor. The enormity of what had just happened sinking in.

'You OK?' he asked.

'Yes, I'm fine. You?' I didn't feel fine, I felt shell-shocked, dizzied from my heart pumping so fast. As though I'd just watched someone else commit adultery, not me.

He nodded, but his smile faded, eyes darkening. 'We didn't use anything.'

I didn't understand what he meant at first until I saw how pale he'd become.

'It's OK, Nicky, don't worry about it. Honestly, it's taken care of,' I said dismissively.

'OK,' he replied, eyeing me curiously as he unlocked the door. Both of us seemingly shaken at what had just occurred.

Without hesitation, we reverted back to our roles. Me the teacher, him the student. It was effortless, like our moment of madness never happened.

'I'd better go,' I said, as Nicky seemed reluctant to move aside.

'OK.' He took a step back, pulling the door open, and paused to turn around, a strange expression on his face. Was it regret? 'Have a good weekend, Miss.'

I walked past him out of the changing room and straight to my car. I didn't look back.

## 15

I wished I had the opportunity to tidy myself up, but my reflection in the rear-view mirror looked the same. There was no scarlet letter on my forehead.

I glanced at the clock, it was already five o'clock and I should have been home by now, although I doubted I'd been missed. On the short journey, I expected to feel wracked with guilt, but instead I was numb, as though what had happened was a dream or a film I'd watched, where it hadn't been me having sex with a student from school but someone else. I needed time to process what I'd done.

'Shit.' It wasn't until I turned into my road, I remembered I was supposed to buy soup and ice cream. Throwing the car into reverse and gritting my teeth, I managed a three-point turn in record time. The tyres screeched and a passing dog walker shook his head disapprovingly as I sped by, back to the convenience store three streets away.

By the time I eventually made it home, it was twenty to six. Before I could get out of the car, Mary our neighbour, appeared on the driveway, gravel crunching beneath her slippers, and handed over a Tupperware box of flapjacks.

'Ah, thank you Mary, do you want to come in for a cup of tea?' I asked, chastising myself that I still hadn't got around to buying her some flowers.

'No, no, I'm off to bingo shortly, my niece is coming to pick me up. I've been baking all day. Can't eat it all by myself.'

'You do spoil us,' I said, patting her hand before she left.

'Where have you been? I'm hungry.' Charlotte sniffed as I passed the living room on my way to the kitchen.

*One, two, three, four; one, two, three, four.* My zipper on my bag moved back and forth.

'I got stuck behind, talking to the head teacher, I couldn't leave.' It surprised me how easily the lie came.

I put the soup straight into a bowl, then into the microwave and the ice cream in the freezer. David walked in to check the oven.

'Mary's been baking again. I really must get her some flowers or something,' I sighed, watching David help himself to a flapjack.

'Delicious! Oh, we're having pasta bake, that OK? Charlotte said she's having soup,' David said as if everything was suddenly back to normal between us.

I nodded in reply. My fingers drumming on my thigh.

'You all right?' David spotted my hand and frowned, knowing it was something I did when I was anxious.

'Fine. How has she been?' I asked, changing the subject and feeling the back of my neck prickle with perspiration. I was waiting for David to take one look at me and know instantly. To see it written all over my face. My heart raced and I felt light-headed, but I did my best not to let it show.

'Yeah OK, on the sofa most of the day. She's had medicine and her temperature hasn't returned. What about you? You look a bit flushed. You're not coming down with it too, are you?' He reached over and placed the back of his hand against my forehead, gauging my temperature.

I squirmed, counting over and over in my head.

'No, I'm fine. Have I got time for a quick shower before dinner?'

David nodded.

'Oh, and these are for you. Happy anniversary.' He pointed towards the enormous bunch of red roses on the table I'd failed to notice.

'Thank you. I'll put them in water once I've had a shower.' I smiled tightly and escaped upstairs, taking them two at a time.

The locked bathroom was my refuge, the scorching-hot shower absolving me of my indiscretion. As soon as I closed my eyes, I could feel Nicky's hands all over me. I wasn't sorry. I had no regrets. When I walked in the door, I thought I'd see David and feel remorse, but I didn't. I felt guilty of course, I wasn't deceitful by nature and David didn't deserve to be lied to, but I wanted what he couldn't give me. I missed the excitement, the longing, the animal attraction that had long since dissolved.

Nicky made me feel desired, but I wasn't stupid, my appeal was likely due to my acquiescence. Yet, at almost forty years old I wasn't ready to accept my role as the patient wife, the one who always had dinner ready for her husband when he returned home. I wanted more. Life was short and the thrill I'd felt in that changing room was like nothing I'd experienced before. Perhaps because it was wrong, forbidden even, but I'd enjoyed it. My groin throbbed, the familiar feeling between my legs of recent sex, a reminder of my dirty little secret. It turned me on.

* * *

We ate dinner in silence, and I was grateful. David assumed I was still angry with him, but I couldn't be bothered to make small talk. He said he'd wash up, trying to get back into my good books, so I curled up on the sofa with Charlotte under a fleece blanket, armed with a spoon each, digging into the ice cream and shivering because it was so cold. Charlotte chose a romantic comedy with an actress I could never remember the name of, sniffing into a tissue periodically. Ten minutes into the film, David came and sat in the armchair with his iPad, but the familiar sound of his work phone rang out and he moved to the kitchen to take the call, closing the door behind him. Was that because he didn't want to interrupt our movie or because he didn't want me to hear who was on the other end? He wouldn't normally close the door. I strained my ears but was unable to hear anything which meant he was talking low. Who was he talking to? The voice in my head chastised me, what right did I have to be suspicious of David after what I'd done?

David didn't return and I tried to concentrate on the movie. It was funny and distracted me from my thoughts. Stella called back, but I didn't answer. I'd call her tomorrow when I could speak properly. Near the end of the film, the two leads had sex. It was a pretty raunchy scene and Charlotte visibly squirmed beside me.

'So gross!'

I giggled and poked Charlotte in the ribs. 'Sex isn't gross, Charlotte. You just have to wait until you love someone, OK,' I said, assuming Charlotte wasn't anywhere near that stage yet. Her cheeks reddened.

'I *meant* watching it with your mum is gross.'

I went to bed alone once the movie had ended, popping into the kitchen to tell David I was going up. He was sat at the table, on his laptop. There had been some crisis to sort out apparently, which couldn't wait until morning. Charlotte had one last hot lemon drink and went to bed; hopeful she would feel better tomorrow. She was gutted that Amy hadn't been able to come over for dinner.

Laying in the dark, all I could think about was Nicky. What was he doing? Was he thinking about me? I hoped Monday wouldn't be awkward when I saw him next.

When Saturday morning came, David brought me tea in bed. He made a big show of switching off his work phone to ensure this weekend was filled with nothing but family time. Charlotte wasn't overly impressed with the idea of spending her entire weekend with us and when Amy called to ask if she could have a sleepover, she begged me to let her go. I wasn't sure as, although she was much better, she still had a bit of a runny nose, but she kept on until I relented. I spoke to Louise on the phone to confirm the arrangements. They were going to take the girls out to dinner for a treat.

Once Charlotte had been dropped off, I returned and began the housework. David was cutting the grass outside and when I made him a drink, he suggested we get the train to London for dinner. I couldn't think of a suitable excuse when David proposed the idea, although I wasn't really in the mood for a night out. He seemed keen to make amends for forgetting our anniversary, so I relented.

At around half past four, David called a taxi to take us to the station. The train was running a few minutes late, and I shivered on the platform as the wind whistled through the fence. David gave me his jacket to put over my dress, lifting the collar to shield my neck from the gale, his face close to mine. This was what he used to be like, the perfect gentleman. Always so attentive. What had happened to us?

We caught the fast train, changed at Gatwick and arrived at London Victoria an hour later. David had managed to get tickets for that evening's performance of *Wicked* at the Apollo theatre, although the seats were at the back. I was looking forward to seeing it as Stella had reported it was good when she went with her mum a couple of years ago. There was a tapas restaurant around the corner and by chance we managed to get the last available table. Pulling out my chair, David commented it was our lucky night.

'Well, this makes a nice change,' he said, pouring the complimentary sangria into my glass.

'It's good to get out. We haven't had a night out in ages.'

A waiter came over and took our order. David suggested we go for the set weekend menu and I agreed.

'We could go the whole hog and stay over?' David raised an eyebrow and winked.

My skin turned to ice. It was one thing to come out for the evening, but I wasn't sure I was ready for a night of passion in a hotel. It had been what I thought I wanted, to get us back on track, but since being with Nicky, it felt tainted. I couldn't just pretend it hadn't happened, or that I wasn't suspicious that David might be playing away. He registered the look on my face and took a mouthful of his drink before he spoke.

'Perhaps not then. I know I need to make it up to you and I'm sorry

I haven't been around. I'm trying to make my mark in this new place, and it means putting the hours in.'

I nodded, unsure whether I believed him. 'You took this job because you wanted to spend more time with us.'

He frowned, but I couldn't pretend everything was fine between us when it wasn't.

I contemplated telling him about Nicky. Blurting it out across the table as we waited for our food to arrive. Would he be consumed by jealously? Or think I was having a midlife crisis? Would he get angry? Throw his drink over me? Raise his fist? I didn't think so, but I was sure he'd shout, maybe even cry. I knew our marriage would be over. David had always made that clear and at the time I'd said it worked both ways. That was in the early days of our marriage when we were adamant we'd be together forever, and our heads could never be turned. How things had changed.

David's voice jolted me from my thoughts.

'Let's pretend it's a date. I'm taking you to dinner and a show. No expectations,' he said with an easy smile and I felt my shoulders ease down.

My stomach growled appreciatively when our food came out around fifteen minutes later. The sangria was making my appetite spike and I dived in straight away. Now I knew I wasn't going to have to dodge sex with David, I loosened up. We discussed St. Wilfred's, how Charlotte was settling in and what Amy's parents were like. Before we knew it, time had run away with us and we had to leave to make it to the show.

The seats we thought weren't so great turned out to be pretty good and the show was amazing. I immersed myself in it and hummed the infectious song about defying gravity all the way home; making a mental note to download the soundtrack. I snuggled close to David on the train, a complete reversal of how we'd sat stoically opposite each other on the way there. The carriage was busy as people made their way home and the train was slow, stopping at every station on its route.

By the time we made it through our front door, it was past

midnight. I'd rung Louise in the interval, they had just got home from Smith & Western. The girls were giggly apparently from sugar over-load and had fleeced Amy's dad for pink sparkly cowboy hats which had subsequently covered the entire back seat of his BMW in glitter.

Knowing Charlotte was fine, I kicked off my heels and made my way upstairs, still feeling the effects of the sangria and later wine at the theatre. David turned off the lights downstairs and checked the doors were locked before he came to bed. I was already cleaning my teeth when he came into the bathroom. I'd slipped into my nightie and David put an arm around my waist, squeezing and kissing the top of my head.

'It was a good night wasn't it?'

'It was,' I agreed and gave him a kiss on the cheek.

He kept to his word and didn't make a move. Instead he reached over to pat my hip and left his hand resting, becoming heavier as he drifted off.

It finally came, what I'd been waiting for, the overwhelming feeling of guilt which washed over me like a wave. Tears pricked my eyes, seeping into the pillow. I lay rigid, not wanting to alert David to my distress. Thankfully he was asleep within minutes, and I lay under the duvet, thinking about what had happened with Nicky. What would Stella say, or my mother for that matter? What about Charlotte? It would be awful if she ever found out, she'd be humiliated. I'd be ostracised for sure, my reputation ripped to shreds. And what for? Yes, things had been strained between David and I, but tonight had proved that there was still hope, we'd been married for sixteen years for good-ness' sake, of course it wouldn't always be plain sailing. I was ashamed of my infidelity and I had to make sure it never happened again.

## 16

On Sunday, I woke to the sound of David gently snoring beside me, it was past eight and I immediately checked my phone to make sure Charlotte hadn't texted. She had sent a message, but it was a selfie of her and Amy in their matching cowboy hats. I smiled at the image, slipping out of bed, not wanting to wake David. Grabbing my dressing gown on the way out, I tiptoed downstairs and put on a pot of coffee, the smell filling the kitchen and instantly making everything better. I'd made the decision to put Friday behind me and forget it ever happened. David never needed to know. It was a blip, that was all.

I poured myself a mug when the coffee was ready and sat in the conservatory, legs curled beneath me, listening to the birds chirping in the garden. I'd missed another call from Stella last night while we were out, so texted her saying it was difficult to talk but I would ring when I could. She'd understand.

Sundays were for lazy mornings with coffee and warm croissants. I remembered I had a batch in the freezer and put them in the oven. Resuming my position back in the chair, a thud came from the hallway. The Sunday papers had arrived. Sighing, I got up again and went to collect them from the doormat. I could take them back to bed, David and I could peruse the headlines over breakfast like we used to before Charlotte came along.

As I scooped up the papers, a single scrap escaped the pile and floated to the floor. I bent to pick it up, a crumpled sliver of paper with a mobile number scribbled on it. Whose was it? Was it Nicky's? I raced to the lounge window to look out onto the street. There was no one to be seen, but I heard a car driving away. Was Nicky trying to contact me? Shit. How did he know where I lived?

I chewed the inside of my cheek and turned the lounge light on and off four times before I could stop myself, hoping Mary wouldn't see the flashing lights and think I'd gone mad or was sending SOS signals.

Snatching my phone out of my dressing gown pocket, I got ready to give Nicky a piece of my mind. What the hell was he playing at? He knew I was married. Why had I made such a stupid mistake in getting involved? With trembling hands, I began to type. My fingers hovered over the screen.

Wait. I had to be smart about this. Did I want to give Nicky my number so he could call whenever he wanted? Definitely not. I imagined my phone ringing repeatedly in the middle of dinner and last thing at night. My nerves were frayed enough already.

I put my phone and the paper back into my dressing gown pocket and went to rummage around the kitchen junk drawer. I knew David had an old handset he'd discarded, so old that even Charlotte didn't want it. It was a Motorola flip-style phone with no SIM card in it. Maybe I could pop out and get one after breakfast? No, I'd ignore it and speak to Nicky on Monday. That would be the best course of action.

The smell of croissants from the oven made my stomach rumble appreciatively. They were browning nicely, little flecks of pastry lifting away in the heat. I retrieved a tray from one of the cupboards and loaded it with butter, jam, two plates and two knives. When the croissants were done, I piled them onto one of the plates and added the coffee. After taking an age to climb the stairs with the precariously balanced tray, I found David still asleep.

'Morning, sleepyhead,' I said, watching him sit up and rub his eyes.

A wide smile spread across his face as he saw what I was carrying.

'Well, that's a perfect vision on a Sunday morning. A beautiful woman carrying coffee and breakfast.' He propped our pillows up and patted my side of the bed.

'I forgot the papers.'

Once I'd retrieved them, we snuggled under the covers, him reading the *Sunday Times*, me the *Sunday Mirror*, reporting on the climate change protest in Manhattan led by Greta Thunberg which dominated the headlines. David read with his glasses on, tutting every so often.

The coffee perked me up and the buttered croissants melted in my mouth. I'd have to be more careful about what I ate this week after last night's heavy meal and now this for breakfast.

'What time are we picking Charlotte up?' David checked his phone for the time, before getting out of bed.

'I'm not sure, she hasn't said. I'll give her a ring once I'm dressed.'

He grabbed his towel and went into the bathroom, closing the door. Seconds later, I heard the shower start. His phone, still laying on the duvet where he'd left it, was unlocked. Curiosity got the better of me and I reached for it, clicking into his messages. There were texts from me, Charlotte, Patrick and one from Paul that came through yesterday morning. That was odd. I'd never heard him mention a Paul.

Can you get away this weekend? Xx

Men didn't put kisses at the end of text messages. It had to be her, logged in his phone under another name. I closed the message and dropped the phone like a hot potato, it bounced onto the bed. Fiery tears streamed down my cheeks and I let them come. I'd been holding back for too long.

I heard the shower stop and the door slide open. My throat constricted and I thought I might heave, the croissants threatening to make a reappearance. I swallowed the saliva that filled my mouth and took the tray downstairs. Waiting down there for David to finish, I composed a text to Charlotte, who replied quickly and asked me to collect her around midday.

When David came out and got dressed, I slipped into the family bathroom to avoid interacting with him. I wasn't sure I could trust myself not to scream in his face. By the time I'd finished showering, I could hear him moving around downstairs. My stomach burned as I rolled my wedding band around my finger. The symbol of an unbroken circle of love. What a load of shit that was. I know I had acted unforgivably with Nicky, but an ongoing affair, which I was sure this was - there had been too many late nights, too many weekends away - was no comparison to a one-off lapse of judgement.

As soon as I was ready, I headed downstairs and out of the front door, calling out before I closed it behind me, 'I'm going to get Charlotte and I need to nip to the shops on my way. Won't be long.' Trying to keep my voice as even as I could.

He shouted something back, but I didn't hear it.

It was half past ten, and my decision to contact Nicky didn't feel deceitful. David clearly didn't care about lying to me. Any sadness I'd felt for the breakdown of our marriage because of the miscarriage had been replaced with pure hatred. Nicky's telephone number was burning a hole in my pocket. I'd been sure to transfer the old phone and the scrap of paper into my pocket before I left.

I drove in a daze to the supermarket, where I managed to pick up a cheap pay-as-you-go SIM card. Sat in the car park, I was all fingers and thumbs as I put the SIM in the old Motorola and listened to the automated voice direct me on how to top up my balance. Two minutes later, I sat with the phone in my lap, now with credit, ready to text Nicky, but unsure what to say. I knew I was acting in anger. A knee-jerk reaction to David's infidelity, which felt like a knife in the back.

Perhaps I should ignore Nicky pushing his number through my letterbox altogether, if it was him at all, and wait until school to speak to him? But David was clearly having his fun, so why shouldn't I?

Typing Nicky's number into the phone, the blank message screen flashed accusingly at me. I swallowed hard, my fingers moving clumsily across the buttons, so different from the ease of the smartphone I used.

Hi.

I didn't want to say too much on text. What if it wasn't Nicky? Even if it was, I wasn't sure what I was supposed to say? Within thirty seconds, a beep, loud and shrill, rang out, making me jump. I fumbled to put the phone on silent and checked the response.

Miss?

The single word sent a thrill through me I hadn't expected.

Where are you?

I wanted to see him, tell him face to face that it wasn't OK for him to put notes through my door.

Home. Can we meet?

Where?

The side road by the restaurant.

Those were his only instructions, but I assumed he meant the last time he'd been in my car. My pulse accelerated making me feel light-headed. I couldn't deny the excitement I felt about seeing him again.

Be there in ten

I had sixty minutes and as I drove, trying to remember my way around, I convinced myself it would only be for a chat. I could tell him that he couldn't contact me at home in future. That was off limits.

When I pulled into the road, Nicky was already there waiting for me, leaning against a lamp post, engrossed in his phone. He could easily pass for being early twenties in his jeans, long-sleeved polo shirt and a brown leather jacket. I hadn't made an effort, throwing on jeans and a jumper, my mind focused on getting a SIM card when I'd gotten dressed. I stopped beside him, and he bent to look through the window. My chest fluttered like delicate wings were beating inside me. I'd forgotten how handsome he was.

I beckoned him inside and he flopped into the passenger seat, squeezing my thigh in greeting. My skin tingled beneath the fabric at his touch and I thought for a second he was going to lean over and kiss me, but he seemed to think better of it.

'I don't have long,' I said.

Nicky rubbed his chin, the stubble catching on his fingers.

'OK, keep going down here and turn left.' He pointed and I started the engine without hesitation.

We drove for about five minutes before pulling into a park. Similar to Tilgate, but with a smaller, car park.

'Where are we?'

'Come on,' Nicky said with a wink.

He jumped out of the car and hurried straight into the wooded area. I followed quickly behind, locking the car using the key fob and glancing over my shoulder, grateful we appeared to be alone. The trees overhead tightly knitted together, making the sky barely visible. Underfoot, my pumps squelched on the damp earth and moss when he veered off the gravel path; moving so fast I struggled to keep up. He stopped abruptly when the car park could no longer be seen. Pushing me back into a tree so I was pinned against it, he kissed me with the same urgency as he had in the changing room. As though we were going to get caught any minute. The bark scraped the back of my head, hair snagging and pulling at my scalp.

For a second, it was as though we were the only two people in the world, the need to feel him inside me was insurmountable. I gasped as he pushed his groin into mine, denim rubbing together. The notion of us just having a conversation was forgotten as his hand pushed inside the waistband of my jeans.

A low groan escaped my lips. I was trying to be as quiet as possible out in the open air. He pulled down my jeans, skin exposed to the elements, and we had sex against the tree. It lasted longer than before, both of us a tangled sweaty mess.

Trying not to laugh, we caught our breath, leaning back against opposite trees for support. My legs trembled, unwilling to steady themselves.

'I've been wanting to do that all weekend,' he said as we hastily pulled up our clothes. I vaguely remembered how much of a sexual appetite I'd had as a teenager. My libido reawakened with the prospect of sex with Nicky. Before I'd met David, I'd had a few wild months at university, excited to be away from home, enjoying the freedom and participating in all the drunken parties. A string of one-night stands followed, but it had been fun and I hadn't regretted a thing.

The desire I felt for Nicky was so overwhelming, it transported me back there. Drunken sex with men I thought were out of my league. Passion I hadn't felt for years with David. It crossed my mind as I watched Nicky secure his belt that he could be doing this with a number of women or girls. How would I know? We should have used something. Too late now.

I hadn't intended on having sex with Nicky again, or maybe subconsciously I had? Either way, I'd hardly put up a fight. I'd known what I was doing. I couldn't palm it off as a moment of weakness. I'd been calculated in my decision and it had served a purpose, to get back at David. A bittersweet victory in the cold light of day.

Nicky looked at me quizzically, trying to read my mind.

'Next time I'll make sure we have somewhere to go, a few hours at least.' He came over and brushed the hair out of my eyes, pulling me in for a long slow kiss. 'I want to make love to you,' he whispered, the top of his lip quivered. Sweat beading there, he licked it away.

I couldn't control the acceleration of my heart, the speed at which the blood was coursing through my veins, but I had to stay in control. I was the adult here after all.

'Nicky, I'm not even sure this should be happening.' I checked my watch, it was ten to twelve. 'Shit. I'm sorry, I have to go.' Already making my way back to the car, with Nicky following behind.

'I'm sorry about the number, I just had to see you,' he said, an underlying hint of desperation in his voice.

'I need to get my head around this, Nicky. Let me contact you, OK, when it's safe. I've got a hell of a lot to lose,' I explained, unlocking the car and climbing inside.

Nicky grimaced. Now his age was showing. He looked like another child had stolen the toy he was playing with.

## 17

I dropped Nicky at the end of his street and switched off the Motorola, hiding it back in the bottom of my handbag. After checking I was presentable, I went to collect Charlotte. I pretended everything was fine at the door to Louise, whilst Charlotte got her stuff together. I felt like my life was one big act and I was playing a part. Louise chatted animatedly and I told her how happy I was that Charlotte had found Amy, mentioning we'd struggled a bit with the wrong crowd in her old school. I didn't disclose how bad things had got there. Louise had encountered similar problems too.

Charlotte gave me a running commentary on the drive home about her meal at Smith and Western's.

'The ribs were gorgeous, Mum, but the ice cream was the best. We filmed ourselves eating this giant sundae. I'll show you when we get home.'

'So, it's somewhere we need to try then?'

Charlotte nodded enthusiastically. A few minutes later, I reversed onto the driveway.

'Mum, what's that?' Charlotte leaned over and pulled at my hair, frowning at the tiny leaf in her hand.

I felt my palms dampen on the steering wheel, but she'd dismissed it, tossing it onto the driveway as she climbed out of the car. Her face was already back on her phone.

'Must have come from a tree.' A nervous laugh burst from my lips.

Once inside, I put a chicken in the oven to roast, knowing I had Aunt Bessie in the freezer to give me a helping hand, and slipped upstairs. After a quick shower, I came back down, enjoying the aroma in the kitchen. How quickly I'd returned to the role of wife and mother. I busied myself with marking, but, unsurprisingly I found it difficult to concentrate. Peace and quiet wasn't a problem: David was watching football in the lounge and other than the occasional swear word I didn't hear a peep out of him, and Charlotte had retreated to her bedroom, supposedly doing homework. However, Nicky kept invading my thoughts.

I knew what I was doing was wrong, even with David having an affair. I wanted to bide my time and gather proof so he couldn't tell me I was mistaken, in case he thought he'd be able to explain it away. But two wrongs didn't make a right and scoring points with Nicky didn't make me feel better. With my stomach in knots, I rang Stella, I needed to talk someone.

'Hello, love, how are you doing?' Stella answered, recognising my number.

'Missing you. Wish you were here, could so do with a girl's night out.' I sighed.

'Ah, miss you too, I'll be there the week after next, so not long to wait now. Tell David he's got a night in with Charlotte as we need to hit the town. I'm dying to wear something other than functional footwear.' Stella giggled.

I wanted to tell her, I really did, but I couldn't bring myself to say it. How could I put it into words? When I formed the sentences in my head, they seemed dirty and dishonest. What would Stella think of me? Would she still be my friend?

'You seem a bit quiet. Is everything OK?' she asked.

'Yeah, I guess. We'll talk about it when you're down.'

'Is it David? Is he being a knob again?' Stella chucked dryly.

'Always.'

Picking up on my reluctance to talk, Stella changed the subject to her dad. Yesterday he'd made his way to the local shop to buy a pint of milk at six in the morning before she'd woken up. She'd gotten a call from the newsagents to tell her he was only wearing his pants; her mum had slept through the whole thing. I shouldn't laugh, it was so sad, but these were the moments Stella said that kept her going. It could be pretty miserable living with dementia.

'In other news, I've met someone.'

'Who?'

I heard a commotion in the background and Stella tutting.

'I've got to go, Mum's struggling to get the pan off the stove. I'll tell all when I see you,' Stella said devilishly. Knowing she'd left me hanging.

In bed that evening, David cuddled in to me and slid his hand underneath my nightie, but I feigned a headache. The idea of having sex with David having only been with Nicky a few hours before made me feel sick. I felt cheap, constantly yoyoing between disgust and enveloped in the excitement of an illicit affair. I guessed that was what was happening? I couldn't say it was a one-off any more. Despite my initial intentions, I'd be lying if I wasn't already thinking about the next time I could be with Nicky.

On Monday morning, I chose a demure navy dress with high heels and hold ups underneath. I also wore matching black underwear, something I hadn't bothered with for a while. I wasn't sure why I got dressed up; I wasn't going to see Nicky outside of school. But it made me feel attractive, plus there was the thrill of knowing I could tell him what I had on that he couldn't see.

After form, I spent five minutes checking my lesson plans were in order for the rest of my day before digging the Motorola out from the bottom of my handbag and turning it on. I hoped a message from Nicky would be waiting and felt disappointed when it remained silent. I'd told him to wait until I contacted him, so what did I expect?

I texted quickly and Nicky responded almost straight away.

Hi

Hi Sexy

Where are you?

Library. Come find me

I grabbed my book of Shakespeare's sonnets I'd borrowed and headed down the corridor. My senses heightened, I felt on edge. The hinges creaked loudly as I pushed the heavy door open. Thomas, the librarian, looked up from his desk and smiled in greeting. Nicky sat at one of the tables, hunched over an open book, taking notes. My stomach lurched, but I approached Thomas and asked him if I could renew the book for another week. He stamped the inside and I wandered along the aisle to where I'd find Shakespeare's works. Within a couple of minutes, Nicky was beside me.

'He's gone off to make tea, regular as clockwork,' he whispered, his eyes fixed on mine. I watched the vein in his neck pulsate. 'You look gorgeous,' he moved closer, gripping my wrist and squeezing it hard. 'When can I see you again?' he whispered.

'I don't know when I can get away.' I eased out of his grip, my wrist stinging like I'd had a Chinese burn. His intensity intimidating but thrilling at the same time.

A door hinge creaked, Thomas had returned.

'I'll text you,' I whispered.

Nicky grimaced, turning to walk back to the table with a random book plucked from the shelf.

I waited a couple of minutes and left the library. When I got back to my desk, there was already a text waiting from Nicky.

Tomorrow? After school

OK

I chewed on my lip. Charlotte had her first netball match, a friendly with another school so I had an hour at least. Maybe more if she got the bus home with Amy. My mind whirred, where would we go? I was trying to think of somewhere we wouldn't be seen when the Motorola buzzed again.

I'm hard just thinking about it

I snorted, feeling like a teenager with her first crush. I knew it was wrong, but I was unable to stop.

It was almost ten and my first lesson of the day was going to start any minute. The bell sounded, and students came streaming in. My year nine class were going to be writing theatre programmes for *Macbeth* including a synopsis on the back and pictures on the front to entice customers to buy. It was a fun lesson and they all got involved in the creativity of the task leaving me to become enveloped in my thoughts.

At lunchtime I caught up with Matilda and Susan. We resembled the witches from *Macbeth*, huddled around the coffee table in the staffroom eating our sandwiches and gossiping at first about the Thomas Cook collapse. Susan's sister was on holiday in Egypt and was having to be repatriated. Then the conversation changed once Mr Scott popped in to borrow Jackie, the school administrator.

Matilda had heard in passing that one of the students in year eleven was pregnant, a shame in someone so young with her whole life ahead of her. Mr Scott was already liaising with the parents on next steps. Apparently, it was early stages in the pregnancy, but the girl wouldn't tell anyone who the father was. It made me shudder to think that, at Charlotte's age, these girls were sexually active. They all seemed too young.

The afternoon assembly was long and laborious. I sat upright on the stage with my legs crossed, trying to keep still and eventually getting cramp. It was a struggle not to look at Nicky. I stole a few furtive glances and, whenever I did, he was staring straight at me, a steely look in his eyes that I hadn't seen before; chin jutting outwards. His friends around him whispered, nudging each other. They'd targeted a girl sitting in the row ahead to terrorise, but Nicky wasn't interested, his gaze focused purely on me.

Knowing I was being watched did nothing to calm my reddening cheeks and I placed my hands upon my thighs, smoothing my dress. I was desperate to drum my fingers and could feel the compulsion rising. I only managed to stop myself by clenching my jaw tightly and squeezing down on my molars. *One, two, three, four; one, two, three, four.*

When the pupils were dismissed, I noticed Charlotte hanging back to talk to me.

'Everything OK?' I asked, my voice echoing around the walls now the hall was empty.

'Seriously, Mum, can you please go back to wearing your normal stuff for school?' I frowned and shook my head, bemused.

'What do you mean? What's wrong with me?' I said, looking down at my dress. It wasn't short or especially tight.

'The boys are winding me up, calling you a MILF,' Charlotte scowled as I sniggered, clapping a hand over my mouth.

'Charlotte, that's ridiculous. Tell them to get a life, for goodness' sake.' I wrapped an arm around her shoulders, but she shrugged me off.

'I've got to get to class.' She hurried out of the hall and I followed. The year eights would be waiting to read their modern take on sonnets.

After school, Charlotte was still stand-offish, barely speaking to me on the drive home even after I promised I wouldn't wear that outfit again. I couldn't take the whole thing seriously, and this enraged Charlotte even more. The hormones were in full swing.

When we got home, I had a message from David to say he would be working late again and not to do him any dinner. It was becoming a joke. I rang him four times, but the calls went to voicemail. I had the urge to leave a message, telling him not to bother coming home at all.

I whisked up a quick tomato pasta dish for me and Charlotte and ran myself a bath. I relaxed for a while, reading a magazine before shaving, telling myself it had nothing to do with seeing Nicky tomorrow.

When I got out of the bath, David still wasn't home. I tried calling him again, but this time the phone was switched off and didn't even ring. The FindMyPhone app was redundant if the phone was switched off. I paced the bedroom, waiting for my vanilla-scented body cream to dry before I went through the pockets of David's clothes.

I found a receipt in the back pocket of his jeans. It was three weeks ago, Saturday 7th September, the day he'd left his golf clubs behind. It was from Miller and Carter: two steaks, one bottle of red wine and one dessert. A heavy lunch? Shared with whom? Was he with the mysterious Paul? Code name for a female? I didn't know what to think, but I believed his time away from home was nothing to do with making inroads heading up the finance department at the PR firm. He had to be having an affair.

*It's exactly what you're doing,* the voice in my head piped up.

Blinking back tears and ignoring the hollow feeling in the pit of my stomach, I got out my clothes for tomorrow and hung them on the wardrobe. Cream blouse and navy skirt, a safe choice, nothing too sensual, although my new peach lace underwear beneath would make me feel good. The idea of a planned meeting with Nicky made my head spin and I chewed my fingernails down to the quick. What did he see in me? I was old enough to be his mother. Did he have a thing for older women? Was I a challenge? Or was he getting the same kick out of it that I was? Half of the attraction was because it was wrong. I knew I should put a stop to it, but discovering David's affair had been like a kick in the gut. My marriage was disintegrating, and Nicky made me feel wanted.

David still hadn't come home by the time I went to bed, but when I woke at three in the morning, he was snoring beside me. He stank of alcohol, it emanated from his pores. I resisted the urge to wake him, to force everything out in the open. Call him out on the affair and demand answers. Wanting to keep my own secret hidden prevented me from doing so. I was a hypocrite and I hated myself for it.

My stomach churned; there was no air in the room and it was claustrophobic. I put on my robe and went downstairs in the dark, with only the sound of the clock ticking in the lounge to guide me. Once safely in the kitchen, I fumbled for the cupboard lights and listened to the gentle hum of the fridge. I felt tightly wound, like a spring, consumed by nerves and stress.

Retrieving the Motorola from my bag, I switched it on and waited impatiently. Two messages came through as it buzzed in my hand.

I can't wait until tomorrow

The second was sent late last night.

Lying in bed thinking about you. My place tomorrow.

I shivered with excitement.

Then I realised, what he referred to as *his place* was the house he lived in with his mum, who could quite easily be the same age as me.

## 18

I sat at the dining table for half an hour, hands wrapped around a warm mug of milk, staring into space. When I did finally head back to bed, it was as though I'd blinked when the sound of the alarm dragged me into consciousness.

The space beside me was empty and I started to wonder if my husband was a figment of my imagination. I sent a text to ask if he was bothering to come home later and received a prompt and apologetic response. He'd be home on time.

An hour and a half later, when I arrived at school, the air temperature had dropped overnight. The classroom was freezing, the old radiators spluttering to life. My choice of floaty feminine clothes seemed idiotic. There was no sun to be seen, only grey skies out of the window. We were early for school, the traffic quiet today and Charlotte waited in my classroom for Amy to arrive, scrolling through her phone. All of a sudden, the classroom door flew open and we both jumped.

Nicky burst through the door, grinning at first until he saw Charlotte and his eyes widened.

'Hello?' I smiled tightly. Outwardly calm but my heart was getting ready to leap out of my chest.

'Hi, umm, sorry... I was looking for Mr Ross?'

I breathed a silent sigh of relief at Nicky's quick thinking.

Charlotte was gazing at him open-mouthed.

'He's not here I'm afraid. You could try the staffroom?'

Nicky nodded his thanks and fled down the corridor.

'What's up with you?' I said to Charlotte whose mouth was still gaping.

'He's gorgeous isn't he, Mum. All the girls fancy him.'

I blushed, turning away to busy myself with writing on the whiteboard.

'I can see why you like him,' I managed.

Charlotte made to swoon dramatically, her hand to her forehead as she walked out of the classroom.

'Hang on, Charlotte,' I called after her and she appeared back in the doorway. 'You OK to get the bus home with Amy after the netball match?'

'You not coming to watch then?'

Guilt twinged at my side, but Charlotte laughed.

'Just kidding, you'll put me off. Are you swimming?'

I nodded, unable to say the lie out loud to my daughter. Charlotte didn't seem to notice and left to find Amy outside before the bell.

There was a couple of minutes' peace before Nicky bounded back through the door, like an energetic puppy, making me jump for the second time that morning.

'That was a close one,' he blurted, and I shushed him, closing the door.

'You've made quite an impression on my daughter,' I said, immediately regretting it. Why on earth had I volunteered that information?

'Luckily, I'm only interested in her mum,' he said, entwining his fingers in mine.

'After school?' I whispered, feeling my nerve endings firing.

'Yeah, my place, 32 Brampton Road. Mum will be at work until after five,' he said conspiratorially.

I swallowed hard. The mention of his mum left me cold, bringing into sharp focus the reality of his age.

His face changed. Gone was the easy-going grin, replaced instead by a hard, thin line, as though he had a bad taste in his mouth.

'Why didn't you answer my text last night?' He sounded like a sulky child, a stark reminder that he was just a teenager.

'Because I can't always answer straight away. You know that.'

He nodded grudgingly but still looked sullen when I shooed him out of the classroom as the bell was about to ring. A minute later, the room was full of children chattering and I had to shout for quiet so I could take the register, but my mind was elsewhere, unable to skim over the knowledge that Nicky was only a few years older than Charlotte. It made me squirm.

The day flew by in a haze; I was distracted for most of it. With each passing minute, I felt my stomach tie itself in knots. When three o'clock finally came, I briefly stopped by the toilets for a quick spritz of perfume and to refresh my make-up. It wasn't until I sat in my car and turned the key in the ignition, I saw my hands were shaking.

I breathed deeply, counting over and over again. *One, two, three, four; one, two, three, four.* I started the car and pressed the clutch so I could run through the gears until I felt calmer. It was silly to feel nervous when I'd been with Nicky before. Twice. But this time seemed different, it was planned, and we would have more time together than our previous fumbles.

I didn't look like a teenager any more. I had wrinkles and stretch marks and had even noticed an age spot appear on my hand in the past year. Trying to shrug off my insecurities, I reminded myself that, according to Charlotte, all the girls fancied Nicky. If that was the case, he could have his pick. But he'd chosen me. I didn't feel thirty-nine any more than he likely felt eighteen.

His nineteenth birthday was right before Christmas, only a couple of months away. I knew because I'd taken a peek at his record while the secretary, Ruth, was out at lunch. She'd left her computer on and Mr Scott had been deep in conversation with Mr Ross in the staffroom. I knew where he lived, that his mother's name was Pat and that there was no father living at the home address. I also looked at his grades; his GCSE results were of a high standard. He'd had a gap year before coming back for A-Levels. Why? Had he had to go out to work to help his mum out? Or maybe there were health issues in the family at that time? I couldn't ask without it being obvious I'd checked up on him and it wasn't an option to ask any of the teachers. I couldn't risk drawing any unnecessary attention to me and Nicky. He was clearly smart and, in a strange way, it made me feel better; I wasn't taking advantage of him.

The weird thing was, I felt like I needed him. I needed whatever it was between us. Without it, all I had was a crumbling marriage, and I couldn't face that right now. With negative thoughts laid to rest, I hurried to Brampton Road, parking further down the street than necessary.

Nicky's home, in the middle of a row of terraced houses, had a dark blue front door. Before I could knock, the door swung open and Nicky stood waiting for me. He wore a salmon coloured T-shirt and lose-fitting jeans. His feet were bare. He stepped aside to allow me in.

'Hi.' I said, my voice low. I could barely meet his eyes.

'Do you want a drink?' he asked and I nodded, following him to the back of the house, into the kitchen. He made me a pint of Robinsons squash and I couldn't help but see the irony as I took a sip. 'How was your day?' He leant on the counter, his posture relaxed. The opposite to how I was feeling.

I stood stiffly, waffling on about my day, the nerves taking hold. I drummed my fingers on my thigh.

Nicky stared, a quizzical smile emerging.

'You do that a lot.' It was a statement not a question.

'It's an anxiety thing,' I replied dismissively, wishing the ground would swallow me up.

Nicky took the plunge, moving first and beckoning me to follow him upstairs.

'No need to feel anxious here,' he said over his shoulder. His bedroom was remarkably tidy; painted a dark blue, with posters of Cristiano Ronaldo and Gareth Bale. A poster of a young Angelina Jolie in a bikini adorned his wardrobe door. I swallowed, feeling my throat close up. It wasn't that dissimilar to Charlotte's bedroom. Aftershave bottles and deodorants lined the top of a chest of drawers and an Xbox connected to a small tv in one corner on the floor, *Call of Duty* games stacked up neatly beside it.

Counting in my head, I placed my coat and bag on the floor. My stomach churned, and I worried I might be sick.

As I considered making a run for it, Nicky approached, raising his hands to hold my face and kiss me so gently that I melted into him, my nerves held at bay. I'd never wanted anybody more. He unbuttoned the top of my blouse, lifting it over my head and letting it fall to the floor. Feeling exposed, I felt the flush creep up my neck as I undressed him. I took my time to appreciate his body, stomach hard and smooth to touch as I ran my fingers across his abdomen. I felt his hands at my back and heard my zip descend, letting my skirt drop. He held my hand to help me step out of the floaty pile of fabric on the floor.

'You're beautiful,' he whispered, as I took my turn and unclasped his belt before tackling the awkward metal buttons of his jeans.

When we both stood before each other in our underwear there was nowhere to hide, no soft lighting and no bed covers to shield our modesty. I kissed Nicky hungrily and we scooted over to the bed. We made love, just as he'd said he wanted to. His hands touched every part of me so tenderly, different from the other times we'd been together. He moved on top of me slowly, fingers entwined, our bodies pressed together tightly. He seemed to know exactly what to do to, how to touch me so I'd respond. I was amazed at his ability to know the way around a woman's body.

Afterwards, we tried not to fall asleep as we laid together, listening to the occasional car driving past. Nicky assured me his mother wasn't due to come home for a while, but every noise set me on edge. The irony of worrying about being caught by Nicky's mum hadn't escaped me. I wrapped the checked duvet around myself and he pulled on his boxer shorts before opening the window and lighting a cigarette, offering me the packet.

'Sod it, why not.' I took one and he lit it for me. 'I didn't know you smoked?' I said.

Nicky raised his eyebrows.

'Only sometimes.' I hoped he wasn't doing it to impress me? No, Nicky was way too self-assured to even think about doing that.

I hadn't smoked since I was a teenager, but it came back to me easily and I remembered how much I used to enjoy it when I was young and carefree.

'I wish we could do it all over again,' I said, wistfully stroking Nicky's arm and kissing one of his many moles.

'We could come here every day if you wanted to,' he said, and I smiled. If only I could. If only I could stay here, all my responsibilities forgotten. But it wasn't real life, I was suspended in a dream.

'You don't talk about me to your friends, do you?' I asked.

He chuckled, smoke billowing from his nostrils. 'No, of course I don't. I've told them there's someone, but that's it.'

The relief washed over me. It wasn't something I'd thought of up until now. The boys discussing their conquests. Sex with a teacher would definitely be something to boast about.

'I just feel like I hardly know you,' I admitted.

'Ask me anything.'

'OK, why did you have a gap year?'

He frowned. 'How did you know about that?'

I blushed, not wanting to confess I'd looked at his school file.

He shrugged. 'I was all set for going semi pro, I had trials at Brighton football club, but I fractured my foot. Fucked it all up.' He squeezed his cigarette tightly, squashing the butt and inhaling sharply. I could see he found it tough to talk about, the bitterness spilling out of him.

'I'm sorry.'

'It's done now. Turned out OK. Bill, a friend of my mum's, got me helping out with the motors at his garage, taught me basic mechanics. I helped out with services and MOTs. I still work there some weekends, when I'm needed. If he gets a rush on. He helped me do up the Fiesta, it didn't run when I bought it.' Nicky flicked his ash out of the window.

'And then?' I probed.

'Then I decided to go back to school, do sports science and biology. If I can't play professionally, maybe I could be a physio? I dunno, I'll see where it takes me.' He paused. 'I think about you all the time,' Nicky blurted, staring at me, his voice cool.

'I think about you too,' I replied, partly because it was true, partly because it seemed like the right thing to say.

We stubbed out our cigarettes and he pushed me down onto the bed, his hands straying to my breasts.

'We don't have time.' I giggled, glancing at the clock. It was ten to five, but Nicky's head was already between my legs making me writhe with pleasure.

Fifteen minutes later, we laughed as we tried to get dressed at speed.

'Mum will be home soon.'

I stood bolt upright, reality crashing in.

'Where's your dad?' I asked, and Nicky's eyes narrowed. I instantly regretted bringing it up.

'He left a few years ago, used to knock my mum about. He's a wanker,' Nicky said flatly, his eyes thunderous.

'I'm sorry,' was all I could say, although I wanted to take him into my arms and tell him he was doing fine without his dad around.

I gave Nicky a quick kiss as I dashed out of the door towards my car, looking up and down the street and praying no one had seen me going in or out.

I drove around the corner and pulled over, sitting for a while to gather my thoughts, not wanting to go home. How could I go back and look at David now? I wanted to be with Nicky, back in his bed. It was ridiculous. *It's just infatuation.*

My bag vibrated jolting me out of my stupor and I reached in to check my phone. There were no messages from Charlotte or David, or

any missed calls. The bag vibrated again, and I realised it was the
Motorola, although I hadn't remembered switching it on. Had Nicky
done it? I had a text from him already.

Don't sleep with David

It was an instruction not a request.

## 19

When I got home from Nicky's, Charlotte was bouncing around as they'd won their first match. I congratulated her and she told me how Amy had scored the winning shot. I found David upstairs, packing. He had to attend a conference in Bristol at short notice, standing in as a representative for his firm as Patrick's wife was unwell.

'Can't someone else go?' I asked, incredulous. David ran the finance department, he was hardly the public face of the firm.

'There is no one else. Simon is on holiday and Patrick can't get hold of Ben the marketing guy. I'll be back on Friday,' he said, shoving toiletries into his bag. I could tell he wanted to get on the road to miss the traffic. He seemed agitated. I asked for the name and number of the hotel in case I needed to contact him and, once he'd left, I rang them. I wanted to make sure the conference was being held there and a room was booked for him. I hated myself for checking but was relieved to learn he was telling the truth. I had no idea if the mystery woman was going to be there too.

In truth, I knew I couldn't say David was completely to blame for whatever was happening between us. The move had been an unspoken last-ditch attempt to bring us back together. Before the miscarriage we were happy, we laughed all the time and made the effort to go out just the two of us, at least once a month. We were a team.

Lately, despite the change of jobs, we were ships passing in the night, barely speaking past the functional. There hadn't been an appropriate time to discuss the state of our marriage. My main priority was Charlotte and her not picking up on the atmosphere. I didn't want her knowing things weren't great between us. She needed to concentrate this year, leading up to her GCSEs. It was a crucial time and I didn't want to rock the boat any more than we already had with the school move.

I couldn't get my head around David entertaining the advances of another woman, though. He was too sensible, too sturdy. He never flirted, only the occasional banter with Stella. He was the reliable one. I was the fanciful one, prone to wacky, outlandish ideas. He made sure my feet were firmly planted on the ground when I got carried away. We complemented each other. To think of him being the object of a woman's desire seemed bizarre. Although he was an attractive man. Tall, dark haired and slim, albeit now with a slight paunch. The thought of him with someone else made my chest cave in. Nicky was the one thing that made me feel better. I looked forward to seeing him. I couldn't get enough. I wanted to consume him. No one had ever made me feel so desired. It was like the last few years I'd been asleep with David and now Nicky had come along, I felt alive. He was intense and, when we were together, we were in our own world. I wasn't stupid, I knew it was infatuation with Nicky, the honeymoon period was yet to wear off. He got a kick out of deciding when and where we met. I was happy to let him be in control. A switch from our roles in real life.

* * *

On Friday, I wandered to the girls' toilets at break time and overheard two sixth-formers talking about Nicky as they vaped in the stalls, a cloying caramel scent spilling out from over the door. I listened for a moment when I heard his name mentioned. One of the girls had been out with him a few times but not recently. She wasn't pleased, her tone bitter. They thought he was seeing somebody, as Amelia, a girl in year eleven, had let it slip they weren't together any more.

One of them couldn't hide their contempt that he was going out with girls in a lower year. I was surprised when they mentioned Amelia; she was in my English GCSE class, but I would never have put the two of them together. She was quiet and bookish but beautiful, a classic English rose.

At lunch, I asked Matilda and Susan if sixth-formers generally dated year eleven students. Matilda told me it was pretty common.

'The year eleven girls are easier to manipulate than the sixth-formers,' Susan said, shaking her head despairingly.

\* \* \*

I couldn't see Nicky after school except at the creative writing class. He scowled when I told him, but my hands were tied; Charlotte had invited Amy to come for a sleepover and after their plans had been cancelled last week, I couldn't refuse.

They hung around until the class was finished and I drove them home as they gossiped in the back of the car. When we got in, they chose pizza out of the list of takeaway options I rattled off and headed upstairs. My heart sank when I saw David was waiting for me in the kitchen, but he planted a kiss on my lips before I could speak, wrapping his arms around my waist. I wanted to wriggle out of his grasp, surprised at the sudden burst of affection. I spied a bunch of flowers on the table.

'What's going on?'

David pushed a cup of tea into my hand and I took a sip, the steaming hot liquid burning the roof of my mouth.

'I'm sorry I've not been around this week. I feel like I've hardly seen you.' He grimaced.

'That's not unusual though, is it? You've been spending more time at work than you have at home. If that's where you've been, of course.

You never answer your bloody phone,' I said brusquely, my face growing hot. It was on the tip of my tongue to ask if he had another woman, but I was scared. Did I want it confirmed? Would I have to admit my affair too? What was the saying? People in glass houses shouldn't throw stones?

His shoulders slumped and he sat at the table. I gripped the edge of the worktop, drumming repeatedly. I didn't have to hide the compulsion around David, although I knew it frustrated him at times. It had only started after the miscarriage. The therapist I saw a couple of times afterwards told me it was common during periods of increased stress to develop a tick of sorts. She told me it may well go of its own accord at some point.

'How was the conference? Did you go into the office today?' I pressed.

'The conference was fine, not really my thing, but I flew the flag like I was asked. I popped into the office on the way back. Had to debrief Patrick.'

'I'm glad it went well,' I said stiffly.

'A colleague's wife died suddenly today. She had a heart attack. The entire office was in bits this afternoon. I guess it was a bit of a wake-up call.' David shook his head, his eyes glistening, tears threatening to fall.

My body, that had been held so rigid, softened. I went to David, pulling him into a hug.

'I'm so sorry,' I said. Things may not have been perfect between us, but I still loved him. Though, I wasn't sure whether that was enough.

'Urgh, get a room,' came a voice behind us.

With a quick wipe of the eyes, I pulled away from David, fixing a smile upon my face. Charlotte stood in the doorway to the kitchen, Amy behind her, peering over her shoulder.

'Come in, what can I get you?' David said, playing the host.

Five minutes later, they were heading back up the stairs with cans of Diet Coke and two large packets of Doritos.

When we were alone again, a lump formed in my throat and I struggled to swallow. I felt claustrophobic, as though a panic attack was building. I turned away, searching for the pizza takeaway menu, taking slow steady breaths to ward it off.

'Is that what they've chosen?' David asked, when I found the brightly coloured leaflet.

'Yes, they must have got the memo pizza is your favourite.' I pursed my lips. David had to have pizza at least once a week. He always said it would be his death-row meal.

Once I had the girl's order, I rang it through and put some plates in the oven.

David sat reading the paper at the table, laptop nowhere to be seen. I wanted to comment as it was so unusual but thought better of it. He'd had a difficult day and I didn't want to make it any worse. Instead, my mind turned to Nicky as I unloaded the dishwasher and tidied the kitchen, if only I could get out and see him later, but I knew I couldn't. I had to be at home, my focus here.

It was surreal, leading a double life. It made the home one, where I was wife and mother, seem boring. When I was with Nicky, I was a teenager again, free as a bird, with no ties or responsibilities. I knew it wasn't real and couldn't last. Sooner or later, the bubble would burst, and my real life would come crashing in.

'Stella's coming tomorrow, isn't she?' David's voice interrupted my thoughts.

'Not for another two weeks. She's told me to tell you, you're looking after Charlotte as we're going out.' I laughed and David joined in. He'd always liked Stella, she was easy to get along with, hilarious and frequently spoke her mind. A quality I was envious of.

'Not out-out?' he asked in mock horror, his face aghast.

I nodded, raising my eyebrows dramatically.

Twenty minutes later, there was a knock at the door and the pizza arrived. We gathered around the table and dived into the two large pizzas, one pepperoni, one Hawaiian. I was astounded at how much Amy could put away for such a small girl. She must have been having a growth spurt, either that or she had hollow legs.

'So, what's the plan, girls, are you taking over the TV tonight?' David asked, a twinkle in his eye.

'Yep, back-to-back episodes of *Pretty Little Liars*. Amy's only seen the first season,' Charlotte replied.

'And ice cream,' Amy added.

'Of course, you mustn't forget ice cream, there are two tubs of Ben & Jerry's in the freezer with your names on,' I said with a smile, pleased Amy felt comfortable at our house. Charlotte had spent so much time at Amy's, it was nice for them both to be here for a change.

David opened a bottle of wine and put the television on in the kitchen. He looked to be settling in to spend the evening there. I cleared the mess from dinner and nursed the glass he'd poured for me while we watched a programme about garden makeovers. The girl's high-pitched squeals came from the front room.

I peeked my head in to see they'd just put on *Fatal Attraction*.

'Odd choice, isn't it?'

'It's a classic,' Amy said. 'My mum loves it,'

'Never seen it,' Charlotte volunteered.

'Mind if I join you?' I asked and they nodded. I settled down on the sofa in front of the window. Amy and Charlotte were sitting on the floor, having a mock picnic on the rug of the leftover Doritos and ice cream.

David followed, bringing in the wine.

'Oh, this is a good one,' he said, sitting beside me.

I shifted in my seat and he rested his hand on my thigh.

We watched the movie, sometimes from behind cushions. Glenn Close's Alex was chilling, and it was just as good as I'd remembered. I eyed David curiously, wondering if the plot rang home, but he didn't flinch. He wrapped his arm around my shoulders and pulled me in to him at the end as the girls took their empty wrappers and spoons into the kitchen. It was easy to play happy families for the sake of Charlotte and Amy.

A loud bang came from out front, making us jump. Our nerves were still on edge from the shock ending of the film. We both got up, realising it had got dark and we hadn't closed the blinds. The security light illuminated the driveway; one of our bins was on the floor. A chill ran down my back, settling in my toes.

'Foxes. I'll go pick it up,' David said.

Foxes? It had to be one hell of a fox.

David came back a minute later and locked up as I closed the blinds and curtains.

'Right, be good, you two. We're heading up to bed,' I called into the kitchen, where it sounded like they were raiding the biscuit tin. Where were they putting it all?

Upstairs, as I was about to close the curtains, I thought I saw a shadow on the driveway; a figure standing in the dark by my car. The security light timed out, plunging the driveway into darkness and then it was gone.

Squinting, I scanned the road as far as I could see, but nothing moved. I froze, sure I'd seen someone, but the light didn't come back on.

After a few minutes, I heard David come up the stairs and drew the curtains. Perhaps I'd imagined it.

## 20

David nudged me awake the next morning, holding a tray laden with coffee and toasted crumpets. I sat up, my head still a little fuzzy.

'Morning. You look like you could do with this,' he said, placing the tray on the bed beside me.

'Thanks. What time is it?' I asked, already turning to look at the clock on the bedside table. It was nine o'clock. I took a sip of my coffee which was steaming hot and sweet. 'How are the girls?' I asked.

'Fine, they went to bed after a midnight, I think.' He sat on the edge of the bed.

'Are they still asleep?' I asked, surprised, as Charlotte never normally lay in this late.

'Yep.'

I tucked into a buttery crumpet, feeling more human with each bite. The weather was getting colder and I felt a draught so pulled the duvet up to my chin. Autumn was in full swing, bringing with it grey skies and blankets of rain.

'There's a country fair on today in the next village, think the girls would like to go?' David asked.

I smirked; I doubted it. I was certain my fifteen-year-old self would have turned my nose up at a visit to a country fair.

'I don't think so.'

'Well, we can go this afternoon and if Charlotte doesn't have plans she can come too. A nice family day out.'

\* \* \*

Charlotte was as unimpressed by the idea of a country fair as I was, but as Amy was going home at lunchtime, she didn't have much of a choice. David was adamant that we were going to have a family outing, guilt creeping in from not spending much time with us this past month.

Later that afternoon, just as we were about to leave, David discovered he had a nail in his tyre. It was completely flat, so we had to go in my car. He said he'd change it later on so as not to delay our trip, moaning about the cost of Land Rover tyres.

We made our way along the winding roads to the picturesque village of Wisborough Green. There was a pub, a village shop and a post office. The fair had been erected on the green, where the locals played bowls and cricket in the summer.

Trying to find a place to park was a pain and the temperature was cooler than we'd expected. David was determined to have a good afternoon so tried to encourage us with promises of crepes and hot tea from the food tent. He dragged the fair out for an hour and a half, which was impressive as there were around fifteen stalls, perusing each one, holding my hand and stopping to see what was on offer. Charlotte spent most of the time sulking and staring at her phone. I tried to become enthused when she found a crafting stall with lots of jewellery. Although I did find a stall selling plaques and bought one for Mary. It read, 'The kitchen is the heart of the home'. As a thank you for all the baking.

David finally conceded defeat when the heavens opened, and everyone ran for cover from the rain. When we got back to the sanctuary of the car, wiping the drops from our faces, David spoke.

'OK, so that wasn't the best idea,' he said, putting on his seat belt.

'You think, Dad?' Charlotte smirked.

I chose to stay quiet, perhaps now we could go home, although I was grateful David was making the effort. Perhaps it was a little too late and I couldn't deny I felt guilty that I still wanted to find an excuse to get out and see Nicky.

'How about we go for an early dinner?'

I rolled my eyes as I stared out of the window. I wouldn't be escaping after all.

'Miller & Carter?' I suggested, dryly.

David frowned at me.

'Smith & Western's Dad.' Charlotte almost leapt over into the front seat.

'OK, OK,' he agreed, tapping the name of the restaurant into the satnav and negotiating a three-point turn back towards the main road.

The meal was nice, lots of meat to choose from, so David was in heaven. Charlotte loved the menu too and the whole cowboy feel to the place was fun. It was like we'd walked into a west coast ranch, complete with country music pumping through the speakers. There were only a few customers as it was a bit early for the dinner-time rush, so we munched on nachos to begin with, waiting a while before our mains came out. I'd made my peace with not seeing Nicky and ensured I enjoyed time together as a family.

Feeling stuffed after sharing a huge sundae for dessert, we rolled out of the restaurant and made the journey home – none of us could wait to get into our pyjamas. Charlotte wanted to rush back to watch an influencer called Saffron on *Strictly Come Dancing*.

'What the bloody hell is an influencer?' David asked, rubbing his bloated stomach.

'Don't worry, Dad,' Charlotte sighed as though she couldn't be bothered to explain.

'Saturday night in for *Strictly*, rock and roll, eh!' David turned to me, grinning.

'Yep, that's us,' I replied, unable to hide the bitterness in my tone.

'What's wrong? You've been in a funny mood all day,' he said, exasperated.

'Nothing,' I replied, my voice a tad too high.

When we got back to the house, I stopped off at Mary's to deliver our gift, trying to delay an awkward conversation with David.

'Ah, thank you, love, it's beautiful,' the crinkled skin around her eyes glistened.

'Just a little thank you for the baking since we arrived.' I squeezed her hand.

'Did you have a visitor late last night? My light on the driveway was going on and off all night, yours too when I checked,' she said.

I shrank back from the door.

'Perhaps it was kids?' I offered, the general term for anything unexplained, but someone had been there. Could they have purposely put a nail in David's tyre? Nicky wouldn't do something like that, would he?

She shrugged and went on to spend a few minutes telling me how she'd won a line at bingo.

When I got into the house, everyone was getting changed and I had a chance to grab the Motorola out of my bag and sneak it into the bathroom without anybody noticing. I turned the taps to run a bath, uninterested in *Strictly*, and switched the phone on. Ten messages buzzed through, one after the other. My stomach churned as I read them one by one.

Hope you can get away over the weekend x

Can you get out? X

I miss you. Try to get out X

You must have your phone switched off again!

Where are you?

Dying to see you!

Are you ignoring me?

What have I done?

Don't Sleep with Him!!!

TEXT ME BACK!!!

Nicky sounded like he was getting angrier and more desperate with each text.

I replied quickly, my fingers fumbling over the ancient keys.

I'm so sorry, been dragged out all day and haven't been on my own at all. Miss you. Will try and meet tomorrow xxx

I hoped it would be enough to placate him. I knew it was difficult for him to understand as his home life was the opposite of mine. I had to carry on as wife and mother like nothing had changed, whereas he didn't have to pretend.

I slipped into the bath, leaving the phone on the toilet seat. The door was locked. I'd heard Charlotte and David chatting as the theme to *Strictly Come Dancing* boomed out. The phone lit up, buzzing as a message came through.

Finally! Hate it when you don't reply

His message was stand-offish, and it showed the difference in years between us. He had no idea what it was like for me.

I'm sorry, it's difficult. Just because I'm not texting doesn't mean I'm not thinking about you.

I hoped it would soften him and when his next message came through, it seemed to have worked.

OK, can't wait to see you tomorrow!

\* \* \*

On Sunday morning, we woke to more grey skies. According to the weather reports, it was going to rain for most of the day. David decided it was a perfect opportunity to make his quarterly visit to his parents back in Weybridge. Charlotte was happy to go as she always got spoilt whilst they were there. I hadn't got along with David's father for a few years. They never made me feel good enough for their only son and eventually I stopped trying, so I had a ready excuse to stay behind.

When they left at ten, I was already showered and dressed, trying to stop the palpitations in my chest as I text Nicky. I hadn't considered where we'd meet. It has started to drizzle and no doubt his mum would be home, so I assumed it wouldn't be there.

I'm free, let's meet

I'll come to you

Nicky's response startled me; the text came through within a minute of mine being sent. I didn't want him at the house. It didn't seem right. As I worded a reply, gently suggesting we go elsewhere, there was a knock at the door, so loud I gasped. Was it a delivery? I wasn't expecting a package, but it was one of those impatient forceful knocks. I crept down the stairs, my body held in an icy grip.

Pulling the door open amidst another knock, I stepped back, my mouth dropping open. Nicky stood on the doormat. The welcome doormat that David had chosen in the hardware shop, the one he'd picked out for our new home.

I opened my mouth to speak, but nothing came out. Nicky stepped

over the threshold without invitation, walking past me into the hallway, turning to close the front door before scooping me up in a
passionate embrace. I pulled away. The hair at the back of my neck
prickled. How did he know where I lived?

'I know he's gone. I watched them leave, so I knew it was safe,' he
continued to nuzzle my neck.

'Nicky, I don't feel comfortable with this,' I managed, but he was
already pulling me upstairs by the hand.

A revelation dawned, like someone had flicked a switch in my
mind.

'Have you been sitting outside my house?' I asked, trailing
behind him.

He stopped, turning around in the hallway.

'Maybe.' He winked, laughing at the horror in my eyes. The sound
set my nerves on edge.

'Were you here last night?' I asked, but he shook his head.

Pausing at the top, he spun around, deciding which room was
mine. A pink dressing gown hung on the edge of the door. It was the
giveaway and Nicky pushed it wide, surveying mine and David's
bedroom.

'I want to fuck you in his bed,' he said, and I whipped my hand out
of his. He saw the revulsion on my face and backtracked. 'I'm joking.
Come and sit down, I've got something for you.' He patted the space
beside him on my bed and pulled out a flat square box.

I lowered myself next to him, muscles tense. The situation made
me uncomfortable. What if David or Charlotte had forgotten something or had a problem with the car and had to come back? I strained
my ears, on high alert for any sounds of cars approaching.

Nicky handed me the box and I opened it; revealing a pair of silver
earrings shaped like apples on a bed of pink tissue paper. They were
gorgeous and I couldn't help but smile.

'Apples for teachers, right?' he whispered, kissing my neck whilst
reaching his hand inside my shirt.

I closed my eyes as my skin tingled beneath his touch, nipples standing to attention. I didn't stop him when he kissed my lips or when he moved lower and began removing my clothes, even though I knew I should have. It was so easy to get caught up in the moment with him.

'Turn over,' he said breathlessly, and I did as instructed. Without hesitation, he pushed inside me, and I cried out. He wasn't normally so rough but he seemed caught up in the thrill of being here. It was against the rules, dangerous and his need was urgent.

Once it was over, Nicky reverted to his charming self, but I couldn't help feeling like I'd been involved in some kind of pissing contest. More to do with his ego and marking of territory than him wanting to be with me. We went downstairs and I made us a drink, unable to shake off the feeling of unease. I couldn't wait to get him out of the house.

'What's up?' He snaked a hand around my waist, pulling me to him.

'I don't feel comfortable here, Nicky,' I sounded whiney and a spike of self-loathing drove into my side.

I caught the slightest eye roll and he chucked his glass in the sink. I winced, waiting for it to shatter, but thankfully it didn't. I had one sulky teenager already, I didn't want another.

'Let's go to Reigate Hill, we can take a picnic. We'll be fine if we wrap up and it'll be dead apart from the dog walkers.' This seemed to pique Nicky's interest and he agreed.

I sped around the kitchen and cobbled together a picnic from what I could find in the fridge. Packing it into a cool bag, hidden away in a cupboard, normally reserved for trips to the beach.

'I'm going to pop upstairs and get a jumper.' I took the stairs two at a time, not wanting to leave Nicky alone in my kitchen for too long. My sheets were a mess and I hurriedly stripped the bed, throwing them in the washing basket, before getting a jumper out of the wardrobe. I put the earrings in my jewellery box, knowing David wouldn't have a clue what was in there.

When I returned, Nicky was looking at photos on the fridge; the happy family snaps taken over the years on numerous day trips and holidays. He was frowning at one of David and I, sat on a rock, squinting at the camera in bright sunlight. Charlotte had taken it two years ago, when things were better. Nicky quickly changed his expression when he realised I'd entered the room.

'Ready?' he said, and I nodded.

I cast my eye around, checking nothing was out of place. Nicky had nothing to lose if we got exposed, whereas I had everything, and I didn't get the impression he had any qualms about David finding out.

I put a baseball hat on and kept my head low as we left. It was great having Mary as a neighbour, but I didn't know if she watched all the comings and goings from the house. It was only once I'd climbed into my car and driven away that I relaxed.

Nicky drove ahead and I could see his eyes, cool and piercing, in the rear-view mirror, staring at me every time we stopped in traffic. I felt goosebumps creep up my forearms. What was Nicky doing sitting outside my house? Had he done it before? Was he the shadow on the driveway last night, and if so, how had he even found out where I lived?

Watching his face as he drove, he looked calm and peaceful, but what was hiding beneath?

## 21

When we got to Reigate Hill, there were only a handful of cars in the car park, most likely people scared off from the weather warning. It hadn't started to properly rain yet, but I'd brought my waterproof coat just in case.

In the café, I bought two hot chocolates in takeaway cups. Nicky stood beside me in the queue, pulling faces at a baby in a pushchair as I looked on. The pinch of my heart caused me physical pain, as though it was in a mincer and he was turning the handle. I looked away, zipping my purse back and forth whilst I waited for my change. It was still raw, and I struggled to be around babies without tearing up.

'You OK?' Nicky slid his arm around me as we left. I tensed at his touch, grateful there was hardly anyone around to see us.

'Fine,' I replied.

We walked for about twenty minutes before finding an area of grass on top of the hill where the surrounding trees were tall and thick, giving us some shelter from the elements, as well as privacy. It was a dry patch and out of the way of the mud, and Nicky laid out a blanket he'd had in the back of his car. As I sat, I wondered how many girls had been on it before.

'Are you seeing anybody else?' I blurted, as I sat down.

'No,' he smirked, amused by my question. 'Are you jealous?'

I shook my head, pulling a can of Coke out of the cool bag.

'I'm sorry about earlier,' he said.

I turned to look at him, his eyes downcast.

'I struggle with you going home to him and sleeping in his bed. I'd be lying if I said otherwise. I want to be with you all the time and I'm jealous he gets to be.'

I took Nicky's hand before I replied, choosing my words carefully.

'I'm sorry, Nicky, I get it, I do, and I want to be with you too.' I almost added, 'but this can't last forever', but something in Nicky's eyes made me stop myself. Was he hoping I would leave David? Because I couldn't. There was no way. I'd done a lot of thinking this week and though I was hooked on how Nicky made me feel, eventually the infatuation would end, and our lives would resume as they were before. I thought he understood this was temporary.

We ate our picnic of sausage rolls, cheese, and cake, washed down with Coke. Laying back and staring at the sky, I felt content. I put my worries aside and enjoyed the moment, just being Izzy. Carefree Izzy, not a wife, not a mother.

Rolling onto my side, I leaned in to kiss Nicky, but our kiss turned into a fumble and soon we were making love atop the hill as the sky desperately tried to rain on us. When it got to three o'clock, I told Nicky I had to return home. I hoped I'd get back before David. I didn't want to have to explain where I'd been.

Nicky held me tight in the car park, a little too tight, kissing me hard. His stubble was like sandpaper. I found it unnerving, having to pry him off me so I could get away.

When I got in, the house was quiet and I showered and stripped Charlotte's bed, replacing all of our sheets, and managed a quick spurt of housework. When they got home, I was waging war with a pile of ironing in front of the television. David carried in a large tray of pre-cooked lasagne which he put straight in the oven. Whenever he went to visit his parents, he always returned with food as if he wasn't fed enough at home. He gave me a kiss and laid the table.

'Lasagne OK for you? It was cooked yesterday so needs reheating. Be about twenty minutes,' David called from the kitchen.

'Sure,' I replied, distracted by an exchange between two actors on the television.

Charlotte disappeared upstairs under the proviso she was going to complete homework due in tomorrow. I finished off the ironing and was about to climb the stairs with the folded pile of clothes when David sneaked up behind me, slipping his arms around my waist.

'Can we be friends?'

'We are friends,' I said, turning back to look at him. He winked and I had the impression he might try it on tonight. I'd need to feign a headache and pre-empt his advances unless I was going to ask who 'Paul' was. Put him on the spot and get him to admit he'd been elsewhere. Although it would mean having to face up to my own affair and I wasn't sure that I could.

I felt cheap, sneaking around with Nicky, and no matter how hard I scrubbed afterwards, I couldn't wash the sin away. I still felt disgusted with myself later, but when Charlotte went to bed and David came upstairs, I didn't reject him. When he kissed me, he felt so different to Nicky, like a comfy pair of shoes, so familiar. It was easy to have sex with him. I knew I wouldn't be able to keep the pretence up indefinitely. At some point I'd had to give in, and I couldn't deny that I'd enjoyed the intimacy, more than I thought I would.

Afterwards, as David lay snoring, I slipped out of bed to use the toilet. The security light was on outside and when I opened the window, unable to see through it because of the privacy glass, I was sure I saw Nicky's car driving away from the house. Creeping downstairs, I checked the Motorola and there was a text from him.

See you tomorrow. X

I didn't reply, plugging the phone in to charge as it was running out of battery. I wandered around the kitchen aimlessly, looking for something to do to fill the time whilst the battery charged. It was after eleven and I wanted to go to my warm bed but couldn't risk leaving the phone out. I glanced at the photos on the fridge. One was missing. They'd been rearranged so the gap wasn't obvious, but the one of David and I eating dinner in Mexico as the sun set behind us had disappeared. I loved that photo, taken on our honeymoon by the waiter. We were both so happy.

Had Nicky taken it? I was concerned that he saw this as more serious than it was. That what we had was long-term. I wanted him to see it as a bit of fun. It would make ending it easier.

It got to quarter to midnight and I was so tired I gave up when the phone was at fifty per cent and put it back in my bag.

The following morning, David left a cup of tea and a note to tell me he loved me, by my bed, which I discovered on waking. Wracked with guilt, I couldn't bear to drink it, instead getting my caffeine fix with instant coffee.

I still felt unsettled when I got to school and didn't involve myself in the chat about what went on at the weekend during form room. I was relieved when the bell rang out and the room was quiet once more. I stared at my lesson plan for the day but couldn't absorb it. Since letting David back into my bed, I felt much worse about the deception. What sort of woman was I, sleeping with two men at once? On the same day.

I switched the Motorola on and almost immediately a text came through from Nicky.

I'm in the library

I hesitated, not sure what to do, but another text quickly followed.

Where are you?

I gritted my teeth and switched the phone off, turning my attention back to lesson planning. I was not in the mood to be bossed about.

Five minutes later, Nicky was at my door.

'I've been waiting for you.' His eyes narrowed.

'I've been busy. I can't just drop everything when it's convenient for you,' I snapped and saw his face darken for a second before his expression changed.

'Can I help?'

'No, I'm sorry. I need to finish this. Can we catch up later?' I suggested, my heart sinking at his face. My feeling out of sorts wasn't his fault.

'Sure.' He gave the back of my neck a squeeze, then fingered my earlobe. Brushing his thumb across the apple earring I'd put on this morning. Reminding me they were a gift, from him. I'd worn them, hoping it would pacify him when I reiterated that our arrangement was a casual one.

The day started badly, and my lessons didn't go particularly well. I forgot a student's name in my ten o'clock lesson, something which I prided myself on rarely doing. In the next lesson, the entire class seemed sleepy and disinterested, causing me to snap and unintentionally reduce one of the girls to tears. It was one of those days where I wished I'd stayed in bed.

To minimise any further damage, I spent my lunch hour alone, trying to make sense of my jumbled thoughts. The knot in my stomach seemed to be growing larger. Perhaps it was time to end this short-lived affair and see if there was any possibility of David and I repairing our relationship? He'd been more attentive recently, maybe he was trying to take steps to bring us closer together? Regardless of that, I wasn't sure how much longer would I be able to get away with it, because I was positive, regardless of David's likely infidelity, if he found out, it would be the end of our marriage.

After much soul-searching, I resolved to end things with Nicky the following afternoon. Charlotte would be at netball practice, so it was the perfect opportunity.

After school, I convinced Charlotte to join me for a swim and we swung home to pick up her costume. It had been a little while since I'd been and it was great to get back into the water. We managed forty lengths in adjacent lanes. Charlotte was in a good mood, humming to herself constantly and unable to tear her eyes away from her phone in the car. She wouldn't go into any details as to why she was so happy, which automatically made me think it was boy related. Did she have her first boyfriend? Was someone on the horizon? I made a mental note to keep my eyes peeled on playground duty.

On the drive home, she asked to cook dinner again.

'Absolutely, what are we having?' I agreed with a grin.

Charlotte rolled her eyes laughing at my enthusiasm. 'The only thing I can cook.'

'Pasta,' we both blurted out at the same time and laughed. I tucked my hair behind my ear.

'New earrings, Mum?'

'Um yes, Stella sent them to me,' I lied, instantly cringing, but Charlotte didn't probe further.

When we got in, Charlotte busied herself in the kitchen and I went upstairs to take the earrings out and put them away.

'Ah we're in for a treat tonight then, I see,' David said, when he walked through the door later, on time for once. He held a bunch of gladioli out to me in yellow, white and orange, my favourite colour. I took them, inhaling their scent and giving David a kiss.

'Thank you, they're beautiful.'

'Not as beautiful as you.' He gave my behind a playful smack.

'Gross, guys!' came Charlotte's disgusted voice from the kitchen, which resembled a bomb site.

David noticed me frowning at the mess.

'Don't worry, I'll clean it,' he whispered into my ear as I arranged the flowers into a vase.

Later, I escaped into the bathroom to check my messages from Nicky. I was well aware that he didn't like to be kept waiting and because he'd turned up at the house before, I was concerned he'd do it again. Thankfully there was only one text.

Wear your purple dress tomorrow

I wasn't sure what to make of the request, it sounded more like an order. Feeling my heckles rise, I text back.

Why?

Nicky replied a minute later.

Because I said so

I had to admit, it was a bit of a turn-on being told what to do, but I wasn't going to sleep with him. Our meeting had one purpose and one outcome. It was time for it to end. I wasn't sure what was happening with David, but he'd definitely seemed more considerate recently, and perhaps he'd decided to make this marriage work. He was making the effort and I had to as well.

The phone buzzed again, and I could see there was a picture message coming through, painfully slow to download.

When it finally filled the screen, I gasped in surprise. It was a picture of Nicky, naked, only his torso, with his hand holding his erection. My hand flew to my mouth, and I flushed red, unable to tear my eyes away. He looked amazing and I bit my lip, desire pummelling my insides.

Another message came through, no photo this time.

Your turn

## 22

I snorted, considering my options. What could I send him that wasn't too revealing? Perhaps some cleavage? I placed the phone on the sink and took off my clothes, standing naked in the steamy bathroom, moving around assessing my angles. The wake-up call hit me around the back of the head and feeling foolish I snapped the phone shut and thrust it into my pocket.

What was I thinking? I'd almost sent a naked photo of myself to him. Was I crazy? A teacher sending explicit photos to a student. It was like a headline from a tabloid newspaper and I cringed.

Sitting on the toilet, my head in my hands, I drummed my fingers repeatedly, *one, two, three, four, one, two, three, four*. I was glad I'd come to my senses. The thought of photographic evidence of my naked body out there for Nicky to show to anybody made me feel physically sick. My heart skipped, like I'd almost fallen down a flight of stairs and only just regained my footing. I comforted myself that by this time tomorrow it would all be over. It was only lust after all. I had to get a grip, get back to reality. Right about now my previous life that had once seemed boring would be a welcome relief.

On Tuesday, the first day of October, I agonised over what to wear. A river of clothes strewn across my bed, but still I struggled. I put the purple dress on at first and then took it off again. What message was I sending to Nicky by wearing it?

Charlotte teased me as time was getting on.

'Mum, wear the purple one, it looks great,' she said as she walked past the open bedroom door and witnessed me still standing in my underwear, holding clothes up against me. Running out of time, I put on the dress, telling myself it was my choice to wear it and not Nicky's request that had swayed me. After today was over, I'd be walking away from him once and for all.

In the car, Charlotte told me that she'd heard a girl in her year was pregnant. She looked genuinely horrified, as though it might be catching.

'How did you hear that?'

'Girls in the corridor, calling her a slut.'

I winced. Girls could be so cruel to each other.

'Well, I haven't heard anything,' I lied, 'and you mustn't talk about such things without knowing them to be true. And if they are, how would you feel if everyone was talking about you?' I couldn't risk divulging what I'd heard to Charlotte, not when it was sensitive information about a girl in her year.

Charlotte chewed her nail, not meeting my eye. I changed the subject to netball, and she told me she'd been moved into wing defence, an ideal position with her being short and fast.

\* \* \*

Determined to be a better teacher than I was yesterday, I threw myself into my lessons, making sure I was jovial and enthusiastic with the students. When I saw the girl who'd cried in my class yesterday, I apologised and told her how impressed I was with the homework she'd handed in over the weekend. It seemed to make amends and I felt much better.

At lunchtime, I popped into the staffroom to catch up with Matilda and Susan as I hadn't seen them for a while. We chatted about Boris Johnson and his alleged womanising in the paper that morning.

'I'm so bored of politics and Brexit. It's all we bloody hear about now,' Susan said.

Mr Scott came in looking harassed. Susan whispered that he'd just met with the parents of the pregnant year eleven girl and he had a meeting with the Board of Governors this afternoon.

'I heard that they had sex on school premises,' Matilda hissed.

'Jesus, do you know who the girl is?' I asked.

'Amelia Jamieson, I teach her in Textiles.'

Amelia was one of the group of girls I'd chastised for swearing in the playground last month. I'd made them give me all their names at the time.

'Who's the father?' I asked.

'She won't tell.'

My mind strayed to the girls' toilets, eavesdropping on a conversation not meant for me. Didn't they say that Nicky and Amelia dated? A wave of nausea washed over me and for a second, I felt a little light-headed. I made my excuses to Matilda and Susan and left the staffroom.

Nicky was waiting for me when I returned to my classroom, perched on the edge of my desk, flicking through pages of my diary. It was only for reminders and appointments, but still an invasion of my privacy. He looked mischievous as I walked through the door, catching him in the act. He didn't apologise, simply closed the diary and swung around to face the door.

'OK for later?'

The corridor was empty, but with the classroom door open, I winced at the volume of his voice.

I nodded, confirming our plans.

He stood and peeked out of the door and each direction of the corridor.

'Take off your knickers,' Nicky said, eyes glinting, as if he was asking for an extension to a homework deadline.

I shook my head, unable to believe he'd been so brazen as to ask. I didn't feel turned on, in fact my body shivered, and I froze, clenching my jaw.

He held out his hand impatiently.

'No,' I hissed.

'Come on. Don't be such a killjoy,' he said, curling his lip back in a sneer.

'Nicky?' The sound that came out of my mouth was like a whimper. I felt like I was pleading.

'Go on,' he said coldly. There was something in his voice that told me he wasn't going to give up on the idea.

We stood there as the seconds stretched out, glaring at each other. Eventually when I realised he had no intention of giving an inch, I knew the quickest way to get rid of him was to give him what he wanted. I stepped back, towards the corner of the room, out of view from the windows and classroom door and reached under my dress. I eased my knickers down my legs, stepping out of them and snatching them from the floor in one quick motion. I rolled them into a ball as small as I could to conceal them in my fist.

'Happy?' I asked sarcastically, glaring at him.

Nicky held out his hand again and I reluctantly handed him the balled-up fabric, which, to my horror, he raised to his face and breathed through the black lace taking in my scent.

'Very. Trust me, you'll enjoy the freedom,' he said, slipping them into his polo shirt pocket and casually strolling out of the door.

I felt mildly panicked and exposed. Although my dress was to my knees, going out without underwear was something I'd never done before. I sat behind my desk and opened and shut my drawer repeatedly until the room stopped spinning and the crush of my lungs began to subside. *One, two, three, four, one, two, three, four.*

Why had I given in? I wasn't exactly sending the message that I wanted to end it. Things had gone too far. It had escalated into something I hadn't prepared for. Now I was playing with fire. There had been a shift in power, him exerting more and more control all the time.

It reminded me how little I knew about him and what sort of person he was. I felt foolish, he wasn't a boy at all, he was an expert manipulator.

* * *

Mr Scott called an assembly in the afternoon, as he was out on Monday, so, unenthusiastically, the teaching staff trotted into the school hall to take their positions on the stage.

I pulled my dress tight around my knees and squeezed my thighs together. Not moving for twenty minutes was torture. I interlocked my hands on my lap, drumming my fingers repeatedly throughout. When I looked over at Nicky, he winked and patted the breast pocket of his polo shirt. Revelling in my 'going commando'. My stomach heaved and I tasted bile in my mouth, coughing as Mr Scott was midway through his talk on the upcoming Harvest Festival that I'd heard nothing about.

After the last lesson of the day, as soon as all the children had disappeared, I rushed to Nicky's, eager to retrieve my underwear. When I knocked on the door, Nicky opened it, naked from the waist up, his jeans already unbuttoned. The sight of him rendered me momentarily speechless. Even though I'd seen him naked before, I still hadn't got used to how my body reacted when he was around.

He led me upstairs into his bedroom and I realised I'd made a mistake not meeting him on neutral ground.

'We need to talk,' I said weakly as he placed gentle kisses across my neck. I felt my resolve waver as I was walked over to the bed.

He lifted the skirt of my dress and feigned surprise that I was naked beneath.

'I agree,' he whispered pushing me down, so I was sitting on the corner of the bed. Lowering himself to his knees, he drew my legs apart. 'But not yet.'

'Nicky stop.'

He leaned back on his heels, frowning as I pulled the skirt of my dress over my thighs. I couldn't deny the pull of desire. I wanted more than anything to lay back and let Nicky do whatever he wanted, but it had to end.

'I think I love you,' Nicky said, staring at me.

I felt the hairs on my arms bristle as the sinking feeling took hold.

'You don't, Nicky, you're too young. You'll meet a nice girl your own age, someone you can—'

'Don't patronise me,' he snapped, cutting me off mid-sentence.

I visibly recoiled at the venom in his tone, standing up and moving towards the door.

'I'm sorry, I can't help how I feel,' he said, his voice softer. I looked at the floor, struggling to find the words, but I had to make it clear.

'You know I care about you, but we can't be anything more than this. I can't leave my husband. In fact, it has to stop now.'

Nicky's face was expressionless. The mood in the room changed. It felt like a cloud had descended, the air turning cold around me. He turned around, grabbing his T-shirt from the bed and pulling it on in one swift motion.

'OK.' His face was passive, a smile on his lips, but it didn't reach his eyes, they were empty.

'I have to go. Can I have my underwear back please?'

Nicky laughed spitefully, the sound chilling my core.

'Tomorrow,' he said flatly. The subject not up for discussion.

I thought about arguing, but I just wanted to get out of there. For the first time since we'd met, I felt scared of him. It reinforced my feeling that I'd done the right thing finishing it. The whole affair had been a mistake.

\* \* \*

When I walked in the door at home, I could tell immediately something had happened. Charlotte was in tears at the kitchen table, David sat beside her holding an ice pack.

'What's happened?' I asked, dumping my bag in the hallway and rushing into the kitchen.

'It's fine, don't panic. Charlotte had an accident at netball and twisted her ankle.' David sighed.

'Sprained,' Charlotte sobbed, correcting him.

'Maybe sprained. They called me at work as they couldn't get hold of you. Where were you?' David couldn't hide the irritation in his voice.

My mind momentarily went blank as guilt washed over me. Charlotte had needed me, and I'd been ending my affair with my eighteen-year-old lover. What sort of mother was I?

I recovered just in time. 'In the library, my phone was on silent. I didn't think to check it.' I crouched beside Charlotte, wrapping my arms around her, hugging her tight.

David stood, seeing Charlotte wanted her mum, and started to get pans out of the cupboards to make dinner.

I propped Charlotte's injured foot onto a cushion and held the ice pack on it. Eventually she stopped crying, her face still red, and sniffed occasionally.

'How did it happen?'

'I clashed with another player and landed badly. It hurt so much, Mum, and I cried in front of the others. I feel like an idiot,' Charlotte explained as I blinked back tears of my own. Tears of regret, guilt and self-loathing.

'Don't be silly, everyone cries. I always cry when I hurt myself. Remember when I bumped my head on the kitchen cupboard? Remember how I cried? No one is going to think any less of you. A good dose of Nurofen and an early night will sort you out, my love,' I added, brushing Charlotte's fringe out of her eyes.

After dinner when we were washing up, David and I discussed taking Charlotte to the hospital to get an X-ray in case there was a fracture but decided it might be better to wait until the morning. She could still put weight on it, and it hadn't swollen up too much.

I was so wracked with guilt I couldn't concentrate on the television or on the conversation David was trying to have with me about booking a holiday. In the end, he got frustrated with me being vague and gave up trying.

I feigned a headache and went to bed at the same time as Char-lotte, leaving David watching a programme about great white sharks. Once upstairs, I wept into my pillow. I'd been a fool. What if something serious had happened to my daughter today and no one could get hold of me? At least it was over now. My family had to come first.

## 23

A week passed in which I felt on edge, expecting Nicky to be around every corner, but I didn't see him once. Perhaps he was hiding away, licking his wounds. I knew I was hiding, worried there would be a confrontation when we saw each other again. I'd taken to holing up during break time in the staffroom, even swapping playground duty with Mr Ross. Matilda and Susan both commented it was a nice change, as often I was too busy to join them. I glossed over their observation, laughing that for once I'd been organised and my lesson planning was done for the week. In reality, I was taking solace in the only place I knew Nicky couldn't go, as students weren't allowed in the staffroom. If they needed to see a teacher, they had to knock and wait outside. It was cowardly and I knew it, but I couldn't face him.

On Wednesday, after school, Charlotte hobbled into my classroom, but I'd forgotten Mr Scott had asked us to stay behind so he could inform us about the Ofsted inspection that had been sprung on us. Charlotte wasn't impressed but refused to wait, instead stomping theatrically down the corridor, yelling that she was going to get the bus. I called after her, standing outside the classroom with my hands on my hips, watching her go, but was ignored.

I watched her until she turned the corner to the exit and headed to the information technology classroom. I was the last one to enter and the chatter hushed, obvious they were all waiting for me before commencing the meeting. I flushed red as I quickly took a spare seat.

'I'm sorry, I got caught up with a pupil.'

Mr Scott smiled tightly before beginning.

'Right I've just found out we've got an Ofsted inspection tomorrow. Typical, as we're all winding down just before half-term. Obviously, I need you all to make sure you've got no marking backlog and you're on top form tomorrow. They will be moving around the classes, checking our engagement with the students, looking at their work. Please ensure your lessons are thoroughly planned, get your best pupils to have their work out and ready to be looked at.'

Generally, tensions were high whenever Ofsted visited any school. Mr Scott would want it to run like clockwork. Some of the newer teachers asked questions on what they would be marked on and how best they could prepare. Discussions went on for over half an hour until Mr Scott was satisfied that we all knew what we were doing and closed the meeting. By the time we reached the car park, it was already four o'clock. Matilda was moaning that Mr Scott had decided the clay was too expensive to warrant an after-school pottery class, but he'd given Mr Ross money to fix the netting in the football goals.

'It's because it benefits more students that's why,' Susan said, a hint of sarcasm to her tone. I left them to it and said my goodbyes.

When I got home, I was surprised to see David's car outside. I found him in his usual spot at the kitchen table, frowning at his laptop. We had an office upstairs, so I wasn't sure why he liked working at the kitchen table so much. He looked up as the door closed, smiling when he saw me take my coat off and hang it on the bannister.

'Hello, love, want a tea?' he said, getting to his feet to fill the kettle.

'That would be lovely,' I replied, kicking off my heels.

'Charlotte at Amy's?' he called from the kitchen.

'No, I don't think so. I thought she'd be here. She didn't want to wait for me. I had a meeting about an Ofsted inspection. She said she was getting the bus.'

My palms perspired as I felt the panic rise, the voice in my head telling me to calm down.

I reached inside my bag for my smartphone to dial Charlotte's number. It rang and rang and went through to voicemail, where I left a message asking her to call me as soon as possible. I stared at David, not really seeing him, thinking of all the places she might be. He came to join me in the hall, concern etched on his face. We were overreacting, but my body wouldn't comply. I drummed my fingers on my thigh. Charlotte was always where she was supposed to be. What if she'd fallen on the way home and done her ankle in again, or worse?

I looked up Amy's home number, which Charlotte had given me before their sleepover. As I was about to dial, we heard a key in the lock. Charlotte opened the door mid-conversation with someone, who I assumed was Amy, but as she came into the hallway, Nicky stepped out from behind her, an enormous grin on his face. I gasped.

'What's up with you two?' Charlotte asked, frowning and slightly embarrassed to find her parents stood in the hallway.

I took a step back and froze, unable to speak. The back of my neck felt hot and damp as though I was standing under a spotlight. I glared at Nicky before turning my attention to Charlotte, but David got there first.

'We didn't know where you were, love, that's all. Mum said you were getting the bus, so she thought you would have got home before her. We were worried about your ankle,' he said, his voice even.

My heart raced and I thought I could feel my ribcage shaking beneath my skin. Why was Nicky here? Was he about to expose me in front of my husband and daughter?

Feeling dizzy, I gripped the bannister to keep myself steady, counting silently in my head. *One, two, three, four. One, two, three, four. One, two, three, four.*

Charlotte's forehead wrinkled, her eyes boring in to me.

'Hi, I'm Nicky. Pleased to meet you.' He stepped forward and offered his hand to David to shake. As they shook hands, I thought my heart was going to burst out of my chest.

'Hello, Miss,' he said warmly, glancing at me and then back to David. 'I saw Charlotte at the bus stop, so I offered her a lift. I'm sorry she's home later than expected. There's some roadworks near the school and we got stuck there for a while.' He smiled, he expression cheery and open. Like butter wouldn't melt, my mum used to say. He passed me Charlotte's school bag, brushing his fingers over mine as it exchanged hands. I felt bile rise in my throat.

'Thanks for the lift,' Charlotte said in a husky tone I'd never heard her use before. David noticed this too and glanced at me, hiding his amusement. I hoped this would explain the reason for the colour draining from my face. I glared at Nicky, who maintained his perfect façade as he stepped back over the threshold.

'See you later, Charlotte. Nice to meet you.'

'Thanks for bringing her home, Nicky,' David said as he waved him off, turning back down the hallway.

I made to close the front door, watching Nicky leave. He turned and waved a small pair of black knickers in the air, twirling them around his finger. His grin twisted, revelling in my discomfort. I slammed the door, my breath catching in my throat and headed into the kitchen.

'Love's young dream eh,' David said as I slumped in a chair, oblivious to my distress.

'You two are so embarrassing,' Charlotte huffed before storming upstairs.

My stomach churned like I was on a ship in stormy seas. A wave of nausea washed over me, and I worried I might be sick. When I saw Nicky, I thought life as I knew it was about to end, that my husband and teenage lover were going to start fighting in the hallway. It wasn't a coincidence. Nicky picked up Charlotte on purpose, to make a point. He could come here whenever he wanted. Nicky was sending me a message. It was easy to infiltrate the Cole household, so I'd better play nice.

Watching Charlotte all doe-eyed at someone who'd kissed every inch of my body made my jaw clench. Nicky only had to click his fingers and she would come running.

David's phone rang, jolting me into action, and as he exited the room, gesticulating wildly about profit margins, I snatched the Motorola from the bottom of my bag and disappeared into the utility room, out of sight.

I had four messages throughout the last few days from Nicky, all questions:

Where are you?
It's not over!
When can I see you?
Are you avoiding me?

I felt my blood pressure spike and furiously punched the keys on my phone.

What the fuck!

I clicked send on the message before I considered whether it was a good idea or not. Within seconds, the phone vibrated in my hand.

There's my girl

I growled, gritting my teeth as anger surged through me, but I didn't want to get into a conversation with Nicky. I wanted to pretend I'd never met him.

Should I have a chat with Charlotte? It seemed pointless; he'd only given her a lift home after all. Perhaps that would be it? Instead, I switched my phone off and busied myself making dinner: beef in black bean sauce and noodles. It was a family favourite that could be rustled up in fifteen minutes.

There was no chatter around the dinner table as everyone was preoccupied; David was frowning at a printout of a graph that I couldn't make head nor tail of and Charlotte was engrossed in her phone.

I messaged Stella to check she was still coming on Friday and she replied that she couldn't wait. I was desperate to see her, I wanted to talk to her about what was going on, although I was worried how harshly she would judge me. Stella never minced her words and would give it to me straight, whatever her opinion. She sent me the arrival time of her train, and I confirmed I'd be there to pick her up.

David carried on working long after dinner, trying to solve a problem with the office in the United States, and Charlotte took her phone into her bedroom and never came out. I could hear her Face-Timing Amy, giggles and hushed voices. The thought of Nicky wheedling his way into Charlotte's affections made me want to punch something. I couldn't bear it. If I'd been swept away by his charm, his looks, what possible chance did Charlotte have? I couldn't stand by as he came in and out of the house as a guest of my daughter's.

Trying to force my mind elsewhere, I sat at the kitchen table, ensuring every book I had was marked in preparation for the inspection. Afterwards, I rang Mum and pretended everything was fine, that I was just stressed about the inspection like the rest of the teachers, although in reality it was the last thing on my mind.

I tried to watch a movie, but my mind kept straying to Nicky. What if he made trouble for me? If I'd been sensible, I'd have considered these things before embarking on an affair, but I hadn't. I'd jumped in head first.

## 24

The following morning, I woke with my stomach in a knot. I couldn't face breakfast, and the dreamy smile on Charlotte's face as I drove to school was compelling me to count in my head. My skin felt itchy and I had to stop myself scratching. Something I did when I was stressed; a habit I'd thought I'd broken, but the long red streaks left behind from my nails across my forearms taunted me. On top of Nicky turning up last night, I had the pressure of an Ofsted inspection to concede with. My mind kept flitting between the two.

I didn't want Charlotte to have a crush on Nicky. It was too awful to comprehend. Not only was our recent dalliance an issue, he wasn't at all the sort of boy I envisaged she would bring home. I'd expected someone shy and polite. Not someone as worldly as Nicky. Plus, there was almost four years between them. Too much of an age gap.

As soon as we pulled into the car park, Amy was waiting and they hurried away, heads bowed together conspiratorially. No doubt she was recounting her romantic trip home from school in Nicky's car, although I'm sure she'd already told her about it last night.

I winced as I knocked my knee on the car door and swore loudly before checking no one was around to hear me. I opened and closed the door four times, then pressed the key fob another four times.

Locking and unlocking, locking and unlocking. My anxiety peaked. I had to regain control. I concentrated on counting the days left, until half-term.

I had a year ten class first thing and we'd reached a pivotal moment where we would be reading the balcony scene in *Romeo and Juliet*. The children giggled and it helped to laugh along with them. Trying to explain love to fourteen-year-olds was surreal. Some of them thought they already knew, holding hands in the playground and snogging behind the bike sheds. I didn't tell them it was only the practice run before they were let loose in the big wide world to get their hearts broken a few times before they found 'the one'. I certainly couldn't claim to be an expert on the subject now.

I got through my lessons fine, not daring to switch on the Motorola. I was still too angry to speak to Nicky. We were done. I sought refuge in the staffroom, chatting to Matilda and Susan about their walking holiday in the Lake District booked for half-term next week, which had crept up on us all. Neither of them were married, they had no ties and walking was something they both enjoyed. Susan said that as it was out of season, the holiday was relatively cheap, but they were expecting to have to rough it.

'We've got lots of jumpers and waterproofs, just the walking boots to buy now,' Matilda said. I could do with a break from life to walk until my feet ached and my head was empty. Susan wanted to curtail lunch, as she had an inspector sitting in on her next lesson.

Most of the teachers were on edge throughout the day, and it showed. Mr Collins, who was usually scruffy, wore an ironed shirt and a bow tie. He jumped ten feet in the air when I knocked on his classroom door to see if the inspectors had been in to see him yet.

One came to me during my final lesson, taking in the classroom and chatting to twelve-year-old Henry, who I'd strategically seated at the front of the class. He was the most articulate boy I'd ever taught, with a limitless passion for reading. I felt like the visit had gone well.

When school finished, I waited for Charlotte to come to my classroom and when she finally arrived, ten minutes after the bell, we drove home. The car park by then was empty and most of the pupils had left for the day. I needed to plan what I was going to teach in my creative writing class the following day. I'd not been on top of it and I felt a twinge in my side at the thought of seeing Nicky.

That morning David had left a note to say he would be home late as he had a video conference with the States again. I hoped that was the case as I couldn't know for sure. I cooked sausage and mash for dinner, and we ate in front of the television for a change.

Whenever it was just the two of us, I tried to make the effort to watch a movie together or a programme of Charlotte's choosing. It was lovely to spend a bit of time together. She had two episodes of *Love Island* season two recorded and we watched them together. I had no idea how raunchy it was, parts were difficult to watch with Charlotte beside me and we both squirmed in our seats a few times.

'Is this what all of your friends watch?' I asked, sipping a glass of wine I'd poured, whilst Charlotte fast-forwarded through the break.

'Yep, it's so addictive Mum. Everyone loves it. All the men are fit, and some of the girls are proper skanky,' Charlotte said, absent-mindedly twisting her hair around her finger. It was refreshing to see the double standards were still in full force.

After the second episode was finished, it was approaching ten o'clock and Charlotte and I headed upstairs to bed. I put on my nightie and cleaned my teeth but didn't feel overly tired. I read some of my book and lay there tossing and turning for around twenty minutes before going downstairs to get a drink. I stood in the kitchen waiting for the kettle to boil when the sensor light came on in the back garden and there was Nicky illuminated outside the conservatory door. His scowling face pressed up against the glass. I nearly dropped my mug, catching it as it slipped from my fingers.

He waved and beckoned me outside as I stared, open-mouthed, at the figure looking in. I drew open the patio door, immediately hearing the tapping of rain on the conservatory roof. Unlocking the back door, I pulled it open and, before I could object, Nicky stepped inside, wiping the rain from his face.

'Hello, beautiful.' His eyes roamed my body as though he could see beneath the flimsy nightie.

'What are you doing here?' I hissed, looking over my shoulder, but the house was dark and quiet.

'I wanted to see you. Where have you been hiding?' He stepped forward, wrapping his arms around my waist and pulling me to him.

'Nicky, you have to leave. I told you, it's over.'

'You don't mean it.' His brow furrowed and he looked almost menacing.

I stepped back out of his reach, crossing my arms over my chest, my flesh a mass of goosebumps. The freezing night air seeped in.

'I do. I told you. Is that why you gave Charlotte a lift home? Trying to get at me?'

Nicky shrugged as though it wasn't a big deal. 'I thought I was being nice.'

'Stay away from my daughter, Nicky,' I warned. My voice sharper than I'd intended. I had to get him to leave. David could come home at any time.

Narrowing his eyes, he stepped towards me, closing the gap between us. I had to force myself not to take a step back. Refusing to be intimidated. This was my house and even though he towered above me, I didn't waver. Not even when he slipped his hands around my neck.

I tilted my chin up in defiance, even though my knees trembled. The chill in the conservatory leaching to my skin. My insides were like ice and I desperately tried not to flinch as he stroked my collarbone, eyes piercing mine.

'Are you going to give me detention, Miss?' he whispered in my ear, trailing his hand down my side and across my behind, taking his time to feel the slippery material of my nightie in between his fingers.

I pushed his hand away and slapped his face. The sound of my palm on his skin echoed against the glass. I recoiled straight away, unable to believe my kneejerk reaction. I clutched my hand, palm stinging, I'd never hit anyone before, but Nicky had the ability to push my buttons.

'You shouldn't have done that.' His lip curled back into a snarl.

I'd overstepped the mark. I could feel myself shaking.

'Get out.' The tremor apparent in my voice.

Pulling open the back door, Nicky didn't take his eyes off me as he stepped out into the garden. The cold air blasted in and I shivered, feeling exposed in my nightie. He let out a mirthless laugh and disappeared into the darkness, out of range of the security light.

How had he got in the back garden? Had he jumped over the back gate? It was always locked at night. What was he doing here, prowling around the house, under the cover of darkness, trying to find a way inside? I shuddered. He was dangerous and unpredictable; I'd been naive, swept along by our affair, choosing not to see what was right in front of me.

I resolved to tell Stella everything when she arrived tomorrow. She would know what to do.

I locked the conservatory door and then the French doors before creeping upstairs, spending ten minutes peeking through my curtains to ensure no one was loitering outside in the shadows before I worked up the nerve to climb into bed. I no longer felt safe in my own home.

## 25

I woke with a start, sitting bolt upright and patting the mattress beside me as though David was hiding beneath the sheet. A nightmare that Nicky had crept in during the night had left a cold sheen upon my skin. The bed was empty, but as soon as I opened the bedroom door, I was reassured by the loud snoring which came from below.

David must have come home so late he'd crashed on the sofa, a half-full glass of bourbon on the floor. I picked it up and took it to the sink to pour away. Charlotte was already dressed and eating breakfast at the table. She nodded a greeting, as if it was a game to use the least amount of words possible in the morning.

I toasted a bagel and ate it as I put together my lunch box for the day. Charlotte had school dinners, so I didn't need to worry about her, but I slipped an apple into her bag anyway, in case she got hungry.

'I'm picking Stella up after school, she's coming to stay for the weekend. I bet she can't wait to see you,' I said, feeling the ball of excitement growing already at seeing my best friend. 'Will you be OK to get the bus as she's not coming in until five? I've got Creative Writing.'

Charlotte muttered it was fine and carried on spooning Cheerios into her mouth rhythmically.

The weather was overcast, so I wore trousers and a white shirt with heels. I was on playground duty too so made sure to put my black mac and umbrella in the car.

*Tess of the d'Urbervilles* was on my mind as I drove to school, my first lesson with the A-level class and I knew the book inside out. It was a going to be a pretty straightforward day as far as lessons were concerned, but I still had to cobble something together for the creative writing class. My dedicated time for lesson planning had been pushed aside for other things, namely Nicky. But not any more.

When I got into the classroom, narrowly missing a downpour, I spied a bright red apple on my desk. It was so perfectly round and shiny, it looked almost fake. Had Nicky left me another gift? The story of Snow White crept into my mind, had he delivered me a poisoned apple? Holding it by its stem, I tossed it into the bin.

The children poured into the classroom before the bell rang with soggy bags and dripping coats, grimacing at the weather. Their mood improved though when I let out a squeal, jumping as a flash of lightning strobed past the window, followed shortly after by a loud clap of thunder.

The children were fascinated by the storm and once I'd done the register, we gathered at the window to watch. The sky was dotted with streaks of light, zipping across the clouds. It was a sight to behold. As the storm continued to rage, the bell rang, signalling the end of form room, and they shuffled out to their classes as I awaited the arrival of my A-level students.

By break time, I was grateful the storm had passed and made my way outside. I enjoyed strolling around to see what the students were up to but, in truth, there was only one student who I was looking out for today.

Nicky was easy to spot. He was always playing football and although my chest tightened the closer I got, I strode past the court, head high and with purpose, deliberately not looking his way. As I passed by, he came to a stop, gazing at me as the ball sailed past him and into the goal he was supposed to be defending.

I carried on, walking past groups of girls and boys, some playing various games and some huddling around phones which hadn't already been confiscated. I saw Charlotte and Amy sitting on a bench and wandered over to say hello. I never lingered too long, not wanting to cramp my daughter's style but I was relieved to see she was keeping out of trouble and nowhere near Nicky.

When break finished, I had another lesson before lunch. I'd been worried after last night how Nicky would react when I saw him, half expecting him to turn up at my classroom at some point. My nerves were shot and every scuffle in the corridor made my anxiety rocket. My fingers were sore from repeated drumming on my desk. Although no contact had been made when I walked past him at breaktime, maybe he was beginning to get the message?

All was quiet over lunch too as I planned out the tasks for the Creative Writing students. No messages had been left on the Motorola either. I should throw it away, but I wanted to wait until things were calmer and Nicky had accepted the situation. He was the first student to arrive in the classroom after the bell to signal the end of the day.

'Hey,' he said as he walked in and sat in his usual spot in the front row.

'Hi,' I replied stonily, as the rest of the class came in. 'Right, OK, nice to see you all on this glorious day,' I said loudly, silencing the chatter. 'What I'd like to do today is talk about characters. Have a think about what books you've read or films you've seen where a character has stood out. Why did he or she stand out, was it their behaviour? What they wore? How they spoke?'

I saw them all listening attentively, their eyes wide, heads tilted upwards, nodding as I spoke.

'Can anyone think of one?' I asked, but the class was silent, still contemplating. 'OK, so for me I'd say Hermione Granger out of the Harry Potter series. She stands out to me because of the transformation she goes through. She comes across a bit snooty and full of herself, but underneath she's shy and isn't sure of the best way to make friends.'

Faye raised her hand to speak and I nodded towards her encouragingly.

'Voldemort too, Miss, when you see him as a boy, he's angry as he's misunderstood and lonely, but even Dumbledore didn't think he would turn out the way he did!'

'That's right. Good example, Faye. Now, I'd like you work in one big group today and talk about a character that stands out to you, whether it's from a book or a film or programme, write some bullet points about your character.'

I sat behind my desk to do some marking, while keeping one ear on the group. They were talking animatedly about *Star Wars* at one point when I had to intervene and steer them back on topic. At the end of the class, I joined them, and they each spoke about their chosen character and why they had picked them.

Nicky stared at me; I could feel his eyes boring in to me as the children took their turns.

'Nicky, how about you?'

'Have you seen *The Graduate*, Miss?'

I winced, biting my tongue and tasting blood on the tip. I glared at Nicky and watched as the other students looked at each other, seemingly confused.

'It's a film about an older woman who seduces a younger man. It's old, from the sixties, but a classic,' he explained.

They all shook their heads, obviously not having seen it. Most hadn't even heard of it.

'The main character, Ben, is seduced by an older woman but falls in love with her daughter and eventually they run off together.'

'Thanks, Nicky, right I think that's all we have time for,' I said, cutting him off.

He grinned at me, winking.

I set homework to write a short story surrounding their character, to be handed in next week. Nicky hung back as always, putting his book into his bag deliberately slowly.

'Have a nice half-term,' he said as he passed by me.

I wanted to slap the smug smile off his face, but I had to play nice. He had the upper hand.

'I'm sorry, Nicky, let's put this behind us,' I whispered.

He stepped towards me, wrapping his arm around my waist to pull me in close.

'No, sorry, no not like that. Let's be friends,' I stumbled back, out of his grip. He'd got the wrong end of the stick, clearly hoping for a reconciliation. His touch left me cold and I couldn't believe I was ever infatuated with him. He wasn't a charmer at all, just skilled in coercion.

'Make your fucking mind up,' he sneered as he left.

I felt my eyes prick with threatening tears. I'd been an idiot to offer to smooth things over. He didn't want to just be friends. I counted in my head as I put my things away, breathing deeply until the unsettled feeling dissipated.

Mr Scott stepped out of his office as I passed, and I turned and waited for him so we could walk to the car park together while I gave him an update on how the creative writing class was going. It was good to think about something other than Nicky. Mr Scott's enthusiasm was infectious. After we said goodbye and he wished me a lovely weekend, I went straight to the train station.

I found the journey easy and where I assumed there would be traffic, it was clear, and I sailed through, even managing to grab a space outside, eagerly awaiting the arrival of Stella's train at ten to five. I had fifteen minutes to kill and gave Charlotte a quick ring to make sure she got home OK on the bus, which of course she had, and was exasperated that I felt the need to ring and check. After I got off of the phone, I sat staring out of my window at the grey sky. Should I come clean to Stella about Nicky?

I was so looking forward to seeing her and enjoying a girly weekend, I didn't want anything to ruin Stella's stay with us. David was going to take Charlotte and Amy over to the Spectrum in Guildford and had booked in ice skating, a break for lunch and then swimming whilst they were there. That would keep them entertained for the day. I was sure David would sit in the café glued to his laptop but at least the girls would enjoy themselves. I had planned a morning of shopping and a massage as a surprise treat for Stella, with a night out in Horsham town centre afterwards. Sunday would no doubt be a lazy day before Stella had to get the train back in the afternoon.

Realising it was ten to five, I jumped out of the car and headed up the steps into the station. A swarm of commuters flooded the tunnel, returning from their day in London, and I stood on tiptoes, catching sight of Stella at the end of the corridor dragging her bright red suitcase, which, by the look of it, only had one wheel working.

Once through the ticket barrier Stella dropped the case and I threw my arms around her, squeezing her tight.

'I've missed you!' I said, my voice breaking and, to my horror, tears materialised from nowhere and spilled down my face.

## 26

'I've missed you too,' Stella's hug enveloped me as I tried to wipe away the tears from my cheeks. 'Come on, silly, let's get in the car, I can't wait to see the house,' she said, linking her arm through mine and pulling me towards the exit. 'Bloody suitcase, it's got a mind of its own,' Stella swore, laughing as she struggled to control it.

'How are your parents?' I asked, always slightly nervous about enquiring on their health.

'Not bad, there hasn't been any more naked wandering thankfully. Although I couldn't find my keys the other day, Dad had put them in the microwave to keep them safe. I almost blew the sodding house up,' she sighed, noticing the wide-eyed look on my face. 'Honestly, its fine; you have to learn to laugh. I don't think about it too much, it's just one day at a time. Anyway, it's Robert's problem for a couple of days.'

We reached the car and I opened the boot. Together we hauled Stella's suitcase in.

'Christ, what have you bought with you?'

'Mostly shoes,' Stella shrugged, and we burst into laughter.

On the drive home, Stella told me more about the man she'd met back in Nottingham. It was early days, but I could tell by how animated she was that she liked him a lot. I was thrilled by the news. I'd wondered how she was going to meet someone, caring for her parents' full time, but, as it turned out, Adam was a carer. He worked with dementia patients and had visited the house to help adapt it. They'd hit it off straight away and he'd asked Stella if he could take her out for a drink. Since then, they'd been on a few dates and things seemed to be going well. I thought about telling her about Nicky, but it wasn't the right time, we were almost home.

When we arrived, I gave Stella a quick tour and let her unpack in the guest room while I made tea. Stella loved the house and its cottage feel; unable to believe we hadn't touched it since we moved in.

'I love the kitchen floor; those tiles are gorgeous. It's all so pretty.'

'It suited us perfectly, all of our furniture fitted in, although they are probably a bit too modern, but it's so neutral, everything seemed to go together well,' I said, delighted Stella loved it as much as I did.

'Stella Crowley,' David exclaimed as he came downstairs, giving Stella a hug. They proceeded to throw insults at each other about their aging appearance, which was something they'd always done. I was surprised David was home early; he must be making an effort. Stella couldn't believe how tall Charlotte had grown too, when she emerged from her bedroom.

'My goodness, you get prettier every day, Charlotte. Won't be long before those boys will be knocking,' teased Stella and David rolled his eyes.

Charlotte's cheeks glowed pink and she exited the kitchen as fast as she could.

'Or perhaps they are already?' Stella said, her voice sing-song, raising her eyebrows at Charlotte's sudden departure.

'Anyway, dinner,' David said, changing the subject and trying to persuade us to order takeaway pizza as he put some menus on the table.

I made tea for everyone and David took a look at the wheel on Stella's case whilst we discussed options for dinner. He managed to tighten the nut holding the wheel on and it turned smoothly.

'Hmm, not sure about pizza. Curry instead?' suggested Stella, slipping into one of the chairs around the table and leafing through the menus.

'Perfect,' I said before David could disagree.

He wrote our order and left the kitchen to ring it through. Stella and I sat sipping our tea and discussing the weekend ahead. When I revealed I'd booked us in for a joint massage at a nearby hotel, Stella squealed in delight.

'Well, if anyone deserves a bit of pampering, it's you, Stella. Plus, I missed your birthday too, so it's my treat!' I said, beaming at my friend.

'Don't be silly, you didn't miss it, you sent a card,' Stella protested.

When the curry arrived, we gathered around the table to dig in. David had ordered a feast and we opened a bottle of red wine. Afterwards, Charlotte went to watch more episodes of *Love Island* in the front room and Stella grilled David about his new job. Eventually he was allowed to leave too. Stella and I carried on chatting, our voices getting louder the more we drank. We were beyond merry and before we knew it, we had to put the light on as it was gone eight and dark outside.

'Come on, let's go and have a sneaky fag,' Stella giggled, trying to whisper but failing miserably. David and Charlotte must have gone upstairs as I could no longer hear the television from the front room.

We stepped outside the back door and moved around the side of the house so as not to be directly under Charlotte's bedroom window. I didn't want little ears overhearing us.

Stella pulled a packet of cigarettes out of her pocket, handing me one and lighting it for me. When I sucked in appreciatively, Stella stared in amusement, waiting for me to cough and splutter.

'Been smoking recently, have you?' she asked with a comical look on her face.

'Might have,' I wiggled my eyebrows and Stella bumped her hip against mine, giggling.

'Are you and David OK?' Stella asked. Her voice had taken a serious note. Had I been acting strangely?

'Yeah fine, why?' I replied, and Stella took a drag of her cigarette before answering.

'I don't know, you just don't seem very... together. I could tell when we chatted on the phone that something's been upsetting you.'

I relaxed, relieved Stella didn't know more than she was letting on.

'I mean he's been working a lot, so I don't see him that much at the moment. I think he might be having an affair, but I'm not sure.' I felt my eyes prickle, a mixture of pent up emotion and alcohol.

'Oh god I'm sorry, Izzy.' Stella gripped my hand, her warm fingers interlocking through mine as we stood side by side, staring out into the darkness.

Flicking my ash into an empty plant pot; I told Stella about the receipt I'd found and the text message, but that I hadn't confronted David about it. I didn't tell her why though.

We remained silent for a few minutes; Stella digesting the news. I sniffed, wishing I had a tissue in my pocket.

'Midlife crisis?' Stella suggested.

'Probably. There'll be a Ferrari on the driveway next week,' I said, snorting. 'Things haven't been right between us since...' I continued until my voice trailed off.

Stella rubbed my arm, her hand soft and warm. 'It's been a tough time for both of you since the baby. It's like you need your heads banging together. You need to sit down and get everything out in the open. You know he never blamed you, don't you?'

'How do you know?'

'Because I've known David practically as long as you have. He loves you, Izzy, I'm sure he did from the moment he clapped eyes on you!'

Stella would be there, whenever I wanted someone to listen, but I could hardly drag David over hot coals. 'Anyway, show me a photo of this Adam,' I said, changing the subject.

Stella got out her phone and opened up Facebook, clicking on the profile picture of a young, blond, wavy-haired man who looked like he should be carrying a surfboard.

'This is Adam,' she squealed.

'He's lovely,' I said, not failing to notice that he looked younger than us.

She went on to show me some of the text message exchanges between them. He seemed like one of the good ones. The opportunity was there for me to tell Stella about Nicky, but I chickened out.

I finished my cigarette and suggested we turn in for the night.

The next morning, I woke before nine feeling dehydrated and a bit fuzzy. Stella emerged from the guest room looking like she'd been on a wild night out. David and Charlotte thought it was hysterical as they zoomed around getting ready for their day out whilst we sat at the table drinking coffee, moving in slow motion.

'It still smells of curry in here,' Stella laughed.

I nodded, opening the kitchen window to air the room. It always took ages for the takeaway smell to go and we were having far too many of them lately.

'Pizza tonight, whilst you two are out gallivanting,' David said with a grin at Charlotte.

'I'll do a proper food shop next week. We all need to be eating much healthier,' I said, even though all I wanted to eat at that moment was something covered in grease.

'Right we're off, got to pick Amy up and their skating is booked in for half ten.'

I smiled at the laptop tucked under David's arm; I knew him so well. He leaned down and gave me a kiss and Charlotte waved goodbye from the hallway.

'Have fun,' I called.

'Bye,' they called back and the front door slammed shut.

'Peace at last,' I said.

'Bliss.'

We got showered, dressed and headed into town so I could show Stella the shops Horsham had to offer. Stella had always loved shopping and the pair of us could spend hours with the intention of window shopping but still coming home with a multitude of bags and sore feet. She wanted to buy something to wear out that night and chose a slinky cold-shoulder top in black.

'This will look good with my skinny jeans and heels, right?'

I nodded. What on earth was I going to wear?

Stella picked out an off-the-shoulder top in bright orange, demanding I try it on immediately. By the time we stopped for lunch, we had pretty much bought an entire outfit each.

'Just like the good old days,' Stella said.

We grabbed a sandwich from Boots and got back in the car to go to the hotel for our massage. I was excited, it had been ages since I'd had one and I knew I was holding a lot of tension in my shoulders.

When I'd booked, I requested we were in a room together. The room was small but lovely and warm, our massage tables only three feet apart. I had a lady who used a lot of pressure, but she eased into it gently and the small amount of chatter back and forth between Stella and I diminished the more relaxed we became. All of the tension rubbed away and the knots in my back dissolved over the fifty minutes.

'Ooh that was lush. Thank you, honey,' Stella said, easing herself up, clutching the towel to cover her as she stretched one arm out.

'Agreed,' I yawned. I didn't remotely feel like going out on the town, I was more ready for an early night.

We got dressed, giggling and bumping into each other as we put our clothes on in the small space.

'It's like we're drunk already.'

'I hope you'll be all right to drive,' Stella said.

'I'd forgotten how relaxed they make you feel.'

After we'd had a drink of orange juice at the bar, I felt happy to set off on the short drive home.

When we got home, it was gone three, but David still wasn't back.

'I bet Charlotte's had a great day,' Stella said, smiling wistfully.

I knew Stella had always wanted children and she was a couple of years younger than me, so there was still time for it to happen. My insides nagged with a sadness I'd been pushing down. I longed for the baby I'd lost; my family had felt incomplete ever since. Not wanting to dwell and ruin the mood, I put on some music and we painted our nails whilst I took the opportunity to let Stella talk more about Adam.

'He's so lovely, a really nice guy. Sends me flowers every week, takes me on surprise dates. You know the ones where you get a text or a note – pick you up at seven, wear a dress – and he'll whisk me away somewhere.' Stella's eyes glazed over as she talked, and it was fantastic to see my friend so happy. I wanted to open up about Nicky, to tell her I'd made a terrible mistake. How I worried about Nicky's stability and that my secret would be revealed. Instead, I swapped our tea for Prosecco and poured us a large glass.

'Shall we go get ready? I've booked a table at Turtle Bay, it does Caribbean food and I've heard its good.'

Stella got up from the table, blowing on her nails to ensure they were dry. 'Sounds fab, let's go get glam.'

## 27

Getting ready with music from the noughties booming around the bedroom brought back memories of when we were younger. We danced around to Kylie Minogue's 'Can't Get You Out of My Head' and the bedroom looked like the dorm at university: a bomb site with clothes and shoes everywhere.

When we were finally ready, our winged eyeliner and brows groomed to perfection, we headed downstairs. As we descended, the front door opened, and David walked in, with Charlotte and Amy behind him.

'Wow, look at you two. Lock up your sons,' he said, and Stella winked.

My stomach clenched at the comment, the glasses of Prosecco momentarily threatening to make a reappearance.

'Doesn't your wife look hot?' Stella said.

Charlotte cringed, pushing Amy onwards into the kitchen as David wolf-whistled.

'She certainly does.' He leaned forward and kissed my cheek as I slipped on my coat and checked the contents of my clutch bag.

'You look lovely, Mrs Cole,' Amy called back from the kitchen.

'Thanks, Amy.'

* * *

Turtle Bay was dimly lit but decorated with bright colours. The tables and chairs were rustic wood and there was driftwood and beach signs on the walls. It was already packed when we arrived, but I'd booked ahead and we were directed to a table for two in the corner.

Stella picked up the enormous cocktail menu, taking her time to decide which concoction she was going to try first.

'I was thinking about Sex on the Beach.'

'Aren't you always?' I retorted and Stella pretended to scowl at me, her eyes peering over the menu. 'I'm going for a piña colada,' I said decisively, putting the menu back onto the table.

'Classy chick.' Stella laughed and gave our order to the waiter who had materialised at our table. The food menu was proving harder though. With so many choices, Stella and I both struggled to decide, but eventually Stella chose jerk ribs and I settled on jerk salmon.

'It's lovely in here, really nice. So busy too, considering it's quite early.' Stella was right, all of the tables were full and there were many serving staff dashing around to reggae background music. What struck me most was the smell, the spices wafted around the room and I couldn't help salivating.

The waiter brought us another round of cocktails, which were going down far too easily. Shortly after, our food arrived on enormous plates, the meat accompanied by spicy rice, corn on the cob and salad.

'God, this is going to get messy,' Stella said, diving straight into her ribs once she'd tied her napkin around her neck like a bib. It was one of the many things I loved about Stella, she didn't care what other people thought. Whereas I always worried about everyone else's perception of me. I would have given anything to be so carefree.

The salmon was fantastic and Stella loved the ribs, she would put one in her mouth and extract the bare bone seconds later. It was a sight to behold.

'Do you think this Adam might be the one then?' I asked between mouthfuls.

Stella's eyes became dreamy at the mention of his name. 'I don't know; I can't believe he's into me. He's so good-looking and nice. I can't believe he hasn't been snapped up already.'

'What are you talking about, you're awesome! Why wouldn't he want you?'

'It's not that, I'm just waiting for someone to pinch me, you know. Or for there to be something wrong with him. I mean, he even bangs like a barn door in the wind... I'm in heaven!' Stella exclaimed, finishing her last rib and tucking in to some rice.

I giggled, Stella always was insatiable, but it was easy to be, with a new lover and no children to look after. David and I were once, but no marriage is the same sixteen years later.

I knew I should tell Stella about Nicky. I desperately wanted to be able to share how I felt. But what if she was so disgusted with me, she told David, or packed her bags and went back to Nottingham and we never saw each other again? I wasn't sure of Stella's views on infidelity as it had never come up. Stella had always played the field, but I couldn't remember her ever cheating.

'You OK? You drifted off there?' Stella said, dabbing her face with the napkin and laying it across her plate. She had finished already, and I made an effort to catch up, but my eyes were bigger than my belly.

'Just jealous,' I replied with a wicked grin and Stella laughed.

When I'd finished, we ordered more cocktails. I had a feeling if we carried on at the same pace, I might be seeing my dinner again later. I told Stella all about my new job in more detail and filled her in on Matilda and Susan and what characters they were. Stella seemed relieved she hadn't been replaced, but I assured her she never could. I was about to suggest moving on somewhere else when another two cocktails arrived at our table.

Stella frowned at the waiter. 'Umm, we didn't order these,' she said to the waiter, who was checking his watch.

'They're from the bloke at the bar.'

Stella and I both stared over but couldn't see who he was talking about. A second later, a crowd of women moved away with their drinks and I saw the outline of Nicky propped up the bar.

I panicked and almost knocked my drink over. He had his back to us, but I knew his shape anywhere.

'I think we've pulled,' Stella said, throwing her head back and laughing, tossing her blonde mane over her shoulder.

I took a sip of my drink, unable to tear my eyes away.

'What is it?' Stella asked, taking in my expression which must have resembled a deer caught in the headlights.

I turned back to Stella, opening my mouth to speak but no words came out.

Her eyes narrowed and she leaned in to touch my arm, her face full of concern.

'Was your meal good?' interrupted a voice beside us.

I knew it was Nicky before I looked up. He was wearing my favourite aftershave. Had he done it on purpose? He looked sharp, in jeans and a white shirt with the top two buttons undone, exposing a slice of smooth skin. He could easily pass for being in his twenties. I felt a rocket of desire shoot through me.

'Lovely thanks, and thanks for the drinks.' Stella smiled politely, rescuing me as I was still trying to engage my brain with my mouth. Bewildered eyes darted from him, back to me.

'This is Nicky. Nicky this is Stella,' I managed, taking a mouthful of my cocktail to relieve the sudden dryness of my throat.

'Pleased to meet you,' Nicky said and shook Stella's hand firmly.

I noticed Stella raise her eyebrows a fraction as she took him in.

He pulled a packet of cigarettes out of his back pocket and offered one to us both. 'I'm going for a smoke if you'd like one?'

I looked at Stella, who shrugged and, with a flirtatious smile, pulled two out of the packet.

Nicky nodded towards the smoking area on the balcony. We finished our cocktails, leaving the empty glasses on the table, and carried the new drinks with us. I was apprehensive, aware of the icy sliver descending my back but I couldn't leave the two of them alone.

What if Nicky told Stella what had gone on between us? Maybe it was nothing? It could be his way of making amends for behaving like an arse at school?

On the balcony, there was a view of the street which was starting to come alive with people. Nicky pulled a lighter out of his back pocket and lit both of our cigarettes before his own.

'How do you two know each other then?' Stella asked, her voice slightly higher than usual.

I cringed inwardly and knew immediately from her tone the game was up.

Nicky made eye contact with me as I took a long drag of my cigarette and tried not to cough. He leaned in close to whisper in Stella's ear.

'I go to St. Wilfred's, but don't tell anyone,' he said mischievously.

Stella's eyes shot to me, unable to contain her expression. 'You teach him?' Stella hissed.

'Only the after-school class, he's doing Physical Education and Biology A-Levels.'

'Yep and creative writing of course.' He nodded.

'That's an odd pairing?' Stella said, her eyebrows climbing off her forehead.

I swallowed hard; thinking she meant me and Nicky, until I realised she was talking about the subjects.

'He's brilliant, you should see the poems he writes,' I said, my panic subsiding. As long as I played nicely, it seemed Nicky would too. It didn't stop me feeling like I was treading on eggshells though.

Nicky blushed, something I'd never seen before.

'I have a good teacher,' he said, a broad smile spreading across his face. His blue eyes twinkled mischievously, making my groin ache. I'd ended our affair, but I couldn't deny the pull I felt to him physically. 'Anyway, have a great evening you two. I might see you later. I'm off to Bar 10 to meet some friends.' He smiled politely, shook Stella's hand and we thanked him for the drinks.

Standing alone on the balcony, listening to the thud of the base from the inside spill out, we finished our cigarettes.

'Jesus fucking Christ, Izzy! He's sex on a stick,' Stella exclaimed, blowing out a long breath.

I smiled at her weakly.

'How long?' she asked, her tone softer.

I couldn't hide it any longer. Stella knew me too well.

'About five weeks, but it's over now.'

The knot in my stomach tightened as Stella picked up her bag from the floor. Was she going to leave? I held my breath, feeling my head begin to swim. Would she tell David? If she did, everything would come crashing down like a tower of cards. My job, my marriage, my family, everything.

## 28

Instead of swinging the bag over her shoulder and marching off, she pulled out a box of her own cigarettes.

'I think I need another,' she said, pulling out two, lighting both and handing one to me.

My whole body felt as light as a feather, and I couldn't control the rush of love I had for Stella at that moment. I threw my arms around her in a sort of bear hug.

'I thought you'd be angry with me.' My eyes welled up.

'I'm not angry. It's your life, Izzy, you do whatever you want. Don't get me wrong, I love David to bits, but unless you're leaving, don't tell him.'

'I'm not leaving.' The words rushed out of my mouth without hesitation.

'OK, so it was just a fling?'

I nodded and we both breathed a small sigh of relief.

We smoked in silence for a minute until Stella spoke again.

'He's young too.'

'I know; it was a stupid thing to do. I should never have got involved.'

'No, I mean Adam. He's young too. Early twenties,' Stella said, her voice barely audible. I had a feeling he was from his fresh-faced profile picture on Facebook.

'As long as you're happy, Stella, then I don't care. I mean, I can hardly talk, can I?' I bumped shoulders with Stella.

She looked relieved to be spilling her secrets too. It was as though a weight had been lifted for both of us.

'How old is he?' Stella asked.

'Eighteen. He drives me crazy, Stella. I can't describe it, I haven't felt this way in years. In fact, I don't think I've ever been so bloody horny,' I laughed.

'It's because it's new, and it's forbidden fruit of course. Not to mention the fact he is as fit as a butcher's dog. Why did you end it? Because of David?'

I stubbed out my cigarette and took a long slurp on my cocktail.

'Yes and no. He was getting a bit too attached, a bit controlling. It was creepy to be honest. He turned up at the house and...' My voice tailed off as I remembered the underwear Nicky still hadn't returned.

'Best rid then. Fun while it lasted though.'

Stella finished her cigarette and we headed back inside. Our table had been cleared to make way for new diners as we'd been out for so long and we paid at the bar before we left. When the fresh air hit, both of us were a bit wobbly in our heels and linked arms to hold each other up.

'Come on, let's go and see what this Bar 10 is all about,' Stella said, cackling. I felt a weight had been lifted. Stella knew my darkest secret and yet she was still here, still my best friend. With things smoothed out with Nicky there was no reason not to go on to the bar. We were grown-ups and it would all be fine. Plus, it was too early to go home and there was more alcohol to be consumed.

The bar was in the next street, it's neon sign flashing. Inside, I was pleasantly surprised to see a variety of ages, so I didn't feel out of place. Pumping music blared from the speakers, tracks that I knew from the radio, and feeling giddy from the cocktails, I swayed in time to the music at the bar. Stella got served first and ordered mojitos before we sashayed over to a corner. Propping ourselves against a railing to survey our surroundings.

'Not bad for totty in here,' Stella shouted over the music.

I rolled my eyes. 'And there was me thinking you were in love.'

I spotted Nicky standing with a mixed crowd over the other side of the bar, his arm slung around a blonde in over-the-knee boots. Who were the girls? I didn't recognise them from school, but, to be honest, I couldn't tell with the amount of make-up they were wearing.

I adjusted my orange top and smoothed my hair, suddenly feeling self-conscious. Stella followed my gaze and we both watched a girl wrap her arms around Nicky and lean in close. I held my breath, ready to turn away before they locked lips, but he simply whispered in her ear and turned to talk to his friend. She clearly didn't like what he'd said as she stomped away. It was ridiculous to be jealous when I was married, but I couldn't help it.

I slurped the rest of the liquid of my cocktail, leaving only the crushed ice in the glass. My legs felt like jelly. I had to stop drinking. 'Come on, let's dance.'

Stella followed me as we pushed our way through the bodies on the dance floor. A Calvin Harris track was playing, it was one of Charlotte's favourites. Within a minute, Stella had someone grinding behind her and was happy to play along.

'Let's go get a drink,' Nicky's voice came from behind and he slid his hand momentarily around my waist. Feeling him so close, combined with the alcohol, sent shockwaves through my body. I thought I was over it, the way Nicky could make me feel with a single touch, but I ached for him again.

I motioned to Stella I was going to the bar and she nodded, still immersed in dancing foreplay with one of Nicky's friends.

We stood side by side at the bar, our hips touching. I didn't need another drink; my vision was already cloudy.

Nicky pulled his wallet out of his back pocket, but I put my hand on his arm.

'No, I'll get these, what are you having?'

'Becks please.' I could see his eyes were glazed, and we both swayed slightly. 'Watching you dance made me hard,' he whispered in my ear and I gasped, letting a childish giggle escape from my lips. 'I want you.' Nicky grabbed my backside, but I swivelled my hips away.

'We can't, Nicky.' The alcohol was making my resolve waver as I scanned the crowd to see if there were any faces I recognised. Everything was a blur. My heart pounded, a mixture of fear and desire bubbled inside.

Impatient, Nicky grabbed me by the elbow and steered me towards the toilets. I didn't protest and let him carry me along, through the wave of people, my head swimming. The corridor by the toilets was empty and quiet. With a quick sideways glance, he pushed me through the door marked STAFF ONLY, a broom cupboard of sorts with mops, cloths and the like. Our mouths found each other at speed, hands everywhere and pulling at clothes. Fingers fumbling, he undid my jeans but stopped when we heard the main door swing open and two voices chatting in the corridor. We both froze and Nicky put a finger to his lips.

'She's got a lovely pair of tits, I reckon she'll let me give her one,' slurred one of the men.

'Keep buying the drinks and she will.'

The voices tailed off as they went into the toilets.

It was then I came to my senses. It was over between me and Nicky, what on earth was I doing? No wonder he was getting frustrated with the mixed messages. But before I could say anything, Nicky launched back at me, forcing his lips upon mine and squeezing my breast so hard, I squealed, my teeth catching his lip as I pushed him away. A tiny droplet of blood dripped down his chin. He bared his teeth.

'You bitch.' His fist came towards me but connected with the plasterboard wall, leaving a dent.

Immediately, I shrank down and pushed my way out of the tiny room and stumbled back to the safety of the dance floor.

I made my way to Stella, who was having a rest at the railings.

'I'm worn out. Too old for this,' she said, knocking back her drink.

'Let's go,' I said, my body trembling.

I looked over my shoulder, but Nicky was nowhere to be seen. He hadn't hit me, but I couldn't deny he'd frightened me. I wasn't sure what he was capable of.

Half an hour later, we were home, kicking off our shoes and falling into the spare bed together. It was almost one in the morning and Stella offered to share as we could both hear David snoring from the hallway.

'Christ, he sounds like a pneumatic drill,' she said as we pulled the covers over us, still fully dressed.

'Tell me about it.' I laughed.

'It's been a great night. Thanks,' she said, squeezing my hand.

I squeezed hers back. 'Anytime.' I listened to Stella's breathing become deeper as I stared at the ceiling, unable to push the image of Nicky's arm, pulled back and ready to launch, out of my head. I was stupid to get caught up in that situation. It was weak, a bad judgement call and all I'd done was make things worse.

## 29

Eight hours later, we were woken by the banging of pans and the smell of bacon. We dragged ourselves downstairs for coffee and paracetamol.

'Christ, it's Eddie and Patsy,' David said as he caught sight of us still in last night's clothes and mascara smudged across our faces.

'Ha ha,' I replied, sitting at the table, images from last night running through my mind in glorious technicolour.

Stella hung her head in her hands. David whistled away to himself as he cooked us all bacon sandwiches. Charlotte thought the state of us was hilarious. After having a good laugh at our expense, she announced I had the day off as she'd arranged to cook a roast with David's help. She wanted all of us to go for a walk around the lake at Tilgate Park afterwards, but Stella's train was at three and I doubted we'd make it.

Once dressed, I went into Stella's room so we could put our make-up on together, the both of us only bothering with a bit of concealer and mascara.

'Be careful with him,' Stella whispered, obviously talking about Nicky.

'I will. I think I've really cocked up. I'm not sure he's all there, you know,' I replied, wringing my hands.

'Maintain your distance. Be pleasant, and polite, but don't engage.' There was no judgement in Stella's voice. 'Are you going to ask David if he's been playing away?'

'I don't know. I'm not sure I want to know the gory details. Plus, I can hardly be self-righteous.'

Stella smiled at me sympathetically and hugged me tightly. I was grateful to have such a good friend.

Downstairs, we lounged in the conservatory reading the Sunday papers which had dropped through the door. David kept popping in and out, having snatched conversations with us as he assisted Charlotte with the roast chicken.

Lunch was fantastic and Charlotte beamed with pride at the empty plates that littered the table. David made Eton mess for dessert and it was half past two when we finally got up from the table to take Stella to the station.

'We'll clear up later,' David said, hurrying us all out of the door and into the car.

At the station, Stella hugged us in turn, thanking us for a lovely weekend.

'Don't leave it so long next time,' David called, wrapping his arm around me as we watched Stella disappear into the station.

I had to blink away tears as I watched her go.

'Do you want to go for a walk around the park?' David said, squeezing me tight. I still felt so full, and even though it was cold, a walk was welcome.

Charlotte strolled ahead of us, taking photos of the lake on her mobile phone. Apparently, she'd found a new filter, which was making her photos look professional.

'Are you OK?' David asked, when Charlotte was out of earshot.

'Yes, why do you ask?' I snapped. The chasm Stella had left behind already painfully obvious. I felt lost without her.

David raised his eyebrows and smiled and me. 'You seem very… far away at the moment.'

I cringed inwardly, guilt swallowing me whole. 'I'm fine, just been busy with work and the creative writing class.'

David nodded.

'Who is she, David?' The words came out before I could stop them. I couldn't carry on the charade.

David's hand dropped mine and he stopped dead in his tracks, his face ashen. He'd told me everything I needed to know without saying a word.

I sighed and walked on.

David caught up and fell in step with me. 'I'm sorry. It was a stupid mistake.'

I wiped my tears away; glad Charlotte was too far ahead to see them. I had no right to shed them. I'd opened up Pandora's box and I couldn't shut it. Should I tell him about Nicky?

'Why, David?'

'I don't know, she showed interest, made an effort.'

I snorted, biting my lip. 'No, not like that. I mean she, you know, pursued me.' He sounded embarrassed.

'And you couldn't say no?' I snapped, the bitterness spilling out. I'd been contained for so long and now the anger was bubbling to the surface. Deep down I knew I had no right. His affair was no different to my own. I was projecting the anger at myself on to David because it was easy.

'I'll tell you whatever you want to know, Izzy. Please say you'll forgive me.'

Charlotte took that moment to turn around and wave, taking a photo of us standing awkwardly together. The worst moment of our marriage, captured for eternity.

'Who is she?' I asked.

'Her name is Paula, she's a temp accountant.' The mysterious Paul in his contacts now made sense.

I closed my eyes and shook my head, not wanting to hear any more, but David kept talking.

'It happened three times, just three, and we met for lunch and dinner once, but that was it, I swear. She's divorced, lonely. I guess I felt sorry for her. She started on the same day as me and we got put on a project together, she—'

'I don't want to know any more,' I hissed, interrupting him. My throat felt thick with my own deceit and I didn't want to listen to David go into details about his.

The wind was blustery, and I pulled the belt of my coat in tighter, turning the fabric over and over in my hands, counting silently in my head, until it was winched in against my stomach.

David looked distraught; his chin quivered as he tried to hold back tears.

'I love you,' he spluttered.

'Do you?' I hissed, turning to look at him.

'Of course I do. I broke it off with her because I couldn't live with myself.' He looked pathetic and, although I was angry, I couldn't take the moral high ground.

'It's half-term this week,' I said, changing the subject.

We walked in silence for a minute before David spoke again.

'Any teacher-training days?'

'No, I'm off all week,' I said, relieved I wouldn't have to see Nicky for seven whole days.

'I've got a conference in London on Tuesday. The company have arranged dinner and a hotel.' His tone was apologetic. I nodded, not wanting to think about whether 'Paula' was going to be there. 'She's gone, left. I won't see her again,' he said, as though reading my mind.

'Charlotte have you made any plans this week?' I called and she walked back to us, throwing a stone into the lake.

'Amy's mum is going to take us to a trampoline centre somewhere and said we can have a sleepover. Shopping and cinema other than that.'

I nodded, an idea formulating in my head.

'What day?' I asked

'Tomorrow or Tuesday, I think,' Charlotte replied.

'Will you be OK in the house on your own for the night?' David frowned.

'Of course. I'll be just fine,' I replied.

* * *

On Monday, it was wonderful being woken by the sun streaming through the window instead of the irritating buzz of my alarm clock. David had already left for work and I was going to be spending the day with Charlotte. A mother-and-daughter day at the beginning of half-term before I lost her to her friends for the rest of the week. I'd told Charlotte last night we could do anything she wanted, knowing that by the time we got up, she would have the day fully planned out for us.

Even though the sun was shining, it was bitterly cold, with November only days away. The radio was already slipping in the occasional Christmas song and festive adverts on the television had begun. I rolled over, feeling David's side of the bed, empty and cold. He'd slept in the spare room last night. When we'd unpacked, he'd put some shirts and trousers in the wardrobe, for when he had an early start, so I wouldn't be disturbed. I didn't know how long he was going to stay in there for. I guessed that was up to me. He'd made promises that he'd be home earlier, be a better husband, more attentive. As upset as I was about David's revelations a part of me was relieved to know that I hadn't imagined it, I wasn't going mad. I still felt crushed by the admission and it brought the pain I would be causing David sharply into focus, if he learned of my affair with Nicky.

'You up, Mum?' Charlotte called from the hallway.

I checked the time; it was half past eight.

'Yep, come in,' I replied, and Charlotte perched on the end of the bed.

'How about cinema this morning, lunch at Panini's, followed by shopping as I need some make-up from Boots. Then we could go for a swim in the afternoon before I cook dinner. How does that sound?' Charlotte looked hopeful; her enthusiasm infectious.

'Exhausting! But yes of course. I'll get in the shower. You check the cinema time.'

'One step ahead of you. The film is at twenty past ten.' Charlotte beamed.

'Plenty of time. I climbed out of bed and pulled the covers back.

Two hours later, we were sitting in a packed cinema surrounded by teenagers. Charlotte had chosen a zombie sequel, which was also a comedy. Not something I would have picked, but it was her day. We took in our own popcorn, but Charlotte loved the slushies, so I bought a large one to share, although every time I sucked the straw it gave me brain freeze.

With the movie in full swing and Charlotte engrossed in the popcorn as much as the storyline, I managed to wrestle the Motorola from the bottom of my bag and slip it into my pocket covertly. I motioned to Charlotte I was going to the toilet, making my way out of the theatre. Once safely locked in the cubicle, I switched the phone on and waited. A message came through instantly.

I'm sorry. Please can we sort this out.

I knew Nicky was referring to Saturday night in the club.

I chewed my lip as my fingers hovered over the keys, knowing it was a mistake to get in touch. I'd managed to refrain when I'd been drunk, but the confirmation of David's affair had floored me. I wanted comfort. I wanted to forget. I typed a message back to Nicky.

Tomorrow night. Can we talk?

I felt my chest pounding as I waited for a response and distracted myself going out to the sinks to wash my hands. I took a slow walk back to the cinema screen, still clutching the Motorola when it buzzed in my hand.

Where?

Your place, is your Mum on nights?

If things got out of hand or I changed my mind, I could leave.

Yep.

OK

I sent the message and switched the phone off, my nerves buzzed, and my stomach somersaulted. I was going backwards, not forwards. Seeing Nicky wouldn't help get my marriage back on track, but one last roll between the sheets would make me feel better. I knew I was being petty but, in my head, I reasoned it would help me draw a line under David's affair and move on. He'd had his fun, I'd had mine and then we'd come back together.

Charlotte had barely noticed I'd gone. She was still rhythmically shovelling handfuls of popcorn into her mouth and gazing wide-eyed at the screen. I settled back into my seat comfortably, knowing I'd be able to pick up the storyline again, but found my mind wandering. My eyes welled up in the darkness when I pictured David with Paula. Of course, in my head she was model material, beautiful with an amazing figure. I couldn't stand it.

One last time with Nicky, that's all it would be. I'd have to make it clear, so he knew where he stood. Just one last time and I'd end it for good.

## 30

As we exited the cinema, Charlotte rubbed her stomach, which was as flat as a pancake, and moaned she'd eaten too much popcorn.

'Perhaps a bit of shopping before lunch?' I suggested, pulling my daughter into a hug as we walked side by side.

Charlotte nodded weakly but soon perked up when she was wandering around Boots, trying all the lip gloss testers. She asked if she could get a sugary pink one and I obliged, pulling out my purse to pay. I wasn't sure how many more of these mother-and-daughter days I would be allowed. Charlotte was growing up faster all the time, her world getting bigger and bigger and my part in it was getting smaller. The thought made my heart ache, so when, a couple of hours later, Charlotte was bored of shopping and she suggested afternoon cake and coffee instead of lunch, I decided to forgo the excess-sugar conversation and agree. Strong coffee and a thick slab of carrot cake was placed in front of me. Charlotte chose a large Bakewell tart and a tall decaf latte, and we talked about the movie.

'Next time, Mum, you can choose,' Charlotte said.

'That's OK, I wanted to spend the day with you. Doesn't matter what we do. So, what are your plans for the rest of the week?' I continued.

'Amy's tomorrow, we're revising for maths. Staying over at hers and trampoline park on Wednesday. Thursday and Friday, more revising. Lots of revising. I need to go to the library too.'

'OK, well, I can always take you later on in the week.'

We decided to postpone swimming for another day and went home. Charlotte was keen to get her nose in her books.

David came in at six, as Charlotte was setting the table, having cooked us Bolognese by herself. I knew his day hadn't been great as he went straight to the fridge for a beer. However, I was pleased to see him home at a reasonable time.

'Bad day?' I asked as we sat at the table sprinkling cheese on our plates, going through the motions as much for Charlotte's benefit as our own.

'Not the best, some reporting issues. Internal system needs an overhaul.'

I nodded, there was no point pretending I was interested, finance bored me senseless. I couldn't make head nor tail of the graphs David produced.

'This is great,' he said, his mouth full of pasta. I wrinkled my nose, finding it increasingly difficult to look at David and not imagine his hands all over the mysterious Paula. The idea of it made me seethe.

Charlotte beamed. 'I can't decide whether to become a chef or a journalist.'

'I think you would be fantastic at either,' I replied.

'Do you think it would be weird if I came to your creative writing class?' she asked out of nowhere, pulling apart some garlic bread and pushing it into her mouth. I felt my knee begin to judder beneath the table, as though it had a mind of its own. I didn't think Charlotte was a fan of writing, although I knew she loved to read.

'Not at all. Come and sit in on one. They're running until the end of the year.' It would mean Charlotte and Nicky would be in the same room, which wasn't something I wasn't entirely comfortable with. Although there hadn't been a repeat of Nicky driving her home that I knew of, so perhaps I was overthinking it. Charlotte changed her mind like the wind, so it would all be forgotten by next Friday no doubt.

David loaded the dishwasher and Charlotte disappeared to her room after dinner and didn't resurface, so I poured myself a large glass of wine and we settled in to watch some television. The atmosphere was frosty, although David tried to initiate conversation. We hadn't spoken about his infidelity since the park, although it rested in the pit of my stomach like an undigestible rock. Had Paula really left the PR firm or was he seeing her tomorrow tonight?

I managed another large glass before I went to bed, feeling fuzzy-headed.

David came in and stroked my arm in bed as I lay rigid with my back to him.

'I'll ring you tomorrow night,' he said, kissing my shoulder, before leaving to spend another night in the spare room.

In the morning, Charlotte was keen to get to Amy's. When she wouldn't stop hovering, I gave up on eating my breakfast and drove her over there. It would be a relief to be alone, to not have to appear as though everything was fine. Inside I was wound as tightly as a spring. Lurching one minute from excitement at seeing Nicky later to recognising it would be a terrible mistake to end up back in his bed. Charlotte leapt out of the car and ran to the door, which was quickly opened. Louise waved at me from the window and I waved back before reversing off their driveway and returning home.

The house seemed too large when I was there by myself, and I wanted to keep busy, my mind on something else other than Nicky. I whizzed around with the hoover and duster, washed the floors and put two loads of washing through the machine, briefly stopping for an early lunch before tackling the ironing, which allowed me to catch up on the TV shows I'd recorded. It wasn't until around two o'clock I ran a hot bath and switched on the Motorola. Two messages came through.

Mum's on nights, leaving at six. I'm cooking dinner
Be here at 7. X

My eyebrows shot skyward. He was cooking dinner? What was I in for?

As I slid into the hot water, my skin prickled and I eased myself lower into the bath. Feeling the excitement creep in at the prospect of spending the night with Nicky, knowing I should feel guilty, but the emotion wasn't there. Looking back at my marriage to David, I never thought in a million years either of us would cheat. David was too solid, too dependable. But he had cheated and so had I. I was about to do it again, but this would be the last time. There was no future for me and Nicky. I was risking my career; not to mention my reputation for an eighteen-year-old student. Nothing good would come of it.

After a long soak, I shaved my legs, arms and bikini line, rubbing in some expensive perfumed body lotion I'd been bought last Christmas and spritzing the perfume on my pulse points to match. I selected a pretty pink bra and briefs and slipped my favourite sky-blue cashmere jumper on, with grey skinny jeans. Casual but elegant was the look I was going for, after all I was nearly forty and if Nicky wanted leggings and a midriff-skimming top, he only had to seek out his female classmates for that.

At five, I was ready and sat in the front room clicking through the television channels, trying to find something to watch to fill the time. My stomach bubbled, breathing shallow. I felt apprehensive, knowing what I was doing was stupid retaliation to make myself feel better.

I rang Charlotte and spent five minutes catching up with her, pleasantly surprised she didn't hurry me off the phone.

Still pacing the kitchen forty minutes later, I decided to indulge in a small glass of wine, I'd still be able to drive, and it might calm me down a bit. I texted Stella to see how she was. We had a short conversation before the carer turned up and she had to talk to them about her dad's medication. I told her that David had come clean, but his affair was over. I didn't tell her I was going to Nicky's. I knew she'd talk me out of it.

I moved to the lounge to watch reruns of *Homes Under the Hammer*.

I'd been sat for two minutes when I heard my phone ringing from the kitchen. I hoped it wasn't Nicky cancelling, but the Motorola was silent, it was my iPhone and David was on the other end. I slid my finger across the screen to answer.

'Hi.'

'Hi, hon, just checking in. Everything OK?'

'Yes fine, been doing housework and catching up on the ironing. I dropped Charlotte around Amy's around ten this morning, so it's been a quiet day.'

'She was keen to get there then,' he said with a chuckle.

'Well, of course, I don't think she wants to spend any more time with me. One day out of the half-term was enough for her.' I heard him laugh and smiled. 'How is your day going?' I continued.

'Well, the conference was dull, lots of networking and now I'm back in the hotel about to get ready for dinner. Wish you were here.'

My throat tightened and the guilty feeling I'd been missing arrived with a thud.

'What are you up to?' David asked, filling the silence.

'I'm going to cook a big bowl of pasta and catch up on my soaps.'

'OK, well, have a nice evening. I'll text you later,' he said before hanging up.

The Motorola beeped and a new message came through.

She's gone.

My stomach lurched, the time had arrived and now it had I felt rooted to the spot. My tongue felt thick and heavy in my mouth, was I making a mistake? I took a second to get myself together, before packing up, ready to leave, ensuring everything was switched off and the house was secure. I left the hallway light on so it would look like someone was home and, grabbing the wine and my coat, I headed out of the front door to the car.

It was cold, my windscreen starting to show signs of frost. Winter was well on its way and it took a few minutes with the blowers on before I could see where I was going.

The roads were quiet and when I arrived on Nicky's street just before seven, I was careful to park halfway down the road, staying in the car until the road was empty. I felt like a criminal, creeping in the shadows and walking on my toes so my heels didn't make noise on the concrete slabs.

I could see the light was on in Nicky's kitchen through the glass at the top of the door. I gently knocked on the wooden frame, hoping he would hear it. Footsteps slapped the laminate hallway and my heart started to pound. I was excited and terrified in equal measure.

The door swung open and Nicky filled the doorway, beaming. He stepped aside, rubbing his hand over his head as his eyes devoured me, and in that moment, I wasn't sure if it was the best decision of my life, or the worst.

## 31

'Come in.'

When Nicky closed the door, he pulled me into an unexpected embrace and my body dissolved.

'I've missed you.' His boyish grin made me smile.

'I've brought wine,' I mumbled, handing him the bottle as he guided me down the hallway.

The kitchen was spotless, not how I'd expected to find it. There was a rumble of a dishwasher coming from somewhere beneath the counter. A large wok sat on the stove, filled with an amazing smelling stir fry. Next to it, a saucepan full of fluffy white rice had steam billowing out of the top.

'Dinner is done.'

I detected a note of triumph in his voice.

'I've got a beer on the go.' He raised his bottle and took a swig as I gestured towards the single wine glass he'd retrieved from the cupboard.

'I'm starving,' I said, opening the wine and gulping a mouthful. My hands trembled and I felt jittery. I shouldn't be here. It wasn't fair to play with his feelings. I had to make it clear that it was a one-off.

As if reading my mind, he stepped across the kitchen and slid his hand under my jumper, caressing my breast through my bra. Watching me squirm, he smiled, his lip curled upwards, enjoying my discomfort. Pinching my nipple until I shrank away, out of his grasp.

'Nicky, this is the last time we do this.'

'Really? I've heard that before.' His tone almost mocking, he turned away to switch off the stove and move the pans away from the heat.

'Yes, really,' I said, my voice wavering as he came back to me and started to undo my jeans.

We had quick, rough sex over the kitchen table, still mostly clothed, knocking the cutlery onto the floor. He pulled my hair, thrusting hard behind me until he'd finished. There was no pleasure in it for me.

It occurred to me I'd made a massive mistake as I pulled my underwear up and fastened my jeans. Staring at his back as he reached up to get some bowls out of the cupboard behind him, a feeling of unease wrapped itself around me. The look on his face a moment before we'd had sex was odd, menacing. He was like Jekyll and Hyde.

I clutched at my breast, the flesh still tender. I knew I'd be bruised tomorrow.

He dished up the stir fry and we sat at the table which I'd laid with clean cutlery. I thought about leaving but Nicky sat and began to eat, and the moment passed. Plus, I had to make clear that once I left, it would be finished. I steeled myself to bring it up, but Nicky broke the silence.

'Where's David today?' He asked and I winced at the sound of his name, wishing he hadn't been brought into the conversation.

'At a conference, and Charlotte is at her friend's house.'

'She seems like a nice girl your Charlotte, she looks a lot like you.'

'I think she'd hate to be told that,' I retorted, shifting in my seat, unsettled by the implication of his comment.

'I think you're beautiful,' he said without any hint of embarrassment.

My face reddened and I concentrated on not choking on my mouthful of food.

'I thought it right from the moment I saw you, do you remember... I think you were giving me the finger at the time.' He laughed and I kicked him playfully under the table. My previous misgivings pushed aside. He seemed more like himself now.

'Well, you were driving like a moron,' I said and watched Nicky roll his eyes.

When we'd finished our dinner, we topped up our drinks and had a cigarette. I couldn't deny that I was enjoying myself and keen for us to be at ease in each other's company, as we used to be. Soon we would be climbing the stairs to his bedroom. This time I hoped I would get to enjoy him, and he'd be gentle. We'd make love like we had before, when his touch was tender and I felt safe. The idea, along with the wine, made me unsteady on my feet.

'I think that cigarette is done now.' Nicky laughed, taking the butt out of my hand and putting it in the ashtray.

'Sorry, my mind was elsewhere.'

Nicky stood, pulling me to my feet. 'Where?' he whispered.

I bit my lip and looked up to the ceiling and back into Nicky's blue eyes.

'I'm glad you're back,' he said, placing butterfly kisses on my collarbone.

'I'm not. I mean, I can't, Nicky. This is the last time,' I said, my firm voice wavering as my body betrayed me.

'Hmm you say that a lot.'

I wrapped my arms around his neck and pulled him in. He felt so good, pressed against me. My hands strayed inside his T-shirt, fingernails trailing the muscles of his shoulders down his back and inside the waistband of his jeans. We rushed upstairs to his room, his bedside lamp on, guiding us in. When we made love for the second time, it was much more intense and infinitely more satisfying. Nicky held me so tight, as though he was afraid I might disappear.

Afterwards, at around half past nine we got comfy on the bed, watching *Scream*, a horror movie from the nineties.

'I think I saw this at the cinema,' I squirmed, realising Nicky hadn't even been born then.

'I love you,' Nicky said out of the blue as the credits rolled. The atmosphere felt heavy, the silence all encompassing.

'Nicky...' I began, trailing off. What could I say? It was after eleven, I could make my excuses and go home, although I'd had too much to drink to drive. 'When is your mum back?' I asked, knowing she was working nights. Perhaps I could wait a few hours and drive home when the alcohol had left my system? I hadn't intended to stay the night.

'Not until around half seven tomorrow,' he said, kissing my neck. 'Leave him, run away with me,' he whispered into my ear, but I didn't answer.

We fell asleep soon after, his words forgotten. I woke disorientated at three in the morning needing the toilet and, pulling on Nicky's T-shirt, scrambled out of the bed into the cold hallway half-asleep. I had to get home. Surely, I'd be safe to drive now? He was awake when I returned and beckoned me back into bed, pressing himself against my back and curling around me.

'I have to go,' I said but Nicky didn't respond, his hand was already reaching between my legs.

\* \* \*

The sound of a door slamming woke me with a start, footsteps hastily climbing the stairs. I elbowed Nicky and he moaned as his mother walked past the open bedroom door. I locked eyes with her for a second as she passed before stepping back into the doorway, her eyebrows raised. She wore a light blue nurse uniform with a watch fob attached to her pocket.

'Morning,' she said in a stern voice.

I instantly felt reprimanded, my ears burning. Shit! How could I have fallen back to sleep? What if she recognised me from St Wilfred's, although I couldn't think of a reason as to why she would have visited the school this term. I couldn't recall seeing her before, but she awarded me a steely glare, taking me in. Recognition spreading across her face that the woman in her son's bed was around the same age as her. How could I have ever been so stupid? I was twice his age.

'Hi, I'm Izzy.' I managed, sitting up, thankful for Nicky's T-shirt.

'Pat,' she responded curtly.

Nicky raised his head and squinted at his mother.

'Shut the fucking door, Mum,' he grunted, and she leaned in to close the bedroom door, huffing for effect.

'Shit.' I threw myself back on the bed, hand clapped to my forehead. Glancing at the clock, it was quarter to eight. Why hadn't I set an alarm to get up before Nicky's mother came home? I couldn't believe we'd just been caught red-handed. If I wanted to feel like a teenager again, I certainly did now. Foolish for thinking what we were doing would have no repercussions. I slipped out of bed, searching for my clothes and throwing them on.

'Where are you going?' Nicky asked, rubbing his eyes.

'Your mum's home,' I hissed, gathering my things and flattening my hair in the mirror before opening the bedroom door. I crept down the stairs, hoping Nicky's mother would have come home from the night shift and gone straight to bed.

Unfortunately, I'd left my handbag in the kitchen and, when I rounded the corner at the bottom of the stairs, I saw Pat nursing a cup of steaming coffee at the table I'd been bent over the night before.

'I'm sorry,' I said as I crept into the kitchen, cheeks flaming as I grabbed my handbag off the side. I felt sick, the interaction excruciating. 'I didn't intend for us to meet like this,' I continued, feeling Pat's icy glare. She was older than me, but not by much.

'Aren't you a little old for him?' Pat asked coldly, raising her eyebrows. She didn't seem shocked that a woman had stayed the night, only at my age. How often did Nicky have women to stay?

'Yes,' I whispered. There was no point in lying. I was.

'I don't understand his fascination with older women.' She shrugged. Her words stung. I wasn't the first. 'Be careful,' Pat said, jolting me from my frozen state. Her voice was barely a whisper.

I stared at her, my mouth suddenly dry.

'He can't be trusted.' She lowered her eyes to her coffee, where they remained, fixed, as I backed down the hallway and out of the front door, into the cold morning air. My flesh crawled like ants were dancing on my skin. Racing to my car, I sat inside, with the engine on, waiting for the frosted windscreen to melt away.

*Can't be trusted?* What did she mean by that? What a weird thing to say, about one's own child too. Perhaps she wasn't the full ticket?

I dug in my handbag and retrieved the iPhone, which had only ten per cent battery. I'd missed three texts last night: two from David and one from Charlotte. David had been checking in after his dinner and there was one more from him a little later, wishing me goodnight. I hurriedly text back, to say I'd had a couple of glasses of wine and fallen asleep on the sofa.

The text from Charlotte was asking if it was OK if I picked her up around seven from Amy's. I sent a breezy reply of 'Sure, no problem'. My heart was pounding and my head still fuzzy from the wine. I couldn't wait to get back home and into the shower.

As I drove the short distance, my mind whirled and panic set in. What if Pat found out I was a teacher and reported me to St. Wilfred's? What if Nicky told her I was his teacher? Surely, he wouldn't be so stupid? Suddenly, sleeping with Nicky was altogether too real and the consequences involved felt tangible. I was mortified at being caught in bed by his mother but also concerned at the way she'd reacted. She hadn't shouted or balled, she'd just looked me in the eye, almost pityingly. It sent a chill through me.

Why did I need to be careful? Was it a threat? It sounded more like a warning. Did Pat know something I didn't? What could she have meant? I'd have to broach the subject with Nicky if I had a chance at school next week. With my rushing off, there'd been no time to reiterate it was over. I had to hope he understood that I was serious when I said it was the last time. There was no doubt in my mind about that now. Things had become too real. Nicky was out of my system for good.

When I pulled up at home, my shoulders sagged as relief flooded through me. I hadn't notice how white my knuckles were from gripping the steering wheel.

I took the Motorola out of my bag and quickly typed a text to Nicky.

Don't tell her who I am

As soon as I got through the front door, I went straight upstairs and stripped off. All my clothes went in the laundry basket and I turned the shower to as hot as I could bear before climbing in. The water pummelled my chest and back as I turned around and instantly felt soothed. Washing away my sins from the night before, I slowly felt more like the woman I used to be. Determined to be a better mother and wife. I'd work at my marriage and it would be stronger than ever. David had made a mistake, but so had I. We weren't perfect but we'd drawn a line under it now and there was no way I was going back.

## 32

I scrubbed at my skin and washed my hair, finally feeling like every inch of me was clean. I slipped on some fresh jeans and a long-sleeved sweatshirt, applying the smallest amount of make-up. Downstairs, I plugged in my iPhone to charge and made some coffee, sitting at the dining table absorbing the stillness of the house. The birds chirped outside, it was still early, almost nine a.m. I cradled the cup in my hands, what would I do today? David wouldn't be home until later, around dinner time, and I wasn't picking Charlotte up until later that evening.

The home phone rang and when I got to the cradle it wasn't there, but it flashed to indicate a message had been left.

'Shit,' I muttered, hunting around for the handset, finally finding it on the sofa under a cushion.

'Hello,' I said breathlessly and heard a chuckle the other end.

'What are you up to?' Stella said, bursting into infectious laughter.

'Nothing, I couldn't find the bloody phone. How are you?' I asked, pleased to hear Stella's voice.

'I'm good thanks, nothing new to report here. Dad's still loopy, Mum's got no patience and I'm still dating a man whose young enough to be my son...' Stella tailed off.

'Only just.'

'Yes, well, he's still hot for me, so I can't complain. How are you? Where's David?' I knew Stella was checking the coast was clear before straying on to more dangerous topics of conversation.

'It's OK, everyone's out. David's at a conference and Charlotte is at Amy's.

'I'm surprised you're on your own and you haven't got company.'

I laughed. 'I ended it, remember.'

'Yeah? So where were you last night the five times I called?' Stella chuckled.

'I did end it... after I stayed over at his house last night.'

I heard her gasp. 'You didn't?'

'I did. I know I shouldn't have. David admitted he'd been having an affair and I kind of lost it.'

'Oh, Izzy, I'm so sorry. I love David and everything, but what a bastard.' Stella's voice was grave.

'I know, who'd have thought it.'

'Are you OK?' she asked.

'Yeah, I am now.' *Well I was until Nicky's mother came home and soured it.* I pushed the thought away.

'I can't believe you had revenge sex.' Stella was so good at making me laugh.

'I know. Shallow right? David says it's over now and I've ended it with Nicky. Hopefully we can move on from this.' I sighed.

'Does he know about Nicky?'

'No, I haven't told him. Last night was...' I paused, trying to find the right word. 'Awkward. His mum caught us this morning.' I drummed my fingers on my thigh as I recalled the uncomfortable exchange.

'Oh god. I told you to steer clear. I had feeling he was a wrong-un.'

'His mum said something weird, it kind of freaked me out.'

'What?' Stella asked.

'Well, after stating the obvious, that I was a bit old for him, she said to be careful, that he wasn't to be trusted. Isn't that strange? Why would she tell me that?'

Stella fell silent, pondering for a second. 'Perhaps she meant be careful with her son's heart. I would if I had kids, I'd be that parent packing a shotgun whenever I met a new boyfriend or girlfriend.'

'Maybe... It was weird though. I literally only saw her for a minute, but the way she said it, it was creepy, and what about the "not to be trusted" bit?'

'No idea! Maybe he's a shit son? At least you don't have to see her again.'

'Thank goodness.'

'Listen, I've got to go, I can hear Dad calling me from upstairs, he's probably flushed his glasses down the toilet again,' Stella sighed. I admired her strength.

'No worries, speak to you soon.' I finished the call and went back to my coffee. I needed to speak to Nicky about his mum before school restarted, otherwise if I left it, I'd worry about it all week. Plus, I wanted to reiterate the clean break.

Would he be awake yet? I composed a text to him.

Fancy a stroll around the park?

Within a minute, there was a response.

Meet you there in half an hour

I grabbed my coat and my wellies as it looked as though it was going to rain any minute. The sky had become dark and threatening, resembling a winter's evening rather than a morning. At least the park would be quiet at half past nine, perhaps with the exception of a few joggers. It was too early for mums and their children and most likely too wet.

When I arrived, there were a handful of cars in the car park and not a soul to be seen. Nicky pulled up as I turned off the engine. He looked dishevelled, wearing the same clothes he'd had on yesterday. Had he come straight from bed?

'Morning. What's up with you?' He laughed, looking at my pained expression, and nudged me playfully as we walked into the park.

'Just the weather,' I lied, shivering in the cold.

The park was peaceful and even with the grey skies and rain it still looked picturesque. We had the place to ourselves, bar a couple of dog walkers and an enthusiastic jogger who smiled as she passed, probably thinking we were mother and son out for a stroll. The thought made me squirm. Rain began to fall heavily, and we put our hoods up.

'I was surprised to hear from you so early. I must have made a good impression last night. You told me it was the last time,' he teased.

I cringed inwardly. This was going to be harder than I thought.

'I did have a great time last night, but we have got to stop.' I clenched my jaw and counted in my head, feeling my anxiety spike.

'I don't see why,' Nicky said, eyes narrowing.

'Because I'm married and I'm your teacher. I should never have let it happen in the first place. I'm the responsible adult here.'

He scoffed at my words, stuffing his hands in his pockets.

'I wanted to ask you about your mum. Did you tell her about me?' The question had been eating away at me since I'd left his house earlier. Pat could ruin my entire life if she wanted to. It made my world seem incredibly fragile.

'What do you mean? That we're shagging?' he asked, missing the point entirely.

I cringed. 'No, that I'm a teacher.'

'No, of course I didn't. It's none of her fucking business anyway.'

I was surprised at the sudden flare of his temper, although the relief my secret was still safe flooded through me.

'She said you like mature women?' I offered, trying to defuse him.

'I had a thing for my mate's mum that's all. It was nothing. She likes to wind me up about it,' he said, grinding his teeth.

'There was something else. It was odd. When I left, she told me to be careful.'

He tutted and shook his head. 'Fucking bitch, always poking her nose in.' I could see his nostrils flaring.

'Do you two not get on?' I asked, cringing as I remembered the awful way he'd spoken to his mum this morning. I'd had no time to dwell on it then.

'She's interfering. I can't wait to move out of there.' He stopped, taking down his hood, and turned to face me, gripping my shoulders, his fingers digging into the skin. Water ran down his forehead, onto his lashes. 'Look I know you think you want to end it, but I meant what I said last night, let's do it. Let's just go, take Charlotte and leave.'

I laughed, a knee-jerk reaction at the ridiculousness of the idea, but the thunder on Nicky's face silenced me immediately.

'You can't love him that much if you're fucking me. Why are you even with him?'

'You're being ridiculous. I'm sure Charlotte would love to leave her Dad and shack up with her mother's eighteen-year-old lover,' I snapped. Nicky's hands balled into fists and he strode ahead of me, rounding the bend back towards the car park. We got back to the cars and I stood awkwardly, not sure what to say.

'I'm sorry, Nicky,' I began, but he turned his back on me to unlock his car.

'Don't worry about it.' He climbed inside and tore off, gravel spraying up my legs as I stood in his wake. It seemed at last, it was finally over.

The rest of the half-term week flew by. The weather turned colder, but the rain was persistent. Halloween came and went on Thursday, and we barely had anyone stop by for trick or treating, even though I'd carved pumpkins and bought sweets. Only the children that lived in one of the other cottages further along the lane came, so they got more than a handful.

David took Friday off and we went to London to do some sightseeing, something we'd wanted to do for ages. I'd pushed the infidelity from my mind. It was a new start and we were both making the effort. I was looking forward to us doing something together and we'd always said it was funny how you could live so close to the Capital but never experience the tourist attractions. He surprised us with family tickets to see *Matilda* in the West End. It was Charlotte's favourite Roald Dahl book when she was little.

When the weekend arrived, I used it to catch up on the chores I'd missed. Charlotte went to the cinema with Amy on Saturday to see the new *Joker* movie, and when David and I dropped her off, we decided on the spur of the moment to see a movie as well. *Doctor Sleep* had just been released and I loved *The Shining* so was keen to see it. Going to the cinema was something we used to do a lot.

'You know Charlotte's old enough now really, we should go out more, the two of us,' David leaned over and whispered in my ear.

I flinched at the proximity, glad for the dim lighting in the cinema. It would take a while before we were back to the way we were before our affairs. The fact that we were both willing to try, though, was enough. I thought perhaps I should come clean about Nicky, but Stella's advice rang in my ears.

The adverts finished and the room went pitch black until the trailers came on, illuminating up the room. People were still entering the cinema, blocking the screen as they scuttled past. I sank lower in my seat, getting comfortable, but my mouth dropped open as I spied Nicky coming up the stairs. I focused on his face as he climbed, eyes dropping to see him holding hands with a pretty brunette girl I recognised from the corridors of St. Wilfred's.

Not only the corridors, but from my very own classroom. It was Amelia, the girl in year eleven. The one Matilda had said was pregnant. I couldn't make out whether she had a bump or not, it was too dark. It hadn't taken Nicky long to replace me. Perhaps he hadn't? Perhaps he'd been seeing her all along and her baby was his? I felt a twinge of jealousy and a pang of self-pity as I looked first at Nicky then at David. Thankful for the darkness to hide my damp eyes. Wasn't I enough for one man?

## 33

On Sunday morning, we sat around the kitchen table, Charlotte was finishing her geography homework and David was working on his laptop, tapping away furiously on the keys. Radio Two played in the background and Lionel Ritchie was singing about Sunday mornings. I was trying to plan my lessons for each year group for the upcoming term, but I couldn't concentrate. Seeing Nicky and Amelia together had niggled at me. Not because I felt any love was lost between us, it was a fling and nothing more, but I couldn't help wondering if Amelia was pregnant, could the baby be Nicky's?

'I need to go into town.' I stood from the table abruptly.

David raised his eyebrows, but it was Charlotte who spoke first.

'Bring back some Millie's Cookies,' she said, without even looking up from her books.

I rolled my eyes at David.

'I need to get some books on this list I haven't read,' I explained.

'Marathon reading session today?' David asked and I nodded, grimacing.

'I won't be long,' I said, grabbing my bag and hurrying out to the hallway to put my coat and boots on, before David could suggest we all went together.

I drove a little way down the street, pulled over and dug out the Motorola. It had been switched off all weekend and once turned on, the beeping of messages coming through seemed to go on forever. Looking at the texts in my inbox, Nicky had sent one every day. First apologising for storming off, then each one becoming more desperate to get in touch. My heart raced. Why hadn't I thought to send a text? What if he came to the house again?

Have managed to get out, got to go into town. Will park in the mall. Text if you can make it.

There wasn't much battery left and I made a mental note to charge the phone when I got home. Putting it on the passenger seat, I drove to the shopping centre. The rain was heavy and my windscreen wipers were on double speed as I drove to the top of the car park. The roof was partly empty, mostly because it wasn't undercover. No one wanted to get wet when there were spaces on the lower floors out of the rain.

When I parked, I checked the phone, no response yet. Sending another text to let Nicky know I'd parked on the roof of the car park, I slipped the phone into my pocket and made a dash across the concourse towards the stairs. I went straight to the bookshop, cursing under my breath that I could only remember the titles of the books I needed and not the authors. However, the shop assistant happily looked them up for me. Within minutes, I was walking out of the store with the books in a brown paper bag.

I had no idea where Millie's Cookies was, but if I went home without them Charlotte would be grumpy. Anyway, cookies on a Sunday morning was a fantastic idea. Charlotte definitely had my genes.

I found the pillar that listed a directory of all the shops and where to find them. I had to go to the second floor for Millie's Cookies so took the escalator, checking my phone again, but there was no text waiting for me. I could smell the shop before I saw it and my tummy grumbled. Choosing a selection box, I paid, deciding not to hang around any longer. Perhaps it was good that Nicky hadn't responded? Maybe it meant that he had moved on? I'd see him at school tomorrow at some point and we could talk then.

Even from the top floor of the shopping centre, there were another four flights of stairs to climb before I reached the roof of the car park. Gasping for breath at the top, I flung open the heavy metal door and saw Nicky was parked right next to me. I ran across the concrete, puddles splashing my jeans and pulled open his passenger door, climbing in.

His face was like stone, cold and hard, staring straight ahead out of the windscreen.

'Where have you been? I've been texting and calling.' His voice low and calculated. It put me instantly on edge.

'David had some time off. I haven't had a chance.' I was interrupted by Nicky smashing his fist on the dashboard, the sound reverberating around the car. I recoiled, my hand on the door handle instinctively, ready to get out.

'I don't want to hear about him,' Nicky snapped, louder this time.

I opened my mouth to speak, but no words came out.

'Are you fucking him?' he snarled.

I felt my hackles rise, anger igniting in the pit of my stomach. 'It's none of your damn business what I do with my husband.'

He launched at me, pushing his tongue into my mouth, his hand holding the back of my head so I couldn't pull away. He thrust his free hand down to my waistband and tried to undo my buttons. What the fuck was I doing there? I had to get out. I placed both hands on his chest and shoved him backwards. He released his hold, pulling back to stare at me, eyes devoid of emotion.

'Get in the back,' he said, his tone flat. It was a command not a request.

'What?' I challenged.

Nicky didn't respond, instead he nodded towards the back seat, waiting for me to comply. Was he trying to humiliate me? It was the same when he'd been at the house, in my bedroom, marking his territory.

'Go fuck yourself, Nicky,' I spat, swinging the door open and narrowly missing my car. He tried to grab my arm as I left, but I snatched it out of his reach, slamming the door behind me.

I scrambled for my keys and got in my car as quickly as I could. Locking the doors and starting the engine. Tears erupted down my cheeks as I drove, my tyre scraping the curb. It was the final straw. There was no hope for any civility between us. We were done.

* * *

'We're late,' I shouted as I tore down the hallway, banging on Charlotte's door on Monday morning. I'd spent much of the previous evening in turmoil, regretting ever meeting Nicky. David and I talked things through, although I followed Stella's advice and didn't reveal my affair. We had a long heart-to-heart about the baby; he didn't realise how devastated I was, and in pushing him away, he'd had to grieve alone. I realised how selfish I'd been and we both agreed to work on getting our marriage back to a good place.

As I drove to school, Charlotte was grumpy. She didn't do mornings as it was, especially one where she was being driven to school thirty minutes after she'd woken up. I had managed to get away with a bit of dry shampoo in my hair and a quick throw-on outfit of a pair of black trousers and a red blouse. It would have to do. I'd need my free period to apply some make-up in the toilets, otherwise I might scare the kids.

## 34

---

'Morning,' I greeted my form room a lot more brightly than I felt. Although I was tired, I was pleased David and I had turned a corner last night. Before our heart-to-heart, I'd cooked a lovely roast lamb dinner and we'd shared a bottle of wine as we talked, once Charlotte had gone upstairs. When we finally fell into bed after midnight, both tipsy and emotionally exhausted, a goodnight kiss had developed into something more and I'd let it. I wanted to put our infidelities behind us and move on.

'I hope you all had a lovely half-term. Let me do the register and you can tell me what you got up to.'

I called out each name in turn to tick them off of my list and the children talked about their week off until the bell rang out, signalling their first lesson. One had been to a trampoline park and unfortunately now had his arm in a cast. The rest of the class gathered around to sign it.

When they left, I leaned back in my chair with a sigh. Out of the two books I'd brought in town yesterday, I'd ploughed through one already and was starting the other. So far, I wasn't overly keen on either of them and if I was getting bored with the storyline, I knew a bunch of fifteen-year-olds would too. It reinforced my choice of books for each year group.

My year-nine class was fun. I began by reading my favourite part of *Macbeth*, using my cackling witch voice.

> Round about the cauldron go;
> In the poison'd entrails throw.
> Toad, that under cold stone
> Days and nights has thirty-one
> Swelter'd venom sleeping got,
> Boil thou first i' the charmed pot.
> Double, double, toil and trouble;
> Fire burn, and cauldron bubble.

The children loved it, and it seemed they were still in the mood for Halloween fun. I split them into groups, and they recreated their own spooky verses in Shakespearian English.

The next class dragged as the students were sluggish and unenthusiastic. By lunchtime I needed a lift. I had a quick walk around the playground to get some much-needed fresh air and joined Susan and Matilda in the staffroom where they were eating their sandwiches.

'Hi, how are you? Good week off?' Matilda boomed when I joined them.

'Good thanks, never long enough though, right? How about you two?'

They'd been on their walking holiday to the Lake District and it had rained for most of the week. Susan regaled how many of the fields had been waterlogged and some areas had to be evacuated as there was localised flooding.

'Oh, hi Izzy, I've got some post for you, I'll drop it in shortly,' Ruth the secretary said as she left, carrying a cup of what looked to be soup.

'OK thanks,' I called after her.

'Fancy a curry this week? Seems like it's been ages,' Matilda said, shovelling a handful of crisps into her mouth.

'Sure, why not. Same time, same place?' Susan nodded, as Matilda now had her mouth so full, she couldn't speak.

Ruth came back handing me a white A4 envelope with my name on it.

'Here you go,' she whispered so as not to interrupt us, and turned on her heels.

Susan started talking about the accommodation on their holiday, as I pushed my finger underneath the flap to pull it open. The sheet of paper inside was dark, a grey image. I blinked quickly, a cold sweat beginning on the nape of my neck. It was a black and white photo printed on paper, the photo Nicky had sent to the Motorola. The picture of his naked torso and large erection, zoomed in and enormous on an A4 page. My stomach rolled and I thrust the paper back into the envelope and jumped up.

'Bad news?' Matilda nodded towards the quivering envelope in my hand.

'No, no. I just need to go and see Charlotte about something,' I muttered, my voice shrill and hurried out of the staff room.

Back in my classroom, I stared out of the window into the playground, to see if I could see Nicky, but he was nowhere to be found. What was he thinking?

What if someone had seen? It was a ridiculous and childish practical joke, definitely not funny. I felt twitchy, my muscles ready to spring into action. I spent five minutes tearing the photo into tiny unrecognisable pieces and hiding them at the bottom of my bin. Was Nicky threatening me or playing games?

The assembly in the afternoon was long and the hall was freezing. I sat stoically on the stage. Nicky was at the back of the hall, staring intently at me. When I accidentally locked eyes with him as I scanned the room looking for Charlotte, his expression was blank. Was he trying to unnerve me?

I ignored him, silently grinding my teeth. Who did he think he was? He had no hold over me. If he went public with our affair, I'd deny everything.

I'd been stupid and reckless to get involved with him in the first place. All because he'd played to my insecurities; he'd flattered me and I'd lapped it up. I'd been weak but I wouldn't be any more.

With my resolve strengthened, I left the assembly, my head high, to teach my final lesson of the day. Thankfully, Nicky didn't come to my classroom after school while I waited for Charlotte. Perhaps my lack of reaction had sent the message that I was done entertaining him? Hopefully now he'd back off. We drove home, revelling in the mundane Monday afternoon. There was a lot to be said for normality. Charlotte disappeared to her room as usual to FaceTime Amy, which she often did after school.

David sent a text to say he would be home for dinner, so I began putting together a beef and ale stew. Pleased he'd stayed true to his word and was coming home earlier than before. It felt cold and wintery and when we were all huddled around the table dipping French bread in our bowls everyone agreed it was a good choice. I looked around the table at David and Charlotte as we talked about the weekend just gone. My whole world was sat right there, and I couldn't believe I could ever have risked hurting them. What a fool I'd been to want anything more.

After dinner, David loaded the dishwasher and I carried on reading my book in the bath. I knew I wasn't going to choose it as the fiction text for that year group but wanted to finish it none the less. When I got out, I could hear Charlotte on the phone to Amy, clearly excited about something as her voice was an octave higher than usual. Edging closer to the door, I could hear they were talking about a boy. I rolled my eyes and went back to my bedroom to put on my pyjamas. I didn't want to be that parent who gave their child no privacy although after what happened at Charlotte's previous school, I couldn't help but keep a close eye on her. David and I had managed to avoid boys so far, but it was going to happen sooner or later.

'Hey,' David said, opening the bedroom door.

I sat on the edge of the bed removing my mascara.

'I think Charlotte might be on the verge of getting a boyfriend.' I laughed at the colour draining from David's face.

'I'm not ready,' he whimpered dramatically and slumped beside me.

'Well, it's coming, so you'd better get prepared.'

David gave me a kiss on the cheek and stood.

'Guess I'd better go and polish the shotgun then.' He winked.

\* \* \*

When I arrived at school on Tuesday, a present lay waiting for me. On my desk were a bunch of red roses and even though there was no card I knew immediately they were from Nicky. Without a second glance, I swept them into the shallow bin, their heads poking out of the top accusingly. I moved the bin out from under my desk, ensuring it was in full view of the corridor should he walk past. The message would be clear enough.

After lunch he walked past, I knew he would at some point. I was marking homework in the few minutes before the bell rang. I saw him stop for a second out of the corner of my eye before carrying on along the corridor. I clenched my jaw, the anger from Sunday still fresh in my mind. Later, I checked the Motorola, but no messages came through when I switched it on.

Feeling restless, I went for a swim after school, as Charlotte had another friendly netball match, using the repetitive lengths to clear my head. I swam solidly for forty-five minutes and my legs were weak when I got out of the pool to shower. I arrived home minutes before Charlotte pushed open the front door, her cheeks a rosy red.

'Wow, you're home quick. Did you win?' I said, talking to Charlotte's back as she hurried upstairs.

'Yeah we won, and I got a lift,' she called before slamming her bedroom door. Teenagers, they were on a whole other planet. Trying to communicate with them should be a course taught at the Open University.

When Wednesday afternoon came around and I still hadn't heard anything from Nicky, I began to get worried. The fact he hadn't been in touch was making me uneasy. I had no doubt he could be dangerous and an accusation would be enough to end my career. He held all of the cards and I had no idea after the photo stunt whether he was planning something. Another prank?

I was looking forward to the curry with Susan and Matilda to distract me, but even as I left the house to get into my car, I searched the street for any sign of him lurking nearby. When I arrived at the curry house, my stomach growled as the smell wafted along the pavement outside. My lunch hadn't been particularly appetising, and I'd left most of the dry ham sandwich in my lunchbox.

Matilda and Susan were already sat at the table and, as I sat, the waiter delivered poppadoms. I didn't waste any time diving straight in.

'I tell you, it's awful. Girls of fifteen shouldn't be dealing with things like that,' Susan bristled, and I realised I'd arrived mid-conversation.

Nodding a greeting, I listened attentively.

'I know, the poor love,' Matilda said, turning to me. 'You know the year eleven girl, Amelia, who got herself pregnant. Well, she had a miscarriage at school yesterday afternoon. In my class too. It was awful.'

Matilda's eyes brimmed and I patted her hand gently, my throat constricting. I gripped the seat of my chair with my other hand, drumming my fingers and willing myself not to cry. Matilda's anguish brought it all flooding back.

'That's terrible. I'm so sorry Matilda.'

She sniffed loudly and took a large mouthful of pint, wiping her eyes.

'How far gone was she?' I asked, my voice weak.

'Around nine or ten weeks, I think, but I'm not sure,' Susan chipped in.

We ate in silence for a couple of minutes, as though in a mark of respect.

Matilda pulled herself together, finishing her drink.

'It all goes on at that place, I tell you. Last year it was the English teacher, this year it's students getting pregnant.'

'You never did tell me what happened last year,' I interrupted, remembering Matilda mentioning it the last time we were out.

'Well, the teacher was having an affair with a student,' Matilda whispered.

Susan and I leaned forward in our seats.

'Allegedly,' Susan hissed.

'Yes, allegedly. It was never actually proven, but the teacher left very quickly, it was all hush-hush, but rumours were rife.'

I gasped, afraid to ask the question on my lips.

'The boy is still there too,' Susan spat.

I felt a wave of nausea wash over me. I took a sip of the complimentary water, but before I could speak, the waiter arrived to take our order and offer me a drink. I reeled off what I'd usually have as my head spun. He took away the menus and within seconds was back with my Diet Coke.

'What's his name?' My voice cracked as I managed to spit the question out.

'Oh, I can't remember. He's a good-looking lad, does PE, I think. All the girls like him,' Matilda said, not appearing to register the colour draining from my face.

## 35

I knew they were talking about Nicky. How could they not be? History was repeating itself.

I excused myself from the table and went to the toilet to splash water on my face. Locking and unlocking my toilet door: *one, two, three, four, one, two, three, four.* I was such a fool; knocking off two English teachers in a row really was something to brag about. Not to mention getting an underage girl pregnant. If that was him?

When I emerged from the stall, staring at my reflection in the mirror, I willed my heart rate to slow and my pallor to return to normal, sucking in air to flood my system with oxygen.

'Fuck's sake, Izzy, get it together,' I hissed at the mirror as I used the paper towels to dry my dripping face. A couple of minutes later, looking relatively like my normal self, I returned to the table. It was piled high with food which smelt delicious.

'We thought you'd fallen in,' Matilda said as she pushed some naan bread into her mouth.

'No, I just felt sick for a second. I don't think I've eaten enough today,' I said weakly.

'Dig in,' Susan said as she helped herself to one of the side dishes in the middle of the table.

I did and the nausea began to subside. We didn't talk about Amelia again and Nicky wasn't mentioned either.

Matilda changed the topic to Christmas and it seemed they were big fans. They had been over to Germany to visit a Christmas market after school finished last year and planned to go again, insisting I went with them. I would have loved to get away but couldn't imagine being able to do so the weekend before Christmas.

As we sat with full stomachs, drinking Baileys-laced coffees, I wished I could talk openly about Nicky. To be honest with these two lovely ladies who had befriended me would be a dream, but I knew I couldn't. There was too much at stake. I'd ring Stella tomorrow; she'd know what to do.

A buzzing from my handbag alerted me to the time. It was already half past ten and David had text to say goodnight and get home safe. We paid the bill and headed out of the restaurant to our cars before a tipsy Matilda launched into a group hug which almost pulled me and Susan to the ground.

When I arrived home, the house was in darkness, except for the sensor light by the front door illuminating the driveway. It was strange; I looked around as I walked to the door, my footsteps crunching the gravel beneath. Lifting my key to the lock, I jumped as a figure stepped out of the shadows from around the side of the house.

'Fuck, you scared the shit out of me,' I hissed as Nicky approached.

'I needed to see you.' He tried to take my hand, but I snatched it away, glancing up to make sure my bedroom window was closed.

'It's finished, Nicky, it has to stop now. I want you to leave me alone.' I whispered, sounding harsher than I'd intended.

His face twitched and he glared at me, blue eyes glacial.

I changed tack. I needed to be smart. 'We had a lot of fun. You're gorgeous and I can't believe you picked me. I'm unbelievably flattered.' My life as I knew it depended on keeping Nicky on side, although my head swam with the realisation I was the second English teacher he'd successfully pursued. However, I wouldn't be the second teacher whose life he ruined.

'You know I'm crazy about you,' he said with a mischievous grin, leaning closer.

'I'm sorry Nicky.' I took a step back, but he gripped my sleeve.

'OK, perhaps you're right.' He sounded like he understood, but I couldn't untangle myself from him.

A bin clanged in the distance and I stared at Nicky, unable to read the look in his eyes. The sensor light went out and he took advantage of the darkness, wrapping his arms around me and pushing his lips against mine for a split second until the light came on again.

'Just a goodbye kiss,' he said, chuckling at my frown.

'I'll see you at school,' I said, quickly sliding my key into the door and slipping inside without turning back.

Leaning against the door, I closed my eyes. Nicky's demeanour made me uneasy. He was too calm, and it made me increasingly nervous.

I wanted to believe life could get back to the way it was before we'd met. I had bridges to build with David and that had to be my priority. Otherwise in a few years, when Charlotte eventually flew the nest, what would be left to hold us together?

The house was deathly quiet with everyone in bed and I crept through to the lounge to look out of the window onto the street. Was Nicky still outside? The sensor hadn't been set off and I couldn't see him in the glow of the street lamp.

Ensuring my footsteps were light, I climbed the stairs. David was snoring gently; he'd left the light on for me in the en suite bathroom. I was grateful for the heavy lined curtains that ensured the sensor light hadn't woken him. After a quick brush of my teeth, I got into bed and watched the shadows dance on the ceiling. I hoped Nicky had meant what he said and his turning up tonight had been nothing more than a final goodbye. I soon drifted off to sleep and woke early in the morning feeling as though the dark cloud overhead was clearing. There was light at the end of the tunnel.

David was still beside me and I rolled over to give him a cuddle. He wrapped his arm around me, kissing my forehead.

'Morning, beautiful.'

We lay until the alarm rang out, dozing peacefully. David went downstairs to make coffee and breakfast whilst I got ready, he was working from home as he had an afternoon meeting in the city.

Charlotte was especially quiet on the way to school, furiously tapping away on her phone as I sang along to Post Malone on the radio.

'Who are you texting?' I glanced over at Charlotte.

'Amy, of course,' she replied without even looking up. I couldn't believe the speed at which her fingers flew across the phone.

'What's the urgency, aren't you going to see her in ten minutes?'

Charlotte let out a loud sigh, rolling her eyes at me, frustrated that I wasn't 'getting it'. I smiled, remembering being the same with my mum.

'There's a boy, and he's been texting and stuff,' Charlotte volunteered.

'You or Amy?' I couldn't hide the rising panic in my voice.

'Amy,' she clarified before continuing, 'and she's just sort of waiting for him to ask her out.'

'Oh, I see, well couldn't she ask him instead?'

'Mum, he's older and girls don't do that. Especially with older boys.'

I chuckled despite myself. It wasn't so different for this generation after all. Thank goodness it was Amy and not Charlotte having the dilemma. Or was it? Had she just successfully pulled the wool over my eyes? I frowned at her, but Charlotte had resumed texting and when I parked, she flew out of the car to meet Amy at the gate.

I didn't see Nicky all day, but I wasn't expecting to. We'd gone our separate ways and had no reason to run into each other. I couldn't wait until later to ring Stella and offload. Just before lunch, I had an issue with a year ten student, Thomas, whose attitude was less than desirable, so I made him sit in the corridor for half of the lesson. It was the only way to stop him interrupting the other students. Mr Scott gave the boy a stern talking-to when he passed, and I hoped it would be the last of it. When he popped into my classroom later, I assumed that was what he was coming to talk about.

'Can you come and have a quick chat in my office when you've finished your lunch?' His face was grave, dark circles hung under his eyes.

All of a sudden, I found my sandwich hard to swallow.

'Uh-huh,' I nodded, and he marched down the corridor without waiting for me.

Jumping up, I straightened my blouse and brushed the crumbs from my skirt, still trying desperately to swallow but my mouth was like sandpaper. My stomach churned audibly. Was I in trouble? Had I gone too far asking the boy to sit in the corridor?

When I got to Mr Scott's office, the door was ajar, and I could see him behind the desk but knocked to be polite.

'Come in,' he said, deep frown lines etched into forehead. 'Sit down, Izzy.'

Dread wrapped itself around me like a winter blanket as I lowered myself into the chair.

'I'm sorry, I shouldn't have made Thomas sit in the corridor during the lesson. He was being difficult and disturbing the other students.'

Mr Scott waved his hand and I stopped mid-sentence.

'No, it's not that. I'm afraid I've heard something today which is extremely disconcerting. There's a lot of history here you may not have heard about. A previous English teacher got herself into a... situation.' His voice was measured, tone cautious as he wrung his hands together.

My blood turned to ice and I felt my bladder announce the need to go. The room shifted and Mr Scott's voice seemed very far away.

'The boy involved remains here at St. Wilfred's and I have received something today, most likely idle gossip, about an indiscretion between you and this boy.'

I gripped the chair, drumming and counting in quick succession. *One, two, three, four; one, two, three, four.* In my head, my voice repeated the word: *deny, deny, deny.*

I shook my head and tried to summon an expression of outrage. Wide eyes, raised brows, an open mouth, but my face wouldn't comply. My legs began to tremble as I realised my world was about to implode.

## 36

'It looks to me like you have no idea what I'm talking about, which is a relief. No complaint has been made, nothing official yet anyway,' he went on, but I interrupted him.

'I'm sorry, which boy?' Buying myself some time, my face steaming hot.

'Nicky Stevens. He's a sixth-form student.'

I shook my head slowly, as though considering the name.

'I'm afraid I don't know who you mean. I might know his face, but he's not one of my pupils. I'd recognise the name,' I lied, feeling flustered. Shit. Of course, I would know him, from the creative writing class. Did Mr Scott know that? Was I about to get caught out?

'No, he isn't in any of your classes, I've already checked. As you must appreciate, it was a scandal for the school last year, and I don't want a repeat of it. What I would like is for you to take a few days off, take the next week.' His voice was firm, and I could tell this was not up for discussion.

'But why? If there hasn't been a complaint, surely it will arouse more suspicion if I just disappear.' Jumping out of my chair, I paced the carpet. What would I say to Charlotte and David? Damn it. Why had I lied about knowing Nicky? If it came out that he was in my Creative

Writing class, I'd look guilty. Inwardly, I was kicking myself, but I'd never been good under pressure.

'Because I would like to investigate fully where this rumour has come from and get it quashed before it gains momentum. That will be easier to do if you are not on the premises. Full pay of course. I also have to notify the Board of Governors that I've got an ongoing investigation. The first thing they will ask is if I've removed you, it's safeguarding the children. You must understand?'

I couldn't think straight, my mind whirled. I wrapped my arms around myself. Unprepared for this conversation, I struggled to formulate a sentence.

'You said you received something? What was it?' My mind harping back to the start of our conversation.

'A note, anonymous in my pigeonhole. Girls overheard talking in the toilets that kind of thing.' Who would do that? Another teacher? 'I'm sorry. I know this must come as a shock and you may think I'm being overly cautious, but I'm trying to protect the reputation of the school.'

'What about my reputation?' I snapped. Although what right did I have to ask? I was guilty. I'd caused this, no one else.

'I will tell the other staff members you are unwell if that suits?'

I nodded, shoulders sagging. The fight had left me.

Mr Scott had handled the matter professionally; I couldn't fault him. He was being overly generous and could have suspended me without pay at the mere suggestion of an altercation. He hadn't even asked me if the rumour was true, which allowed me to slip away from his office without having to lie outright to his face.

When I got back to my classroom, thankful for the few extra minutes before the bell signalling the end of lunchtime, I sank into my chair. Opening the drawer and closing it again, repeatedly slamming it shut, listening to the sound echo around the room. Out of the window, children shouted and squealed, but I couldn't focus on them. What was I going to do?

The shrill bell rang out and students came piling in, bringing the cold with them. I shivered and pulled on my coat, packing my handbag to get ready to leave.

I took the register quickly and stared in a daze at the list of names, unaware of the busy chatter around me. My handbag buzzed and I checked my iPhone to find a text from Charlotte, letting me know she was going to Amy's after school so wouldn't need a lift. I wouldn't have to come back to get her and explain why I'd left early. I'd be able to talk to her tonight and prepare for the influx of questions that would come.

The second bell sounded, and the children dispersed. Matilda appeared at the door, filling the space. Her face etched with concern.

'Mr Scott's just asked me to take your afternoon class, is everything OK?'

I stood and grabbed my bag, ready to leave. 'What about tomorrow?'

'He's calling a substitute in now. Are you all right, Izzy, you look very pale?'

'Yes. Fine, listen I've got to go. I'll ring you later,' I said as I squeezed past Matilda into the corridor and rushed towards the exit.

All I could think about was who had started the rumour. Had Nicky and I been seen the last time we were together? In the park or in front of my house? Maybe there'd been another car on the roof of the car park I hadn't noticed was there? We hadn't been that careful in our meetings. Perhaps in the beginning we had, but more recently it had slipped my mind how easily we could be spotted. Was the timing significant? Maybe no one saw us at all, and Nicky was smarting about me ending things between us. What if he had started the rumour?

Inside my car, I felt little comfort and, in a rush to get off the premises, my tyres squealed in protest as I accelerated too fast out of the car park. Driving on autopilot as I made my way home past the newsagents, I stopped and reversed back at an angle onto the curb. Handing over a twenty-pound note at the counter, I requested a box of Silk Cut and was given a few coins and the cigarettes in return. Five minutes later, when I arrived home, I was relieved to see David's car wasn't there. I couldn't remember what time his afternoon meeting was.

Unlocking the door, I took my mobile straight through into the garden, shivering as the wind gusted around the side of the house. I dialled Stella's number, lighting a cigarette whilst it rang. I inhaled the smoke deep into my lungs and the familiar rush hit my head. It tasted awful and, every time I had one, I remembered why I'd quit. This time the nicotine was needed; there was no immediate stress-reliever like it.

'Hello?' Stella answered.

'It's me,' I said, my eyes already filling with tears.

'Are you OK?' Stella sounded worried and I sniffed loudly, taking another drag.

'They know, Stella. I'm so fucked!' I wailed.

'Right, start from the beginning,' Stella said, her tone calm and reassuring.

I regaled the events of last night and today, pausing to light another cigarette with the butt of my almost dead one. Stella remained quiet on the other end of the phone.

'What do you think?'

'Hang on, I'm thinking.' I heard the familiar click of a lighter and knew Stella had slipped outside to smoke too. 'I know you don't feel calm, but I don't think there's any need to panic. Not yet anyway. The headteacher seems to be on your side, he's assuming you're being dragged into this and are as much of a victim of the rumour as the school is.'

'Maybe you're right.'

'Nicky had it off with another teacher then? The one you replaced?'

'So it would seem,' I said, unable to hide the bitterness in my voice.

'Fuck.' Stella sighed.

'Yes... Fuck!' I repeated.

'Take the time off, relax. Remember, deny everything. I don't think you have anything to worry about. Who do you think made the complaint?' Stella asked.

'Well, no one has complained yet, it's just a rumour. But I have no idea who started it. Perhaps one of the students saw us together? Who knows?'

'Christ.'

'Nicky's been a shit though, he sent a naked photo to me at work and there's been times where he's been aggressive.'

'Stay away from him, Izzy. He's bad news. It's done now, over with. You have to pretend it never happened.'

I felt calmer already. Stella was fantastic at being objective in times of need.

We spent half an hour on the phone before she had to go, discussing various scenarios of how the next few days were likely to go. Even though Stella didn't think I needed to worry, adrenaline pumped through my veins regardless. My body was on high alert, fight or flight mode. Should I text Nicky to warn him? Or drive to his house after school? No, he was on his own. If I was seen it would be game over. If his phone was confiscated, all the evidence was there to make my suspension permanent.

No, I had to stay at home and hope it would blow over in the next few days. Surely Nicky would deny everything when he was summoned to Mr Scott's office.

I let the bitter cold wind whip around me as I lit my third cigarette. I should ring Matilda, but I couldn't face it, she'd still be in lessons anyway. My throat prickled, I was in desperate need of a cup of tea. I promised myself it would be my last smoke.

Deep in thought, I didn't hear the conservatory door open and my mouth was full of smoke when David stepped outside onto the patio. His face contorted as he looked first at my tear-stained face and then the cigarette in my hand.

'What's happened?'

## 37

Shoulders sagging, my eyes brimmed with tears.

David came out of the conservatory in his slippers onto the patio where I stood, arms wrapped around myself, teeth chattering.

'What's happened?' he repeated.

'I've been asked to take some time off. A rumour has been spread about me and it's got back to the head.' How far was I going to go in this admission? Had David heard my conversation with Stella?

'What about?' David mirrored my light tone, but his face was awash with worry. He hadn't seen me smoke for ages, only under times of immense stress. The last time was after the miscarriage.

'Harassment.' Telling a half-truth and letting David fill in the gaps. I took the last drag of my cigarette before flicking it onto the grass.

'Harassment of whom? A pupil?' David asked, incredulous.

I nodded.

'I'm going to take the rest of the week, its full pay, pending an investigation.' I turned to face him, rubbing my arms to fend off the cold.

'They can't sack you, surely?'

'I haven't done anything, David, so no, I doubt it. They have a duty of care to remove me from the premises when there has been any sort of accusation, even if it is a joke or a rumour. It's child protection.' I sounded like I knew what I was talking about and that seemed good enough for David as he turned to open the door back into the house, holding it for me to pass through.

'It's outrageous that's what it is,' he said, filling the kettle with water and switching it on.

'It's fine. I'm going to take a week out to relax and whilst I'm away they'll sort it out.' This seemed to appease him, and he muttered to himself as he made tea for us both.

'Why are you home early?' I asked.

'My meeting in London was cancelled, got to Victoria before they sent an email, so had a nice round trip on the train. I didn't bother going into the office as I wanted to be home for when you guys got back. How is Charlotte getting home?'

'She's gone to Amy's, so I'm sure she'll get a lift from Louise.'

I slumped at the table, inwardly feeling like I was going to combust. I was irritated David had come home early; I'd had no time to process the shock before having to act like everything was fine for his benefit. I wanted to cry, to scream into my pillow and pour myself a large glass of wine to drink whilst I sat in the bath. The bath seemed like a good idea, so I went to run one. David followed shortly after with a cup of tea. He placed it on the side and gave my shoulder a squeeze as I sat on the edge, swirling the water with my fingertips.

'I'm here if you want to talk, you know,' he said gently. It was almost too much to bear. My imperfect husband who, besides his indiscretion, was kind and caring; I'd repaid him by jeopardising everything we'd built.

I patted his hand and nodded, too afraid to speak as the lump in my throat expanded.

He left, closing the door behind him and that's when I climbed into the scalding hot bath, turned on the cold tap and sobbed beneath the sound of running water.

I spent an hour there until the tepid water made me shiver and my head throbbed. Putting on my warmest pyjamas, I joined David in the kitchen, where he was rustling up his speciality of pasta carbonara. The thought of eating made me feel sick.

I smiled weakly at David as I pulled a cigarette from the packet sitting on top of my open handbag. He raised his eyebrows at me.

'I'm just stressed that's all, it won't last!' I snapped.

I sat outside on the back step, the disgusting taste becoming all too familiar again when I heard a door slam from inside the house, followed by raised voices. Charlotte must have found out about the suspension; the news would be around the school already. I cringed at the thought.

Seconds later, Charlotte stepped out and sat beside me.

'I heard you were sacked, Mum!'

I sighed, all the crying had worn me out and even though it was late afternoon, I was ready to climb into bed and sleep for a week. 'I haven't been sacked, honey. Someone has started a rumour about me, and I can't be at school while it's investigated.'

'You're smoking?' Charlotte stood, her hands thrust on her hips. More upset by that than her mother's suspension.

'Only temporarily, it's been a bad day.'

'What was the rumour?' Thankfully Charlotte hadn't heard about the accusation and I wanted it to stay that way.

'I can't talk about it, especially with you, Charlotte, but if you hear any whispers, just ignore them. Stick with Amy and you'll be fine.' I stubbed my cigarette out in an empty pot I'd intended to plant some bulbs in.

'I won't let anyone say anything bad about you.' The show of solidarity choked me up.

Once I'd finished pushing dinner around my plate, I took myself upstairs and got into bed. I was exhausted and wanted to pull the duvet over my head and hide from the world. I spent all of Friday in my pyjamas, wandering around the house, feeling sorry for myself. David rescheduled an appointment so he could take Charlotte to school and she was going to get the bus home.

Once the house was quiet, I made myself a strong coffee and took the Motorola out of my bag and into the garden. I switched the phone on and waited for it to come to life. A minute later, no messages had come through. Pacing up and down the garden path, chewing the side of my cheek, I felt incensed there'd been no messages from Nicky. He must have heard what was going on by now. Why would he not have tried to get in touch? Had he hung me out to dry? Or could he have been the one that delivered the anonymous tip? To get back at me?

Unable to relax, I spent the day on edge. Was he was going to turn up at my door? The bell never rang and neither did the phone. I felt alone and resorted to trying to read in bed in an attempt to distract me for a while. When that didn't work, I rang Stella, but it went to voice-mail. I did some ironing and ran a bath to soak in, getting out when a text came through from Charlotte to say she would be getting a lift home about half four. I busied myself making a marinade for dinner and it wasn't long before everyone arrived home.

'Did you have a nice relaxing day?' David asked as I passed him a plate of barbeque chicken and new potatoes.

'No not really, it was quiet.'

'Perhaps we should go away for the weekend?' he suggested.

'I have plans,' Charlotte piped up.

'Who with?' David asked.

'Amy of course.'

'Oh well, it was a nice idea, I guess.' David squeezed my hand.

'I think I'll go for a swim. Hey, we could go to the cinema and get a takeaway Saturday night?' I offered, perking up at the idea of getting out of the house.

'Sounds great, I'm in,' David said. I ignored Charlotte rolling her eyes at us.

David was by my side continuously all weekend, trying to lift my spirits and, as planned, we went to the cinema to see a gentle film called *Aeronauts* which distracted me from my thoughts for a couple of hours. An extra hour in bed as the clocks went back meant a long lay-in on Sunday morning in which I managed to finish my book.

I tried to keep myself busy and the following week came and went.

I swam every day and visited the library, making sure I got out of the house to prevent myself from going stir-crazy. Stella rang every evening to see how I was and if there had been any developments, but I had nothing to tell her. Neither the school nor Nicky had been in touch. I felt isolated and hated not knowing what the future held.

Charlotte spent much of the time out of the house, at school and at Amy's, not returning until the early evening. Trying to get anything out of her was like getting blood out of a stone. I wasn't sure if she was embarrassed or whether she was getting stick at school. She didn't want me to pick her up or take her if she could get around it. I tried to broach the subject but receiving two-word answers as she retreated to her room became the norm.

David muttered something about the teenage years and constant mood swings being upon us and I had to agree.

A surprise delivery of a beautiful winter bouquet arrived from Susan and Matilda on Wednesday. The card read: *Chin up chick, see you next week.*

I could see the flowers made David visibly relax as if with them, the delivery man had carried a confirmation of my innocence. I left a message on Matilda's answering machine to thank them both for the gift. She called me later in the day and I admitted why Mr Scott had asked me to stay at home, although I had the feeling she already knew. It was nice to hear her outrage on my behalf, and she urged me to enjoy the rest of the week, but by Saturday I was bored stiff. The house was spotless, and I couldn't take any more daytime television.

I invited my parents for Sunday lunch and Dad drove them both over at around eleven that morning. I squeezed Mum hard when she arrived, wrapping my arms around her before she'd even had time to take her boots off, feeling guilty I hadn't seen her in weeks and seeking comfort only a mother can provide. She held me at arm's length, looking me up and down.

'Izzy, you're practically skin and bone. Are you all right? Has the move been stressful?'

I replied I was fine and glossed over the comment, whisking my parents around the house for the tour. They loved it, just like Stella had.

After a cup of tea, Dad and David went to take a look at the butler sink, Dad having found something in his shed he thought might work on the stains. Mum and I chatted about what we'd been up to, as I peeled potatoes and she helped me with the vegetables. Charlotte told her grandparents over lunch about Amy and St. Wilfred's, explaining her position on the netball team. They didn't leave until four to make the journey back to Dorking. Their visit had been a lovely distraction from my worries about school. I was glad no one had brought up the subject of me being off, I didn't want to have to explain to my mum that I'd been suspended, and especially why.

There had been no contact from Nicky. I'd charged up the Motorola and left it on all week, switched onto silent at the bottom of my handbag. The battery life on old phones was phenomenal in comparison to smartphones today, but every time I looked there had been no texts. It hit me almost as hard as the allegation itself. Why, if he cared about me so much, had he not been in touch?

Had he taken what he'd wanted, and I'd been kicked to the curb? *Don't be ridiculous, Izzy, you ended it remember. Why would he come knocking?* My inner voice wouldn't let it lie. Perhaps he was looking out for me and was afraid to jeopardise the outcome of the investigation. Either way, I was bitterly disappointed by the lack of contact. I was also a little surprised Mr Scott hadn't been in touch and was unsure whether I was supposed to go into school on Monday morning. Would I be allowed on the premises? The thought of going back made my stomach flip.

Discussing it with David as we dried the dishes, we decided I should remain at home until asked to return. I was being paid after all and, with the insinuated harassment complaint, David said I should be more indignant about the whole thing. Perhaps I wasn't acting as outraged as I should have been, but I had no fight left. I didn't have the energy to pretend.

As David predicted, Mr Scott rang my mobile at lunchtime on Monday and I stepped out into the garden to light the last cigarette I'd been deliberately saving for the call I was dreading.

## 38

'Hello?' I answered, my voice quivering slightly.

'Hi Izzy, it's Steven. How are you?' He sounded relaxed, his tone upbeat, which was a positive sign.

'I'm OK, how are you?'

'Good thanks. I've looked into the complaint and, on the limited information I've had, there's been no evidence to support the rumour. No one has come forward to offer further information and Nicky Stevens denies involvement. On that basis, I'm happy to put it to bed and for you to return to school tomorrow.'

Inwardly, I jumped for joy. A huge weight had lifted to hear Nicky had come through for me. Perhaps I'd judged him too harshly.

'Great. I'm looking forward to getting back to work,' I replied, sinking to the step and flicking the ash of my cigarette.

'I'm so sorry about all of this, Izzy, we'll talk about it more when I see you of course, but because of a similar situation last year, I have to look into everything, however small. Moving forward, I would make sure you have no unnecessary contact with Nicky Stevens, to avoid any continuation of the rumour. Although I'm sure it won't be an issue as you don't have him in your lessons.'

'Of course,' I agreed, my voice strained. Surely Nicky wouldn't come to the creative writing class now?

'OK great, well, I'll see you tomorrow then.'

'Thanks Steven, goodbye.' I hung up and sucked furiously on my cigarette, feeling the relief flow through my body. I'd been wound like a coil, but now the whole thing was going to go away. I'd be able to move on, finally.

Tears erupted and there was nothing I could do to stop them rolling down my cheeks. My shoulders eased down. I'd been given a second chance at a new start.

I smoked the cigarette to the butt and wished I had more; something told me this habit was going to be difficult to kick again. What the hell, I could do with some fresh air anyway. I'd been a virtual recluse since the suspension and needed to blow the cobwebs away. I put on my thick coat and boots. The temperature seemed to have plummeted since we'd reached November. Only seven more weeks or so of the school year left and Christmas would be upon us. It would be a quiet affair as the move had ploughed into our savings. Being holed up with David and Charlotte seemed heavenly right now. Perhaps we could go to Mum and Dad's? Or invite them to us. I'd mention it to Mum when I next spoke to her.

I grabbed my keys and headed out into the street; the closest shop was about a fifteen-minute walk away and I knew I could grab a bottle of Prosecco to go with dinner. I had no idea what we were having, something from the freezer would do. I had a spring in my step, feeling lighter for the first time in a week. There was no need to look over my shoulder any more. Nicky and I were finished. No more sneaking around. No more lies. Perhaps it was time to get rid of the Motorola too? Though, I figured I'd better keep it for a little while longer, just in case. Better than Nicky turning up at my door trying to get hold of me.

I bought Prosecco and cigarettes, not waiting until I got home to smoke one. On the walk back, I called David to tell him the good news and then spoke to Stella briefly, who made me laugh as she said she would have told them to stick their job up their arse. She didn't mince her words for anyone; it never failed to make me smile.

Later, Charlotte turned her nose up at my offering of fish fingers.

'Mum,' she groaned, but eventually, realising it was a fight she wouldn't win, she began to eat.

'I'll be back at school tomorrow,' I announced, joining David and Charlotte at the table.

'Let's hope that headteacher of yours grovels tomorrow,' David replied.

Charlotte raised her eyebrows.

'How was school today?' I asked, concerned she may have been teased because of my absence.

'Fine. I've stuck with Amy, like you said.' The last thing I wanted was to drag everyone into the mess I'd created.

'Charlotte, what is that on your neck?' A greenish bruise that looked suspiciously like a love bite was partly visible above her collar. She tugged at her school shirt, neck lowering into her shoulders like a tortoise until it was out of sight.

'Nothing, Mum, it's just a spot.'

I glared at David who was oblivious. That mark didn't look like a spot to me, but I could see her reluctance to talk about it at the dinner table, perhaps because her father sat opposite her.

Charlotte ate her dinner quickly and hurried back upstairs. I made a mental note to keep a closer eye on her at school. It wasn't such a big deal, teenagers coming home with love bites. It was something every one did at some stage, but it was what it led to that concerned me.

That evening, I spent half an hour on the phone to Stella, having more time to talk than she did earlier.

'Have you heard anything from Nicky?' she asked, once certain I was alone.

'No, he's been as quiet as a mouse.'

'Looks like you've had a lucky escape,' she replied. I believed that too and felt relieved it was over, glad we wouldn't have to talk about him any more.

'All OK with you? Things with Adam still going well?'

'A little too well... I'm going to meet his parents at the weekend,' Stella squeaked, the apprehension in her voice apparent.

'That's fantastic, well, make sure you behave.'

I joined David afterwards in the lounge, where we watched mindless television, sitting side by side on the same sofa instead of us having our own as we normally did. Sharing the bottle of Prosecco I'd bought earlier, we toasted to new beginnings. Stella was right, I felt I'd dodged a bullet in terms of my affair still being a secret. It wasn't fair to throw David under the bus for his. When we went to bed, we made love, more passionate than we'd been for a while, something which had been lost a little over the years together.

Waking on Tuesday morning still wrapped around each other was unheard of and we laughed like teenagers as we got ready for work. I wanted the demurest outfit I could find, so chose navy tapered trousers and a dusky pink blouse. Smart, with no skin on show. I wanted to look like the least likely teacher to be having an affair with one of my pupils. But however I dressed, I couldn't shake the feeling everyone was going to be looking at me.

I was sure it was paranoia, but from the minute I walked through the double doors into the school, it seemed like I attracted the stares of onlookers.

I did my best to shrug it off and engaged my form to tell me what I'd missed since I'd been away. Apparently, they didn't like having a substitute teacher cover for me as she made them sit and read their textbooks quietly until the bell rang.

The first couple of lessons ran fine, with no awkward questions to field. By the time lunchtime came, I couldn't wait to get into the staffroom to see Matilda and Susan and thank them again for the beautiful flowers. I held my head high as I entered, reminding myself that, for all intents and purposes, I had done nothing wrong and I was the aggrieved party. They were already seated, and I squeezed in beside Matilda, placing my lunch box on the table in front of us.

'Thank you so much again for my flowers,' I whispered.

'You're welcome, are you OK? I'm so glad you're back,' Matilda said, reaching over and patting my hand.

'We were worried, and to think we were only talking about it a couple of days before. The problem is, everyone is so hypersensitive now since the last time,' Susan said, leaning forward, keeping her voice low.

'Who was the boy in question?' Matilda asked and I felt myself sit bolt upright. They didn't know? Perhaps it wasn't around the school like I thought it had been. Maybe Mr Scott had managed to keep it contained.

'I'm... I'm not supposed to say,' I stammered.

Susan nudged Matilda's arm reproachfully.

'Ah well, it's done now,' Matilda sighed.

'Yes, over and done with. It's not gone on record, so technically no harm done,' I said, not wanting to make a big deal of it.

'God, I'd be shouting from the rooftops, Izzy. You're too nice. I'd be making a right fuss, compensation, the lot,' Matilda stuck out her chest, reminding me of a pigeon on the prowl. I wasn't sure if she was joking or not.

The rest of the day was uneventful, and I managed to forget I'd been the centre of the latest scandal. I offered to be the monitor for break time so I could get some air, but hardly any of the pupils gave me a second glance. Nicky was nowhere to be seen. Perhaps Mr Scott had asked him to leave? I had no idea and I couldn't ask anybody as I wasn't meant to know him at all, but it was for the best, this way we could both get a fresh start.

I parked my car on the driveway later, relieved to be home. I'd been dreading returning to school, worried I would receive a hostile reception, but had been pleasantly surprised by the support from Matilda and Susan. Mr Scott had popped in to see me as I was packing up and getting ready to leave. He'd thanked me for my patience and understanding in what I could see had clearly been a stressful time for him as well. This made my insides knot together, knowing I'd caused it. I'd repay him in hard work and exam results, which seemed to be all the governing bodies cared about these days. As a result, I was late to leave school; Charlotte had text to say she was getting a lift.

Pushing open the front door, I heard voices coming from the kitchen, it must be David and Charlotte. I was amazed she hadn't shut herself away in her room. Dumping my keys on the console table by the door, I slipped off my shoes and padded towards the kitchen. I was two steps away when I heard a familiar voice. Unable to register it initially, I walked into the kitchen to see Nicky leaning against my fridge with a can of Coke in his hand and an ingenuous grin on his face.

## 39

My mouth dropped open and my body solidified, leaving me unable to move.

'Hi Mum,' Charlotte sang, not noticing the look of terror etched on my face.

I recovered quickly, wide eyes meeting Nicky's as his narrowed, just for a second, before his smile returned and he took a tiny step towards me.

'Hiya,' he said, lifting his hand in a kind of wave.

I moved back, turning my body away from him to put my handbag on the worktop, using the few seconds to recover myself as I tried to work out what was going on. I looked first at Charlotte and then David, who'd I remembered telling me in bed this morning that he was working from home. Everyone was smiling and seemed at ease.

Was I going mad? What the hell was he doing here? The roller-coaster of emotions meant I was struggling to speak. I shivered, icy fingers caressing my back.

'Hello,' I managed.

'Nicky gave me a lift home,' Charlotte piped up, pleased with herself.

'I was hoping to take Charlotte to the fireworks tomorrow, if that would be all right with you both?' His voice was sugary sweet. He had David sucked in for sure, I could tell by his appraising smile.

My head began to spin, and I steadied myself with a hand on the worktop as I counted slowly in my head. I couldn't allow this to happen, but before I could protest David spoke.

'Sure, I don't see why not. Charlotte has to be home by nine thirty though,' he said, and Charlotte beamed from ear to ear. Her father had just made her year.

I wanted to scream and inwardly I was, but everything was happening so fast, I couldn't process the information quick enough to act on it. Nicky was here, in my kitchen, talking to my husband and asking to take my daughter out. The idea was so ridiculous, I couldn't get my head around it. Adrenaline shot around my system like a rocket and I pulled myself up straight, about to let him have it.

'I'd better be off, I've got homework to do,' Nicky said, eyeing me curiously before strolling towards the door.

Charlotte followed behind him like a lost puppy.

'Nice to see you again,' he said, turning back to look over his shoulder.

I glared at him, ignoring David's quizzical look at my lack of response.

'You too, Nicky,' he called after them. They stepped outside together, Charlotte pulling the door closed behind her.

'Where is she going?' I dashed down the hallway, desperate to keep Charlotte where I could see her.

'Saying goodbye that's all, she'll be back in a minute. What's got into you?' David wrapped his arm around my waist. 'He seems nice, don't you think? Good of him to come and ask if he could take her out.'

I shot him an incredulous look. If he only knew.

'He's too old for her, David. He's eighteen, you do realise that, don't you?' I snapped, hoping if I played it that way, perhaps he'd feel more protective over his only daughter.

'She's growing up, Izzy, she'll be sixteen in a couple of months, whether we like it or not.' David seemed surprised I was making a big deal out of it.

I grabbed the packet of cigarettes out of my bag I'd bought on the way home and headed for the conservatory door.

'I thought you quit?' he called after me, irritated to see I was still smoking. I didn't bother answering.

Lighting the cigarette, I paced around the patio, straining to hear any voices coming from the front of the house. What was Nicky playing at? It had to be about us, about me. He was punishing me for ending the affair. Showing he could have whatever he wanted and there was nothing I could do about it.

We were supposed to be keeping our distance. No unnecessary contact, Mr Scott said. Well, this was bloody unnecessary. What was I supposed to do? Charlotte obviously didn't know that Nicky was the other party in the harassment claim. David didn't know either and I didn't want to tell him. I couldn't risk making him suspicious.

One thing was for sure, Charlotte wouldn't be going to the fireworks with Nicky or anywhere else. I had to talk to him, perhaps I'd be able to convince him to leave her alone. I could see she was already smitten, all doe-eyed around him. I could hardly blame her for failing victim to his charm, he'd won me round too but now I knew he was dangerous and unpredictable. Had he been the one to give her the love bite? The thought made bile rise up in my throat, to think he'd had his hands on my daughter.

My head whirled, but I needed to keep calm, carrying on the way I had just now would be foolish. David would soon suspect something was wrong.

When I went back into the house, Charlotte still hadn't returned, and I forced myself to not to go and look out of the window to see what was going on. Instead I wrapped my arms around David's waist, pressing my face into his back as he stirred something in the slow cooker.

'You stink,' he said, patting my arm.

'I know, I think I may have to quit again.'

'Hmmm, I think so,' he agreed.

'Sorry I overreacted; I just wasn't expecting it. She's our baby,' I whispered into David's back.

'Well, she's going to start having boyfriends, she's getting to that age. It's something we've got to get used to.'

'Smells good, what is it?' I asked, changing the subject, amazed at how domesticated my husband could be when he wanted.

'Teriyaki pork. I thought I'd give it a bash and threw it in the slow cooker at lunchtime.'

'So talented,' I said, giving him a playful squeeze before turning back to my bag. I replaced my cigarettes and rummaged for the Motorola, slipping it into my pocket as I heard the front door close.

Charlotte wandered back in to the kitchen, a dreamy look on her face.

David turned around as he heard her come in.

'Think she's in love?' he teased.

Charlotte turned pink and sat at the table, retrieving books from her school bag.

'Is he your boyfriend now?' I asked, unable to keep my voice from sounding incredulous.

Charlotte scowled at me and shrugged.

'He's a bit old for you, honey.'

'Not that old, Mum, he's eighteen, I'm almost sixteen,' Charlotte protested, instantly on the defensive. I could tell she'd expected this kind of objection, but perhaps more from her father than her mother.

'I'm not sure I like it,' I said stiffly, knowing full well I didn't. He'd pursued two teachers and likely knocked up a girl in Charlotte's year. Did she have any knowledge of Amelia's pregnancy? I couldn't ask as it was confidential information.

'You don't have to like it,' Charlotte retorted indignantly before grabbing her bag and storming up the stairs.

David rolled his eyes at me. I made to follow her, but he interrupted.

'Leave her be, hon.'

'I'm going to get changed,' I snapped.

I took the stairs two at a time and closed my bedroom door to put on some comfy clothes. I sat on the bed retrieving the phone from my trouser pocket before slipping them off. There was some battery left, but still no texts or calls from Nicky. I punched the keys hard, my anger rising again.

Stay away from my daughter

I hit send and waited, but a couple of minutes later there was no reply. Once I'd slipped on some leggings and removed my make-up, I checked again, but still nothing. I balled my hands into fists and paced. Nicky was infuriating and I was determined to catch him the following day at school. He had to call off their date. I couldn't have him corrupting my daughter. Charlotte was too sweet, too innocent, to be chewed up and spat out by him.

I stewed on it all night. I had a feeling in the pit of my stomach things were going to get worse. I couldn't shake it off.

On Wednesday morning, I woke as though I was on a mission. Finding Nicky had consumed my thoughts as David slept beside me. Blood boiled in my veins, keeping me awake late into the night. Eventually I'd passed out, waking up tired but motivated to shut down Nicky's attempt to destabilise our family.

I tried to engage with Charlotte over breakfast and on the drive to school, but she wasn't giving anything away. I had the distinct impression something had been going on between them before now and felt stupid for not realising it sooner.

I could tell Charlotte thought I was trying to rain on her parade. When I said I was worried about the age difference, that older boys expected more, Charlotte sank into her seat. I knew I wasn't going to get anywhere, there was no way she was going to walk away from Nicky. I had to hope I could convince him to call it off. Either that or wait until he got bored and dumped her. It made my heart sink. There was no doubt Charlotte was going to get hurt if I didn't stop it before it started.

At first break, I wandered around looking for Nicky but couldn't find him. During lunchtime, I walked the perimeter again. Slower this time, paying attention to every corner, but I didn't have to look too hard. I found him sat on a bench, watching his teammates play football. He only looked up when I was right beside him.

'Oh, hey Miss,' he said dismissively, turning back to the football.

I gritted my teeth. Cocky little shit.

Keeping my voice low, I leaned in. 'Call off tonight.' It was an order not a request.

He turned to look at me, using his hand to shield his eyes from the afternoon sun.

'Why would I want to do that, Mrs Cole?' His blue eyes squinted, a smirk beginning to form.

I crossed my arms, tucking my hands in to stop myself from slapping him around the face. I smiled tightly, so anyone looking would think we were having a pleasant exchange.

'Just do it,' I hissed.

He tutted. 'I don't think we should be seen together like this, do you? I think you'd better go, Miss.' He smiled sweetly and I turned on my heels and marched away. I felt my blood begin to boil; he was right. The two of us seen together would give weight to the accusation against me. As well as the fact that Mr Scott had advised me to steer clear.

## 40

I got back to my desk, all the time grinding my teeth. I tried to keep calm by counting, but nothing worked. I opened and shut my bag so many times, the zip broke and I swore loudly. My anxiety hadn't been too bad lately, but now my hands trembled. Fire burned in the pit of my belly, continuing after break concluded. I couldn't dwell on it, I had to settle my year-eight class into deconstructing one of Shakespeare's sonnets. I wandered around each table, assisting where necessary, but my mind was elsewhere.

Nicky had been so nonchalant, and I had played right into his hands. His intention was to wind me up and I'd let him. I imagined him laughing at me behind my back. Had he told his friends too? There was no way I could stand by and let him take my daughter out. What if he forced himself on her? Had he been the one to get Amelia pregnant or was that just gossip? I had to hope he'd take my advice and call it off. What would my next move be if he didn't? Did he want me to beg? There were no limits to what I would do to protect my daughter.

It continued to play on my mind as I drove home. I fidgeted in my seat and received monosyllables instead of sentences from Charlotte when I tried to broach the subject. I'd been stupid to make my feelings about Nicky known. I had to get her back on side.

'Want me to straighten your hair for you tonight?' I offered and, although Charlotte politely refused, she did soften a little.

She disappeared upstairs when we got home. When I went up, twenty minutes later, she had on a checked shirt, skinny jeans and boots, with a small amount of make-up. She looked beautiful and under any other circumstances I would have felt happy for her, but when the doorbell rang at half past four, my heart leapt into my throat. I slipped into the front room to peak out of the window, letting David, who'd walked in five minutes previously, answer the door. Perhaps if Nicky realised he wasn't getting a rise out of me, he'd soon get bored and leave Charlotte alone.

'Hi, Mr Cole.' Nicky remained on the step, like a vampire unable to cross the threshold.

'Call me David please.'

Charlotte rushed down the stairs, grabbing her coat from the bannister.

'I won't be late,' she said as she whizzed past.

'Drive safely,' David called after them before closing the door.

I saw them walk out on to the road. Nicky looked smart in his brown leather jacket; he'd made an effort. I bit my lip, caught in a mix of hatred and jealousy, turning away from the window.

Perhaps once he'd taken her out that would be it. He would have made his point and he would move on. I'd be there to pick up the pieces if Charlotte needed me to. Kids fell in love so quickly at this age and first love was always the hardest to hit.

I couldn't concentrate on the television after dinner, checking my watch every ten minutes from eight o'clock onwards. Where were they? Had he parked somewhere? Or taken her to the lake? Somewhere we used to go together?

'Relax,' David said, shaking his head at my fidgeting. He assumed I was reacting badly to Charlotte having a boyfriend. The whole situation made me squirm. Nicky touching Charlotte the same way he touched me made me want to vomit.

I ignored him, going upstairs to keep a vigil at our bedroom window, where there was a full view of the street below. If I kept the light off, I wouldn't be seen staring out.

At nine, Nicky parked up, walking around to open Charlotte's door for her to get out.

'Nice touch,' I muttered bitterly under my breath as I stepped back from the window to ensure I couldn't be seen. He took Charlotte by the hand and pulled her towards him. I watched them kiss as they held hands. He was pretending to be the perfect gentleman, but I knew better. They got in range of the sensor and the outside light beamed against the front door, forcing them to pull apart. I watched Charlotte giggle, my heart shrinking in my chest.

I heard the key in the door and moved into our en suite, locking the door behind me. I could hear muffled voices in the hallway and Charlotte's footsteps on the stairs before her bedroom door creaked as it closed. I took off my make-up and cleaned my teeth, settling on the duvet and leafing through my book. A pointless exercise, I couldn't concentrate on the words and spent most of the night tossing and turning even when David came to bed.

Throughout the course of the following week, Nicky took Charlotte out three times. Always bringing her back on time and spending a few minutes to talk to David, who, irritatingly, had taken a shine to him. I couldn't deny it, Nicky was charming, and he had a way with words. David thought he was a nice young man and admitted he was happy Charlotte was dating him, compared to whom she could have brought home. He kept pushing me to be friendlier, but I couldn't do it. I found it easier to avoid all contact with Nicky wherever possible.

How could I look at Charlotte and her new boyfriend when weeks before I'd been in his bed? The whole situation was impossible, but I felt powerless to stop it. Nicky hadn't been in touch at all. I hadn't seen him in the playground, and he hadn't attended the last two creative writing classes. David worked late that Friday evening, and Charlotte was out with Nicky again, bowling this time apparently. I took the opportunity of an empty house to ring Stella, filling her in on recent events. She couldn't believe the audacity of Nicky but agreed that if I intervened, I risked pushing Charlotte further towards him. It was something I'd have to ride out.

I threw myself into my lesson planning and tried to swim as often as I could after school, anything to distract myself. Charlotte was hardly home and when she was, she didn't talk much. I tried not to think about what Nicky and Charlotte got up to when they were alone together. I knew Charlotte was a sensible girl, but it had been about two years since we'd had the talk about safe sex and making sure you love the person before you jump into anything.

That was the problem, I knew how easy it was to fall for Nicky. He was all she talked about whenever she came out of her room. Her physical appearance suddenly became of the utmost importance. Clothes became tighter and skirts slightly shorter, not so much as to cause concern with David yet, but I had noticed. Amy had taken a back seat and now it was Nicky waiting for her in the morning at the gate when we arrived. I'd watch them hold hands in the playground and feel the acid swirl in my chest. I tried to ignore the smirk he'd give me when Charlotte wasn't looking.

I prayed Nicky genuinely felt the same way about Charlotte and would look after her. Until she came home in tears, I couldn't intervene. For now, I was stuck on the side-lines. I could do with a weekend at Stella's in Nottingham, to get away from it all, but I couldn't book anything, I had to be here. A bird protecting my nest.

I cajoled Matilda and Susan into visiting my local pub on Saturday night for a few glasses of wine. I was desperate to get out and fancied a drink, so we settled in a corner of the Bell & Whistle, an old-style village pub with oak beams and a log fire.

'Do you ever get sick of them?' I asked Matilda and Susan, already on my second glass of Sauvignon Blanc, even though it was still early.

'Who?' Matilda asked.

'Sick of children,' I blurted, and we laughed.

'Every day,' Susan said wistfully. It was common knowledge she was desperate to retire.

'Is everything OK? Matilda jumped in, referring to my suspension a couple of weeks ago.

'Yes fine, that's all fine. Just motherhood is driving me mad.' I proceeded to tell them Charlotte had an older boyfriend and I was finding it difficult to adjust to the idea. I didn't tell them who he was or that he attended the school and thankfully they didn't ask. The advice they gave me was pretty much the same as Stella. However, it felt good to talk about it again. To get things off my chest.

We stayed until last orders and Matilda and Susan ordered a taxi. They offered to drop me off, but I declined, they were going in the opposite direction and it was no longer raining. It would be quicker for me to walk, I lived so close.

We said our goodbyes outside the pub before they climbed into the car. I walked down the street, glad to be out in the fresh air. At home, the atmosphere seemed oppressive, although I knew it was me that had created it. I felt unable to relax, wondering if Nicky was going to show up.

Turning the corner into my street, only two minutes away from home, I shoved my hands into my pockets to keep them warm. The streets were quiet and as I walked, I thought I could hear another set of footsteps fall in time with mine. Behind, but not too close. I sped up, counting the door numbers as I walked by.

*It'll be fine, I'm only a few houses away.*

Every fibre of my being told me to run as I heard the footsteps gaining on me, the thudding of heavy shoes on concrete echoing around the quiet lane.

# 41

The back of my neck prickled, tiny hairs standing to attention, alert to the danger I was in. Droplets of rain began to fall, peppering the ground in front on me. The street lights seemed too dim to be of any use. My chest shook from the banging of my heart against its cage. I was desperate to look behind me, but too terrified to do so. My fingers gripped the keys in my pocket, ready to pull them out. They were all I had to defend myself.

At last I saw the house; the hallway light had been left on, but the rest of the house was in darkness. David was in bed. All I could hear was the sound of my heart thudding in my ears. Breathing shallow, I imagined being seconds away from home and safety, before being attacked in the street.

Rushing onto the drive, I reached my front door and spun around. Keys wedged through my fingers, ready to fight.

The driveway was empty. I panted, trying to catch my breath, edging backwards until my shoulder connected with the door, reluctant to turn away. Fearing if I did, someone would launch at me from the darkness. There was no one there, but I hadn't imagined it. Someone had been behind me, getting closer and closer. Perhaps they didn't know I lived so close by and were deterred when I turned into the driveway?

I fumbled with my key in the door, going by touch as I looked over my shoulder out onto the dark street. I'd had seen one too many horror movies to know it would be an error to look away.

'You all right, Izzy?'

The voice made me jump and I saw Mary, my neighbour, putting some rubbish in the recycling bin.

My shoulders sagged and I managed a weak smile.

'Yes, fine thanks, Mary, couldn't find my key,' I lied.

'Night, love,' she called and went back inside.

I slotted the key in correctly and turned it, pushing open the door. Inside, the house was dark and still. I turned on all the lights downstairs, but it gave me little comfort.

To calm my nerves, I sat on the kitchen worktop and smoked a cigarette, leaning towards the open window, the alcohol having left my system. Fear made you sober up pretty quickly.

I knew I wouldn't be able to sleep, I was far too wired. My handbag vibrated making me jump and I snatched it, retrieving the Motorola that had been silent for so long. A text from Nicky waited for me. I opened it and shuddered.

You looked nice tonight

I threw the phone and it clattered onto the worktop. I cringed at the noise, hoping it hadn't woken my family sleeping upstairs. Hands shaking, I lit another cigarette and pushed the window open further. I'd have to light a candle to get rid of the smell, but I didn't care. Had it been Nicky behind me in the street? Or had he seen me at the pub? He hadn't been with Charlotte. David had dropped her around Amy's at lunchtime and Louise had brought her home after dinner.

My skin crawled, and goosebumps crept up my arms and across my back. I had no idea what sort of game he was playing. I wasn't going to respond. I didn't want to talk to Nicky or engage with him in any way. Not while he held all the cards.

I waited a while until I felt calmer and the smell of cigarettes had diminished before retiring to bed.

I didn't sleep a wink. It felt like days since I'd had a good night's sleep.

When morning came, I rolled over, rubbing my stinging eyes, pulling the cover back over my head as the bedroom door opened.

'Morning,' David said brightly.

I grunted from beneath the duvet. I heard him place a cup on the bedside table. My mouth was dry, and I needed caffeine desperately.

'Hungover?' he asked, slowly drawing the cover back, smiling at me pitifully.

'Yep,' I groaned. My hangover was mild, but I felt like I could sleep for a week.

'Well, I hope you'll be hungry later. Roast beef today, with help from my apprentice.' He smiled. David cooked a lovely roast dinner. My forte was the Yorkshires and potatoes, but he had a way with meat, always able to cook it so it was melt-in-the-mouth tender.

'What's the occasion?' I asked, shuffling up the bed and taking a sip of my tea which was frustratingly hot.

'Nicky's coming for Sunday lunch.'

I swallowed the hot liquid, scorching my throat, and coughed.

'I hope you don't mind? Charlotte asked, and I thought it would be nice. He's coming over around midday, I think,' David continued.

My mood plummeted like a ton of bricks; this wasn't something I wanted to face today. Not after last night; not after the text. What had it meant anyway? Was it a poor attempt at flirting or was he letting me know he was watching? Either way, it wasn't good, and I worried that it might have been him following me last night. Would he have hurt me? Or did he only mean to scare me?

'Come on, you can smile your way through one meal, can't you?' David grimaced, frustrated at my lack of response.

'Sure.' I smiled.

He left and I continued to drink my tea, scalding my mouth. There was only one way to get through today and it was to pretend everything was fine, plaster a smile on my face and be polite.

I threw off the covers and jumped straight in the shower. The hot water eased away my stress and once dressed, with hair and make-up done, I felt better. My smile would be my armour.

David wolf-whistled when he saw me, peeling potatoes over the sink. I snorted and put my apron over my head, to get started on the vegetables.

'I think I'll invite handsome young men to dinner every week,' David said, chuckling to himself.

I didn't respond, my jaw tightened and inwardly I cringed.

'I think I'll make a cheesecake, I've got the ingredients,' I said, changing the subject.

When everything was prepared, and the beef in the oven, David made coffee for both of us and we perused the Sunday papers in the conservatory.

At midday on the dot, there was a knock on the door and Charlotte flew down the stairs to open it. They came through to the kitchen briefly to say hello before Charlotte dragged Nicky away to her room. The exchange between us had been pleasant but robotic. I smiled tightly, fixing him with a hard stare, trying to figure out if he was the one who'd followed me last night. He barely flinched, giving nothing away.

'Do you not mind him being up there?' I asked David as I laid the table. The thought of them alone together made the lump in my throat hard to swallow but I guess it was better here, under my roof and within easy reach.

'I've told her to keep the door open.' He winked.

I wasn't sure what sort of deterrent that would be, it wouldn't have stopped me when I was the same age.

Before long, David was serving dinner and I climbed the stairs as quietly as I could. The top faced Charlotte's room and her door was open. Nicky was sat on the floor looking through Charlotte's CD collection and Charlotte was laying on her bed reading the album insert of Pink Floyd's The Wall.

'Dinner's ready,' I called from the top stair and turned to head back down.

Minutes later, we were all seated, but I was struggling to relax. Nicky sat directly opposite me on purpose, waiting until I chose a seat before joining the table. I could feel his eyes burning into me.

'Can I get you a drink, Nicky?' I asked in a voice that didn't particularly sound like my own.

'Yes please, anything is fine. Thanks.'

I got up and grabbed a can of Diet Coke from the fridge, pouring it into a glass and returning back to the table.

He smiled, locking eyes with mine. His twinkled, and a mischievous grin emerged for a second. I felt like I'd been kicked in the ribs.

David made conversation with Nicky and Charlotte, asking them about the fireworks last week and what movies they'd been to see. I didn't pay attention, trying to zone out, tucking into my dinner and stopping every couple of bites to sip some of my wine.

When I looked up, I saw Nicky was smiling at me. My eyes darted around the table. David and Charlotte were both looking at me expectantly. I slowly chewed, finishing my mouthful and feeling my cheeks flush.

'What did I miss?' I said, taking another sip of wine.

Nicky glanced at my trembling hand.

'I asked if the creative writing class was still running?' he said, a gleam in his eye.

I bit my lip. 'Yes, it is,' I replied before turning to Charlotte, diverting the attention away. 'Charlotte, I think at one point you thought about coming, didn't you?'

She opened her mouth to speak, but Nicky interrupted.

'One of the guys I play football with goes, he said it's been really enlightening. You've taught him a lot. He said he's been able to expand on the skills he already had, learn new tricks.'

I felt the room swim momentarily. Bile burned in my throat. *Please, Nicky, not here, not now.*

David nodded approvingly, raising an eyebrow.

I glared at Nicky as he winked at me across the table and was lucky not to be seen. I pressed my nails into my palms. Counting in my head. This was a game to him. He was playing a game with my life for his own amusement. How had I been so stupid to get involved with him?

Something brushed my foot and I jerked my leg back.

'Do you live with your parents?' David asked.

Nicky squirmed at the question, shifting uncomfortably in his seat.

'Just my mum,' he said, trying to sound nonchalant.

'Oh really, is your dad not around?' I asked, my tone light and inno- cent. I propped my chin on my hand, staring at Nicky. The spotlight was now on him. I saw his jaw clench.

'He walked out a few years back,' Nicky replied with a shrug of the shoulders, although I could see his bravado was fading.

'That's awful, I'm sorry to hear that. How come?' I pushed.

'Mum,' Charlotte protested and the atmosphere at the table changed.

David patted my hand and I leaned back in my seat.

'Sorry, sorry,' I said, although I wasn't. 'I didn't mean to pry.'

'He used to beat my mum until one day I stepped in,' Nicky growled, his knuckles white around his fork. Seeing it tremble, he set it down before picking up his glass to take a sip.

'Men who bully women are cowards,' I said before standing and turning to clear my plate.

I felt like I'd won a small victory and grinned, unseen, from the dinner table. It was then I heard the shattering of glass and Charlotte's high-pitched scream.

## 42

I spun around, terrified at what I was going to see. Had Nicky lost his temper and started throwing glasses around?

Charlotte was leaning over him, wrapping his bleeding hand in a napkin. He looked directly at me. A pointed glare and laughed coldly.

'Sorry, Mrs Cole, I don't seem to know my own strength!'

David was mopping the Coke which had spilt all over the table and I carefully collected what remained of Nicky's glass from the tablecloth.

'It's these bloody dishwashers, they weaken the glass, you know,' David scowled.

'Come and wash your hand,' I said, wrapping the broken glass in newspaper and throwing it in the bin.

Nicky joined me at the sink. The cut wasn't too bad, and I tried my best to minimise touching him, but even standing in such close proximity made my revulsion surge. I breathed in his scent, the smell transporting me right back to his bed. I shook my head to dispel the image, trying to ignore his breath fluttering strands of my hair. I didn't like him so close. He made my skin crawl now, any desire I'd had for him had evaporated. Charlotte was the other side, rolling up his sleeve so it wouldn't get wet.

Once he'd rinsed the cut, Charlotte helped him dry his hand and I placed two plasters over the wound. Our eyes met as I pressed it gently over his skin, smoothing it to ensure it would stick. A sense of sadness nagged at my side that things between us had turned so bad.

'I think this calls for dessert,' David interrupted, trying to dispel the fractious atmosphere.

I brought the dessert plates and cheesecake over to the table with a knife, relieved the ordeal was almost over. It was like being on a roller-coaster and I was exhausted.

'Looks delicious,' Nicky said enthusiastically.

'It is, Mum's cheesecakes are awesome,' Charlotte said, and she sounded like my little girl again, before the teenage years had hit.

'Thanks, Charlotte. Here you go.' I delivered the first slice to Nicky, one to David, then Charlotte and lastly myself.

Ten minutes of polite conversation later, we'd finished. Charlotte excused her and Nicky from the table to go back upstairs.

'Thanks very much for lunch, it was lovely.' Nicky said before leaving the kitchen, Charlotte in the lead.

'You're welcome, Nicky, any time,' David replied as he cleared the table.

I loaded the dishwasher and we worked in silence until all the dishes were out of sight.

'What was that about?' David asked as he topped up both of our wine glasses. I'd tried to pace myself throughout dinner, not wanting to let alcohol tempt me into saying something I shouldn't.

'What?'

'The third degree about his parents?'

I snorted. 'Just curious. I didn't realise he'd be so sensitive,' I said lightly.

David tutted and headed into the lounge. He liked lazy Sunday afternoons with a full stomach and a bottomless glass. It wouldn't be long before he'd be nodding off on the sofa.

I bundled the cloth and napkins together and took them into the utility room for a short hot wash. When I returned to the kitchen, I was glad David had gone. I wasn't in the mood to listen to him tell me what a wonderful young man Nicky was.

I sat at the table and marked some homework. I was almost done when, an hour later, Charlotte came into the kitchen.

'Nicky's going now,' she said, her cheeks a rosy red. I didn't have to ask to know what they'd been doing upstairs.

David was snoring on the sofa and I didn't want to disturb him, so I got up and went into the hallway, where Nicky was slipping his chunky desert boots on. I had a vague memory of seeing them discarded on the floor of his bedroom that night I'd stayed over. I wrung my hands awkwardly.

'Thanks so much for lunch, Mrs Cole.'

I smiled tightly. Charlotte was holding his hand and looked like she didn't want to let go.

'Oh, I've left my hoody in your room. Could you grab it for me, babe?' Nicky asked, his voice sickly-sweet.

Charlotte nodded, bounding up the stairs like an obedient puppy. I had to refrain from tutting.

Nicky took a step towards me and leaned in close to whisper in my ear. My hair fluttered as he spoke.

'She tastes like you.'

I gasped, my hand flying to my mouth. Hot tears pricked my eyes and I had to turn away from fear I would launch at him. My entire body shook, and I faltered, holding on to the staircase for support, but then I heard Charlotte's footfall on the stairs. I began to cough, it was all I could think of to mask my angry red face and streaming tears.

'You OK, Mum?' Charlotte said.

'Fine, just a tickle,' I managed, my hand in front of my mouth, hiding as much of my face as possible. 'Bye.' I waved my free hand above my head and turned back towards the kitchen. Carrying on coughing until I reached the utility room, where, after closing the door, I sank to my knees and sobbed. What had I done, exposing my daughter to this monster? Why was he punishing me?

When my chest had heaved enough, and I was exhausted, I got to my feet and opened the door cautiously. The only sound came from David's snoring. Charlotte must be back in her room already. I snuck outside for a smoke in the garden, moving towards the back fence so I could check Charlotte's window wasn't open. Lighting up, I called Stella.

'What the fuck?' Stella spat when I told her what had happened.

'I know. Oh god, what am I going to do? He's got my daughter hooked on him and I don't know what he's capable of.'

'You need to go and see him, make him understand what he's doing to you. Say you're sorry if that's what he wants to hear.'

'I will. I'll go to his house. I can't tonight, I've had too much wine already to drive. I'll go tomorrow after school.' Perhaps Stella was right, if I could make him see sense, perhaps he would stop this charade and leave us alone. I didn't believe he was with Charlotte for any other reason than to get to me.

Stella made me promise to keep in touch and once my face had returned to normal, the blotchy tear stains gone, I went to see Charlotte.

'Come in,' she called as I tapped gently on the door. She was sitting on her bed, reading her Geography textbook.

'Homework?' I asked.

'Always,' Charlotte groaned. 'Do you like him now?' she asked, eyes like saucers.

'I still think he's too old for you,' I said, trying to be as diplomatic as I could.

'Dad said if we had him round for dinner, you'd start to like him more,' Charlotte admitted. Now I understood why the dinner had happened, arranged behind my back. I couldn't blame David; he didn't know his daughter's boyfriend was a psycho.

'I don't dislike him,' I said, trying desperately not to lie to my daughter. If the truth be told, I hated him, but that wasn't going to help the situation.

'Don't let him push you into anything, Charlotte, OK? Make sure you're safe,' I said, cringing inwardly.

She wrinkled her nose. 'Mum! Grim. And, no, he's not pushing me into anything,' Charlotte said in a hurry, as though she couldn't get the words out fast enough.

\* \* \*

The following day at school, I arrived to find a gift bag on my desk. Knowing it could only be from Nicky, I threw it in the bin.

But what if it was something important? A gift for Charlotte or a message? Pulling it out, I opened the bag, slicing the tape that held the sides together. Inside, I saw black fabric and knew instantly what they were. Nicky had returned my underwear. Closing my classroom door, I pulled them out of the bag and found they'd been shredded. The gusset ripped apart, chopped like a child's paper snowflake with pieces missing. My chest tightened and, all of a sudden, I couldn't breathe. I gasped for breath, knowing a panic attack was coming, but I couldn't control it. Putting my head between my knees, eyes streaming, I counted over and over until my lungs opened up.

I avoided the playground and the afternoon assembly, feigning a headache. I couldn't bear to look at Nicky. I didn't want to be in the same room with him, but I knew I had to. I needed to go to his house to speak to him, away from the school grounds.

At the end of the day, Charlotte came to my classroom to ask if Nicky could take her to the library and drop her home before dinner. My talk with Nicky would have to wait.

Remembering my swimming kit was still in the boot of my car, I went for a swim to clear my head. I no longer counted lengths but glided up and down the pool in the cool water, working out what I was going to say to Nicky. Forty minutes later, I felt calmer, and my tightly coiled muscles relaxed after a hot shower.

I got home before David and prepared dinner, chilli con carne. A nice easy dish which was one of my favourites in winter. Christmas songs plagued the radio and adverts were on the television non-stop. I'd done nothing so far, burying my head in the sand that the festive season was fast approaching. I couldn't focus on anything but fixing my problem with Nicky.

I texted Stella to tell her I hadn't been able to speak to Nicky, so had nothing to report and was dishing up when David returned from work. He looked tired, saying he'd had a busy day on the new project and was looking forward to flopping on the sofa after dinner. Charlotte had been brought home from the library as promised and with books, so I knew she'd been.

Later, once dinner had been cleared, I took the opportunity to charge the Motorola, hiding the phone behind the fruit bowl out of sight while it was plugged in. I didn't want to contact Nicky unless I had to, but if he sent a message, I didn't want to miss it.

It was around seven and dark outside when the text came through. The Motorola was on silent, but I heard a humming sound from the corner of the kitchen and immediately knew what it was.

Retrieving the phone, I clicked open the message from Nicky but had to wait, it was a picture message and the phone was old. The screen started to download the image from the top, practically line by line like the old dot-matrix printers. My eyebrows shot up and my jaw hit the floor when I realised what he'd sent.

I stared at a photo of Charlotte, a selfie. A topless selfie of her lying in bed, the phone held from above, exposing part of her breasts with only a sheet covering the rest of her body. In the photo, she was biting her finger. It was provocative, but through my tears all I could see was my baby girl.

## 43

I unplugged the Motorola and threw it into my handbag, flying out of the door in seconds. Anger bubbled like blisters on my skin. I wanted to tear at Nicky until he bled. I drove like I had a death wish, taking corners too fast, way above the speed limit for our sleepy village, arriving at his house in little more than five minutes, screeching to a halt outside. I hammered on the front door with my fist, not bothering to ring the doorbell. I didn't care who heard or saw now, this had gone beyond keeping secrets or shielding reputations.

I waited, but there was no response. Again, I beat the door with my fist and pressed the doorbell for an extended period. Eventually the door opened, and a dishevelled Pat stood in front of me in her dressing gown.

'Where is he?' I snarled, pushing past Pat into the hallway and shouting Nicky's name up the stairs.

'What the hell do you think you're doing?' Pat screeched, still groggy from sleep.

'Where is your son?' I shouted, enunciating each word. Unstoppable tears came, the adrenaline pumping around my body had peaked, and anger and frustration leaked from my eyes.

'What's happened?' Pat stood with her hands on her hips.

'He's going out with my daughter now, did you know? He's sent me photos of her – naked ones!' The words spilled out in a rush. I sounded hysterical.

'I warned you,' Pat sighed.

I shot her an incredulous glare, but she shook her head.

'I told you to be careful, I warned you he wasn't to be trusted. Now get out,' Pat said, pulling me by the arm to thrust me back out of the door. 'He's just like his father that boy, takes everything, contributes fuck all. His dad was an arse; abused me, not only on the outside, but up here too,' she pointed to her temple before continuing. 'I used to think I was going mad. Everyone thought he was a saint, but no one saw what went on here once the door was closed.'

'I need to find him,' I pleaded as I stumbled onto the doorstep, but Pat was already closing the door on me. I pushed back on it hard to stop it from shutting. 'Did you make a complaint against me at the school?' I asked, but Pat let out a spiteful cackle, all the while shaking her head.

'You know what the only difference is between him and his father? He's smarter,' Pat said bitterly before closing the door in my face.

I waited by my car for a while, chain-smoking to calm my nerves, hoping Nicky would come home. I rang his phone repeatedly, but each time it went to voicemail. I sent a text asking where he was but got no response. I threw away my third butt and got in the car. As I was about to drive away the Motorola beeped.

Like mother like daughter

I stared at it, the letters blurring together. He was terrorising us, perhaps I should go to the police. I was backed into a corner now. I'd have to come clean about all of it to stop Nicky. I'd lose my job, my husband and possibly my daughter too, but I had to protect Charlotte at any cost.

Why had she sent him that photo? It was rule number one; I knew I'd talked to Charlotte about it in the past. We'd listened to radio campaigns on the way to school about never sending photos. What should I do? Confiscate Charlotte's phone? How would I do that without admitting I'd seen the photo?

My mind was whirling, and I felt utterly lost. I drove home slowly. When I got in, David was still watching television in the front room.

'Where did you rush off to?'

I hadn't prepared a response, my mind too busy elsewhere.

'Oh, I had to go over and see Matilda quickly, she was upset.'

'What happened?' David asked, but I interjected.

'What if we moved away? Started again somewhere new?' I continued, but David's face said it all.

'What's going on, Izzy? We moved here to "get away". What's wrong with here?' He scowled, his face a mask of annoyance. I immediately regretted mentioning it.

'Nothing, it's fine,' I said, which infuriated him more.

'Why are you shutting me out? I thought after we talked, everything was out in the open. Now it seems you don't want to tell me what's going on. You have to start trusting me again.'

'Not everything is about you,' I hissed.

'Then tell me what's wrong? You've been weird for ages.'

I contemplated blurting it out, but he was already angry, and I knew he'd hit the roof.

I sank on to the sofa and stared glassy-eyed at the television. David, realising he wasn't getting anything out of me, sighed and stalked out of the room. Pat's voice needled in the back of my mind. 'He's just like his father'. If Nicky was his father's son, had he hit his mother too? Is that what Pat meant? Was he violent?

My head spun and it was only after a large glass of wine I felt able to go to bed. David was already there and a hostile silence in the bedroom led me to believe he wasn't asleep yet. I climbed into bed beside him and pulled the duvet to my neck. My life was unravelling, and I was powerless to stop it.

* * *

On Tuesday morning, I had the comfort of teaching the year sevens story writing, which was my favourite lesson. At that age, they were still eager, and their imaginations weren't stifled by whether their ideas were cool or not. It enabled me to take my mind off Nicky and enjoy teaching.

I'd set myself a task, something I'd decided on last night whilst staring at the ceiling and willing sleep to come. At lunchtime I was first in the staffroom, waiting for Matilda and Susan to arrive so we could eat together. The gossip of the day was that slanderous graffiti had been found on the boys' toilet walls, shaming all the teachers. There were various nicknames for us all and some of the teachers had taken offence, but luckily both Matilda and Susan found it hilarious. Susan was called Mrs Witch, which they all decided was rather unimaginative. Matilda was Roly-Poly and I was Mrs Horny.

'My husband wished I was Mrs Horny,' I laughed nervously. I didn't have to guess where that had been dreamed up.

'Crikey, they are an imaginative bunch, aren't they? What are you teaching them in English?' Matilda said.

'Obviously not enough,' I retorted.

'Steven's gone mad, he's having it painted this afternoon,' Susan said.

'Oh well, it'll soon be yesterday's news,' Matilda said.

'The last time he had it painted was when Miss Willis was here,' Susan continued.

Perfect, if I'd got it right, I hadn't even had to steer them.

'Was that the English teacher?' I enquired.

'Yes. Christ, you should have seen the walls then,' Matilda said.

I finished my sandwich and made an excuse that I had to get back to my classroom to print out some sheets for the next lesson.

The sound of the children outside carried through the closed windows, but inside the school was quiet. I checked both phones, but there were no texts or calls. Picking up my smartphone, I typed Miss Willis, St. Wilfred's School into Google. There were a few hits, but none were right. I added the town as well and an article from the local paper loaded. It didn't have much detail but mentioned a teacher had been suspended from the school due to an alleged harassment complaint.

As I scrolled, I realised how lucky I'd been, considering it could have been my name in the paper and potentially my teaching career out of the window. Nothing had been reported in the local press to my knowledge about my absence from work or about the investigation undertaken by St. Wilfred's. Most likely because no evidence had been discovered and no allegation proven. I really had dodged a bullet. It could be my reputation smeared on that screen.

I needed to find Miss Willis, the article didn't provide much information that would help in my search, but it did supply her first name – Hayley. I googled Hayley Willis and various links to Facebook and LinkedIn popped up; it appeared to be a common name. Again, I entered the town to filter the list but got nothing from social media this time. Instead there was a listing from a website called Vital Skills, which looked to be a company which helped young people from the ages of sixteen to twenty-four transition from higher education into work. Clicking on the link took me through to the Personnel page, where there was a list of five employees in their various roles and Hayley was halfway down the list. I clicked on her name and it opened a profile page, with a large head and shoulder shot. She was pretty and looked of a similar colouring to me. She had long auburn hair and dark brown coffee-coloured eyes which were looking into the distance wistfully.

Nicky clearly had a type. Hayley was listed as a youth worker, and the contact address was in Rudgwick, heading back towards Surrey. I'd driven through it a few times when we were house-hunting. There was a telephone number too, but I thought it better to approach Hayley in person.

After school, I checked Charlotte didn't need a lift home from netball, but as I suspected, she was going back to Nicky's. To do homework, *apparently*. I bit my tongue, knowing the amount of homework that would be going on would be minimal. Instead of letting my feelings show, or tearing her mobile phone from her hand, I gave Charlotte a kiss and wrapped her into a hug. She squirmed awkwardly until I released her.

'Home for six please, and be good,' I said as I got into my car. I could see Nicky at the other side of the car park waiting, but I refused to look at him. I couldn't trust myself if we crossed paths. Fortunately, he'd had the sense to stay away since sending the photo of Charlotte, but he knew he had me exactly where he wanted me. I planned to change that.

## 44

The traffic to get out of the village was bad but expected during the school run. I used the time to think about what I was going to say to Hayley. She'd obviously moved town and changed job to get away. There was no presence of her on social media. Hayley must have fled the rumours and gone into hiding of sorts, deleting her Facebook and Twitter accounts to stay anonymous. I was sure she wouldn't appreciate a stranger dragging up the past.

I got lost trying to find the office of Vital Skills and had to pull over to key the postcode into the satnav. When I arrived ten minutes later, it wasn't an office I sat outside of, more a row of shops. The buildings were white with dark oak beams and quaint front doors. Looming windows showcased products on display, although the office Hayley worked in had frosted glass so you couldn't see the employees at their desks, only shapes moving inside. The whole street had a chocolate-box-village feel.

It was four o'clock and I got comfortable in my seat, sipping on a bottle of water I retrieved from my bag. I assumed Hayley would work until about five and I would catch her as she left the office, sure I would recognise her from her photo on the website.

My iPhone beeped; David had sent me a text message.

Where are you?

The tone of his text looked like he was still upset about our row. He was working from home more often, coming home earlier, making the effort to be present and here I was on a wild goose chase.

I sent a reply back.

At the library. X

Less than a minute later, I had a reply.

OK, I'll start dinner

I didn't respond, instead returned my concentration to the door of the office, but there were few comings and goings. As time wore on, my legs complained of pins and needles and I got out of the car to have a cigarette. When I'd finished and was putting the stub in a bin, I saw Hayley come out of the office, turn left and leisurely stroll along the street. Hurrying after, I called her name when she was about ten feet away.

'Hayley?'

She turned around and smiled politely at me, trying to place my face. Her eyes narrowed as it became clear she didn't know me.

'Hayley, I'm sorry to bother you. My name is Izzy. I work over at St. Wilfred's.'

As soon as I mentioned the name of the school, Hayley retreated, backtracking with her hands out in front of her.

'I'm sorry, I've got to go,' she said, turning away.

'Please, it's about Nicky.' I followed as Hayley quickened her pace, trying to get away. Desperation took over and I blinked back tears. What a fool I'd been to approach her in such a way. No wonder she felt cornered.

'Leave me alone,' she hissed in a low voice, turning around for a second to make eye contact with me, her eyes darting around to make sure no one was watching the exchange between us.

'He's got my daughter,' I wailed, tears starting to fall. The embarrassment of crying in the street hadn't escaped me, but once I'd started, I couldn't stop.

Hayley came to a halt and turned around, making her way back to where I stood, her face full of pity.

'Let's get a coffee, shall we?' she sighed and took my arm, steering me into a café which was practically empty.

Hayley sat me at the table by the window and disappeared to the counter to order. I dug in my handbag for a tissue to wipe my face. I wasn't sure where the wave of emotion had come from, but I felt better for the release.

Hayley returned a minute later with two cappuccinos in large white mugs and placed one in front of me.

'I'm sorry about that. I don't normally...' I said, trailing off.

'It's all right. I'm sorry, I just don't want people round here knowing about what happened there. My reputation has been destroyed and I've had to start again.'

I nodded, feeling awful for this young woman sat in front of me. Hayley was around ten years younger than me, possibly in her late twenties. Pretty, although restrained, her face free of make-up, long hair plaited. Even her clothes were reserved, a plain beige shirt buttoned to the neck and ankle-grazer trousers with black loafers.

'I'm your replacement,' I said and Hayley's eye's blinked rapidly. 'At St. Wilfred's. I'm the new English teacher. I met Nicky on my first day, in fact he almost ran me off the road on the way into school. He came to apologise, we got chatting and...' It was hard to say the words out loud. To admit to the ethical low point I'd hit.

Hayley remained stony-faced. Her eyes were rigid, and she nodded for me to continue.

'He flirted and I was flattered initially, but it got serious.' Could I tell a complete stranger I'd had a liaison with a pupil?

'You had an affair?' Hayley said incredulously, filling in the blanks. Her eyebrows shot up her forehead.

'Yes, but I ended it. Surely you know what he's like, how persistent he is,' I said, irritated that Hayley was taking the moral high ground in a situation so like her own.

Her eyes narrowed as though she'd read my mind. 'Ah I see, you heard the gossip. Another one who thinks they know what happened. Well, you don't. You shouldn't believe everything you read in the newspapers, you know,' Hayley spat before taking a deep breath and lifting her coffee to take a sip.

'I don't understand,' I muttered.

'I never had any sort of relationship with Nicky. Believe me, he tried, he wore me down, and when I wouldn't give in, an anonymous complaint was made against me. Although I know it was him. There was evidence found apparently, texts on his phone, photos, supposedly from me. I'd never sent them, but it was enough for Mr Scott to suspend me indefinitely.' Hayley's knuckles were white around her mug. 'I walked out of school knowing I'd never teach again. My fiancé moved out and I had to sell up. That little shit took everything from me. All because he couldn't get what he wanted.' Hayley's anger was evident, her face had turned a reddish purple, like she was about to explode.

'I'm so sorry, Hayley, I had no idea.' I felt terrible. I'd accused her all over again, like everyone else had.

'It's done now. I've had to move on, there's nothing I could do about it. I couldn't prove he was lying or even that it was him who made the complaint, but I knew.' The bitterness in Hayley's voice was heavy. Time had not healed her wounds yet. 'You said he had your daughter?' Hayley asked.

'Yes. The affair, it only lasted a couple of months and I came to my senses and finished it. He seemed fine at first, but I have a fifteen-year-old daughter at the school and one day she brought him home as her boyfriend. She's besotted and has no idea what he's like. She won't listen to me and he's sending me texts and photos she's sent to him of herself.' My voice trembled and I couldn't stop the tidal wave of emotion flooding out.

'He's using her to get to you?'

'Yes. I don't know what to do. I guess I thought if I knew what had happened with you, it might help me figure out how to handle him,' I said, lowing my head to my hands.

'Well, he hounded me out basically. He kept on and on, romantic gestures, flowers, to full on groping me when no one was looking. It got to the point where I was going to make a complaint against him and warned him I would if he didn't stop. The next day, I went in and Mr Scott was waiting to show me texts on Nicky's phone which were sent from my own. I didn't send them, and I have no idea how he did it. The texts were suggestive to say the least and, of course, it was open and shut for the school. The board of governors got involved and they had to let me go.'

'Did you ever hear from him again?' I enquired.

'One text, a week after I left, which read "I wish it didn't have to end this way". I didn't respond. He's a psycho and he'll keep on and on until he gets what he wants,' Hayley said.

I sank back into my chair. My phone started to ring, and I knew it would be David. It was half five already. He would be thinking about serving dinner soon and wondering where I was.

'Thank you for your time, and for the coffee,' I said, trying to keep my voice steady.

Hayley stood and lifted her bag onto her shoulder.

'What will you do?' she asked.

I shook my head. 'I don't know. Come clean, I suppose.'

Hayley nodded as if she agreed it was my only option.

'Take care,' she said and left the café.

I went back to my car, praying the traffic on the way home would be kind.

Throughout the journey, I contemplated what options I had. The only way I'd be able to separate Charlotte from Nicky would be to tell her the truth. In doing so, I would no doubt lose my job, my marriage and potentially Charlotte too. It was unthinkable, but at least Charlotte would be safe. Alternatively, I could let it run its course and ignore all contact from Nicky, perhaps when he'd got bored of tormenting me, he would move on to someone else. Although I couldn't be sure what he would do to Charlotte in the meantime. That option made me increasingly nervous. I had to protect my daughter.

When I opened the front door, I saw from the hallway Charlotte and David were already seated at the kitchen table eating. My dinner was there waiting for me.

'I did ring you,' David said.

I dropped my bag and slipped into the chair, the plate in front of me full of lamb chops with mash and broccoli. It looked delicious.

'I was driving and couldn't answer,' I said, before turning to Charlotte. 'How was your day, honey?'

'Fine,' Charlotte said lightly, not volunteering any further information.

'How was the library?' David asked.

'Fine,' I replied, and David sighed.

We ate in silence after that. I had too much going on in my head to be dragged into an argument with David and he looked as though he'd given up trying to figure out what was going on with me. I knew I couldn't carry on, something had to give, I just wasn't sure what.

## 45

We spent the evening in separate rooms again, David downstairs watching Boris Johnson and Jeremy Corbyn go head-to-head in an election debate, whereas I went to bed early to read. I spent much of my time going around in circles trying to figure out a way to get us out of this mess. I rang Stella, who thought it was hilarious I was in my bedroom whispering down the phone like a teenager, until she heard how upset I was.

'All I'm saying is before you blow up your entire life with this, make sure it's your only option left. There's no coming back from this, Izzy.' Stella was right and the last thing I wanted to do was break up my family. I was so grateful I could talk things through with her; she helped me see things from a different perspective and was almost always spot on with her advice.

'Thanks so much. Miss you.' I wished for the hundredth time my best friend was closer.

'I know, me too. Listen, how about you come up here for Christmas? All of you. Get away from it all? It'll get Charlotte away from Nicky. My brother will be up too. We can have one big celebration here?' Stella suggested.

Christmas was a month away and I had nothing prepared. I hadn't bought any cards or presents or even thought about retrieving decorations from the loft.

'Oh god, Christmas!' I groaned.

'Yes, Christmas. Talk to David about it, come on, it'll be fab. You can help me chase Dad when he goes out for a wander in his pants,' Stella laughed loudly, and I shushed her, stifling a giggle.

'OK, I'll see what he says. Love you. Bye.' I hung up and had to agree it was a good idea and when David was in a better mood, I'd talk to him about it.

I climbed out of bed and put my dressing gown on. It was half past nine and I wanted to see if Charlotte was still awake. Her door was closed, and I listened, sure I could hear the tapping of fingers on a screen, so I knocked.

'Come in,' Charlotte called, and when I pushed open the door, she was sitting up in bed, her phone in one hand and a book in the other.

'You OK?' I asked, my eyes fixed on her phone.

'Yeah, was going to finish my page and go to sleep,' Charlotte replied with a yawn.

'What do you want for Christmas?' I asked.

Charlotte frowned.

'I don't know, um, some GHDs? Yeah, I'd love some of those, pink ones please,' Charlotte said, looking more awake by the second.

'OK.' I smiled.

She looked so sweet and innocent in her emoji pyjamas, the excitement of Christmas and presents now on her mind. I leaned over and kissed the top of her head.

'Night, beautiful,' I said, and turned to leave.

'Night Mum.' Charlotte put her phone on the bedside table, book on the floor and rolled over.

I turned out the light, a warm glow spreading through my body as I left to go back to bed. Charlotte was my only daughter, the most precious thing in the world to me and hell would freeze over before I'd let Nicky ruin her.

* * *

The week dragged. I was still in a quandary about what to do. Every time I thought I was brave enough to tell Mr Scott, my knees buckled as I approached his office and I turned in the opposite direction. I couldn't wait for the weekend to arrive and spent my free time swimming countless lengths at the pool. At school it felt like I would bump into Nicky around every corner and my nerves were frayed. In reality, I rarely saw him or Charlotte. My iPhone rang around four times a day, there was never anyone at the end of the line when I answered. I was sure it was Nicky; he'd got my phone number from Charlotte somehow. He was slowly driving me mad.

On Friday lunchtime, all teachers were summoned to the staffroom for a quick debrief on the Ofsted inspection. When the meeting was over, I told Matilda and Susan I had to run an errand and left to catch up with Mr Ross. I found him striding down the corridor in his jogging bottoms back to the sports hall.

'Mr Ross,' I called, and he turned around. He didn't exactly smile, but his usual stern face softened. Mr Ross was Scottish and notoriously grumpy, although, by all accounts, he was an excellent teacher and the kids liked his firm but fair attitude.

'How can I help you, Mrs Cole?'

'I wanted to ask you about one of your pupils, Nicky Stevens?'

I hoped Mr Ross hadn't heard or, more likely, hadn't been concerned with any of the gossip which may have done the rounds. He struck me as someone who would pay little attention to the rumour mill.

'Ah yes, the elusive Mr Stevens. I know him well. Why do you ask?' Mr Ross stroked his stubble as he waited for me to answer.

'Well, he's dating my daughter and she's in year ten...' I trailed off, but Mr Ross nodded.

'Aye, well he's a waster, shows effort only when he can be bothered, and he's close to being kicked off the course. If you want my opinion, I think he's only here as he's got no idea what else to do.'

'Oh,' I said, taken aback by his abrupt assumption.

'Yes, afraid so. He plays the system well and seems to know what he can get away with to maintain his place on my course. I'm not sure what he's like for Mrs Howe, the biology teacher, you'll have to talk to her. Shame, as he's a smart lad. Could be an A* kid if he applied himself.'

'Thanks for your help. I appreciate it.'

I turned to walk away, building a picture in my head of who Nicky really was.

'Keep an eye on your daughter. He's a bit of a lady's man,' Mr Ross called after me.

*Tell me something I don't know.*

I pushed open the double doors to the playground, intending to stroll around to my classroom on the other side of the building, wanting to blow the cobwebs away, but immediately regretted the decision when the cold wind hit my face. I'd left my jacket in the classroom and sped up so as not to prolong my time outside.

A flash of red caught my eye and I saw two figures wrapped around each other by the large industrial recycling bins. Moving towards them, I recognised the red bag that had been slung on the ground as Charlotte's. My hand flew to my mouth as I saw her and Nicky locked in a passionate clinch, oblivious to their surroundings. They'd chosen their location well, no one else was in that part of the playground as it was close to the school gates. As I got closer still, I saw Nicky had his hand halfway up Charlotte's shirt. I felt my insides engulf and quickened my step towards them.

'Seriously?' I raised my voice to almost a shout and they abruptly stopped and pulled apart, untangling themselves from each other.

Charlotte looked horrified to not only be caught, but to be caught by her mother. Nicky looked unabashed, smug even.

'Get to my classroom now,' I hissed through gritted teeth at Charlotte. She scuttled off and I turned back to Nicky, pushing him against the fence.

'Woah,' he laughed, his palms raised in a submissive gesture.

'In the school grounds? Really?' I spat, outraged at his audacity.

'What are you going to do, Miss?' he asked, his chin raised skyward.

He knew I couldn't do anything. Our past history meant I had to tread carefully, and he knew it. It was my job which was in jeopardy, after all, not his; he could still swan around like he owned the place.

'Why can't you leave us alone?' I hissed.

'Because I can't.' He shrugged nonchalantly.

'Why not?'

'You really want to know why?' he asked, enjoying every minute of this exchange between us, the power he held.

'Yes, I really want to know why.'

'I fuck your daughter because I can't fuck you.' He leaned in close as he spoke and, instinctively, I shot out a hand, slapping him around the face.

He held his cheek, where I'd struck him, looking surprised at first. Then a slow smile spread across his face. I didn't care who had seen but judging from Nicky's eyes darting around the playground for witnesses, we were still alone.

'That was silly.' He raised an eyebrow and tilted his head a fraction to the side.

'Can't you see how much you're hurting me?' I said, tears now erupting from my eyes, the realisation of what I'd done involving myself with him, struck me around the head like mallet.

'Come back to me,' he whispered, his demeanour changing at the flick of a switch.

I took a step back, open-mouthed. He was delusional.

'Come back. I love you. Come back and I'll leave her alone.'

'You're crazy,' I said with a shake of my head.

'Well, if I can't have you, then I'll have to have the next best thing.' His voice was so matter-of-fact, it chilled me to the core.

## 46

I turned and marched away, quickly drying my eyes before I reached the main playground, which was full of pupils. As I walked past my classroom window, I could see Charlotte sitting in one of the seats at the front, waiting for me. I strode into the classroom and closed the door.

'What were you thinking? You could have got suspended for that display,' I said, trying to remain calm, but I was furious with her, with Nicky and myself too. In fact, anger was all I had, and it was eating away at me.

'I'm sorry, Mum.' Charlotte was hunched over in her seat, ears tinged pink, unable to make eye contact with me.

'I don't want you seeing him any more, Charlotte.' It was a command not a request and she began to sob.

'But I love him,' she cried, reaching into her pocket for a tissue.

'He doesn't care about you, Charlotte. I hear things, things from the other teachers, about him all the time. He's not a nice person.'

'He says you all hate him here. You've got a vendetta against him and you want him out,' Charlotte bit back.

'That's rubbish.' I was getting nowhere, so I decided to change tack.

'You know that girl Amelia, in your year, there's rumours he got her pregnant.'

'I'm not having sex with him, Mum!' Charlotte insisted, her eyes brimming with tears. My shoulders sagged, she looked like she was telling the truth.

'Good, because he's an adult and you're a child.'

'I don't care. I won't stop seeing him. I love him and he loves me,' Charlotte said, sounding like a petulant child.

'Oh, and you're going to run off, get married and live happily ever after, are you?' I said sarcastically.

'Maybe. It's none of your business.' Charlotte looked wounded.

I sighed, the fight gone out of me. I sat next to Charlotte, who shifted her body away in defiance.

'Charlotte, I don't want to fight with you. He's too old for you and today he could have got you in a lot of trouble had another teacher seen. Think about how it looks for me. You're my daughter, yes, this is your school, but it's also my place of employment. What would Mr Scott say?'

'I said I'm sorry,' Charlotte snapped, although she didn't sound sorry in the slightest.

The bell rang out shrill in the corridor, signalling the end of the break.

'Go back to your form room. I'll see you here after school. You're coming home with me,' I said, at least knowing my daughter was safe from Nicky for tonight.

'What about your writing class?'

'I'll have an extra student won't I,' I said, my voice firm.

Charlotte left the classroom as my form piled in for the second register of the day. I wasn't sure what to do. I could put my foot down, and I wanted to, but what if Charlotte snuck out to see Nicky, or worse, ran away with him? I'd snuck out all the time when I was her age because my parents were strict. I'd climb out of my bedroom window and down the trellis, out into the night. She was obviously besotted and at that age it was all-consuming. I remembered it well. Nicky's offer to leave Charlotte alone came with conditions that made my skin crawl. I'd never let him touch me again. There had to be another way.

After creative writing, which thankfully Nicky didn't attend, we drove home in silence.

'What did you think of the writing class? Do you want to come again?' I asked, attempting to defuse the tension between us.

'Nope.' Charlotte folded her arms and stared out of the window.

I felt a sting of irritation.

'You do realise I should ground you, so not seeing Nicky for one night is hardly life or death,' I snapped.

'You don't understand.'

I had to stifle a laugh. Why did all teenagers think they were the first to go through something?

'No, clearly I don't. You can forget seeing him this weekend.'

Once we were home, Charlotte stomped theatrically to her room, slamming her door.

David raised his eyebrows questioningly and I explained, hoping he'd be as enraged as I was and ground Charlotte until she was eighteen. But he was as laid-back as ever, blaming teenage hormones on their public display of affection. I wasn't even sure he was fully listening, his eyes straying to his laptop screen.

'You didn't see his hand up her shirt,' I said.

David's head snapped up at that. 'Well that's not on. I hope you intervened?'

'Of course I bloody did,' I rolled my eyes at him and headed to the fridge to pull out the ingredients for dinner.

Later that evening, I heard my bag vibrate and froze. I hadn't put the Motorola back onto silent. Luckily David was in the lounge watching a dull programme about canal journeys. I flipped open the phone and saw I had two text messages from Nicky. I hesitated for a second before opening them. My hands shook as I read the first one.

Reconsidered?

And then:

Shame

The first message was sent a couple of hours ago and the second just now. I didn't respond. He wouldn't be reasoned with and it might do more harm than good to open communication between us. I'd carry on as before, ignoring the texts and the goading. Eventually he would get bored. He had to.

My iPhone rang on the worktop, the screen flashing, it had been on silent since the anonymous phone calls started. I didn't want to alert David, still hoping I could handle this myself without blowing up my world as I knew it.

I realised it was yet another anonymous call and I stabbed the red button on the screen to decline it. Nicky had found a new way of harassing me, but these missed calls I could cope with. The thing I couldn't cope with was him using my daughter. I wanted to believe her and that she hadn't slept with him already, although I knew how persuasive he could be. His words rang out in my head: *I fuck your daughter because I can't fuck you.* I had to try and get through to her, try and make her see he was bad news although I feared I was too late. She was already lost to him. I tapped on her door, no reply came, but I entered anyway.

'Do you want me to take you to the doctors? Get you on the pill?' I suggested gently. It was the last thing I wanted. The thought of Charlotte and Nicky sleeping together was intolerable, but as her mother, I had to make sure she was safe, and protected. I didn't want her to end up like Amelia.

'Mum, how many times? We're not having sex!' Charlotte was exasperated. It felt like she was missing a word from the end of that sentence. *Yet.* We're not having sex *yet.* The idea Charlotte would lose her virginity to that little shit didn't bear thinking about.

'OK, well if you change your mind, let me know and I'll book an appointment.' For now, I had to be grateful for the reprieve and just hope I could change her mind before Nicky did something that couldn't be undone.

* * *

On Saturday, Charlotte remained in her room, practically on hunger strike, refusing to speak to me. Only David was allowed to deliver her food and I was annoyed that he was pandering to her. What message was that sending?

When Sunday came around, she tried a different tack and bent over backwards to be nice. She begged David and I over lunch to let her see Nicky. I was happy for the separation to continue for as long as possible, but under the imminent threat of tears, David rolled over.

'OK, he can come around here tonight.'

Charlotte bounced away from the table clutching her phone.

I scowled at my husband. He used to have a backbone; where it had disappeared to, I didn't know. I chided myself; I wasn't being fair. David didn't know the circumstances; he had no reason to be overly concerned about Nicky.

'I wanted to talk to you about Christmas,' I said, putting down the paperback I was reading and taking a sip of my tea.

'It's four weeks away, I believe,' David said wryly as he lowered the newspaper in front of his face.

'Stella invited us to Nottingham.'

David's gaze returned back to the newspaper.

'Well, I thought as this was our new home, perhaps it would be nice to spend Christmas here? The first Christmas in this house. We can invite your parents over and I can go and see Mum at some point, the day after Boxing day perhaps?'

I felt deflated, he was right of course, but I wanted to be away from here, away from Nicky.

'OK.' I got up to throw my remaining tea in the sink and headed upstairs to put some ironing away.

'Stella can come here if she wants too?' David called after me, and I knew he was trying to compromise, but it couldn't work with Stella's parents to look after. I didn't bother shouting downstairs to reply.

Christmas wasn't the same for me now. My miscarriage last year had happened on the 22 December and I'd spent most of the festivities trying not to cry in front of Charlotte. The anniversary was approaching, and I wasn't sure what to do. Should I do something in remembrance or try and pretend it was a normal day and keep myself busy?

Later, after dinner, David received a phone call from his boss to ask whether he could prepare a presentation for the board tomorrow. Of course, he agreed and locked himself away in the office upstairs to get started. I knew better than to disturb him when he was busy so left him to it. I lingered by the door, listening to hear if he was on the phone but heard nothing but the tapping of keys. The effort we'd been making since his affair had been revealed had stalled. I knew he felt like I was shutting him out, but I couldn't talk to him about Nicky.

I rustled up some pasta, quick and easy, delivering David a bowl to his desk. Charlotte was unusually talkative over dinner, obviously looking forward to Nicky's arrival. I said they could have the front room to watch a movie as I would be doing some ironing but he had to be gone by ten. Charlotte asked if she could microwave some popcorn, and before Nicky arrived, dinner had been cleared away and everything made ready for him: a large bowl of popcorn, a can of Coke chilled and ready to be opened, and a movie downloaded from Sky.

I shut myself away in the back room. Muffled voices and giggling came from the lounge as I tried to concentrate on not burning one of David's work shirts. I turned the volume up on the TV, so I didn't have to listen to them. David was still upstairs in the office and it was unlikely he'd be out until after I went to bed.

Just before ten, knowing Nicky would be leaving shortly, I went upstairs to put my pyjamas on, discarding my clothes on the bed. I liked to lay with the iPad and go through my emails and social media stuff before turning in. I heard them giggling whilst I was getting changed but I wasn't concerned anything untoward was going on downstairs. Hopefully Charlotte was staying true to her word about refraining from sex with Nicky, although I had no idea how long it would last. I was certain it wouldn't be happening under my roof tonight.

I was scrolling through Twitter when I heard heavy footsteps on the stairs and, thinking it was David, I hurried to the bedroom door and opened it.

'You finished?' But it wasn't David, it was Nicky standing there with his T-shirt crumpled.

He stepped forwards into my bedroom forcing me to take a step backwards.

'You shouldn't be in here.' I hissed, acutely aware David was only feet away behind the office door. 'Where's Charlotte?' I asked.

He ran his fingers over his stubbled jaw. 'She's using the toilet downstairs. I said I'd use the one up here,' he whispered, stepping forward again, but this time I held my ground. He was so close, I could smell the popcorn on his breath.

'Please leave,' I said, sounding a lot calmer than I felt.

'Ah come on, I can be quick,' he whispered, reaching forward and tugging at the waistband of my pyjamas.

I recoiled, slapping his hand away. I vaguely registered David's muffled voice down the hall; he must be on the phone.

'Get out!' I hissed and he retreated back into the hallway, giving me a wink and heading into the bathroom. I locked myself in the en suite, shaking as I sat on the toilet with my knees pressed against my chest.

I had no idea what Nicky was capable of. I thought I knew him, but since I'd ended the affair, I realised I didn't know him at all. Five minutes later, I heard the front door shut and I unlocked the door to the en suite, hurrying around my bed to peer out of the window. I watched Nicky get into his car and drive away. Still feeling unsettled, I got into bed, pulling the covers right up to my chin. I put an old episode of *Friends* on the iPad and halfway through let my heavy eyelids fall and drifted into a fitful sleep.

I dreamt Nicky and Charlotte got married and, during the speeches, he projected a naked photo of me as he presented the benefits of trying the mother of the bride out first. I woke in a panic, damp hair stuck to my forehead, until I remembered I'd never sent him any pictures of myself, naked or otherwise. The room was pitch black, the iPad digging into my side. It was three o'clock. David wasn't beside me, had he slept downstairs?

Curiosity got the better of me and I slipped on my dressing gown and crept down the stairs. I heard David snoring from the sofa before I reached the bottom step. Peeking into the front room, I saw he was positioned half on the sofa, half on the floor and still fully clothed. He must have finished working and gone downstairs for a drink before falling asleep.

Entering the kitchen to get a glass of water, I noticed a light illuminating my bag in the darkness and realised the Motorola must have a text as the light flashed until the text was either opened or the battery died, whichever came first. I fished the phone out of my bag, put it in the pocket of my gown and took my glass of water back upstairs.

In the safety of my room, with the door closed, I opened the text message. The picture was slow to download as usual and feelings of dread crept through me as it came through. It was a black lacy bra laid on out on a bed – Nicky's bed, I recognised the pattern of the duvet cover. The text underneath made me baulk.

Got myself a souvenir

I switched on my light and rummaged through the clothes I'd pushed onto the floor when I climbed in bed. My top and jeans were there, and underneath were the knickers, but the matching bra had gone.

## 47

I stood in my room, aghast at what Nicky had done. He must have come back and taken my underwear. The dirty underwear I'd been wearing all day. I ran to wretch into the sink. Whatever I did, I couldn't escape him. The torment was getting worse and I felt backed into a corner. There was nothing left to do, I had to confront him at school. I had to admit everything to David. I didn't know if my marriage would survive it or if my daughter would ever speak to me again but there was no other option now. I wasn't sure what lengths he would go to.

I switched off the light and slipped the Motorola into my underwear drawer. I hadn't bothered replying to Nicky, what was the point? I tried to go back to sleep and did at some point, around half past five, waking again before seven. I dressed in a black pinstripe suit with a white blouse, as business-like as possible. I felt empowered and it would enable me to do what had to be done.

I was devoid of energy and it was obvious in my lessons. At lunchtime I scoured the grounds looking for Nicky but couldn't find him. After searching the football court and playground, I ventured to the sports hall. My breath caught in my throat when I found him alone, practising his basketball moves.

He grinned when he saw me, eyes lighting up, no hint of remorse in his expression. His demeanour sent a chill that descended the length of my body. He was unhinged.

'I want you to leave us alone,' I said slowly and clearly, as I walked over to him. My words echoed around the empty hall, bouncing off the bare brick walls. He rested the ball on his hip and lifted his T-shirt to wipe the sweat from his face. It was done to showcase his perfectly toned stomach, but I didn't blink. It wasn't going to work.

'Come on, Izzy. Stop playing hard to get. We were good together.' He sounded so sure of himself. I could see he thought it was only a matter of time before our affair was rekindled.

I took a deep breath and tried to remain calm. 'Listen, Nicky, I don't know how much plainer I can be. What happened between us is in the past, it will never happen again. I want you to leave me and my daughter alone. If you don't, I'm going to tell David and Charlotte all about us and then I'll tell the school.'

Nicky shrugged and turned his back on me, shooting the ball and watching it land perfectly through the basketball hoop.

'You won't do that.'

'Oh, I will, trust me,' I spat. Anger was bubbling to the surface. I leant towards him, our faces inches apart and lowered my voice. 'You'll be kicked out of school, then you'll have to be a grown up and go out and get a job. I'll move away and you'll never see me or Charlotte again. I'll tell everyone about you, how you're a manipulative little stalker, a pervert with a fascination for older women, English teachers especially,' I whispered into his ear, the venom in my voice unmistakable.

Nicky took a step back, picking up another basketball from the side lines. A grin emerging as he took in my words.

'You heard about Miss Willis then?' He laughed, before continuing. 'Don't worry, Izzy, there's only ever been you,' he sneered.

'I went to see her, so I know all about you, Nicky, and soon everyone will if you don't back off.'

He raised his eyebrows and the basketball rolled out of his hand, bouncing to the floor.

I walked away from him, out of the school hall, hoping the message had finally sunk in.

I didn't see Nicky for the rest of the week. I threw myself into my lessons and swam after school. My shoulders loosened more each day that went by that I didn't see him. Charlotte said he was busy putting hours in at the garage, so he wasn't around much. I hoped he was trying to let her down gently. Perhaps it was finally over? When I drove out of the car park on Friday afternoon, I was looking forward to a week away from school, hopefully one where I wouldn't have to see Nicky or even hear his name.

Charlotte had other ideas as she told me about his upcoming birthday celebrations at the weekend and how she was going to surprise him with a T-shirt she had designed in Textiles class. My heart plummeted, but I continued to smile and nod along to Charlotte, who bounced in her seat the whole way home, glad that he'd finally got in touch with her. His birthday was on Sunday so she was going shopping tomorrow to search for the perfect card and would I drop her in to town?

I'd made zero progress as far as Christmas was concerned so decided I'd brave the crowds and make a start.

'Sure, I'll drop you in, I need to do some shopping myself. Want me to wait for you?'

'Nah, Amy is going to come too and we're going to have lunch at Ed's Diner.'

I loved seeing her so happy, although I knew her heart was about to be broken.

'We need to go shopping,' David said when I got in the door. He'd discovered the kitchen was bare.

'I just haven't got around to picking anything up this week,' I snapped. I knew David wasn't trying to get at me, he was simply making a statement, but I bit anyway. Running the house wasn't solely my responsibility.

'Mum's dropping me off in town and she's going Christmas shopping tomorrow,' Charlotte explained as she riffled through the cupboards for an after-school snack.

'I'll go tomorrow, if you're going Christmas shopping. It'll give me something to do.' He'd read my mind. Although I remembered the last time he went, I had to go back to the supermarket the next day and get all the things he'd forgotten. 'I'll write a list this time,' he said, catching my eye roll. I couldn't help but smile, David knew me better than anyone.

Mum rang, asking if we'd seen the news. She wanted to check David hadn't been in town as there'd been a terrorist incident on London Bridge where a man had stabbed random members of the public before being shot by the police.

'No, David worked late last night so he stayed home today. We're all safe.' Mum had been glued to the BBC News channel since it had happened, watching the drama unfold on the bridge. Although I hated it when David went into London, he was more likely to be struck by lightning than get caught up in a terrorist attack. Mum went on to tell me that Dad had finally rigged up the camera, inside the bird box we'd bought him for Father's Day, now their Wi-Fi was strong enough to connect to the house. I was looking forward to seeing babies in nesting season.

Later that night, after we'd enjoyed a takeaway and shared a bottle of wine, David tried to coax me upstairs for an early night. I didn't feel like it but could see he was put out, although he pretended he wasn't. It irritated me. Why should I apologise because I wasn't up for it? Why did men always take it so personally when they were rejected? My head was focused on other things, it hadn't even crossed my mind that David might be missing some intimacy between us.

The following day, I woke before everyone else and was downstairs drinking coffee when Charlotte emerged looking like she'd not been to bed.

'I think I'll have some coffee too.' She yawned, taking some from the pot and pouring it into a mug before adding lots of milk and sweetener, seeming far too old for her years. 'Can I see Nicky over Christmas?'

'We'll see. I'll speak to your father,' I said, satisfied I'd sidestepped that one for the time-being. 'Speaking of Christmas, what time do you want to go shopping?' I asked.

'I'm not meeting Amy until eleven, but I have things I need to do anyway, so whenever you're ready,' Charlotte replied as she went back into the kitchen to retrieve her favourite cereal, which she carried back to the table, eating straight from the box.

'Charlotte, that's gross. Get a bowl.' I frowned, but Charlotte didn't stop munching.

An hour later, we parked in the multi-storey car park at the top of the mall. I gave Charlotte twenty pounds and she walked in the direction of the card shop I needed to go to later. I didn't want to cramp Charlotte's style so went to look for something for David and Stella. My first shop was a success and I picked a beautiful printed scarf with birds on it for Stella in a lovely cerise colour and a contrasting turquoise across-the-body bag which was gorgeous and functional all in one. I wandered around the men's department looking at the ties and the cufflinks but had no idea what to get David.

Would we even still be together at Christmas? If I had to make good on my promise to Nicky and tell everyone about the affair, then I doubted it. I hoped the threat would be enough and I might be able to save my marriage. Even though we'd both made mistakes, I still loved my husband.

I pushed on with shopping, next stop was Rush, the hair salon where I'd had my hair cut and coloured. I pushed open the door and saw the manager standing behind the desk chatting to Rebecca, my stylist.

'Izzy! Hi, how are you?' Rebecca said, smiling widely at first and then frowning at her appointment book.

'Hi Rebecca, I'm fine thank you. Don't worry I don't have an appointment, I came in to buy some GHDs.'

Rebecca came around the desk to the shelves where all the products were for sale. Reaching to the top, she brought down a sleek black and pink box.

'For you or a gift?'

'A Christmas gift, for my daughter.'

Rebecca slid the box open, inside were fuchsia slimline straighteners, a heat protector spray and a small hairbrush.

'Charlotte is going to love it. I'll take it.' I knew straighteners were expensive as I owned a pair myself, but it would be worth it to see her face on Christmas morning.

'Great, I'll wrap them up. That'll be £120 please,' Rebecca said, tapping the till. We spent five minutes chatting about our plans for Christmas and I booked my next appointment.

I decided to peruse the bookshop where I'd bought the school paperbacks. I loved everything about bookshops; the displays were colourful and eye-catching, and the smell was divine, especially those with coffee shops. I remembered seeing some brightly covered notebooks last time I was there, which made me think of Matilda. After ten minutes of browsing and getting side-tracked by the bestseller list, I found a vibrant orange leather 2020 diary which screamed Matilda and a muted forest green one for Susan.

They'd been good to me since I'd arrived at St. Wilfred's and I hoped the gifts would be viewed as a token of how much I appreciated their friendship. Soon they'd be off to a German Christmas market and I wished I could join them. Perhaps next year. Once I'd visited the card shop to get some cards and wrapping paper, I couldn't bear the crowds any longer. My toes were being pinched by my boots, which were obviously the wrong choice of footwear for the trip. I hadn't given it much thought when I got dressed.

When I got home, I'd go online and order the in-laws a hamper, as I did every Christmas, a different variety every year, and I'd seen a wine cooler in Debenhams that I knew my parents would love in their kitchen. Disappointed I hadn't found anything for David, I sent Charlotte a quick text to let her know I was leaving, in case she wanted a lift.

I leaned against the barrier, waiting for a reply, watching people scurry around on the floor below. A man caught my eye as he looked like Nicky, walking with purpose through the crowd. Repositioning myself to get a better view, I saw it was him. He walked past a few shops, paying them no attention before pausing outside Ann Summers and staring at the lingerie in the window. I watched intently from my safe viewing platform above as he went in and came out a few minutes later with a bag, before carrying on towards the exit.

My stomach churned. Had he bought something for my daughter from a sex shop? My fifteen-year-old daughter? Nicky turned nineteen tomorrow, but even now Charlotte was a minor dating an adult. If I found any evidence of a sexual relationship between them, it would be a criminal offence. He'd pretty much confirmed it, but I was sure he'd say anything to hurt me. I hadn't wanted to believe they had gone that far so quickly. They hadn't been dating long but I remembered how persuasive Nicky could be.

## 48

I walked back to my car chewing the inside of my cheek, fingers drumming on my handbag. Perhaps our chat almost a week ago hadn't made any difference at all? Maybe Nicky believed my threats were empty, and perhaps before they were, but I could see he was going to make me tear my life apart to get away from him. I sat behind the wheel of the Audi and cried, ignoring the stares from drivers who lingered, wanting my space in the full car park. They could drive around again, I didn't care.

I drove home slowly so my face could return to its normal colour after my tears had been wiped away. I didn't want David to know I'd been crying as it would provoke questions I couldn't face answering today. When I got home, I was pleasantly surprised to find he'd been food shopping and the cupboards were full. I hurried upstairs to stash my presents and came back to join David at the table for a cup of tea.

'I'm starving,' I said, jumping up to fix myself a sandwich.

'Good job the fridge is stocked.' He was clearly pleased with himself.

'Was it busy?'

'Heaving! Saturdays are not good days to go food shopping.'

'Well, I appreciate you going out so we can all eat tonight. I have also had a successful day and got some Christmas presents. Although I've got no idea what to get you this year.'

David raised his eyebrows. 'I don't know, I have everything I want,' he said, and I squirmed, my throat thick with guilt.

'I hear Charlotte is out for the day tomorrow with Nicky. His mum is taking them for lunch apparently. Not very rock and roll, is it? He must be down the pub with his mates tonight surely?'

My blood ran cold and I felt my limbs stiffen. Pat knew I was Charlotte's mother. I'd told her. Suddenly the sandwich became difficult to chew and I put it back on my plate. David hadn't noticed and carried on.

'There's a Christmas market in Redhill tomorrow, do you fancy a wander around there, the two of us? We could have a pub lunch somewhere?'

'Sure.'

David laughed at my unenthusiastic response.

I swallowed hard and added, 'Well, it's not a German Christmas Market with Matilda and Susan, but it'll have to do.' I smiled to show I was joking, and David seemed satisfied with my poor attempt at banter.

'Perhaps next year.' He patted my hand.

I picked at my sandwich again and nibbled. My stomach seemed to be constantly in knots. Sometimes I felt like I couldn't catch my breath.

My phone rang on the table and *Unknown Number* flashed up on the screen. I stared at it, knowing who it would be.

'Not going to answer that?' David said, reaching for the phone.

I snatched it up and slid my finger across to answer, my heart in my throat. There was no way I was letting Nicky speak to David.

'Hello?' I wandered into the hallway as David frowned at me. All I could hear was breathing. Ending the call, I turned around and smiled. 'Wrong number.'

I grabbed the laptop from the office and booted it up.

'Right, let's get your mum's hamper ordered, shall we? I was thinking John Lewis this year?'

David nodded, feigning interest. Twenty minutes later, I'd ordered the hamper and the wine cooler, which only left a few stocking bits to get and David's present.

When Charlotte arrived home in the early afternoon, David suggested we all went to see a movie before dinner. Charlotte was in high spirits and with teenagers you had to capitalise on it when you could. We waited until we arrived at the cinema and picked the film with the closest start time which happened to be *Last Christmas*. I loved George Michael and it had all of the Wham songs in it.

We used to do it a lot, head out together for the day or the afternoon like the three musketeers. I knew those days were changing and it was only to be expected, but with Charlotte sitting between the two of us, shovelling popcorn into her mouth, I wished she'd remain a child forever. I couldn't bear to think of her handing her innocence to Nicky, gift wrapped.

On the way home, we laughed about how it was far too early to be watching Christmas movies. Charlotte headed straight to her room, phone in hand, and I got a bottle of wine out of the fridge. David pulled two glasses out of the cupboard and I poured.

'Well, that was a lovely afternoon. Thank you.' I smiled at David and enveloped him in a hug.

'You're welcome, lovely being out with my girls again,' he said, rubbing my back.

I was lucky to have David and ever since the longevity of our marriage had been thrown into question, I appreciated him more than ever. It was true, you didn't know what you had until it was gone.

'I'm glad you've quit smoking; I was getting worried about you for a while there.'

'I know, it's been a stressful time. All sorted now though,' I lied, hoping I wasn't going to have to tell David everything. I was clinging on to my marriage by my fingertips.

We made love later, but I was going through the motions to keep David happy. My head was so full, I struggled to relax and enjoy it. I didn't know if he could tell or not, but soon after he was snoring loudly.

I crept downstairs, fed up after an hour of listening to David. I wanted to check the Motorola in case there was a message waiting for me. There was.

Do you know what I really want for my birthday?

I ignored it. I hadn't responded to him for ages, but he was nothing if not persistent. I hoped he'd appreciate the effort Charlotte had gone to for his birthday and let her down gently. Was he out getting drunk with his friends and chatting up other girls? Older girls who'd finished school and would be only too keen to drop their knickers if he showed an interest? Did he truly care for my daughter or was he playing games with her for fun? I prayed they weren't having sex. If Nicky got Charlotte pregnant, he'd be in our lives forever. I couldn't allow that to happen.

I lay on the sofa, my mind whizzing and tried to read my Kindle.

The next thing I knew, David was patting my leg to wake me, and daylight flooded the front room as he pulled the curtains back.

'What are you doing down here?' he asked. I was stiff and cold where I'd fallen asleep without a blanket.

'I couldn't sleep, and you were snoring,' I groaned, rubbing my neck.

David went into the kitchen and I heard the kettle boil. It was half past eight and I toyed with the idea of going back to bed, although a minute later David placed a mug of hot coffee in my hand. I sipped it slowly and listened to him rattling around in the cupboards and the clang of saucepans hitting each other.

'I'm doing eggs and bacon,' he called brightly.

I chuckled to myself; he was always so cheerful the morning after the night before.

Ten minutes later, Charlotte came down, also in a jolly mood.

'The smell woke me up, Dad,' she said, wishing me a good morning as she walked past. I felt like I was in the twilight zone.

Shortly afterwards, we sat at the table eating eggs, bacon, tomatoes and bread with lashings of butter.

'Are you meeting Nicky's mum today?' I asked.

'Yes, I've met her before but only briefly. She's a bit scary actually,' Charlotte giggled nervously.

I nearly agreed out loud but caught myself in time.

'I'm sure she'll love you,' I said instead, knowing it would be true. She was likely ecstatic that Nicky had brought home a girl of his own age.

'What time are you going over there? Do you want a lift? We can drop you off on our way to the Christmas Market,' David offered.

I didn't want to go anywhere near Nicky, Pat or the house with my family, but what could I say?

'That would be brilliant, Dad, I'll text Nicky and let him know. What time are you leaving?' Charlotte asked.

'Whatever time your mum is ready,' David joked, squeezing my knee under the table. 'Say ten-ish?' David said and Charlotte nodded, her fingers flying across her phone at an alarming rate.

When I was ready and in the car on our way to Nicky's, my gut wrenched. The closer we got, the harder I found it to breathe. I desperately tried to hide my discomfort from David and Charlotte by looking out of the window. *One, two, three, four, one, two, three, four.* I counted repeatedly and drummed down the side of my seat, where I couldn't be seen. When David pulled up outside the house after Charlotte had given him directions, she said goodbye and jumped out quickly.

Nicky must have been watching out for us, as the front door opened, and he was sprinting towards the car. Luckily the driver's side was closest, and I leaned back to keep out of view as much as I could, but Nicky gave Charlotte a kiss and walked straight to David's window.

'I'll drop her home later, David. About nine, will that be OK?'

'Sure, and happy birthday. I can come and get her if you want to have a drink?' David winked and I cringed inwardly.

Nicky shifted his stance so he could see me squirm in the passenger seat.

'Well, I might, but if I do, my mum will drop her home. She's inside if you want to meet her?' Nicky asked innocently.

David turned to look at me to gauge my thoughts.

I formed my lips into a tight smile. 'No, there's no need. Let us know if you need David to come and get her,' I said stiffly.

Nicky nodded and turned back towards the house. David narrowed his eyes at me, and I felt the need to defend myself.

'David, if we don't leave now, we won't get a parking space and you'll moan if we have to drive around for half an hour to find one.'

This seemed to placate him, and he turned on the engine and we drove back to Surrey.

The market was busy, but we found a parking space. I tried to enjoy the festive feel, but I couldn't help but wonder what Charlotte was doing. I had a bad feeling in the pit of my stomach, I couldn't stop thinking about what Nicky had bought in Ann Summers. David's suggestion of roasted chestnuts at an old-fashioned cart didn't entice me, instead we opted for a glass of mulled wine and a slice of Christmas cake by the reindeer enclosure.

'They've gone all out this year,' David said, gesturing towards the reindeer.

I nodded, my mouth full of cake. 'We have to buy some of this cake, it's delicious.'

I wanted a minimal-effort Christmas this year, and if it included an M&S dinner in foil platters and a shop-bought cake then so be it. I had too much on my mind. When we finished our drinks, I went to the stall selling the cake and bought a medium-sized beautifully decorated one with snowflakes on top, as well as some chutney, a bottle of mulled wine, and some decorations, spending well over fifty pounds.

'You're stocking up.' David laughed, taking the bags from me to carry.

'I'm unprepared this year, and the less baking or cooking I have to do the better,' I said, putting my arm through David's. The weather was turning cold and I huddled closer to him as we strolled along.

'I haven't forgotten, you know, that the anniversary is coming up. I never know whether to mention it or not. I don't want to upset you,' David said softly, laying his hand over mine, the warmth seeping into my fingers.

'I don't know whether to ignore it, or fall apart,' I replied, feeling tears prick my eyes. The mere mention of the miscarriage felt like my heart was being ripped out. I understood why David felt it was a minefield bringing it up.

'We'll do something, buy a rose plant or name a star, something like that. We should have done it last year.' David grimaced, that awful time replaying in his mind.

'A rose sounds like a nice idea.'

'Are you upset we're not going to Nottingham?' David asked and I was grateful for the change of subject.

I contemplated for a moment. 'Not upset... disappointed perhaps. I must let Stella know later on today, I haven't called her back yet,' I said. I would have preferred we all get out of the area for a blissful few days where I knew we would be free from Nicky. Charlotte would likely ask for him to come over on Christmas Day, but there was no way he would be. Hopefully by then things would be over between them. With any luck, Nicky would end it today.

My handbag vibrated against my side and I knew a text had come through on the Motorola. I hoped David hadn't heard the buzz it made, but the hustle and bustle of the market was loud.

On the way home, he stopped at the newsagents to buy the Sunday papers, which for some reason hadn't been delivered that morning. While he was in the shop, I pulled the Motorola out of my bag and flicked it open, frowning at the text.

Your daughter is a star

## 49

I had no idea what it meant, although it sounded ominous. I slipped the phone back into my bag and swapped it for my current one, checking there were no texts from Charlotte. As expected, there weren't.

David climbed back into the car passing the papers over for me to hold. On the front page, there was an image of a priest who had been found molesting young boys. I tutted as I read the headline. David turned and looked before he plugged in his seat belt and drove away.

'I know, paedos. They're everywhere. Should be strung up,' David spat. Would he consider me a paedophile too? I guessed as Nicky was an adult I couldn't be, but he was still half my age. I knew in the eyes of the law, it was illegal, even though Nicky was eighteen, because I was in a position of trust. If it was reported, I could end up on the sex offenders register.

Blood drained from my face and I shook the thought from my head. The affair was over now, but was the damage yet to be done? I had no idea whether I would come out of it unscathed.

When we got home, I busied myself with chores. I had a mountain of washing to get through and all the sheets to change. David prepared a casserole, which he put in the oven for a few hours. When I got to the ironing, it was almost seven and Charlotte still wasn't home. She came through the door at nine, having been dropped off by Pat. She was rosy-cheeked and grinning from ear to ear, flopping onto the sofa opposite David.

'Did you have a nice day?' I asked, trying to hide my disappointment there'd clearly been no break-up. Nicky's message had been whirring through my mind all afternoon. I'd been trying to decipher it but had been at a loss. Obviously I couldn't ask Charlotte what it meant.

'Yeah great, we went bowling and then to the restaurant, where they had those enormous sundaes. Oh, Nicky said thanks for his card by the way.'

I frowned and looked at David.

'Charlotte brought it. I signed it from both of us as you weren't around,' he said.

*Great, he'll think it's an endorsement.*

'Did he like his T-shirt?'

Charlotte nodded enthusiastically. 'Yep. I've got a tiny bit of Geography homework to finish, so I'm going to go and get it done,' Charlotte said and went upstairs.

'You still don't like him, do you?' David said.

That was an understatement.

'I just think he's too old for her, that's all. He's going to break her heart,' I said defensively. I was starting to think my ultimatum hadn't worked, that Nicky wasn't about to toe the line and finish with Charlotte. I felt on edge, constantly wondering what he was he playing at.

When Monday came, I struggled to get out of bed and, in a bizarre reversal of roles, had to be cajoled by Charlotte, who was already dressed. It was so cold, I wore long boots and trousers and, mainly because I didn't feel like it, I put on lipstick too. If I couldn't feel ready for the day, at least I could look like it. Fake it until you make it was the phrase, wasn't it?

Mondays weren't so bad with the free period in the morning and the assembly in the afternoon. They went pretty quickly.

Along the corridor some of the sixth-formers and Matilda were putting up intricate snowflake decorations that must have been made during Art class. I stopped to say hello, commenting on how beautiful they were. Ruth, the school secretary, walked past, lugging an artificial Christmas tree, still in its box, towards the trophy cabinet. Christmas had officially begun at St. Wilfred's, although still a little early for me at home.

After a brief chat with Matilda, I visited the library to change some books, in the hope I'd see Nicky, so I could ask why he was still dating my daughter when I'd expressly told him to end it. Nicky was nowhere to be seen, although he was at assembly in the afternoon, sitting at the back, staring first at me and then at Charlotte to unsettle me. I ignored him, knowing it would annoy him more that I wouldn't play his silly games.

At the end of the day, I collected my things and as I was about to leave the classroom to find Charlotte, Nicky walked in. He sat on the first desk opposite me, dropping his bag to the floor and pulling his phone out of his pocket.

'Hi Miss!' he said, a hint of sarcasm in his voice.

'I thought you were breaking up with Charlotte this weekend?' The words spilled out of my mouth.

'What, on my birthday? Now that wouldn't be very nice, would it? Especially after she made me such a lovely present.' His eyes focused on the screen of his phone, his fingers moving silently across it.

'I'm not doing this any more, Nicky,' I sighed and picked up my handbag, ready to leave.

'I think you are,' he said and I felt an icy grip take hold. 'You know I said your daughter is a star. Well, she will be, when this video does the rounds.' Nicky held the phone out towards me, showing the unmistakable image of Charlotte on the screen. I froze to the spot, a lead weight in my feet, unable to move as the video played out in front of me. Vomit burned my throat and I squeezed my lips tightly together as I pushed Nicky's hand away.

I sprinted down the corridor to Mr Scott's office, the sound of my heels echoing on the floor. Unstoppable tears streamed, I couldn't eradicate the image of Charlotte from my mind. I reached his office, but it was locked. I beat my fists against it, but there was no response. Ruth had gone home, so I ran around to the school office to ask Jackie, the administrator, but found her deep in conversation with two parents, their child sitting on a chair inside the office. I didn't have time to be polite and interrupted their discussion.

'Has Mr Scott gone already?'

Jackie looked on, surprised at my outburst, but then saw how upset I was.

'Yes, he's been called to a meeting at the local council office. Mrs Cole, are you all right?'

I didn't answer, I turned and ran back to my classroom. Nicky had gone, but my bag remained on the desk. I found my phone, which had a text from Charlotte, saying she was going to Nicky's after school but would be back for dinner.

I slumped in the chair, my head in my hands. Nicky had played me a video of Charlotte giving him oral sex in his bedroom. It had the potential to ruin Charlotte's life; her reputation would be in tatters. Even beyond high school, things like that could follow a person to university or into employment. The image was now ingrained in my mind. It sickened me.

What had I seen in Nicky? I'd been such a fool not to see him for what he was. Nicky was a narcissist and enjoyed exerting control over people. I had to take back control. He was banking on me staying quiet because of everything I could lose. None of those things mattered any more. Charlotte's safety and future were in jeopardy; there was no time to hang around. I toyed with the idea of calling the police, but first I had to speak to David and come clean about everything. Then, after the initial shock, we could deal with Nicky together. However angry he'd be at me, I knew I could count on him as far as Charlotte was concerned. He'd step up for his daughter without a doubt.

As I drove home, my temperature climbed. Underneath my arms, patches appeared; I felt like a lamb to the slaughter. I had no idea what I was going to say to David. How would I even begin? I felt shaken to my core, knowing, after tonight, life would change forever.

When I got there, David's car was nowhere to be seen. It was only four o'clock, so it was likely he was still working. I went inside and paced around the front room, wringing my hands as I tried to form the words in my head of what I was going to say. David was going to be so angry with the mess I'd dragged our family into.

I called Stella, who spent the first ten minutes trying to get me to stop hyperventilating so she could understand what I was saying.

'Fuck, Izzy, you've got to get that video. Christ, poor Charlotte. You'll have to go to the police. It's proof of him with a minor.'

'You can't see his face,' I whimpered.

'It doesn't matter, it'll be possessing indecent images of a child or something to that effect. They'll seize the phone.'

I felt dizzy, my blood pressure skyrocketing.

By six o'clock, I'd already downed a glass of wine when the front door opened. My heart leapt, but it was Charlotte coming home for dinner. In my fretful state, I'd forgotten to prepare one.

'When's dinner, Mum?' Charlotte called as she trudged upstairs, oblivious anything was amiss.

'In about fifteen minutes,' I called back, my voice higher-pitched than normal.

I ran around the kitchen, pulling bowls out of cupboards, and got a pan on the stove to boil some water for pasta. I had a jar in the cupboard I could use. If I threw in some tomatoes and peppers I had left over in the fridge and covered it with cheese no one would notice it had been thrown together at the last minute. As the pasta cooked, I chopped vegetables, which gave me something to focus on, although my mind kept wandering. Where was David?

I checked my phone, there was nothing. I checked the Motorola and opened a new message from Nicky, containing the video he'd shown me earlier. I'd only watched a couple of seconds of it. I was about to delete it, when something stopped me. Stella was right, the video was evidence of an adult engaging in a sex act with an underage girl. What did they call it? Grooming, that was it. If he shared that video with anyone, he was going to go to prison for a long time. He intended to ruin my life, but I was damn well going to make sure I dragged him down with me.

## 50

'Shit!' I accidently cut my finger chopping the end of the pepper. Raising it to my lips to suck the blood, I braved a look, but it wasn't too bad. A plaster would fix it.

I threw the sauce and vegetables in with the cooked pasta and stirred it through, letting it simmer gently whilst I grated cheese into a bowl. My hands trembled as I scooped the pasta into two bowls and the front door opened. David came in. I heard the thud of his laptop case hitting the floor and my pulse quickened. *It's OK, he doesn't know anything yet.*

'Oh wine. Brilliant, another glass?' he said, giving me a quick kiss on the cheek and filling my glass before pouring one for himself. I could tell he'd had a drink as I could smell the beer on his breath. He must have stayed after work to have a drink in the pub with his colleagues before coming home. Either that or he'd been with Paula? No, he'd told me it was over and she didn't work there any more. I had to trust him otherwise what was the point? However, it would have been nice for him to let me know.

I filled another bowl with pasta. There was barely enough for the three of us. It looked a bit measly with no bread or salad, but no one seemed to notice.

I slid into my seat at the table and pushed the pasta around with my fork, unsure how to even broach the subject with David, let alone drop the bombshell that I'd been having an affair. We'd discussed his infidelity and I'd been willing to move on with the assurance it wouldn't happen again. Would he be so accommodating with mine?

Charlotte looked up from her bowl and glanced surreptitiously at David and then me. The dinner table was unusually quiet, and it made Charlotte suspicious.

'Is something wrong with you two?'

David shook his head, bemused. 'Not that I'm aware of,' he said, glancing at me.

I shook my head; glad my mouth was too full to speak. Our fifteen-year-old daughter had noticed the atmosphere which my husband was oblivious to.

Charlotte went back to playing with her phone and clearing what was left in her bowl. I stared at her, trying to put together the girl sat at the table and the one on the video. My brain wouldn't comply. I had to make sure David never saw that video. I needed to save him from that. I felt fraught, on the edge of bursting into tears.

David finished his glass of wine quickly and poured another, topping up my now half-full one. If I carried on, I was going to be tipsy when I spoke to him. It wasn't a good idea for David to be drunk either. I couldn't be sure how he'd react with the unpredictability alcohol brought into the mix.

After dinner, Charlotte went back upstairs to get changed as she was going out with Nicky again that evening. Apparently to 'shoot pool' with his friends, she informed us as she left the table, promising to be back by nine o'clock.

'I'm going to get changed too,' David said, leaving his empty bowl on the table and following in his daughter's footsteps. His second glass of wine was almost empty, and I looked around at the mess in the kitchen, but tonight it could wait.

I followed David to our bedroom, where he was getting out of his suit to put comfier clothes on.

'We have to talk,' I said, pushing the door to behind me.

'Oh god, what about now?' David sighed. He sounded exasperated.

I frowned, was this the drink talking? 'What's that supposed to mean?'

'Well, there's always some bloody drama, isn't there?' he said, unbuttoning his shirt. His words stung like a slap around the face.

'Why are you acting like an arse?' I asked, losing my temper all too easily, my voice louder than I'd intended.

'I'm an arse, am I?' David bit back, his volume matching mine. He looked ridiculous standing in his boxer shorts and socks, with his shirt hanging open.

'Right now you are, yes. I create drama, do I?' Feeling more frustrated by the second, ready to let the anger I'd buried resurface.

'It's one thing after another, even when we were in Wallington. First it was Charlotte's bad-influence friends, then Stella moving to Nottingham. Then you not liking Charlotte's boyfriend, then you went and got yourself suspended. You jump from one crisis to another. Or have I got it wrong? Did you come to talk to me about the gas bill?' He reached for his jeans and pulled them on, first one leg, then the other. He rocked unsteadily on his feet.

'Well, I'm sorry my life is so problematic,' I shot back, annoyed I'd bitten. I hadn't intended for our conversation to go this way.

'I'm sorry, I've had a shit day at work, and I was hoping to come home and chill. It just seems there's always a problem; you haven't been the same since you found out about the baby,' David sighed.

I gasped. He rarely brought up the miscarriage; at the weekend when we were at the Christmas fair, it was the first time he'd mentioned it in months. Using it against me now was like a knife in my side. Tears erupted and his face instantly softened, regret echoing in his eyes. He reached for me, but I jerked away.

'How could you say that?' I shouted, my voice full of hatred for my husband.

'We moved to get away from it all, to put it behind us,' David said, his voice wavering.

'And you found it all so easy, didn't you,' I spat, trying my best to hurt him. Looking at his face, I'd succeeded.

'Fuck you, Izzy! It was my baby too.' He flung off his shirt and pulled a jumper over his head, before shoving me out of the way of the door. Hurling it open, he froze in the doorway and I looked past him to see Charlotte on the stairs, gaping at us. Her eyes widened before she scurried away, knowing she'd bore witness to something she shouldn't have. David tore after her and I thought he was going to explain, but I heard him grab his keys and then the front door slammed.

A couple of minutes later, I heard the door again and I looked out of the window to see Charlotte climbing into Nicky's car. The house was quiet once again and only then did I let myself sob into my pillow. Everything was such a mess right now and I didn't know what to do. I'd ruined my chance to talk to David and now I'd have to wait to tell him about Nicky. His car was still outside, so I assumed he'd walked to the pub to prop up the bar there.

I wrapped the covers around me and cried until my eyes were swollen and head ached. I felt numb. There would be another day where the video of Charlotte was out in the world and there was nothing I could do about it unless I went to the police. I felt utterly helpless. Throwing the duvet off, I ran downstairs to text Nicky.

OK you win. I'll do whatever you want. Just delete the video.

I clicked send and hoped it would be enough. Surely, he would be basking in the glory of getting me to agree to his terms. It would buy me some time to speak to David again, hopefully before Nicky showed the video to someone else. If I could get him to meet me, I could convince him to delete the video, threaten him with the police, sex with a minor, whatever it took.

I took the left-over wine upstairs and changed into my pyjamas. Sitting in bed drinking straight from the bottle, I mourned my marriage which was soon to be over. Once the wine was finished, I got cans of premixed gin and tonic from the fridge and brought them up to the bedroom. I didn't care that it was a school night. My job would soon be snatched away too.

I rang David to make sure he was OK, but there was no response and no answers to my texts. I called Stella instead and told her about mine and David's row, drunkenly sobbing down the phone about how I'd messed our lives up. I shouldn't have rung her in such a state. I had to talk her out of jumping on a train to come down to me. Desperate for a cigarette, I chewed my nails, cursing the day I'd met Nicky.

The near miss at the roundabout was just three months ago. If only I'd been a couple of minutes earlier or later. Fate had it out for me, I was sure of it. Without its intervention I could have been getting ready to celebrate my second child's first birthday. Fate could fuck itself, I thought as I finished another can of gin and tonic and tossed it to the floor.

I managed to stay awake until I heard Charlotte return and then I passed out, too drunk to keep my eyes open any longer. When I woke, struggling to lift my head off the pillow, I saw Charlotte sat on the end of the bed staring at me. It took a while for her to come fully into focus, but when she did, I saw she was dressed in her school uniform.

'I was getting worried you were in a coma,' she said, standing.

I tried to speak but only produced a grunting sound.

'Are you OK?' She sounded concerned.

The floor of the bedroom was littered with empty gin and tonic cans as well as the discarded wine bottle. It looked as though I'd had a party for one. I saw Charlotte surveying the room, wrinkling her nose at the smell.

'I'll tell the office you're throwing up, OK, and you'll call in later. Dad's giving me a lift to school on his way to work, he looks awful as well. What's got into you two?' Charlotte scolded as she left the bedroom, closing the door behind her.

I looked at the clock, it was half past eight in the morning. A wave of despair washed over me, along with a monstrous thudding headache. When I heard the front door shut, I crept downstairs to check the Motorola. Two texts from Nicky were waiting for me.

So glad you finally came around


Your daughter was very upset last night, she wouldn't tell me why. Good job I was there to comfort her


I vomited over the discarded cereal bowls in the sink. Washing it away, I dug out some paracetamol and headed back to bed, pulling the duvet over my head.

A couple of hours later, when I woke for the second time, my headache had subsided, but I felt awful. I was weak and shaky, my stomach hollow and mouth dry. The stress had finally caught up with me and I couldn't face what was to come today. Instead I'd hide from the world. I wrapped myself in my dressing gown and gingerly made it down the stairs, my stomach churning. Everything ached and I felt like I'd been run over by a bus.

It was the worst hangover I'd experienced in a long time, no doubt due to mixing gin and wine. Even the strongest coffee didn't scratch the surface. Instead, I sat slumped at the kitchen table, staring into space. There was no way I could bring myself to eat anything, but I looked in the fridge anyway. It was eleven o'clock already and I didn't know where David was. Had he gone to work? What time would be home? He must have thought I'd gone way overboard after the fight we had. He had no idea his world was about to come crashing down around his ears.

Hair of the dog would do the trick. I opened another bottle of wine, one David had brought home as a gift from work. It was an expensive bottle, to be saved for a special occasion, but it was the only alcohol left in the house. I necked a small glass and poured another to take upstairs for the bath. I knew I was drinking too much, topping up my alcohol content from the night before, but I wanted to block everything out. I was yet to have my real showdown with David, and it would be much worse than last night. I drained my glass before the bath had been filled. Starting to feel the alcohol hit, providing a nice buzz, I closed my eyes, sinking beneath the water.

The heat felt good, spreading through me. I'd had a bath after the miscarriage. It was the first thing I did after coming home from the hospital. The bath had been so hot, nearly scalding, but I got in regardless. At the time, I saw it as some sort of punishment to the body that had let me down. I had sat there for hours, topping up the water, my skin itching from the heat. The baby had been unexpected but desperately wanted and I'd lost it.

It wasn't anyone's fault, I realised that now. It took a while to forgive myself and come to terms with the bereavement. I found it hard to talk about, but that's because David never spoke of it. All of my feelings were bottled up, his were too. We never got the chance to grieve together. The anniversary was near, and it was a day I was dreading. It hit me like a sledgehammer that this time last year my baby would still have been alive inside of me. I caressed my bloated alcohol stomach, knowing it was empty of anything good. With that thought, the tears began to fall.

## 51

I cried in the bath until I had nothing left, feeling numb until the water turned cold. Perhaps I was having a breakdown. Maybe this was what it felt like? I hadn't checked my phone or rung the school office, but I didn't care, not today.

When the shivering became unbearable, I quickly washed and got out of the bath. I slipped into clean flannel pyjamas and removed the cans and bottle from the bedroom floor. My hair was a mess and eyes red-rimmed and sore. Blotches peppered my neck and chest from crying. It didn't matter, I wasn't going to see anyone. David would pick Charlotte up from school or Nicky would bring her home, and she had her key to get in.

Lowering to my knees, I rummaged amongst the storage boxes under my bed. In one of the clear plastic cases, I found what I was looking for. I took out the small white satin box and placed it carefully on the bed, sitting beside it. I unhooked the clasp and lifted the lid, folding it all the way back. The box hadn't been opened for months, not since before we moved. It contained some keepsakes from what would have been my second child.

Inside was a hospital bracelet, mine from when I was admitted to undergo what is referred to as a D&C, where part of the foetus gets left behind after a miscarriage. It was the most awful experience and something I'd never want to go through again. At the time I felt like I deserved it, for not managing to hold on to my baby.

Laid on top was a beautiful yellow new-born sleepsuit. I couldn't resist. It was the only item I'd bought for the baby and in my state of mind after the miscarriage I thought I'd cursed myself by buying it so early on in the pregnancy. Stella had bought me a small statue of an angel in white porcelain which was exquisite, but I couldn't bear to have it out on display as a constant reminder so had added it to the box. There were a few more items such as a tiny baby name book, a cross-stich pattern I had intended to do for the nursery and a packet of folic acid, which, on reflection, I had no idea why I'd kept.

I laid everything out, looking at each item in turn before gently placing them back in the box. My heart burned with the future we should have had together; about the mother I never got to be a second time. I stood, about to put the box away, when I heard a noise behind me.

Whizzing around, expecting to see David, I cried out when Nicky stood in the doorway. How had he got in? His eyes were wild, they seemed to glaze over as he clenched and released his jaw. I'd never seen him look so angry. My legs buckled, bladder weakening as he stepped towards me.

'You're pregnant,' he spat.

I didn't have time to move before he shoved my shoulder. Legs weak, I fell backwards onto the bed, bouncing on the mattress. Pregnant? I didn't understand. Alcohol had dulled my brain and I scrambled to work out what he meant.

I shook my head. No, I'm not pregnant. I couldn't be pregnant.

'Lying bitch,' Nicky hissed as he loomed over me, forcing me back down and pining my wrists over my head.

My body finally reacted, and I felt my muscles contract. I thrashed, my heart pounding in my ears. What was he going to do to me?

'Nicky, please. I'm not,' I pleaded, struggling to get my words out, but he was enraged. Letting go of my wrists, he pulled his arm back and belted me across the face with the back of his hand.

My cheek felt like it shattered, pain like a hot poker shoved into my flesh. I raised my forearm across my face to defend myself and managed to push up to a half-seated position. Tears pooled in my sockets, blurring my vision. My teeth chattered uncontrollably, and I felt the warmth of my urine dampen the sheets beneath me.

'Shit, I'm sorry, I'm sorry,' he said, straddling my lap and wiping my tears away with his fingers.

I shook my head, trying to get him to stop touching me.

'You're going to have my baby.' He trembled with each spoken word, resting his hands on my stomach.

I blinked rapidly. What did he mean? Was he going to rape me? I opened my mouth to speak, to beg.

'No,' I managed, but his face contorted, and he bared his teeth, lashing out again. His fist connected with my nose and I was conscious for long enough to see blood splatter across the duvet and wall. Eyes rolling back, darkness threatened to envelop me. His weight on top of me, pinning me to the bed as I coughed, choking on blood flowing down the back of my throat.

I tried to fight, but he was so heavy, my arms flailed, beating his chest with my fists, but he pinned them to the bed with ease. I coughed again, the metallic taste of blood on my lips.

He leant over, face warped beyond recognition. 'You're pregnant and it's mine. I know it is.' Pregnant? He must have seen the baby things laid out on the bed and assumed? Why was he here?

I felt dizzy, my cheek already beginning to swell. It throbbed rhythmically. I had to make Nicky see sense.

'I had a miscarriage...'

His hands were at my throat, cutting me off mid-sentence and my words faded.

'Liar!' he yelled, spit flying through his teeth. He was deranged and even if I could speak there was no way I'd be able to calm him down.

I couldn't focus as his hands tightened their grip and I struggled for air. He squeezed his eyes shut tight as though my death would be too painful to watch. I clawed at his fingers, but he carried on crushing my windpipe. My lungs burned from lack of air and I felt my head begin to swim.

'I love you,' he whimpered, and I felt his hands loosen, but not enough.

I was going to die, murdered by the man I'd been foolish enough to have an affair with. Charlotte's blurred face formed in my mind spurring me on and with one last burst of strength, I raised my hand to fight back. Scraping his face with my nails, unsure if I'd even made contact. My arms fell back to the bed with an insignificant bounce and my eyes rolled back, the light slipping away.

## 52

I stared out of the window onto the street. The bedroom I stood in bore no trace I'd ever lived there. Packing was almost finished and now I was moving from room to room, checking nothing had been forgotten.

I paused in the bathroom, inspecting my puffy face, gingerly touching the bruises around my neck which were still a dark purple, soon to go green, I'd been told by the nurse. My face was a mix of the two, with a cut across the bridge of my nose. I looked away, glancing back into the bedroom, at the space on the walls where my blood had been. I was sure I could still see a slight smear of crimson that had been poorly wiped away.

I was discharged from hospital last week, and although bruised, I was otherwise in good health. Since then I'd been to the police station to give a statement and had photographs taken of my face and neck. Nicky was charged with Actual Bodily Harm the same day and released on bail. Mostly because he had no history of violence on record and no previous convictions. I was relieved to hear the terms of his bail meant he couldn't come anywhere near me and thankfully he'd stayed away.

Detective Groomsland, who was in charge of the case, told me

Nicky hadn't uttered a single word in interview. He'd stared at his hands, refusing to even deny the allegations. I didn't tell the police about our affair, instead I described how Nicky had become fixated on me whilst dating my daughter and had come to the house to assault me. David had persuaded me to keep quiet, damage limitation he'd called it. Said there was no point admitting to a crime I hadn't been accused of yet.

I was told that Nicky would likely get a suspended sentence, he'd never see the inside of a cell, so I didn't feel too guilty, not after what he'd done. Groomsland said the CPS couldn't prove Nicky had intended to kill me, but I knew different. I'll never forget the look on his face before he shut his eyes. Unable to watch as he squeezed the life out of me. He wasn't in control. If David hadn't come home early from the office to check on me, if he'd been a few minutes later, it would have been game over.

Charlotte struggled to get her head around how the boy she loved could cause so much destruction. How could he inflict so much pain on her family? Her first love had ended in lies and violence. I was worried she'd be scarred for life. Now she was being torn from her best friend and new life for the second time in so many months.

I didn't understand why Nicky had attacked me, until Charlotte told us she'd confided in him that she'd overheard us arguing about a baby. She thought I was pregnant, and he'd automatically assumed the baby was his. He'd panicked that I was going to get rid of it and stole Charlotte's house keys out of her bag when I didn't turn up to school.

I knew he hadn't had the best father figure. He wouldn't talk about his childhood much. Perhaps he wanted to break the cycle? I'll never know.

When the bed was dismantled, I found Nicky's phone underneath. It must have fallen out during the struggle. I made sure it found its way to the bottom of the nearest drain, right after a good downpour. Charlotte's video wouldn't be seen by anyone. All of the texts between us were gone forever and I hoped any evidence of our affair had now been eradicated.

I had to tell David about the affair from my hospital bed in a crowded ward, my voice raspy and throat sore. He was upset and angry, as I'd expected him to be, but he stood by me. I think he knew, after his own infidelity, that he couldn't claim the moral high ground. The only way for us to move forward, we agreed, was to pack up and leave. Rent somewhere for six months until we found another house. A house we could lay our demons to rest and start again. Nicky or Pat could blow the whistle at any time, and if they did, it wouldn't be long before reporters turned up at my door. I had to shield my family from that.

I had no intention of returning to St. Wilfred's. The police had been in touch with Mr Scott and informed him of the attack. Even with Nicky's expulsion, I told him it would be too traumatic to return. I had to walk away from the school altogether. Eventually we came to the agreement that I'd be replaced in the New Year, my record clean and with a good reference. I knew he had his suspicions after the incident, no smoke without fire after all, but he couldn't prove it and St. Wilfred's had had its reputation smeared enough. I'd miss Matilda and Susan; they came to visit once I was home from the hospital. Bringing with them a huge fruit basket. I promised to keep in touch and come to the occasional curry night depending on where we ended up.

The house echoed as I lugged the last heavy suitcase of clothes down the stairs and passed it to David, who was loading the van. Everything was going into storage and we were heading to Dorking to spend Christmas with my parents. Charlotte was leaving school early for the holidays and David had wangled two weeks off. We'd booked four nights in Tenerife over New Year. A cheap getaway. It was Stella's suggestion, her and Adam were coming with us.

Taking one last look around at the house that was supposed to be our new start, I bit my lip. Perhaps it would be third time lucky? I had no idea where we'd go.

I closed the front door and handed the keys to David. He was going to drop them off at the estate agents so they could get potential buyers through the door. I was amazed at how fast it had all happened, but I couldn't live there now. I couldn't sleep in the same room I almost died in.

Both Charlotte and I had a lucky escape. I needed to take owner-ship of what I'd done. Learn from my mistakes. It had all come down to vanity. My fragile ego flattered by a schoolboy during a rocky patch in our marriage. One moment of recklessness. It could happen to anyone.

# EPILOGUE

NICKY

**January 2020**

I rubbed the black lace between my thumb and forefinger, breathing in the fabric, her scent still lingered. It was the closest I could get to touching her and I carried it with me everywhere, like a talisman. The only part of her I had left.

Izzy was gone, her house empty. I'd driven past every day at first; waited outside for hours but no sign of her. I'd hidden across the street, breaching my bail conditions, unable to accept she'd gone. The house remained locked up until, two by two they came, delivered by the estate agent. The bitch had abandoned me. Taken her family and left me behind. Now all I had were memories and thoughts of what could have been for us. For our child, if there was one? Now I'll never know. It had been fate, her replacing Miss Willis. A sign sent just for me, but it wasn't supposed to end the way it did.

St. Wilfred's asked me not to return and suggested Chichester College, closer to the coast, where I could continue my A-Level courses without interruption. It's a bit of a trek but no one knows me there. A chance to start again. I'm going to move out of mum's, get my own place as soon as I can get the money together. The college seems all right, there's no school attached so everyone's older, but I'm going to keep my head down and finish the qualifications.

The click-clack of heels echoed from the corridor and I shuffled in my seat, putting the bra back in my bag. I'd arrived early, to get the best spot, at the front, where the show was good.

She arrived soon after, an extra button of her white blouse undone. Too low to really be appropriate. When she turned to the side, I glimpsed her flesh coloured bra, the smooth mound filling the cup. It made me hard instantly and I had to sit forward to hide the bulge. She knew what she was doing. They all did. It would be the mental snapshot I'd use later, when I was alone.

'Hello Nicholas. You're keen today,' she said, awarding me a flash of perfectly straight white teeth and tucking her dark hair behind her ear. She glided to her desk, reaching into her satchel and pulling out her notepad and books. I spied the rock on her finger, she was someone else's, not that it mattered.

'Hello Miss Evans, how was your weekend?'

# ACKNOWLEDGMENTS

Firstly, thank you to my mum, who read *Reckless*, chapter by chapter, as I wrote it back in 2016. The first novel I'd finished. An amazing achievement that you encouraged. I'll forever be grateful for your support.

Thanks to my reader Denise Miller, for always being honest and willing to lend your time. You're stuck being my guinea pig forever now!

A massive thank you to my fabulous editor Caroline Ridding, part of the wonderful team at Boldwood Books who are so supportive and nurturing. The final product is very much a team effort and I couldn't do it without all of you. Jade Craddock, you've been amazing at turning this beast of a manuscript into something more refined! Thank you so much.

To the many ladies who helped with different research aspects of the book. Philippa East and Lisa Sell particularly. I really appreciate you giving me an insight on anxiety and the teaching profession.

I would like to thank Becky Poulsum for raising money for the charity, Cancer Research UK, by arranging the auction of a character's name in the book. Stella Crowley, I very much hope you enjoy *Reckless*.

Lastly, thank you to Dean, Bethany and Lucy for putting up with me.

# MORE FROM GEMMA ROGERS

We hope you enjoyed reading *Reckless*. If you did, please leave a review.

If you'd like to gift a copy, this book is also available as an ebook, digital audio download and audiobook CD.

Sign up to the Gemma Rogers mailing list for news, competitions and updates on future books:

http://bit.ly/GemmaRogersNewsletter

If you'd like to read more from Gemma Rogers, *Stalker* and *Payback* are available now.

# ABOUT THE AUTHOR

**Gemma Rogers** was inspired to write gritty thrillers by a traumatic event in her own life nearly twenty years ago. *Stalker* was her debut novel and marked the beginning of a new writing career. Gemma lives in West Sussex with her husband, two daughters and bulldog Buster.

Visit Gemma's website: www.gemmarogersauthor.co.uk

Follow Gemma on social media:

facebook.com/GemmaRogersAuthor

twitter.com/GemmaRogers79

instagram.com/gemmarogersauthor

bookbub.com/authors/gemma-rogers

# ABOUT BOLDWOOD BOOKS

Boldwood Books is a fiction publishing company seeking out the best stories from around the world.

Find out more at www.boldwoodbooks.com

Sign up to the Book and Tonic newsletter for news, offers and competitions from Boldwood Books!

http://www.bit.ly/bookandtonic

We'd love to hear from you, follow us on social media:

facebook.com/BookandTonic

twitter.com/BoldwoodBooks

instagram.com/BookandTonic

Printed in Great Britain
by Amazon